VIENNA

by

JULI ANA ANDREW

DORRANCE PUBLISHING CO., INC.
PITTSBURGH, PENNSYLVANIA 15222

The contents of this work including, but not limited to, the accuracy of events, people, and places depicted; opinions expressed; permission to use previously published materials included; and any advice given or actions advocated are solely the responsibility of the author, who assumes all liability for said work and indemnifies the publisher against any claims stemming from publication of the work.

Dorrance Publishing Co., Inc.
701 Smithfield Street
Pittsburgh, PA 15222
Visit our website at *www.dorrancebookstore.com*

ISBN: 978-1-4809-0144-5
eISBN: 978-1-4809-0413-2

VIENNA

A
Novel

JULI ANA ANDREW

For my beloved girls,
Cheryl, Kayla and the real Vienna

Chapter One

Hawthorne, 1981

The day was cold; the sun was a big, yellow ball in the deep, blue January sky. The dogs were still pulling hard as if the boisterous crowd gave them extra energy to speed up for the last half mile of the race. Something—no, someone—caught Rainey's eye. There, among the crowd of spectators, a face from the past sent a shiver up and down his spine. She was laughing and jumping up and down, cheering the dogsleds to the finish line. He couldn't believe what he was seeing.

"Yates," he said, and he was sure that his voiced must have sounded strained. "Who is that woman over there?"

"Well, buddy, you are going to have to be a little more specific. What woman?"

"Okay," Rainey agreed. "She is right beside the last red flag and she is wearing a red coat and white scarf; long, brown hair. Do you see who I mean?"

"Hell, do you mean the one who looks like V?"

"It can't be Vienna. She can't look the same as she did twenty years ago!"

Zane and Jimmy had returned with the hot coffee.

"What took you guys so long?" Yates asked.

"Had to go back to the car to get some creamer, you know what I mean?" Zane winked. "What's got you looking so perplexed, Rain?"

Yates answered for him. "See that girl over there by the red flags? He thinks it's V."

"I didn't say that exactly, Yates," Rainey argued.

"Well, that is just crazy, Rain," said Zane. "Did you expect her to look like she did in the '60s?"

"It's probably her daughter." Jimmy cursed to himself and wondered if V was here.

"Her daughter is here?" Rainey asked. "How come nobody told me?"

"I didn't say that it *was* her daughter, but it could be," Jimmy replied. "I don't see any other explanation. It's been a long time since I've seen her."

"You've met the daughter? When and where?" Rainey demanded.

"I am sure that I told you, Rainey. Maybe ten years ago. I met them on the street in Bridge. There were two girls with V. They were both very young then."

"Wait a minute. Are you saying that you have actually talked to Vienna? Jimmy, I feel like I have been kept out of the loop here. Is she here now?"

"I honestly don't know." Jimmy had the feeling that V was indeed here, and sooner or later, he was going to have to confess everything to his old friend.

"There is something that you're not telling me," Rainey surmised. "Do you all know something? Has Vienna come back to the valley?"

"No one is keeping anything from you, Rain. Why are you so paranoid? You haven't even talked about V in years. I thought that you were, at long last, over her. You knew that she was married. Do you think that she knew you were married? I'm sure she did."

"When you've seen her, did you ask her out, Jimmy?"

Jimmy was ticked. "So what if I did? Do you think that you still have a monopoly on someone from so long ago? Yeah, I did ask her out and she refused. 'Too much history,' she said. Anyhow, the thing is that you two were a long time ago and this is the here and now. You're still carrying a torch for her, aren't you? Yeah, I can see that you are."

Yates stepped in between his two old friends. "Hey, you two, let's not come to blows over this. Rainey, you all right?"

"Yeah, I'm good. Sorry, Jimmy. I didn't mean to get on your case. I guess seeing her, the daughter…it must be. Who else could look like Vienna?"

"Her sister's daughters maybe. Does anyone know if there are any? Why don't we settle this and go and ask her?" Zane suggested.

Jimmy disagreed. "That's a little crude, don't you think? I'm sure we will get an answer one way or the other before the day is over."

"In the meantime, how about we head over to the Revada and get some drinks? How long has it been since the four of us have caroused together anyhow? We haven't even congratulated the Kinney boys on their valiant effort yet. What do you say?"

"You're right as usual, Yates. What do you say, Rain?" Jimmy offered his hand to his best friend, and the four of them lit out for the hotel and the presentation of the awards.

The crowd had all gathered at Geranium Park to welcome the mushers and their exhausted dogs. Jimmy was all set to congratulate one of the Kinney brothers on their third-place finish when he spotted her among the onlookers.

Damn it! he thought. *Damn it, she is here. I guess it's all going to hit the fan now.* He debated with himself for a brief second as to whether he should tell Rainey or not. "Do you think that you can handle seeing her, bro?" he asked.

"What?" Rainey looked puzzled.

"Your Vienna." Jimmy nodded in her direction. "Oh yeah, she is here."

Rainey turned and froze. It wasn't the girl in the red coat who looked like Vienna at seventeen. It was Vienna at what? How old would she be...thirty-seven? Was it really her? After all these years, was she really standing 20 feet away from him? He felt something in the pit of his stomach—was it jubilation or was it anger? He knew Jimmy was watching him for his reaction. "I don't think I can, Jimmy." But he was already walking toward her.

Jimmy put his hand on his shoulder. "Take it easy, Rain. Later, I am going to have to confess a few things to you. Now, go."

Rainey looked back at his old friend. "I don't like the sound of that, Jimmy."

"No two ways about it. You're going to be pissed with me."

Yates and Zane had seen her, too. "Well, isn't this a fine turn of events? What do you think, Jimbo, how's it going to go? I'm a might feared."

"Rain's a big boy, Yates. He can handle it."

"Hell, it's not him I'm worried about."

"V?"

"Yeah, I ran into her at J.B.'s funeral a few years back. You guys were at the auction in Potsdam. She asked how you were. We danced around, not mentioning Rainey, and then it was there. She asked about him. I gave her a short version of what I knew. She surprised me when she said she knew all that but how was he really? I told her that if she was going to stay in the valley, I was sure that she would run into him sooner or later. She said, and I quote, 'I pray that I never ever see Rainey again. I could not deal with the consequences. It's too late now.' She sounded resentful."

"Hell, why didn't you mention that encounter before?"

"Same reason you haven't mentioned any of yours with her...same reason, Jimmy."

"Vienna?"

She froze. Time stood still. No one was moving. She couldn't hear a sound. The wind had lost its chill. She was sure that she wasn't breathing. She could pretend that she hadn't heard the velvet voice speak her name. Only one person ever called her Vienna. She thought of ignoring him and walking away. Could she chance having him reject her and getting her heart broken all over again?

"Vienna, are you going to speak to me?" Rainey asked.

She took a deep breath and turned around. She knew that for everyone's sake and her own sanity, she had to pretend that seeing him had no effect on her whatsoever. That wasn't going to work because one look at him and she wanted to melt into his arms. Why hadn't he aged? Why didn't he have white hair and ugly warts?

All the while, Rainey was thinking, *My god, she is still my raven-haired beauty, but with one difference: she isn't mine anymore. And what happened to her black hair?*

"Hello, Rainey," she said. "How are you?"

"Vienna, do you know how long it has been since I last saw you?"

Did he think that she was oblivious to the fact that it had been twenty years, four months, eleven days, and a million lonely nights? "It has been a long time, hasn't it, Rainey? Life has been good to you. You got married, as I always knew you would when you found the right woman. And you have children, and I understand that you became the architect that you always wanted to and have a thriving business. I guess you got everything that you ever wanted. I am very happy for you."

Was she kidding, everything? He didn't have her, and until this moment, he hadn't realized how much he still wanted her. "You're married also. You have a daughter?"

"Yes, actually, I have two. Ava and my adopted daughter, Rosalyn. I married her father. He passed away four years ago."

"I am sorry, Vienna." He wanted to comfort her.

"Thank you. He was a good friend to me and a very good dad to the girls. His first wife, Maveryn, passed away before Rosalyn was two."

"How sad…just a minute, I know those two names." Rainey was puzzled as to why he felt some strange connection to those names.

"I can see that you might know the name Rosalyn, as it is fairly common I imagine. On the other hand, Maveryn is rather unusual."

"I seem to associate those two names together. Could you have mentioned them before?"

"I met Maveryn when I was twelve or so and doubt that I ever told you about her. Rosalyn wasn't even born yet. She was not even two when I went away."

"And just where did you go, Vienna?"

She could not answer him. Instead, she said, "I really must go. I seem to have become separated from my party. I am glad to see that you are well, as reports are sometimes not always accurate. Please give my regards to your parents." Was this all she wanted to say? No, but it was all that she could manage right then.

Rainey wondered how she knew about him and from whom…maybe Lara. It had been years since he had spoken to his cousin about Vienna. Like everyone else, she thought he had finally forgotten about her, and maybe he had. Well, that wasn't the case anymore. One more try. "Vienna, are you coming over to the hotel? I would really like to buy you a drink and continue our conversation."

"I do not drink anymore, Rainey. I may see you over there; I can't promise. Bye."

With that, she was gone. He watched her walk away, but she wouldn't be going too far if he had anything to say about it. Still, there was the nagging at the back of his memory banks. *How do I know those names…Maveryn and Rosalyn?*

She had to get away from him while she could still walk and before the tears started to fall. She closed her eyes and tried to regain composure, but not before a salty droplet slid down her cheek.

"Mama," Ava asked her mom. "What's wrong?" She slipped her arm around her.

"This darn wind. I'm afraid that it blew something into my eyes. Darling, I think that I going to head back to Bridge." She had learned to lie a long, long time ago.

"Oh, Mama, you are shivering. We need to get you warm. Randy, we are going to go over to the hotel."

"Okay," he answered. "See you in a couple."

"Come on, Mama. A nice, hot drink and then I promise that I will take you home." Ava hugged her mother. "You are soooo cold, I can feel you shivering."

"I am all right, dear. Maybe a quick coffee first." She didn't know in which direction Rainey had gone and kept herself from looking for him. She had never expected to see him here today. Why would he even be here in the middle of winter? Lara said that she hadn't seen him in years but knew that he visited his parents once or twice a year. If Randy hadn't met one of the sled teams in the bar the other day, they probably wouldn't have been here, either. Was this how it was all going to end? Was he going to settle for anything she told him and then go back to his family and leave her to her lonely, loveless life? What was the matter with her? Why couldn't she tell him that she still loved him and then suffer the consequences? She was sure that his rejection would be more than she could bear and she couldn't risk losing herself again.

Rainey had watched the encounter between mother and daughter. At least he had assumed that it was one of her daughters. This wasn't good, was it? He was talking to himself. Running into Vienna was the farthest thing in his mind when he had let Jimmy talk him into coming to Hawthorne for the winter carnival. He had given it much thought, debating whether he should bring the boys. As it turned out, they had sports events scheduled and couldn't come, so he had decided that he would come alone. He hadn't seen his parents since late summer and could use a break from his hectic life. That was all that he had that mattered, his boys and the business. His marriage had been in the dumpster for years and the only reason he was holding on was for his sons. He had often wondered if staying in a failed relationship was good for them, but he couldn't uproot them in their teenage years. He could hold out a while longer…but now, here he was, and, after all these years, so was Vienna. He felt as though he had been wallowing in quicksand for the last twenty years and she was the only one who could pull him out.

Chapter Two

June 1960

I t was hot and humid, not unusual for Bridge Falls in the summer, but it was only June 11. If this was an omen of what was to come, then the summer was shaping up to be a scorcher.

Rainey and Jimmy had travelled the 18 miles from Hawthorne to see what trouble they could get into at Bridge. That meant drinking the day away in some establishment that catered to you whether you were underage or not. This was the first year that they were both the legal twenty-one. Rainey hadn't been "downtown" since returning from university in late May. That was how the people from the surrounding smaller hamlets referred to Bridge Falls. He was getting used to small-town living again and working long hours at the family ranch in Hawthorne. The name Quinn Brothers Horse Ranch was really a misnomer, as it was primarily a cattle and hay farm. There were horses all right—horses that you saddled up and rode out over the hundreds of acres, checking on the cattle, repairing fences, changing sprinklers, and, of course, haying in the summer. A far cry from life in the big city. Rainey didn't consider university as work. He loved learning and nothing was going to stand in his way of acquiring his degree in architecture. Though the work on the farm was hard and tedious, he was glad to help out, as he had been doing it all his life. The pay was not great, but he had free room and board and got to spend time with his parents and longtime friends.

Theirs was only one of a dozen such farms in the area. Hawthorne and the other small villages were in the fertile Black River District. The land was flat and ideal for farming. In contrast, Bridge Falls was a vast expanse of rolling hills, sylvan forests, and cascading waterfalls. Mountains framed the town on the east and west with the Black River flowing through the valley. As the river meandered through the Hawthorne fields, it dipped and climbed, producing numerous waterfalls along its path. When it reached the summit, it dropped into a deep cavern cascading down 40 feet into the calmer Founder River. The two rivers traveled peacefully most of the time through Bridge Falls.

The boys were sitting in Jimmy's red convertible on Main Street, looking for some excitement. "Hey, Lara!" Jimmy called out. "Look, Rain, it's Lara."

Lara came over to the car and leaned on the open window where Rainey was sitting.

"So you finally came down to see your little cousin, did you?" she said to him.

"Been busy, hon," Rainey said. "Can't you say hello to Jimmy?"

Lara planted a big kiss on Rainey's cheek while waving to Jimmy.

"Okay, you kissing cousins," Jimmy said. "You doing anything interesting, Lara?"

"Waiting for a friend, just hanging around, and going to work later. Here she comes now. Over here V."

"V?" Rainey queried.

V came over to the car, noticing its rich interior. The guys in it weren't bad, either, she thought.

"This rogue here is my cousin, Rainey Quinn, and that handsome character behind the wheel is Jimmy Douglas," Lara told her. "Have I told you about them? Guys, meet my best friend, V."

Rainey opened the car door, catching the girls by surprise, and they had to back up quickly. "Sorry. Is it V?"

"Yeah, V," Lara stated.

He smiled, took her hand, and kissed it gently. "Delighted to meet you, Lady V."

A game, V thought. *Okay, I can play.* "Charmed I am sure, Lord Rainey."

Jimmy said, "Get in, girls. Let's go for a spin."

Rainey opened the door for them.

Lara didn't need to be asked twice. She said, "Boy, Jimmy, this is sure some hot rod. I guess work up north paid off for you. Come on, V, what are you waiting for? These guys are all right."

"Are you sure about that, Lara?" Jimmy kidded. "I'll tell you how hard I had to work to get this beauty. I call her Jezebel."

V was a little hesitant, but she wasn't sure why. Since moving to Bridge last winter, she was constantly meeting new guys. The "new girl in town" syndrome, she guessed. As long as she was with Lara, she had always felt safe before. Why did she feel something ominous coming?

Lara took her hand and practically pulled her into the backseat. "What's wrong with you?" she whispered.

Rainey jumped into the front and turned around. "What has my little cous told you about me?"

"Honestly, I don't even remember her mentioning you," V replied.

"Ouch." Rainey winched.

"Thank God your reputation hasn't preceded you this time. Right, Lara?" Jimmy teased.

"V, have you met Jimmy before?" Lara asked.

He started up Jezebel. "Well, I know for a fact that I have never met V. I would have surely remembered. I guess that we are the last of the boys from the country to make your acquaintance. Howdy." He waved at her in the rearview mirror.

"Hello, Jimmy," V said. "I think that I have met quite a few of your friends. Hawthorne, right? Lara has mentioned you but said that you were away, working. Rainey? That is an odd name."

Rainey's arm was on the back of the seat as he looked at her. "Really? You think that my name is odd...and V, that is not? How do you spell it anyhow?"

V only smiled. Lara answered for her. "V, that is how you spell it. The letter V. Got that, you college boy?"

"Whoa there, girl!" Rainey replied. "It must be short for something—Valentine, Victoria, Virginia... Come on, help me out, Jimmy."

"Vera, Valerie, Viola...that's all I can think of off the top of my head, Rain," Jimmy added.

Lara laughed. "You will never guess it, not in a thousand years. She never tells anyone."

"Do I hear the offer of a bet in the air, cous? Do you even know yourself?"

"V's not the prize like in one of your rowdy poker games, Rainey. If she wanted you to know—"

"Vienna," V stated. "It's Vienna."

"Your right, Lara, I would never have come up with such a romantic name." *Vienna.* Rainey let the feel of it roll over his tongue. "I like it. May I call you that?"

"No one calls her Vienna. No one. Not even me or her family," Lara declared emphatically. To herself, she wondered why V had revealed her full name. She never had before.

Rainey removed his arm from the back of the seat and turned around. He decided to let the name thing go for now. "Where are we going, Jimmy?"

Jimmy eyed the girls in the backseat. "Do you really have to work later, Lara?"

"Yes, we both do."

"You are both working on a Saturday night? Sounds strange. Is that just an excuse because you both have hot dates?"

"No, honestly. We start at 4 and finish by 8:30, hopefully. It all depends on how busy the restaurant is."

"Just where is this place?" Rainey asked

"Lily Lane's. It is where the old Neon was. V's mom owns and runs it."

"I've heard about it. Good food, right? We are looking for a place to eat later. What do you say, Rain?"

"Sounds good to me. Will you girls be serving us?" Rainey asked.

"If you're lucky," was Lara's answer.

"Okay, that is settled. We've got a few hours…how about heading down to the beach at the falls? The river must be down now." Jimmy didn't wait for an answer and took the turn that would take them there.

Rainey tried to see Vienna in the side mirror, reaching out and slyly tilting it so he could see her without being obvious. She hadn't said a word since blurting out her name.

The parking lot was sparsely occupied despite the heat of the day. Later in the year, it would be overflowing, as the best swimming hole in the area was here. A ten- to fifteen-minute walk from downtown made it an ideal spot for the kids. During high water, the whole area would be securely cordoned off, as the falls would be roaring and spewing foam from both sides of the precipice. The water level could get as high as the forty steps that led to the beach. The last actual flood was back in the late '40s, when many homes and properties had been badly damaged. The Black River had already crested and the danger was over, thanks to God and Mother Nature.

They emerged from the car in tandem. Rainey grabbed the back door from Vienna to keep it from slamming. She was off and running down the steps, kicking her sandals off as soon as her feet hit the sand. He picked up her shoes when he reached them, watching her as she ran into the water.

"V!" Lara yelled. "You'll freeze!"

V hiked up her pedal pushers and turned and tried to splash them, but they were too quick for her and backed away. She started for the shore, laughing and shivering.

Rainey reached out his hand for her. "My lady, I am fresh out of towels. Should I get my jacket for you?"

"Burr," she stammered. "No, I will warm up fast; the air is so warm. Thanks, though." She let go of his hand rather hastily, and when she shivered this time, it was not from the cold. Why did Shakespeare's words come to her mind, "by the pricking of my thumbs"? She shrugged it off.

Lara and Jimmy had moved on down the beach.

"Shall we join them?" V asked. She didn't wait for an answer and started toward them.

"Tell me about yourself, V." Rainey emphasized V.

"There isn't much to tell. I am not very old you know, so I haven't done much but move from town to town. Dad was in the construction business and so we moved wherever his work would take us. Mother would never stay put. She always had to follow him, so guess what? I, too, have been following them all over the country. If it weren't for my sisters, I would be in Wales. Someone has to look out for them. Then, out of the blue, they bought this house and diner, and here we are. End of story."

Rainey didn't think that was the end of the story at all, but had to ask, "Wales, what is that all about?"

"Oh, just that I want to live there with my Aunt Jannie. She lives on the Isle of Anglesey, in a lesser castle. She has no children of her own and has promised me that I will always have a home with her whenever I want. My parents will not let me go, and then there are my sisters, and so I am just bidding my time. My mother's family are Welsh Gypsies, and between that and my French heritage, I am forever doomed." She sounded bitter and melo-dramatic at the same time. Her dark, almost black eyes stared into his. She was looking for a reaction. She smiled and then laughed. "Now, tell me about your life. It has to be more interesting than mine."

Has she been pulling my leg? I really need to find out more about this young, raven-haired beauty. Do I want to be drawn into her fantasy? Too late. If there was a game to be played, then he was in. "You enchant me, Vienna." Now what made him say that? He had only just met her.

What a funny choice of words. Can one be an enchantress when she is only sixteen? I do love that word. He thinks that I am enchanting and we only met an hour ago. What is happening here? When I first met him, I felt my heart flutter, and I got weak in the knees when he kissed my hand. Is this the feeling that I have been hearing and reading about? Do I like it? Too soon to tell. Why did I tell him my real name? I never tell. Who is this Rainey? What is he going to do to me? She heard the words, *"Something wicked this way comes"* in her head and brushed them off again. She broke the spell of the moment. "Let's catch up."

She ran ahead of Rainey and he wondered if she wanted to get away from being alone with him.

Jimmy and Lara were so close to the falls that they could feel the cool, re-freshing spray. They were sitting on top of a picnic table, having a cigarette.

"Well, Missy, did you enjoy your cold bath?" Lara asked Vienna, handing her a cig.

Jimmy leaned over to light it for her.

She looked over at Rainey, who had a pack of spearmint gum in his hand and popped a piece in his mouth. "You don't smoke, Rainey?"

"He doesn't have any bad habits," Jimmy answered for him. "Unless you call gambling, drinking, and women bad habits. Oh yeah, and higher learning."

"Very funny, Jimmy," Rainey groused.

V butted out her cigarette. "I thought that everyone in this country smoked. May I have a stick of gum please?"

Rainey handed her a piece, saying, "You didn't have to do that for my sake you know."

"Yes, I did. Had enough of a shower, everyone? We should be getting back. Don't want to be late for work. Race you all to the car."

Rainey said to Lara as soon as Vienna was out of hearing range, "Is it true what V told me about herself?"

"Well, I don't know," Lara answered. "What did she tell you, that she was raised by wolves, that her father found her in a cabbage patch when she was a baby, or that she was adopted by really horrible people?"

"No. She said that she was from a family of Welsh Gypsies."

"Oh, that one. Probably true. Does it matter?"

V was waiting for them at the foot of the stairs, where she had just taken the gum out of her mouth and tossed it into the trash can.

"Hey," Rainey said. "I just gave you that!"

"Well," V offered, "I never chew gum for more than a minute or two, just enough to make my breath kissing fresh; not that I am going to be kissed or anything." She kind of winked at Rainey. "Have you seen those women who chew gum with their mouths open? They kind of look like cows."

Rainey looked at Lara, and she shrugged her shoulders. "What can I say, guys? She's right. I'm learning a lot about etiquette since I met her."

Vienna only smiled again.

Jimmy dropped the girls off at Lily Lane's diner, saying that they would be back when they got hungry. They drove over to One Bridge Hotel to grab a couple of beers before supper.

"What do you think, Rain?" Jimmy asked.

"You mean about the girl known as V? Don't know yet; ask me later. What can you tell me about her? How old is she, eighteen?"

"Doubt it. How old is Lara?"

"Let's see, I think that she is four years younger than me, so seventeen. Yeah, she will be seventeen in August."

"That sounds about right," Jimmy agreed. "I really don't know much about her, as she moved here while I was still up north. I do know that Yates and his kid brother, Jamie, and even 'the only girl for me is Marley,' Zane, have all gone out with her. Only once or twice, though. Apparently, that is her limit. I guess she learned not to get involved after her disastrous fling with Bobby Dumb Ass Evans."

"What happened there?" Rainey asked. "Didn't anyone warn her? I sure hope that she didn't find out the hard way. She is way too nice for the likes of him."

"Well, I guess you will find out later tonight just how nice she is."

"I'm not looking for anything, Jimmy. You know that."

They arrived back at Lily's shortly after 5. Upon entering, they were a little stunned by the décor of the place. They weren't expecting vivid pinks, yellows, and oranges. The pale-yellow walls were lined with signed autograph pictures of Doris Day, Rock Hudson, Liz Taylor, Marilyn Monroe, Frank Sinatra, Dean Martin, Humphrey Bogart, Kirk Douglas, Charlton Heston, and Elvis, just to name a few. There were booths with orange vinyl seats and chrome tables in red, yellow, or white tops.

The long counter was a tangerine color and the stools were covered with the orange again. The tables and chairs were wooden. Bright tablecloths and napkins decorated the tables. In one quick glance, they could see cakes and pies under glass-domed lids. Over the serving counter were cupboards full of coke glasses, white mugs, tulip sundae glasses, banana split bowls, and water jugs.

"I like it," Rainey said.

"I thought this was the '60s, but wrong again," Jimmy mused. "We are right back in the swinging '50s. No wonder Yates likes this place, a little nostalgia."

Lara had seen them and came over to where they were admiring the place. "Booth or table, boys?"

"What do you say, Rain, booth?" asked Jimmy.

"Sounds good to me," Rainey replied, looking around for Vienna.

"This is quite the place. Are you always this busy?" Jimmy asked.

Lara led them to an empty booth near the back. "It is every day that I am working. Here are your menus. Now don't go crazy. I will be right back as soon as I get a couple of orders out."

They were studying the menus while glancing around at the other patrons. They were mostly families with children, a few teenagers, and several lone oc-cupants sitting at the counter. Jimmy kicked Rainey under the table. "Look at that sign, Rain." He pointed to it on the wall, above the kitchen doors. It read: *We do not tolerate noisy children or unruly customers. Said offenders will be sentenced to kitchen duty under the watchful eye of the wicked witch of Bridge."*

Vienna came through the swinging doors with an order and, seeing them, waved. Rainey had thought that she looked cute in her short pants and peasant blouse this afternoon, but now, it was a whole new grown-up look. Her dark, shoulder-length hair was piled up on her head while little curls framed her face and forehead. Lara and she were both wearing form-fitting pink uniforms. Vienna filled it out in all the right places, no skin and bone here. She was short but somehow appeared taller than she was this afternoon, although she was not wearing heels. He wanted to whistle.

Jimmy interrupted his thoughts. "I can see the wheels turning, buddy. What is going on in that heavy brain of yours?"

"Not much. Just wondering what we are going to do while we wait for the girls to get off. Any thoughts?"

"Have we even asked them out or are we just assuming that they want to do something with us? I am pretty sure about Lara, but what is your take on V?"

"I guess you are right. We only said that we would see them here at the diner. I guess we should have asked if they had plans. If V would get over here, I would ask her."

"Lara will be back soon and then we will find out. How does a movie sound? That should time it just about right."

"Sure, sounds good to me. Have you decided on what you are going to order yet?"

"No, I cannot decide. Geez, are you really starting to hay tomorrow?"

"Yeah, the weather is perfect. We could really use an extra hand if you are not too hung over."

"I make it a point not to drink too much now that I have Jezebel."

Lara returned to their table, carrying two glasses of water. Jimmy asked her if they served booze and she told him no.

"Have you decided what you want yet?" she asked.

"Geez, Lara, I can't decide. What's good?"

"Everything is good Jimmy," she told him. "I can attest to that. If I had to choose, it would be Lily's goulash."

"Goulash?" Rainey questioned Lara. "I don't even know what that is."

"Sure you do. Your mom makes something like it…hamburger and noodles and other stuff. Lily adds some sort of sweet and sour sauce. You'll like it."

"Sounds good enough for me," Jimmy said. "What about you, Rain?"

"Yeah, sure, I'm taking your word on it, Lara."

"What do you want on your salads?" she asked.

"You mean like lettuce and vegetables?" Jimmy scowled.

"Quit being silly, Jimmy," Lara said. "You know it is. House dressing for you both then?"

They both nodded.

"Send Vienna over here, will you, Lara?" Rainey smiled smugly.

"This isn't V's station. I am your waitress, Rainey." Lara turned and left with their orders, pretending to be offended.

"I just want to know if she is going out with me later."

Lara turned with a big grin on her face. "You can only hope, cous, you can only hope. Be right back with your orders."

Rainey was fiddling with the tray of condiments. "Do you see Vienna over at the counter? She is flirting with those guys who just came in. Do you recognize them?"

"Yeah, so what? They are probably friends. What's with you anyhow?"

"Do you know them or not, Jimmy?"

"I think they are some of the Southerly Gang, is that what you are thinking? They are the boys that Yates and company had a run in with a while back. Don't tell me you are jealous, ole boy." Jimmy laughed. "I don't think that I have ever seen you so affected by a girl before, especially one that you just met. Here she comes."

Vienna smiled at them. "Lara said that you wanted to see me?"

Rainey took her hand. "I wanted to be sure that I will be seeing you later."

"Are you asking me out? You will have to ask my mama about that," V teased. "I'll send her over after you've had dinner." She let go of Rainey's hand and winked at Jimmy in her funny way of only half closing one eye.

A few minutes later, Lara returned with their salads and steaming-hot biscuits. "Do you guys want anything to drink?"

"Maybe coffee later," Rainey said.

"I'm not spoiling my appetite with this rabbit food." Jimmy pushed the salad away.

"You never have known what's good for you, have you, Jimmy? Make Mama Lily happy and have a few bites." Rainey said.

"Geez, you're already calling her mama!" Jimmy said.

Lara returned with their entrée and scolded Jimmy for not eating his salad.

"So," Rainey said, "V's last name is Lane? She was kidding when she said I had to ask her mom if I could take her out, right?"

"I don't think that she was kidding," Lara answered. "But with V, one never knows."

"Anyhow, her last name is not Lane, it is LaFontaine. But don't ask her, she will probably tell you it is Bronte."

"Bronte…like the sisters? *Wuthering Heights* and the like? Why?"

Lara shrugged her shoulders. "She's a bit of a romantic."

They struggled with the huge dinner.

"We should have had split a meal," Jimmy sighed.

"We'll know for the next time," Rainey agreed.

Vienna's mom came through the swinging doors. She definitely was V's mom. Her hair was reddish brown, not black like her daughter's. She was a few inches taller than V but had the same build, only more matronly. She had the same dark, intense eyes. He estimated that she was in her early forties. He took this all in as she crossed the room to where they were seated. Lara was with her and did the introductions.

"This is Jimmy Douglas and that rogue there is my cousin, Rainey Quinn. Boys, say hello to Lily Lane."

Lordy, did she have to call me a rogue?! Rainey stood up, as did Jimmy, to acknowledge the introduction. "Mrs. LaFontaine, the meal was absolutely delicious!" Rainey complimented her, assuming that she was the cook.

"Left room for dessert, I hope," she replied.

"Oh no, we couldn't eat another bite," Jimmy moaned.

"Nonsense. Bring them each a cruller, Lara. Please call me, Lily. Everyone does."

They made small talk until Lara returned with a plate in her hand covered by a tea towel. Lily pulled the cloth off and handed them each a fork. "Or," she said, "you can just pick them up with your fingers and eat them."

Not wanting to or daring to offend V's mom, they took the forks and took a bite of the delicate confection. It was sweet and crunchy, and was covered in liquid honey and icing sugar. Tasted something like a donut, only better.

"To heck with that," Jimmy said as he discarded the fork and picked it up with his fingers. He ate it all and then licked his fingers.

Rainey followed suit and he didn't even have a sweet tooth. He licked his lips. "My compliments, Mrs.…Lily."

"Now what is this I hear? You want to take my daughter out? Hmmm, I guess it will be all right, seeing that Lara vouches for you and you seem like decent chaps. Have her home by 10 o'clock. Nice to meet you." She started back to the kitchen, and then turned and said, "You boys do know that the girls have to work until 9, don't you?"

Jimmy said, "Yes, Ma'am."

"Vienna has a curfew of 10?" Rainey asked Lara.

"Some nights, I guess, but she is sleeping at my house tonight. I'm pretty sure that Lily was fooling with you. What are you guys doing until we get off work?"

"I guess we will head over to the Bijou and see what is playing. Unless you girls want to go to the 9 o'clock showing?" Jimmy asked.

"No, thanks, we have seen it," Lara said. "We'll meet you there or else we will be at V's. It's the old Doc Lewis house. You remember where that is, don't you?"

"Yeah, I remember. About four blocks over on River Street, right?"

Lara nodded. "See you later, and oh yeah, don't forget to leave a big tip!"

Rainey glanced in V's direction. She was too busy to see him leave.

While the girls were getting dressed for work, V had the chance to talk with her best friend about her cousin. "Tell me about Rainey, Lara."

"I can't believe that I haven't mentioned him before."

"Maybe you have, but honestly, I don't remember. It would be pretty hard to forget his name, though."

"He has always been my favorite cousin and I do have a few, as you well know. He is five years older than me and so he has always been protective of me. Every now and then, I would go up to the ranch with my mom. Rainey's dad is her brother. He taught me how to ride, how to saddle a horse, how to put the bit and bridle on, and most importantly, how to brush her down after a ride. That was my favorite part. I say her because the horse I rode was Belle. She was a beautiful chestnut. Unfortunately, she died a long time ago. Rainey and his sister are the only ones in the family to continue their post-secondary schooling. He is very serious about becoming an architect and he says that nothing will get in his way."

"Sorry about Belle. Hasn't Rainey been serious about a girl...I mean enough to make a commitment?"

"Not that I know of and I have never heard of him bringing a girl home to meet his parents. What do you think of him, V?"

"I like him. He is different from all of the others I have dated. He is quite the gentleman, which seems to be a rare quality these days. He is dashing in his casual slacks and loafers, and I have to say that I like the open white shirt. Definitely preppie. Plus, he is dashingly handsome and I love his voice, and even his name is dreamy. Very romantic. Why haven't you introduced him to me before?"

"He just got back. He is quite the ladies' man, I am afraid. I hope he doesn't break your heart."

"Lara Jacobs, what a strange thing for you to say." There it was again, the sensation that something—or in this case, someone—was warning her...tread lightly, oh so lightly. Vienna shivered.

They weren't waiting for the boys outside of the theatre.

"Good God, did we really sit through two hours of agonizing dialogue and questionable acting?" Rainey asked Jimmy as he stretched and yawned. "The girls should have warned us!"

"Well, I caught up on my sleeping," Jimmy answered, starting the car. "You may have to give me directions, Rain."

"Surely you remember the early years in Doc Lever's chair?"

"Oh, I remember all too well. That rubber chair and the drill that sounded like a jack hammer, and what did we decide that smell was? Rotten eggs?"

Rainey laughed. "We sure did celebrate when we heard that the old guy had gone bonkers and had been carted off to the loony bin."

"Yates was so happy that he cried. The doc gave it up two days before his appointment."

They were laughing so hard that they missed the turn unto River Road. Jimmy backed up. "It should be the last house on the left, if I am not mistaken." He slowed Jezebel down to a slow crawl and parked at the curb.

"What an impressive piece of nineteenth-century architecture! I never appreciated it before. I can hardly wait to see the inside."

"And just what makes you so sure that you are going to see the inside, bro? This is the girl who only sees a guy once or twice."

"There are always exceptions to the rules, and believe me when I tell you that I am going to see the interior. Make no mistake about that."

The girls came running down the steps. They were dressed in identical white slacks and green blouses with white sweaters draped over their shoulders. They had been waiting patiently for their dates. Lara had carried a torch for Jimmy for years. He had started to notice her as more than a kid sister just a year ago. They never really dated, but got together now and then in Hawthorne when Lara was visiting or at parties in Bridge. She hoped that maybe tonight might lead to a new and meaningful relationship.

V didn't know what she wanted. There were too many prospects out there for her to consider. But then, she had never met anyone before who took her breath away like Rainey Quinn. She wasn't sure how she was going to play it with him.

Rainey hopped out of the front seat and motioned Lara to take his place beside Jimmy. At the same time, he opened the back door for V. She got in and slid across the seat as far as she could. Rainey joined her and, with a big grin, said, "I don't have leprosy you know."

Vienna laughed. "Oh, thank goodness. I have been worried about that all day. But should I just take your word for it, Sir?"

"Sir? I like it, shows respect."

"I have nothing but respect for my elders," V teased.

This is going to be a fun evening, Rainey thought.

"Where are we going, guys?" Jimmy asked. "Lara wants to go to the Opera House. Do you think the road will be all right, Rain?"

"Don't know. It's up to you. What kind of clearance has this gal got?"

"Pretty good. We'll give it a go."

The Opera House was a local parking spot for the young people of Bridge Falls. It was 6 miles up the old highway and then a couple more down a dirt road that then veered down a grassy, well-worn trail. It sat on a knoll overlooking the river and a multitude of fire pits. It had been so named because it was a haunt for several coyote families whose eerie songs echoed through the valley, especially during the full moon cycle.

Vienna always felt restless and edgy during a full moon and so was glad there wouldn't be one tonight.

Jimmy was a little hesitant going the last mile, but he coaxed Jezebel at every corner, talking to her like she was a person. He had worked hard in that logging camp, and as soon as he had earned the $5,455 for her and pocket money to last a while, he had called it quits with the northern job. He let out a sigh of relief. "I think we made it with no harm to Jezzy."

"I'm sorry, Jimmy," said Lara. "I am used to coming here in beat-up jalopies so I never notice how bad the road is."

"Hey, no problem." He pulled up to the edge and engaged the parking brake. "I've been wanting to come out here myself. It's been a while. You going to get the hooch out of the trunk or what, Rain?"

Rainey got out and sunk into the soft, mossy grass. It had rained a few days ago and there was still a sweet smell in the air.

"Well, I have never been here before, so I am looking forward to the choir. They had better be in tune," V quipped.

"Don't count on it, girl." Rainey passed a beer to everyone. He assumed that Vienna drank. He wasn't wrong. She took a long drink, savoring the cool liquid running down her throat. *God*, he thought, *she is sensuous.* "I've been meaning to ask you how you keep your figure around all that food. I take it that your mom is the dessert person."

"In case you haven't noticed, Mister, I am not what one would call skinny. But to answer your question, I don't eat," V replied.

"Oh, I have noticed all right. Don't tell me that you don't eat, you have to."

Lara was giggling because she knew what V was going to say next.

"If I ate, I would look like Little Lulu," V said.

Rainey almost choked on his beer but was quick enough to spit it out of the open window.

Jimmy turned around. "Little respect for the upholstery, bro. V, don't you mean Chubby?"

"No, are you insinuating that I look like a boy?"

"I don't think that is what Jimmy meant and, no, no one would ever make the mistake of thinking that you were anything but a girl," Rainey answered for his friend.

Jimmy had turned the interior lights on and Rainey had a chance to study V. Her smile was telling him something, but he wasn't sure what. It was mysterious, like the one Mona Lisa wore. He tossed a few bags of chips up front and said to Vienna, "I guess you don't want any of these?"

"What? Aren't they right up there on the food chain with celery and carrots? Sure, toss me a bag and another beer please."

The next hour or so was spent with the guys telling stories on each other. The radio was on low and Elvis, Little Richard, Brenda Lee, and the like were trying to break through the static. During one hysterically funny anecdote that

Jimmy had told on Rainey, V was laughing so hard that she spilled some of her drink down her blouse.

"Oh, for crying in the sink!" she exclaimed.

Jimmy looked at Lara and said, "Did I just hear her say that she was crying in the sink?'

Lara answered, "You haven't heard anything yet."

"Quit talking like you think I can't hear you," V complained.

Jimmy said, "Let's go for a walk, Lara. I have to water the horse. Pass us a brew, will you, Rain?"

"Be careful out there, guys. The ground is saturated." He was finally alone with Vienna and was plotting his next move. He didn't think that she would take kindly to being pulled over and kissed, and it certainly didn't appear that she had any intention of moving closer to him.

Vienna made the decision for him. She had suddenly jumped up and was leaning across the front seat. A Connie Francis tune was playing on the radio. "I just love that song!" She was halfway over, trying to reach the volume with one hand while holding on to her bottle with the other. She realized that she was stuck and could not go forward or backward, and was in danger of doing a face plant on the dashboard. "Fiddlesticks! Help me, Rainey!"

Now it was his turn to laugh. "You have got yourself into some predicament, haven't you? You could always drop the beer."

"On Jimmy's nice seats? You have to be kidding!"

He grabbed her around her legs and pulled her back, right onto his lap.

"Well, isn't this a fine kettle of fish? If I don't quit laughing, I am going to pee my pants and that won't be pretty." She was struggling to free herself from Rainey's grasp.

"Hey, hey, hey. You don't think that you are going to get away from me, now that I have you right where I want you, do you?"

"Oh, and is this where you want me, Sir? And what are you going to do with me?" Her eyes were wide open as he pulled her closer for that long-anticipated kiss. *Cherry*, Vienna thought. *Why does he taste like sweet cherry wine? And how would I know? I have never even had cherry wine.* She only knew that she didn't want the kiss to end and, apparently, Rainey didn't, either, as he wasn't releasing her.

Finally, their lips parted and Vienna took a deep breath. "Well, you certainly know how to shut a girl up, don't you?"

"Believe me, Vienna, I was not trying to. I only wanted to taste the mouth that has intrigued me all day."

"Just what does that mean?"

"Don't get defensive. I only mean that I have been looking forward to kissing you ever since I met you, and I must admit that the wait was well worth it. I hope there is more where that came from."

"We'll just have to wait and see, won't we? Have you been chewing cherry gum?"

"It's funny that you should ask, as I was going to ask you the same question."

She had dislodged herself from his lap but had not moved away. "Maybe there are cherry trees in blossom. Oh, I so hope there is."

"Now, it is my turn to ask, what do you mean by that?"

"I never kiss and tell, but I will tell you one thing, Rainey Quinn. I may be only sixteen but I know what a kiss is, and most of them are mushy and awkward, and that one was…I don't know."

"Sure you do. I felt it, too. It was a kiss waiting to happen and I think that we were meant to also."

She was shivering and Rainey put his arm around her, pulling her close again. She couldn't bear it if he kissed her again and she would die if he didn't.

They decided to head out as the night had developed a sudden chill. Lara lived a few miles out of town with her parents, Anne and Lance Jacobs. They ran a retail nursery that catered to the local florists and public domain. They employed five people at peak periods. Lara much preferred working at the diner than at the garden center. She made 65 cents an hour and a few dollars in tips every day, and she got to wait on all her friends. The wages were enough to keep her in cigarettes and beer, and occasionally, new clothes.

Rainey walked Vienna to the door as Jimmy and Lara were saying good night in the car.

"I'm glad Jimmy talked me into coming to Bridge today. May I call you tomorrow?"

"I'd like that, Rainey. I'm glad that you came, too. Good night."

He took her face in his hands and said, "Good night, Vienna." Then he kissed her, and again, she tasted the wine.

Lara came running from the car and they tiptoed quietly through the house to Lara's bedroom. They struggled to hold back the giggles. As soon as they reached Lara's room, V flopped on one of the beds, pulling the chenille spreads over her.

"Aren't you going to get undressed?" Lara asked her.

"Eventually," V replied. "I just want to dream right now."

"You like my cousin, don't you?"

"He calls me Vienna."

"That's because you let him, V."

Vienna's little voice was warning her. "Go away, go away," she whispered to her imaginary mistress of destiny.

The boys drove slowly through the deserted streets of Bridge Falls. Jimmy asked his friend what he thought of the girl known as V.

"I think that I could be in trouble here, Jimmy."

"Well, you know what to do about that, don't you?" He looked at Rainey with a big smile and answered his own question. "Don't ever see her again, bro. If you want to have a summer romance, well, all right then. Just don't let it turn into anything more . You can't afford to jeopardize your future."

"That's not going to happen, Jimbo. That's just not going to happen."

"Good. You did mean that you're never going to see her again, didn't you?"

"No, that's not what I meant at all."

Jimmy let out a long sigh and changed the subject.

Rainey couldn't wait to talk to Vienna the next day. She answered the phone.

"I was hoping that you were home from Lara's by now. I managed to track down your number, seeing that I forgot to ask you last night. Seems like I had other things on my mind. I slept like a baby, how about you?"

"Ummm, I did. I had very pleasant dreams."

"You have to work today, right?"

"Yes, for a few hours, as I have to get home and study for exams."

"I guess that it is okay that I can't get over until next weekend then. We will be haying all week into the dark of night. I might not get a chance to call you until Friday. I will be done by noon on Saturday… Will you spend the rest of the day with me?"

"I have to work until 4 but will try to get off earlier. Will you be coming alone?"

"I think so. Is that all right? I hope you are not afraid to be alone with me?"

"I'm not Rainey. Don't work too hard. Bye Rainey."

"Good luck with your exams. See you on Saturday Vienna."

She loved hearing him say her name. She danced up to her room hugging herself. It was going to be a very long week.

She wrote her last exam on Friday. She knew without a doubt that she would be repeating math next year. English, French, socials, and home economics had been a cinch; science was another story. She hadn't been studying or applying herself; she had been too busy having a good time. Oh well…

She walked the short distance to the diner and found Lara on a break, sitting with some of the guys from Hawthorne.

"Hey, V," Yates called out. "Come join us."

She sat down next to Zane, wondering why they were here. Shouldn't they all be haying? She soon found out that they weren't farmers but worked at the quarry.

Lara brought her a coke. "How did the exams go?"

"Just like yours, they're over," V answered. "Enough said."

"Amen," Yates said. "What time are you off work, Lara? We thought that we would get a bunch together and have a little party down at the pond. Hope that you girls will join us. We have already seen Mary, Marla, and Lizzy, and they are game."

Lara moaned. "I have to work until 9."

"I'm sure one of us will come back for you," Yates said. "How about it, V?"

She wanted to say no but instead said, "Sure, sounds like fun."

The pond was a runoff from the rivers, and at this time of year, it was a much warmer place to swim in. The beaches went on for a mile or so. It was frequented by the local constabulary now and then, when they felt like driving down the rough, dusty road.

V tried to enjoy herself but found that she was thinking about Rainey far too much. These were all his friends, but somehow, they were very different from him. Jimmy must be helping out with the haying. She didn't want it to get back to Rainey that she was having a good time with his buddies. She wondered if he had phoned. She decided to go back with Mary when she went to pick up Lara.

Everyone was surprised when she said that she was leaving . Yates asked her if she was feeling all right and told her that she was going to miss the fireworks if she left. She asked him what he meant by "fireworks." He said that she would have to stick around to find out, but she wasn't that interested. She had Mary drop her off before she picked up Lara because she was sure that her best friend would talk her into returning to the party.

To Vienna's dismay, Rainey had not phoned.

Her mother remarked on how early it was and why was she home so early.

"You are always telling me not to stay out late," replied V. "I guess I can't win."

"School is over now so you are cleared for later nights. Girl, have you been smoking again?"

"Bonfire smoke, Mom. I'm tired, going to bed." She agreed with her mother, she smelled horrible and should bathe but decided to wait until morning. Bedding needed changing anyhow. She just wanted to crawl into bed and dream about Rainey. What was wrong with her anyhow?

Vienna was in the bath when she heard the phone ring downstairs. Then she heard someone running up the stairs and down the hall. She expected the door to burst open, but instead, there was a knock.

"V, someone named Rain or something is on the phone."

"Well, Addy, I cannot come right now. Ask him to call me back in fifteen minutes please." V rinsed the soap out of her hair, and then rinsed it with a vinegar solution and more water until her hair smelled clean. Satisfied that there was no remnant of smoke left, she climbed out of the tub, wrapped a huge towel around her, and ran to her room. She rubbed her hair vigorously and set it in large rollers when it was barely damp. She slipped into a clean housecoat and ran downstairs. She wasn't going to miss Rainey's call again.

Her mother came by and saw her sitting on the floor, under the phone. "Anxious are we then? Your father is driving me to work as I have the pies to take and thaw. Don't be late."

V nodded. The sharp ring startled her: two short and one long…that was theirs.

"Hello," she said in a little voice.

"Hello, Vienna. It's Rainey. How are you? I'm sorry that I didn't call you last night. I'm afraid that I fell asleep right after dinner and didn't wake up until late."

"That's okay. I was at a bonfire with Lara and some of your buddies anyway."

"Is that right? Are you still up for tonight or do you have other plans?"

Did she detect annoyance in his voice? "I'm looking forward to seeing you."

"Me, too. I'll see you at the diner at 4 then."

"Bye, Rainey." Too late, she realized that Lara had not been at the bonfire when she was.

Her day dragged on. At 3:30, she went to the ladies' room, combed her hair, and applied a fresh coat of lipstick. She didn't wear mascara or rouge. If she was pale, she would pinch her cheeks just like the Bronte sisters used to do. Sometimes, she wore black eyeliner and she decided to today. She thought that it gave her a provocative look…like Liz Taylor. She was refilling the salt and pepper shakers when Rainey walked in.

"Hello, Vienna." His velvet voice caught her by surprise.

She took a breath and turned to face him. "I wasn't expecting you so soon."

"Happened to be in the neighborhood," he teased and winked at her.

"Can I get you anything?"

"Are you on the menu?"

V passed him a coke. "Here, keep your mouth busy." She knew that she was blushing.

For the next half hour, she flitted about the diner, clearing tables and chatting with customers. Rainey watched her every move.

Now I know how a goldfish feels, Vienna thought.

At 4, she emerged from the kitchen with a picnic basket. She grabbed two cokes from the cooler and motioned for Rainey to follow her. He ran ahead of her to open the door. He led her to his car and placed the basket on the backseat.

"A picnic, eh?" Rainey said. "I haven't been on one since I was ten."

"Well then, you are long overdue! You boys sure do like red, don't you?" Vienna walked around his two-toned, red-and-white automobile, caressing its sleek lines. As she came around the front, she said, "I like it."

He opened the door for her. "I'm glad you like her. I'm kind of fond of her myself."

"What year is it and why do guys always call their cars 'she'?"

"I guess because the car owns us…something like a mistress would."

Vienna blushed again. "I'm sure I would know nothing about that."

Rainey smiled all too knowingly. "It's a 1956 Oldsmobile 88."

"All my father ever owned were station wagons. It always seemed that we carried half of our possessions with us on our moves. What do you call her, Rainey?"

"Sometimes I call her 'Ole Betsy'—nothing exotic like Jezebel."

"Isn't that the name of Daniel Boone's gun, or was it Davy Crockett's?"

"I haven't the foggiest idea. How would you even know anything like that?"

"I have no idea…from watching too much T.V., I guess."

"Do you think I should change her name to Marilyn, or how about Vienna?"

"Don't be silly. I need to go home and change. You can visit with my father; that is, if you don't mind older men. Apparently, I don't." It was her turn to wink at him.

As they entered the hundred-plus-year-old house, Rainey let out a low whistle. He assumed that the front door was solid oak. The staircase was a delicate maple color. The banister had a curvature that was unique and it was polished to a golden sheen. V walked him down the hall, noticing that he was admiring the freshly decorated plastered ceiling and newly painted walls. *He's going to love the library*, she thought and opened the doors that led into it.

"My God, is that a tin ceiling?" he exclaimed.

Vienna laughed. "Dad, meet Rainey Quinn. He is studying to become an architect. Rainey, this is my dad, Joe. I'll leave you two to talk shop."

Joe LaFontaine was a man about Rainey's dad's age, maybe a little older. He got up from his desk to shake Rainey's hand. "Architecture? A man of good taste. There is nothing more rewarding than to see the wondrous buildings of the world and feel the wood and stone that carved out our heritage. What do you think of this monument created in the last century? I call it Infinity Castle. That's how long it is going to take me to restore it to its original grandeur." He had a hearty laugh and Rainey liked him immediately.

"Well, Sir, if what I have seen so far is a sample of your work, then I would say you are well on your way. Is this all you're doing? It all looks original. The ceiling is glorious!"

"Please call me Joe. I can't take any credit for this room. It's pretty much as we found it, minus the cobwebs. This and the master bedroom are the only ones that didn't require a lot of work. I am trying to track down the origin of this tin ceiling, but it is proving to be a formidable task. Here, have a gander at the plans for the kitchen. Lily and V do most of the baking for the diner here, so I need to make it a priority."

Rainey was busy studying the blueprints so he didn't hear Vienna enter the room. "I can hardly wait to see the rest of the house. Did you know that when I was a kid, I used to come to this very house and be tortured by Doc Lever's drill? He had his practice somewhere at the back of the house."

Joe laughed. "Yes, I have heard some pretty gruesome stories about the man."

"And that is a story for another day. Come on, Rainey, we are losing what is left of the day. We are going on a picnic, Daddy. See you later." Vienna kissed her dad on the cheek.

"Looking forward to talking with you again, Sir." Rainey shook Joe's hand again.

Vienna pulled Rainey along as they ran from the house. "Come on, slow poke, we don't have all day." She was making him feel like a teenager again. "Where shall we go for our picnic? You know the area a lot better than I do."

"How about Hudson's Crossing?" Rainey asked. "Have you been up there yet?"

"Sounds wonderful. I have only been there once. The river was still very high." Rainey held his door open for her and she scooted in past the steering wheel.

He grabbed hold of her. "Don't go any further, young lady. I want you right here."

Vienna giggled. They shared a quick kiss. "Let's go, let's go."

"Is that all I get? I've been a good boy."

She turned the radio on. "Quit kidding, Rainey, and drive."

Hudson's Crossing was idyllic. They found a grassy spot along the river, away from the other visitors. Rainey laid the blanket down and Vienna took out their dinner. She had brought potato salad, chicken, fresh rolls, and grapes and strawberries. Rainey admitted that he was hungry. He opened a bottle of fruity wine and poured her a small glass. She took a sip; it had a cherry flavor.

She smirked. "You knew that Superman died last week, don't you?"

"Excuse me, did you say that Superman died? You mean he was killed off in the comic books?"

"No, the actor who played him on T.V. died. You have watched it, haven't you?"

"Oh, of course. I really don't have much time for television. What happened?"

"His name was George Reeves, just in case you are interested. He may have committed suicide. I think he was murdered."

"You know something that no one else does?" He was teasing her.

Well, she could tease, too. "We Gypsies know things."

That brought howls of laughter. "I wish Jimmy was here. He is quite taken by you."

"Now what does that even mean? Here, have a piece of my white chocolate fudge cake." She handed him a big slice of a decadent-looking layer cake.

"You're kidding me! You expect me to eat all of this?" He took a bite, exclaiming, "My God, this is absolutely sinful! Where is yours?"

"I can't afford it." She patted her hips.

"You won't mind if I take some home? My mother is going to want your recipe. I am exploding from your exquisite cuisine."

"You have such a way with words, my lord."

"And can I have my way with you, Lady V?"

Vienna was disturbed by his request. She got up quickly and started packing the picnic basket. Rainey jumped up and took her in his arms.

"Hey, hey. I am sorry. I shouldn't have said that." He tilted her head and kissed her. "We have had such a wonderful time, I am sorry if I spoiled it."

She caught her breath. "Don't be a daffy duck. You didn't spoil anything. You surprised me, is all. This is only our second time that we have been together."

"Is there going to be a third, Vienna? I understand that two dates is your limit."

"Now where did you hear that? If it is, what are you going to do about it? Now come on. You promised to take me to the movies."

Three hours later, they emerged from the Bijou hand in hand. Rainey asked her if she enjoyed the show. "I mean," he said, "you were sobbing so much I didn't even think you would make it to the end. If I had of known that it was going to be such a tearjerker, I would have brought a bigger hand-kerchief."

"Rainey, don't you know that if you don't cry or laugh, then it wasn't a good movie?"

"No, I don't think I knew that. Thanks for telling me. Still, I didn't laugh or cry, and I thought that it was a pretty darn good movie."

"I loved the movie...Ava Gardner is the most beautiful woman in Hollywood; next to Liz and Marilyn that is."

"Of course... You know, you remind me of a young Elizabeth Taylor."

"There you go, being silly again. I don't suppose you knew that Mike Todd died on my birthday last year?"

Rainey had no idea who Mike Todd was but decided not to ask in light of being ignorant regarding the Superman thing, so he said, "No, I didn't know that."

They arrived at her house and talked for a while until V decided it was time to go in.

Rainey took her face in his hands and kissed her tenderly. "Vienna, you take my breath away. When can I see you again?"

"Anytime you want, whenever you want." She smiled and danced into the house.

He watched her as she twirled and whirled into the house. Was nymph the right word to describe her? He truly was enchanted by her ways. She was without a doubt the most delightful creature that he had ever met. He shook his head as he drove down River Street. *Don't get carried away with this charming young girl, you can't afford to. We'll see*, he told himself. *I'll see her again and then I will decide.*

Rainey, like his sister, Claudia, who was five years older, had been born in Bridge Falls. He had lived all his life in Hawthorne with his parents, Patsy and

Paul Quinn. His sister had left home after graduation, and lived in Toronto with her husband and two young children. She was a substitute teacher. He, like all the other kids from the valley, spent his senior year at Bridge Falls High. He knew early in life that he did not want to be a farmer. After a family visit to Quebec City, he had decided that he wanted to be an architect. He had been truly amazed at the buildings of one of the oldest cities in North America. Their tour had led them to the great churches like Notre Dame Cathedral, and then there was The Palace Royale, The Citadel, and the most impressive of them all, The Chateau Frontenac. The images of the city that had been founded in colonial Canada stayed with him through boyhood, and now he was well on his way in mastering the work of the great architects. In just another year, he would be off to France and Italy to continue his studies. There would be nothing that could hold him back.

His mind started to compare Vienna to other women. That wasn't fair. He had not dated anyone this young since he himself had been a teenager. Yes, he had known plenty of women…loved them and left them. No, that wasn't right; he had never been in love. They were all just passing fancies; dancers and would be actresses, promiscuous college girls, and bored rich girls. He was cautious and had rules. No married women or single mothers. But of course, some of them lied. Sometimes, he was so ashamed of himself that he would avoid women for months. He had never taken a girl home to meet his parents. There was no room in his life for a lasting relationship. Besides, he had never met anyone whom he thought enough of that he wanted his parents to meet.

This summer was to be a quiet one. He was going to work on the ranch and hang out with Jimmy and the guys. He was going to take a hiatus from women. Then Jimmy had talked him into going to Bridge a week ago. They were only supposed to spend the day haunting the bars, and then they had run into Lara on the street. Damn that Jimmy!

Chapter Three

Vienna, 1959

I was fifteen years old in the fall of '59. My parents had left me in charge of my sisters; Sissy was eleven and Addy was seven. They had gone on one of their instant vacations, which meant that we would be moving again. Later that morning, as I was straightening up, I found pages in a real estate magazine circled. They were for British Columbia. *Okay*, I thought, *we're moving back to the coast.* I read on. The listings that had been outlined were for Bridge Falls and Valley.

> *For sale: A large, century-old house on the banks of the Black River. Built in the 1850s by an American railroad magnate. This house has great potential to be great again in the hands of the right person. It will require hard work and TLC (tender loving care). It features a huge library, which boasts a tin ceiling, hardwood floors throughout, two baths, and a conservatory. It is nestled in the quiet valley of Bridge Falls, 300 miles from Vancouver. It must be seen to be appreciated. It has sat empty for ten years. It was owned by the local dentist until his retirement. It has just come on the market and is listed at the low price of $15,599! Please apply to 911 Hobart Ave., Bridge Falls, B.C. Phone no. 1- 933. Listing is 112.*

Underneath was another listing that had been highlighted. It made no sense to me.

> *For sale or lease: A once-thriving restaurant. Property is in receivership. Some upgrades needed. Listing is 121. See address above for Bridge Falls.*

I sighed and started packing the china cupboard. I didn't like it here in Alberta anyhow. We moved every year and so it was no big surprise, as I knew that my father's job had been winding down. He was a construction consultant.

True to form, we were gone in a few short weeks. I was in grade ten and already struggling with the new math. I wondered how the move would affect my schooling, as it was in the middle of the school year.

My parents had actually bought a house. They had never owned one before to my knowledge. We had never lived anywhere long enough to lay down roots. Not only had they purchased the old house, but also the restaurant! Apparently, mother had always wanted to run a diner. News to me, and even stranger was the fact that father had inherited a good sum of money from some unknown (to me) uncle. We spent the whole of December in a motel while the house was made livable. The room I was to have as my own was in the worst shape, so I had to sleep in the library for a few weeks. I didn't mind, as it was filled with a thousand old and treasured books. My passion was reading.

Father did the needed repairs to the diner and mother opened it in May of 1960. She called it Lily Lane's. I worked at the diner after school and on weekends, so did my best friend, Lara. We were inseparable; father called us the "Gold Dust Twins." I was very happy and had a whole new life.

Unfortunately, it was not all good. I had started smoking and drinking, just like everybody else who we hung out with did. I had discovered "boys." I hadn't even had a date until I moved to Bridge Falls, and now I was going out with a different guy every week. There was either a party or a dance every weekend. I was finally a normal teenager. Then on June 11, I met Rainey and my carefree and uncomplicated life went to hell in a handbasket. The prophecy of the Gypsy fortune-teller echoed in my head.

"Be very wary of the one who will call you Vienna."

A chill ran up and down my spine.

Rainey and I spent every possible minute together. We didn't date other people, we didn't talk much about it, we were just together. Yet, we had made no commitments. Rainey had to attend a seminar at the University of British Columbia and would be gone for a week. I decided that our relationship was not progressing and that I should probably quit seeing him before I became any more involved. While he was away, I partied with Lara and friends, many of them the boys from Hawthorne. I drank a little too much and made some poor decisions, none of them too serious. I told myself that I didn't care if word got back to him. He had not asked me to sit at home and wait for him. It was a Monday morning late in July when I heard from him again.

"Vienna," he said over the phone. "Are you busy tonight?"

The sound of his voice sent chills up my spine as usual, but I thought he sounded different somehow. "No, I have the whole day off. Did you have a nice vacation?"

"Well, it was hardly a holiday. Shall I come over then, say in an hour or so?"

There it was…annoyance. I put the phone back on the hook. Okay, he was going to tell me that he didn't want to see me anymore. He probably met up with one of his old girlfriends at the coast and decided that he wasn't interested in me anymore. Being the gentleman that he was, he would tell me to my face, not over the phone. Well, I had prepared myself for this. It was nice while it lasted. I couldn't have been more wrong.

I didn't give Rainey a chance to get out of the car. I didn't want him prolonging the agony by visiting with my father. I walked over to his bright, shiny car. He reached over and opened the door for me.

"Hi," was all that I could manage. I sat squarely on my side of the seat.

"Hello yourself," he said. "I'm glad that you have the day off. I think that we need to talk."

Here it comes, I thought. He didn't start the car. I guess we are going to have it out right here. "Okay," I said. I couldn't look at him.

"I am not very happy with you, Vienna. I hear that you had yourself quite the time while I was away. Is that true?"

I didn't know if I was angry or hurt. I turned to face him. "I guess you might say that. Yes, I did a little partying. What are you getting at specifically? You just got home. Who have you been talking to? I would be interested to know what is being said about me."

"Never mind. Oh, you may as well know. I talked to Jimmy this morning and he said that he had been out with you several times, and you really knew how to cut loose."

"Not that I owe you an explanation, but I was never out with Jimmy on a date. We were always with a crowd. Did he say that I danced on the tables and took off all my clothes? And what would you care if I did?"

Rainey looked hurt. "I wouldn't go that far, Vienna. And, yes, I do care. I thought that we had something special. Did I not tell you that I didn't want you seeing anyone else? Well, I am telling you now. How do you feel about that?"

Okay, this is going in a whole other direction, I thought. *Should I tell him that I never want to date anyone else and that maybe I am in love with him?* Instead, I said, "I care for you, too Rainey. I don't want to see anyone else. I won't if you don't." I was so relieved that I thought I might cry, but I managed not to.

"This summer is only you, Vienna. Let's not lose the rest of it by quarrelling. Can we kiss and make up?"

"I wasn't aware that we were fighting."

"Maybe I just want to kiss you. Now will you get over here?"

I smiled and moved closer to him. My heart was beating rapidly. No more was said, but I heard from Lara that Rainey had laid down the law to Jimmy and his friends. He told them that he did not appreciate their loose tongues and that I wasn't on the market for any of them. That week we spent by ourselves hiking up to the fossil pits, swimming, and becoming more aware of our feelings. One day, Rainey asked me what I intended to do after graduation.

"That is still two years down the road. Perhaps I will go to Wales and get a position as a governess. Maybe I will even find some Gypsy relatives."

"Is that so? I thought that maybe you would join me at the coast?"

I laughed. "Are you propositioning me?"

"Maybe."

By the weekend, we were back hanging out with everyone else again. We double-dated with Zane and Marley and went to the drive—in to see a double feature horror film. I hid my face in Rainey's shoulder throughout *House on Haunted Hill* and *Creature from the Black Lagoon*. I told him that he was never to take me to a scary movie ever again. The last horror movie that I had seen was *The Thing*, when I was about nine. I did not do well being scared to death.

Rainey laughed and said that he liked me thinking that he could protect me from monsters, and that it was my idea to come tonight. I hit him ever so slightly. We had many more fun nights and one that wasn't.

One very hot evening, toward the end of August, we were at the Opera House with the gang. I had decided to go swimming. I hadn't brought a bathing suit and so had to jump in fully clothed. I felt chilly after and tried to warm myself up on Rainey.

He held me at arm's length and said, "Oh no, you don't, young lady! Come and take your clothes off and I will wrap you in the blanket, and then I will really warm you up."

"What do you mean, Rainey?" I demanded.

"I think that you know very well what I mean, Vienna. I want to make love to you."

"That is not going to happen. I think that we have had this conversation before. I am not one of your little floosies. Now I want to go home."

I walked back to the car with Rainey following me. He tried to open the door for me but I pushed him aside. Lara came running over to see why we were leaving, and I told her that I was cold. I was sure she doubted that it was the reason, as it was still 90 degrees. I yanked the blanket from the backseat to sit on, as I didn't want to get the upholstery wet. I sat as far away from Rainey as I could.

He said in a teasing voice, "I sure know how to ruin a party, don't I?"

"Don't be flippant, Rainey! You want what I can't give and I am tired of fighting about it. You should have found someone older and more sophisticated to spend your summer with. I am glad that summer is over and you will be leaving soon!"

"You don't mean that, do you? Tell me you still want to see me, because I want to keep seeing you. I don't want any old, experienced girl. I just want you."

"Oh, I want to see you all right. I just can't."

"Get over here, Vienna!"

"I can't, I am all wet."

"I don't care. I will take you any way that I can get you."

"You can't have me the way that you want me. That's it. Please take me home."

"You know what? I kind of like it when you are feisty…it's a turn on."

"Quit it, Rainey! Don't make fun of me. I know that you are in your prime years of sexuality and I am only a naïve teenager, so take me the way I am or leave me."

"Now how would you know that, Lady V?"

"I read and I'm not completely innocent about the facts of life."

"I can attest to that and I wouldn't want you any other way. I'm sorry that you think I want more from you. It's true, but I don't expect it. Am I making any sense at all?"

"Yes and no. I don't want you to be angry with me."

Rainey started the car and said, "I'm not and I hope you are not with me."

"I'm not, Rainey. I just feel so helpless when I am with you."

"Helpless? What does that mean?"

"I know that you are frustrated with me, as I am with my feelings for you. I sometimes think about you and all your other girlfriends, and I know that I cannot compete. I have to be me."

"Who says there are other girls? If there were, I would only be comparing them to you and they would lose."

"There is nothing special about me."

"Don't sell yourself short. You are special, you make people happy, and you make me happy. The minute I am gone, the boys will be lining up at your door. I'm jealous already."

"Oh, Rainey, I am sorry that I am such a prude." He had his arm around me and I was trying not to cry. He kissed me on my forehead.

"Whatever am I going to do with you? Is there a glimmer of hope for me with you?"

"Does this mean that you still want to see me?"

"You know I do, Vienna."

We arrived home and made plans for the next weekend. It would be the last one before Labor Day. I was becoming increasingly restless. I didn't want the summer to end because I was sure that when Rainey went back to college, I would never see him again and it would all be my fault. I was the master of my ship, but I had a foreboding that I was going to capsize it, and I did. The day was here and I was powerless to change what was going to transpire. Rainey and I had our plans for the day all laid out. We were going to take Sissy and Addy to the Labor Day parade and then to the carnival.

Everything went according to plan. Rainey took the girls on the Ferris wheel and some crazy Tilt-A-Whirl. I watched from a safer place—the ground. We ate popcorn and candy floss. He won stuffed teddy bears for the girls and a tiny unicorn for me at the midway. The girls were very fond of him. Afterward, we went to the diner for burgers, fries, and milkshakes. Mother and father joined us and said it was their treat. We thanked them and dropped the girls off at home. Rainey asked where I wanted to go, and I told him to Lookout Point. We had never been there together, so it held no memories, good or bad.

Labor Day, 1960

I think I lost my happy face the second that we dropped the girls off. I loved Rainey's kisses, and if only we could be like this forever…but passion leads to lovemaking, and that wasn't going to happen, not even if he was going off to war. Elvis was singing "It's Now or Never." I turned the radio up and suggested we go outside. There was a full moon coming over the mountain. *Perfect*, I thought.

"Why are you so quiet, V?"

That must have been an omen because Rainey never called me V. "That'll Be the Day" came blasting over the airwaves. Nonchalantly, I said, "Do you know where you were when Buddy Holly was killed in a plane accident?"

He laughed as he usually did when confronted with one of my trivia questions. "Well, let me see. No, I don't. There were others with him, right?"

"Yes," I replied, "Richie Valens and the Big Bopper. It was on February 3, 1959."

"And I suppose you know exactly where you were?"

"I guess that I was sleeping, as I heard about it the next day."

"You know, Vienna, I think that you have a photographic memory."

"If I did, I wouldn't be repeating math next year now, would I? Apparently, it only works on useless facts."

Rainey opened a beer for us to share and I told him, "No, thanks. "I'm glad that summer is over. I have been drinking far too much. I suppose that this is how alcoholism starts."

"I don't think that you are in any danger of that happening. I have never seen you have more than two drinks at a time. Did you ever think that it is the company that you keep?"

"I love being with you, Rainey. I can't stand to think that I am not going to be seeing you after tonight. I love you, Rainey." *There, I had said it, and there is no going back.*

He took his arm off my shoulder and slid off the hood of the car. He couldn't wait to get away from me. "Oh God, Vienna, you can't love me. I'm no good for you. I'm no good for anyone, but most of all, you. You don't know what I am really like. Please don't say you love me."

"I think that I am a pretty good judge of character, and from the moment that I met you, I knew that you were special. I thought something wonderful was going to happen, and it did…at least for me. I'm sorry you don't feel the same way. On the other hand, I had the sinking feeling that our relationship was going to end badly. I shouldn't have let it go on for so long. Do you know how many times I decided not to see you anymore? No, of course you don't. But hearts are a dime a dozen, right?"

"Vienna, please—"

"Please what? I was your summer fling. You think that once you are gone, I will forget you. Well think again, Mister. Unfortunately for me, my heart wins over reasons why I should forget you. I'm just some silly girl with a crush on an older man—that's what you are thinking, right? I can't stop how I feel. I love you and that is that. I will never regret knowing you. Now please, take me home."

I felt his warm breath on my face as he lowered me to the ground. I wanted to kiss him and was pretty sure that he wanted to kiss me, but it was just as well that he didn't.

"You're not silly and you are not young, Vienna. You possess a wisdom that I have not seen before in anyone, no matter their age. I am sorry if I led you to believe that there was going to be more for us. I'm ashamed of myself for letting our relationship go this far."

When we arrived at the Palace, Rainey put the car in park and turned to me. "I won't soon forget this summer, Vienna. Believe me when I say that I was not playing with your affections. Promise me that you will forget me."

"I will do no such thing, Rainey Quinn!"

Connie Francis was singing another heartbreaker. I shut the radio off and undid my red lacy scarf that Rainey kept on his rearview mirror. "You won't be wanting this anymore. Good-bye. Have a great year and life."

He reached for me but I was already out the door. I heard him say to me as I ran up the walkway, "You are very special, Vienna, and don't ever forget it. Good night and take care of yourself."

I didn't look back. *Well*, I told myself, *you handled that with a lot of class.* What had I been expecting him to say, I love you, too? If he had, then I would have followed him to the end of the world.

As I climbed the stairs to my room, mother yelled out to me, "You're home awfully early, dear. I suppose that Rainey wants to get an early start for the coast tomorrow?"

I yelled back at her, "You're home early, too. It's been a long day. Good night."

I could barely hear her as I reached the top step. "We closed early; it was dead."

She was right, it was dead. The clock chimed nine bells.

I laid out my new black sweater set and red tartan skirt for tomorrow, and the words of Scarlett O'Hara came to mind. Yes, tomorrow was indeed another day. I cried myself to sleep and wished that I could take back tonight, but if wishes were fishes, then pigs would fly.

Rainey watched her as she disappeared behind the huge oak doors. She hadn't looked back. He slammed the steering wheel over and over again as he drove down River Street. "Damn it, damn it!" he cursed. This wasn't the way he envisioned the evening ending. "Why did the girl have to say that she loved me? If it was two or three years down the road, maybe I could love her, too.

Who am I kidding? Love is a foreign word to me. I need to get back to the bright lights, wild nights, and loose women. Say good-bye to the idyllic life of the valley and romance with a sweet sprite. Time to go away, Vienna."

He hadn't planned on leaving until next weekend; he hadn't even told Vienna that. There was no reason to stay now. He'd go and say good-bye to the boys tomorrow and hope that no one asks about her.

He spent a restless night and woke up in a sweat. Geez, what was that about? He must have been dreaming. He turned over and tried to get back to sleep. As soon as he closed his eyes, he found himself in a verdant forest. The ground was covered in lush mosses. He had been here before but couldn't decide where it was exactly. He opened his eyes again, or did he? This was so strange. He found himself back in the woods. He was running. He was chasing something or someone. He couldn't make out what it was. A unicorn? Suddenly, the dense trees opened up to a meadow overflowing with wild flowers. The apparition seemed to be gaining momentum as it neared a cliff. He reached out to grab it, but he was not quick enough. He watched in horror as the figure turned and smiled, and then went plummeting down, down into the dark, murky water. All he had left in his hand was a piece of red lace...a piece of red lace from Vienna's scarf. The clock read 4:44.

Chapter Four

Autumn, 1960

I was very surprised to see Jimmy in the school parking lot the next day. He called my name and I walked over to his car. "Hi, Jimmy. Are you coming back to school?"

He laughed and said that he was picking some parts up for his dad. He was back working with his dad, who had a machine shop in Hawthorne. Their main business was repairing farmers' equipment. He asked if he could give me a lift downtown.

"That would be nice. Do you have time to grab a coke before you head back?"

"I'd like that very much. Hop in, V."

Of course, I wondered if Rainey had asked him to see if I was all right, but I doubted it.

We sat and talked about the summer, and neither of us mentioned Rainey. Before he left, he asked if I would like to go to the movies with him and the others on Friday for the showing of *Ben-Hur*. I said that I would love to go. I hoped that he wasn't thinking of starting anything up with me, but then, why not? Rainey and I were most assuredly over. However, they were still best friends and it wouldn't be right. Why was I assuming that he was interested in me as anything more than a friend?

For the next two months, I was invited everywhere with the gang from Hawthorne; Zane and Marley, Yates and whomever, and Jimmy. Sometimes, Lara and her new boyfriend, Dean Murdoch, would join us. He lived and worked in Potsdam, which was 60 miles away to the west. He tried to come over every weekend, or else Lara would go over there.

Jimmy was not seeing anyone and I failed to see why he didn't have a steady girlfriend. He was darn good looking, had a job, and was fun to be with. Then to my bewilderment, I found out why. We had all gone to the movies as usual and I started sniffling at a sad breakup scene. It had not gone unnoticed that the leading man bore a huge resemblance to Rainey. That only added to my misery. Everyone was aware that things had not gone well for Rainey and me before he returned to university, so they never brought up his name. Jimmy put his arm around me and tried to get me to quit crying.

"It's okay, hon. You're going to forget him and whatever it was that he did to you."

I excused myself and went to the ladies' room. I was not happy at what had just transpired. Jimmy and I were always the extras. Did he want us to be more than friends? He was like a big brother to me. There really wasn't anything wrong with him calling me "hon." Rainey never even called me that. Why was I making such a big deal about it? I decided that this would be the last night that I would be accepting invitations to join the gang anymore. I begged off going to a party after the movie, citing a headache. Jimmy was disappointed. When he dropped me off at home, I felt like I was losing an important part of my life. He promised to call me in a few days. I wanted to tell him that there was no future for us, but I couldn't, so I just smiled and said, "Good night."

He did call me, but I always made excuses as to why I couldn't go out. I could only hope that the Hawthorne gang would quit coming into the diner. Just like that, I had alienated myself from all of my friends, except for Lara.

All of that was behind me when I met someone new on Halloween. His name was Jack. I was at work when I first saw him. He was sitting with the Southerly boys. I had heard via the grapevine that they had a run in with Yates and friends at the pond—that was the fireworks that I missed.

Paddy Reynolds noticed Jack and I looking at each other and clued in that we hadn't met. "Hey, V, this is my good buddy, Jack Jennings."

We said hello to each other. He was very handsome in a rugged way—brown eyes and dark hair, which he wore in a duck cut. He was very muscular and I was sure that he would tower over my 5 foot 2 stature by 10 inches. He was the exact opposite of Rainey. I was attracted to him and soon found out that he was attracted to me also.

Paddy asked if Lara and I would like to go to a party in the Barrens that night.

"You are kidding." I laughed. "I don't think that I am up to partying in the graveyard on Halloween night."

"I can promise you that there won't be any ghouls except for these guys," Jack assured me, taunting his friends. "Anyhow, I will be there to keep you safe." He looked at me in a way that made me want to say yes, and so I did.

I found Lara and asked if she would come; she was game. I asked her what she knew of Jack and she said that she didn't know him very well. He was usually out of town, working at a mine or something. She thought that he had a sketchy past. She asked me why I wanted to know and was it a Rainey-rebound thing.

"Don't get caught up in his brooding good looks. He is nothing at all like Rainey. I think he could be dangerous," Lara cautioned.

"Oh, Lara," I answered. "Don't be so melodramatic! It's only a party. I want to meet some new people, and didn't you tell me that it was high time that I got over Rainey?"

Lara warned, "Still waters run deep."

I poo-pooed her and let Jack drive me home after work. He had rode in on a motorcycle but said that he would change it for his truck if I preferred. I had never been on a bike before, so I asked him to take me for a little ride. I still had my uniform on and found it a little risqué but enjoyed the wind blowing through my hair and everyone staring at us. I daren't let my father see me on it, so I had Jack drop me off a block from home. I showed him where I lived and he said that he would be back in half an hour with the truck.

When mother heard that I was going out with him, she was not impressed. She called him a hoodlum and wanted to know what Rainey would have to say about me hanging out with his kind. I told her that she knew darn well that he was at university and that we were most assuredly done with each other.

Jack treated me okay, but he was by no means the gentleman that Rainey was. He was crude in his ways and language, and he took some getting used to. He drank a lot and was a smoker, and I took to the habit again. I had fun with him and his friends. As it turned out, most of the girls I already knew were girlfriends of his buddies.

Jack was becoming more and more demanding. I told him that I was going to quit seeing him unless he changed his tune. I wasn't going to sleep with him, or anyone else for the matter, and that was that. He backed off and we called a truce. He told me that he had never had feelings for a girl before like he had for me. He wondered what would happen to us when he went back to work and was worried that I wouldn't wait for him. I surely had no idea myself. I was only sixteen and wasn't about to make a commitment to him. Why would I wait for someone who I would only see once in awhile? There had to be many more fish in the sea. It didn't matter anyhow, because on December the 19, I heard from Rainey.

I had been to the mail for Mother. I was surprised to see my name on an envelope, and even more so when I saw that it was from Rainey. It was a Christmas card. I read it while walking back to the diner.

Merry Christmas, Vienna. I hope this finds you well. I am flying with my parents to Claudia's for the holidays. We will be returning to Hawthorne on the 30th. I am hoping that you will accompany me to the New Year's Eve dance at the Grange. Do you think that you would want to see me? May I phone you when I get in? Please say yes, Vienna. Convey my best wishes to your family.

As Always,
Rainey

What? Why had he done this to me? No damn way was I going anywhere with him! That night, I was out with Jack and we made plans for New Year's Eve. There was going to be a party at Paddy's and that was where I would be.

It was December 29 when I answered the phone. I said in a cherry voice, "Happy holidays."

"Happy holidays to you, too, Vienna."

No one had called me that in four months. *It's not him*, I told myself. He said that he would call on the 30th, and that was tomorrow. I hadn't planned on answering the phone all that day. The hall clock chimed 9. I said nothing.

"Vienna, are you going to talk to me? I really hope so."

I finally found my voice. "Hello, Rainey. How are you? I hope that you had an enjoyable holiday at your sister's." I wanted to keep listening to his sweet voice.

"I am well. We just arrived from the airport. It is too late to travel, so we are staying at my house here in Vancouver. Did you receive my card?"

"Yes, I did."

"Have you given my invitation any thought? I am hoping that you will say yes."

"I am not sure that is a good idea. What purpose would it serve?" I felt my knees give way and had to sit down on the floor.

"I really want to see you, Vienna. Please tell me that you don't have other plans."

"As a matter of fact, I do, Rainey." *Will he please quit saying my name?*

"Of course you do. I should have known that you wouldn't be free. I wish you nothing but the best for the new year and—"

I didn't let him finish. I said the words that would seal my life forever. "What time will you pick me up? Mother is cooking a special dinner. Would you care to join us? I am sure that my family would like to see you." That was an understatement. Of course they would—anyone who wasn't Jack.

"Thank you, Vienna. I am so glad that you changed your mind. I promise that you will not regret it. May I phone you tomorrow?"

"Yes. Good night, Rainey."

"Until tomorrow, Vienna."

I ran upstairs, threw myself on the bed, and cursed for not being able to say no to him. I cried because the sound of his voice turned me to putty. I knew that the day would come when I would be sorry that I had ever met him. I tried to convince myself that it was just a harmless date and nothing more would come of it. He had told me to forget him, hadn't he? Perhaps he just needed a date—yes, that was it. I had better get busy and come up with a plausible lie to tell Jack.

Later in the day, Mother had taken me upstairs with the girls following closely behind. She took us into her bedroom, where she removed a plastic bag and unzipped it. She took out the most beautiful dress that I had ever seen. It had cap sleeves and a deep, rolling neckline. It had a fitted waist and looked as though it would be knee length. I believed that it was crepe or taffeta, but it was the color that was so remarkable. It was a dark, emerald green that was almost black when turned away from the light.

"I was saving this for your seventeenth birthday but thought you may like to wear it tonight. Would you like to borrow my little black pumps? And I think that your black diamond earrings and necklace will look lovely with the neckline."

I asked her where and when she had bought it. She said it was when she and dad were at the coast last fall. I couldn't believe that she had thought ahead that far. I hugged her and told her that I loved it, which I did. Addy and Sissy were giggling, and I gave them each a big hug, too. Apparently, Mother had told them about the dress when Rainey had phoned to ask me to the dance. Mother handed me a black lace petticoat, new underclothes, and black hose also. I went to my room and laid everything on the bed, praying that the dress would fit me.

I was still upstairs when I heard the doorbell ring. I crept to the landing, standing so as not to be seen. My father answered the door and welcomed Rainey. My heart quickened as usual when I saw him. He was dashing as ever in white, tucked-in shirt and dark, brown pants. His blazer matched and I just knew that it would have leather patches on the elbows. He had worn a long trench coat over his attire and short rubber boots over his shiny brown loafers. No tie…good. He hated ties.

I quietly entered the library where everyone was sitting and talking. Rainey saw me and attempted to get up, but I motioned him to stay seated. I thought that I looked the same as I had last summer. My hair was longer and I had it pulled into a ponytail, as I wasn't sure how I would arrange it later. I had lost some weight but doubted that he would notice. He was staring at me, though.

Father said, "Here's our girl."

My mother came to the rescue and ordered them all out to help in the kitchen. The girls protested but Mother shooed them out.

"Hi," I said. I was not shy but was suddenly at a loss for words. I was glad that there was a big ole coffee table between us.

"Hi yourself." He was smiling and my temperature went up a few degrees. "I am so glad that you agreed to see me and invite me here. I've been on edge, wondering what I was going to say to you. I think I owe you an apology."

"Whatever for? You owe me nothing. We are friends, aren't we?"

"I would like to think that we are a bit more than friends."

I didn't know what to say to that remark, so I said, "Come on into the dining room. I am going to have to put a towel or something on you so that you don't spoil your white shirt." He followed me and touched my hand as we passed through the doors. I turned and smiled at him.

Dinner was very pleasant. Mother had prepared a lovely meal as usual. She had cooked a honey ham and scalloped potatoes, baked rutabagas, cabbage salad, and melt-in-your-mouth biscuits. I had made a strawberry cake for dessert. Our kitchen was still unfinished but the pantry had been fully restored.

I loved to prepare delicacies for home and the diner in there. It had a north-facing window and so did not receive the morning sun, but father had made sure that it had adequate lighting. The original cupboards had been modernized, with the top shelves open for easy access to boxed ingredients and utensils. The counters were over 2 feet deep and the pantry itself was 7 feet long and 6 feet wide. Mother, the girls, and I could all be in there at the same time and not get in each other's way. I preferred to be alone so that I could have the radio turned up loud. Today, I had been singing along to all the hits. Even the sad songs didn't make me sad. Rainey was coming and I had another chance.

We had no sooner started to eat when Addy cried out, "Where's the jam?"

Mother said, "Who set the table?"

"I'll get it," I offered. "What kind, Addy, strawberry or raspberry or both?"

Rainey looked at me strangely as I got up. "Why do you want jam, Addy?" he asked.

"You don't know?" I asked.

He shook his head and looked at my father, who shrugged his shoulders and said matter-of-factly that he lived with four women and so we had a lot of idiosyncrasies.

I returned with the jam jars and handed them to Addy, who slapped some on her ham and passed them to Sissy, who did the same thing. I also put a small spoonful on mine and passed one jar to Rainey. "Try it, you might like it."

He looked at me peculiarly but tried it and said, "This isn't bad. I will have to pass this on to my mother. Ham and jam…who would have thought?"

We all laughed and I said, "Stick around. You might just learn a thing or two about Lane cuisine."

He looked at me, winked, and said, "Don't worry, I intend to."

After dinner, Mother sent me upstairs to get dressed. Father and Rainey retired to the library, where I knew they would be talking about all things related to buildings.

The dress fit perfectly. I put on light-green eye shadow, black liner, and peachy lipstick that matched my nail polish. I piled my hair upon my head in a modified beehive and pulled down long tendrils that cascaded down my face. I sat down on the bed, not really believing that Rainey was downstairs, waiting for me. How could this be? I must be dreaming. I pinched myself.

Addy entered my room. "What's the matter, V? You look like you are going to cry. Don't cry. You'll ruin your makeup. Aren't you happy that Rainey is here? You don't wish that he was Jack, do you?"

"Oh no!" I got up and gave her a hug.

Addy took my hand and led me down the hall. "Rainey, come and see V. She's ready!" she squealed.

He was waiting for me at the bottom of the stairs. I hoped I wouldn't stumble.

"Oh, V, you are so beautiful!" Sissy half whispered.

"I agree." Rainey smiled a smile that would stay with me forever.

I felt like Cinderella and prayed that my life with Rainey wouldn't end at midnight.

We put on our winter garments and I put my black pumps in a tote. My dancing slippers fit in my clutch purse. Addy called them my elf shoes. Mother passed us an umbrella, as it was snowing ever so slightly. I declined, saying that I had enough hairspray on to hold up Dorothy's house in the worst of tornados. Of course, Rainey found this amusing. We had only driven a few blocks when he pulled over and parked. I asked him if anything was wrong.

"Yes," he replied. "Could you please move a little closer to me?"

I moved over a few inches.

"Was I wrong to call you, Vienna? Should I have stayed away? I understand that you are seeing someone. It is none of my business, but did you break a date with him to see me? If you did, I am grateful."

I chose my words very carefully. "Rainey, what you do is your business and what I do is mine. We don't have commitments to each other, and if we choose to see each other now and then, that's up to us. It was my choice to see you."

"I hope he sees it that way. Is it serious?"

"Maybe, I don't know. I'm living day by day."

That seemed to satisfy him, though it wasn't entirely the truth, but I wasn't going to say anything that may rock the cradle, like I was still in love with him.

We arrived in Hawthorne amid a howling blizzard. Rainey tried to let me out in front of the Grange but I wanted to stay with him and make a run for the doors together. We shook ourselves off and shed our coats and boots. He held me up while I changed into my shoes. I wanted to slip into his arms.

"Before we join the gang at the back, I have some people I want you to meet," he said.

I walked with him to a table where three older couples were sitting. One was Lara's mom and dad, and I knew right away that one couple was Rainey's parents. I took a deep breath as he introduced me to them.

"Mom, Dad, I want you to meet V. This is my Aunt Mavis and Uncle Saul, and of course, you know Anne and Lance."

I nodded hello. His dad stood up and said, "A pleasure to meet you, young lady."

His mother got up and hugged me. "I am so delighted to finally meet the girl who kept our son so busy last summer, and I can certainly see why. I know you're eager to join your friends, but bring her back soon, Rainey, so we can chat. Now, go have fun!"

He squeezed my hand and I said to him when we were out of earshot, "You could have warned me! Do you have any more surprises for me?"

"We'll have to see about that, won't we?"

Thank goodness our table was full of friendly faces—Yates and June, Zane and Marley, Shorty and Katie, and Jimmy. There was a new face, and I soon learned that her name was Ruth and that she was Jimmy's date. He winked at me and I smiled.

"You dog, Rain! Why didn't you tell us you were bringing V? Did you know, Jimmy? Nobody tells me a thing." Yates gave me one of his big bear hugs and whispered, "We have missed you, girl."

I gave him a little peck on the cheek. "And I have missed you all."

It was a fun evening. I loved listening to all the stories they had to tell. I really had missed them. Rainey danced me off my feet. Thank goodness I had my little elf shoes.

Jimmy said to me while we were dancing that as far as he knew, Rainey had never introduced a girl to his parents before, and that gave him cause to worry.

"Why would you be worried, Jimmy?" I asked. "And I don't think he had much choice. They were sitting right there at the first table. I'm sure that they know a lot of his old girlfriends."

"Local gals don't count, and anyhow, they were few and far in between. No, I think our boy is smitten but good."

"So why would you be worried?"

"Maybe I am worried for you, V."

"Don't be. I can look after myself. You know, I never once heard from him for four months…out of sight, out of mind. I am only his holiday girl."

"Don't sell yourself short. By the way, where is Lara? It's not like her to miss a dance."

"You do know that she has a new beau? She's with him in Potsdam. By the way, Ruth seems like a lovely girl."

Around 11:30, Rainey whispered something to me that I couldn't understand. He took my hand and led me off the dance floor into the cloak room. He closed the door and pulled me into his arms. "I couldn't wait any longer, I had to kiss you."

"You've been kissing me all night."

"Not like this."

Minutes later, we emerged and I went to the ladies' room to fix my blotched lipstick. I had told Rainey that as soon as the bewitching hour was over, we could steal away and really be alone. He liked the idea, but not half as much as I did.

We made the rounds at midnight, kissing and wishing everyone a happy new year. Rainey let me loose after a thirty-second kiss and I knew it was time to leave. He told the crew that we may not be back, depending on the storm, as he had to get me home. I didn't think anyone believed his story. He told the same thing to his parents, who wished me well and cautioned him to drive safely.

There was 3 inches of new snow on the ground.

"We're not going very far in this weather, Vienna," Rainey said. "Do you want to go back in while we wait for the snowplow to come?"

I was breathless from the last kiss and managed to get out a firm, "No."

In a few minutes, it was warm enough for me to take my coat off and I considered myself lucky that was all that came off. I knew that I was letting myself in for another fall, but I didn't care. The plow came by and we followed it slowly down the highway to Bridge. Rainey was pretty quiet until we drove into my yard.

"What now?" he asked. "I really don't want to say good night."

"Then don't. Come in and I will make some coffee." I took him into the newly finished conservatory. It overlooked the river. I turned on the outside lights so that he could see how spectacular the view was, with the snow falling and glistening on the frozen water like diamonds.

He asked why I hadn't shown it to him earlier, and I told him that I had been waiting for this special moment.

"You had a hand in this transformation, didn't you? You are one of my favorite people, Vienna, and you make me very happy."

That was as close as he came to saying he cared. We made some inane promises about not seeing other people. I floated up to my room on a cloud of hope for us.

I was sitting at the kitchen table with a cup of coffee when the phone rang.

"V, is that you, or should I say Vienna?" It was Jack.

"Hello, Jack." My voice was flat.

"You're finally out of bed. Exactly whose bed were you in anyhow?"

"Jack, I am sorry—"

"Don't even try and cover up your lie. A family party, my ass! Thanks for making a damn fool out of me! I am so mad at you that I could kill you!"

He hung up and my headache became a little worse. The phone was ringing again and I let it go on and on. Sissy yelled at me, "V, where are you? It's Rainey."

I picked up. "Good morning."

"Good afternoon, gorgeous. Did you just get up? Are you up for a visit?"

"I have been up for a while. I don't think I want you seeing me like this."

"I don't care how you look. Wash your face and comb your hair, I'm on my way."

He was at the door in twenty minutes. He greeted me with a big kiss. "What did you do to me last night? You put some sort of spell on me, didn't you?"

I laughed. "Of course I did, because I can do those sorts of things! What exactly are you accusing me of, Sir? Do you think I dabble in witchcraft?"

"No, nothing quite so sinister. It's the best night's sleep I've had since last summer."

"It had nothing to do with me. Did you ever think that you were just tired?"

"I think it had everything to do with you, my lady. Do the numbers 444 mean anything to you? This is the second time that I have seen 4:44 on my night clock, and both times, I had been with you the night before. The first time was Labor Day, and that was a nightmare! I dreamt that you fell off a cliff and I couldn't get to you in time to save you."

"Did you have the same dream last night?"

"No, just the contrary, but when I awoke, the time was 4:44 again. What does it mean?"

"Rainey, I am sure I don't know. I am not the interpreter of dreams. I have enough of my own that don't make sense. I can't cast spells, but if I could…well, you don't want to know what I would do to you."

Now it was his turn to laugh. "I guess I am just being melodramatic, but strange things do happen when I am around you."

"You can elaborate while I am making breakfast. How do eggs and waffles sound?"

Rainey followed me into the kitchen. "Sounds wonderful. I really can't explain, but I am not me when I am with you. I'm a nicer, kinder person…you do that to me."

"Well good, because if I turned you into a monster, that would be horrifying!"

After breakfast, we sat in the conservatory and watched the wildlife. There were two deer, one squirrel, and dozens of birds, all vying for a place at the feeders. We sat in the ratty loveseat as we had last night. We held hands and didn't talk for a long time.

I promised myself that I wasn't going to go all girly on him. He thought that I was this strong, composed person, but he was so wrong. It took all my willpower not to blubber and beg him to take me with him. I shouldn't have been so brave.

Our time was limited, as he had to attend his Aunt Mavis and Uncle Saul's anniversary party in Hawthorne. He asked me to come with him, but I declined. I didn't want him to have to drive back and forth over the winter roads. I thanked him for taking me to the dance and said I would remember the evening forever.

When it was time for him to go, he said to me, "I will think of you often, Vienna. I probably won't get down this way until May. This is going to be a particularly challenging period for me. Will there be a place for me in your life when I return?"

"What do you think, Rainey Quinn? Just focus on your studies, but don't forget to breathe. May the sun shine brightly on your joyous days and the rain refresh you through peaceful night."

"Did you just make that up? I don't doubt it for a single minute. Something so intriguing could only come from you."

"As much as I would like to say that they are my words, I cannot take credit. It comes from the Irish. They have many lovely and endearing ditties."

"And just how would you know that? You read something and you remembered it, don't you?"

"Remember the math thing? I wish that some of your arithmetic knowledge would rub off on me."

"You have many other wonderful natural abilities, so I wouldn't worry too much about the math thing. You probably will never need trigonometry and calculus anyhow."

"Whoa there, I don't even know what they are. Just trying to understand algebra and geometry. I may need it someday if I become a governess."

"Do governesses still exist?"

"I am sure they do somewhere. There are still palaces and castles in foreign lands that require teachers for their children, and probably even in North America; the rich can be very eccentric."

"Are they in Wales?"

I smiled. "Maybe I will find out someday. What the future holds is a mystery, as it should be. Would you want to know about tomorrow or next month or twenty years down the road?"

"Maybe."

"That would take all of the fun out of knowing what lies around the next corner. Should you have taken door number two or three instead of one? No, life will play out and we cannot always control our fates. There will always be antagonists to confront us. You know, we may not always be captains of our own ships. Lordy, what got me started on this?"

Rainey laughed and said, "I don't know, but it has sure been fun listening to you. I think Freud could have used you."

We kissed for a very long time. Reluctantly, I let him take his leave. "Until we meet again, Rainey."

"Until we meet again, Vienna, in sunshine or in rain. Stay just the way you are." He blew me a kiss and was gone.

I felt a cold chill enveloping my bones and it wasn't just from the north wind blowing. I heard my little voice laughing. She had been silent for such a long, long time.

Rainey had left and, hopefully, Jack had also. I applied myself to my studies, joined the volleyball team, and helped out with the drama club designing sets. I didn't date, as I wasn't interested in anyone except Rainey. I still hung out with the girls and worked at the diner after school and on weekends. At the end of January, I received a letter from Jack. He said that he missed me. Had he forgotten that I had lied to him and that he had said he wanted to kill me? I didn't answer, as I never intended to see him again.

I received a Valentine from Rainey in the form of a letter. It read:

> *There is this sweet girl that I met who yearns to cross the seven seas. She is the one that I cannot forget, Lord, please have mercy on me. On this Valentine's Day please may she be thinking of me.*
> *As always,*
> *Rainey*

My poem to him read:

> *How often have I thought of thee*
> *And your sweet breath upon my face*
> *I lie awake and dream of your embrace*
> *And hope that when you dream it is of me*
> *Yours,*
> *Vienna*

That was the last time I heard from him until March 29. Jimmy answered the phone. "LaFontaine residence. How may I help you?"

"Jimmy, what the hell are you doing answering the phone at Vienna's?" Rainey said.

"And hello to you, too, buddy," Jimmy replied. "There is a party going on in honor of V's seventeenth birthday. Did you even know that it was her birthday last week?"

"That doesn't explain why you are there and answering the phone. Where is Vienna?"

"I told you that it's a party. Lara threw it for her and her parents wanted it here. Anything else you need to know? You sound a little inebriated."

"I think that does it. Just put Vienna on the phone, Jimmy."

"Sure thing, boss. Here, listen to some Elvis while I track her down."

"Rainey, is that really you?" I said when I got to the phone. "I thought that Jimmy was playing a cruel trick on me."

"Happy birthday, Vienna. I'm sorry that I didn't know it was your birthday. Maybe I thought that you were going to stay sweet sixteen forever."

"Oh, don't be sorry. I don't think we ever talked birthdays. How are you, Rainey?"

"I should have asked. I should have called you after I received your card at Valentine's. I should have done a lot of things. I don't know what is wrong with me."

"Rainey, you sound very melancholy. What is wrong, my love?" *Oh God, I said love.*

"Well, for one thing, you are there and I am here. I feel badly for you because I am such a rotten person. I miss you, Vienna. You are the only one who can keep me in focus. You don't know what I have done."

Okay, this has nothing to do with him not being here at my party. It is something else completely different. I may not want to know what it is. "Tell me, Rain, what has got you so down?" He had definitely been drinking. His words were starting to slur. How could I comfort him when he was so far away? His voice was not at all like the Rainey I knew and loved. I was worried, but when I heard his next words, my worry turned to dismay.

"You will never forgive me, Vienna. I went back on my word...I am so sorry."

What is he saying? I thought to myself.

"I asked you to wait for me…but I can't anymore. If only I could take back these last few months. You just don't know what I have done, Vienna."

I took a deep breath and held back my tears. "You know what, Rainey, I think I know exactly what you have done. I am here celebrating my birthday with your friends and trying not to think of how much I miss you, and listening to you feel sorry for yourself because you have been screwing around. I suppose you want me to forgive you again. Well, that doesn't even enter into the picture because I just don't care anymore. I am breakable and I think that you have just broken me. Now, if you will excuse me, I have a party to get back to. And you can get back to whomever and not feel guilty. I release you from whatever we had, which was apparently *nothing*. Good-bye, Rainey Quinn!"

I was fuming when I returned to my party, which had now spilled out onto the porch.

"How is our boy? He sounded a little off-kilter."

"You were right, Jimmy," I replied. "He is nothing but a playboy. How dumb was I, thinking that we had something special? Well, knock me down and call me stupid! I'm done."

"Stop beating yourself up. You're too good for him. Sure, he is my best friend, but sometimes, I don't even know him. You know what, though, V? He will apologize again, and you, being the wonderful person that you are, will forgive him. Is Uncle Jimmy, right?"

"Unfortunately, you could be right, but it is not going to happen anytime soon."

I went to bed that night wishing that I had never heard of a Rainey Quinn. How many times was he going to break my heart and how many times was I going to let him?

Rainey felt like hell. Vienna had hung up on him and he didn't blame her. He wasn't so drunk as not to care. The thing that bothered him the most was that she was with all his friends and he was at some rotten gala with that bitch, Priscilla. What the hell had happened since New Year's? Why did he crawl into bed with this woman, whom he cared nothing about? How long was he going to keep seeing her? One thing was for certain, he couldn't contact Vienna again until he had broken if off with Priscilla. Why had he sabotaged his relationship with Vienna? Why was he so afraid to be happy? He had to prove it to himself that he could be the man she could be proud of. He put his drink on a table and left without saying a word to anyone. Priscilla tried to reach him, but he ignored her calls for days. The day he decided that it was time to talk to her, he told her that he was going home and wouldn't be back. He felt that a weight had been lifted off his shoulders and that he could finally call the only girl who mattered to him.

"Vienna, its Rainey. I'm coming home. Are you going to see me?"

Her reply was what he expected. "Didn't we already do this? Do you think that I have been sitting around, waiting for you to quit screwing around with anyone who wears a skirt? What would that say about me?"

"I don't expect you to forgive me. I have been an ass. I have no excuses except stupidity. I need you to give me the chance to make it up to you. I haven't been a male whore, Vienna. There was only one and I have no feelings for her at all."

"Well good! That makes everything all right then—it was just sex. You are going to tell me that you were with someone for months and had no feelings for her? What kind of a fool do you take me for? I can't compete with your sluttish women, nor do I want to."

"Does it matter to you at all that I have missed you and everything about you? I have thought of you often."

Here we go again. Secretly, I had been praying that Rainey would call me, but I wasn't sure what I would do when and if he did. Lara and Jimmy told me that I should find someone who wouldn't give me so much grief. Easy for them, they had never been in love with a Rainey Quinn. "So, you have thought of me. I can only hope that it wasn't when you had someone lying in bed next to you."

"Vienna, have I reduced you to thinking that little of me?"

"I have held you in my heart, and when I am in bed at night, you are the only one I dream of being with. When we are together, you make me feel so special and that I can trust you, but that isn't so, is it, Rainey? I am just your stand by and you think that I will forgive you no matter what. How weak do you think I am? Our relationship cannot survive. You want me to give you another chance, and even though I ache for wanting to see you, I think that I have to give you up."

"Please don't say that, Vienna. I have waited over a month to even call you though I wanted to every day. Maybe I was testing myself. I don't know, but when I tell you that I have not seen another woman since last we talked, you can believe me."

"Oh, how I want to believe you, but my heart cannot take you at your word. You tell me, Rainey, if you were me, would you trust you?"

"No, I wouldn't, but you must. For my sanity, I need you in my life, Vienna. Tell me that you need me, too."

"Alas, perhaps I do. I also know that I need to have my head examined for even considering seeing you. I will tell you one thing Rainey Quinn. I will give you one more chance, but remember this: there will be no more seconds. There will be no coming back again no matter what."

"Thank you, Vienna. I am coming straight through tomorrow. Can I pick you up at school? It has been almost five months since I have seen you. I don't know how I am going to get through the night."

Did he not know that I knew down to the minute how long it had been? "All right, I will look for you."

"Till then Vienna."

"Drive safely."

He was shaking when he hung up the receiver. He remembered the day he had met her. What had made him take her hand, kiss it, and call her, "my lady"? He wanted to ask her where she had been all his life, but that was a stupid cliché and she would see right through it. She had made him laugh and feel warm inside. Her voice was melodious. He had thought that she was just a passing fancy, but he couldn't say that anymore. She was all he could think about. Was he going to be able to convince her that he had changed? He wasn't a religious man, but he felt he owed it to the Man up above to say, "Thank you for another chance…I won't screw up this time."

Chapter Five

Rainey and Vienna

I was not as excited as I thought I would be to see Rainey. I went to my classes and the day passed quickly. I had asked Mom if I could have the day off because Rainey was coming down. She had told me of course and that Sissy could fill in for me. Sure, anything for Rainey. She said how nice it would be for me to see him, but I didn't know. My doubt about seeing him all went out the window when I saw him. He waved to me, and I walked over and said, "Hi." He took my books from me and put them in the backseat, never taking his eyes off me. I averted his stare and headed for the passenger door.

He gently took my arm and said, "Where do you think you're going?" He pulled me close to him, kissed me, and whispered, "Hello, Vienna."

I melted but didn't want him to know that. We stood there looking at each other for a few minutes.

"I like your new look. I watched you come out the door and asked myself who was that gorgeous girl? Maybe if I played my cards right and didn't screw things up *again*, she could be mine."

I had cut my hair and had red highlights put in by Lizzie Wagner, who had quit school and was now a hairdresser. It was the fad, a curly poodle cut. "You could be right, but time will tell, won't it?" I slid past the steering wheel as I always did, and of course, Rainey wouldn't let me get very far. How fitting, "Teenager in Love" was playing on the radio…that would be me, I guess.

"I have to return to Van on Sunday to finish up at school and pack up, but I will be home in ten days. I couldn't wait that long to see you, Vienna. I hope that says something of my feelings for you.'

"You needn't have come all that way for me. Nothing would have changed in two weeks, or didn't you trust yourself?"

Rainey felt rebuffed. "You are still angry with me, aren't you? What can I say or do to have you forgive me? I want us to work."

"Let me ask you a question and be honest with your answer. Suppose that you came home and found that maybe I had been seeing someone and even slept with him, how would you feel and would you forgive me?"

"I don't have to think. I would be mad as hell! If you had given yourself to someone else…there are no words for how I would feel. I probably could not forgive you even though it would have been my fault after what I have done. I am sorry, but I can't bear to think of you with someone else."

"Ummm, old double standard. Have you never heard that what is good for the gander is also good for the goose?"

"It doesn't apply to you. You are my Vienna and I will not share you."

"So what happens if we don't work out, are you going to kill me?"

"My God, Vienna, why would you say such a thing?"

"I don't know, I am still confused. You can have sex with anyone you choose but I have to stay pure just for you…am I reading you right?"

"I will not be seeing anyone but you. Can I make it any clearer?"

"Let bygones be bygones as far as your indiscretions go, but in my case, it is another matter, is that right?"

"You make me sound like a dictator."

"If the shoe fits…I am not happy with you, Rainey Quinn, and your actions will speak for themselves. I am still very confused as to whether we will work out or not. I think that it is going to take a lot of work. You may very well rue the day that you said you wanted me back. I do not intend to make anything easy for you. I am very high maintenance."

Rainey was smiling all over his face and it was hard for me to stay angry with him anymore, especially when he said, "It will be my deepest pleasure to see that all your needs are met, my lady."

"Don't smile in that little boy way at me. You can't win me over with your charm."

"Why not? It has worked before, hasn't it?"

"I am different now. I have had my heart torn into little pieces and scattered for all to see. I am cautious now. I can't run helter-skelter into a relationship. My eyes are wide open now."

"Did I do this to you, Vienna, or was it someone else?"

"If you have to ask, then you don't really know me."

"Whoever invented the word 'sorry' must have known I was going to need it a lot. I am serious and I should be kicked in the keester and strung up."

"I think tarred and feathered would suit me fine. Now, do you want to come home with me and see what Dad has been up to?"

"Yes, another pleasure, but not as great as the idea that you might care for me again."

"I do care for you, Rainey. I wish I didn't, but alas, I do."

He squeezed my hand. I hoped that I had the upper hand now. He was my Achilles' heel and I was going to have to deal with that.

Back at the Palace, I took him to the side of the house where a porch wrapped around two sides. We found father hard at work, putting finishing touches on the railings and spindles. He stopped as he saw us. "Great to see you, Son. All done for the year? Are you hear to help V with the painting?"

My parents did not know what had transpired between Rainey and I last March.

"No, Sir, I have to go back for a short time. And, yes, I would love to paint with your daughter." He smiled at me and I knew he was thinking of other things that he would like to do with me.

I hit him none to gently. "He was kidding, Rainey. Surely, you are not cut out to do menial work."

"Let's just see about that. I'm game if you are."

"All right then. I will go and get changed, and get you some old duds to wear. I know that we should have painted the railing before the floor, but it needed so much repair work that I just went ahead and did the floor anyhow. Hopefully, the drop cloths will serve our purpose . You must come and see the conservatory. It is no longer the bare room that you saw in winter. Give me five minutes and meet me in there, okay?"

He saluted me. "Your wish is my command, my lady."

I wondered what my father was thinking about all of this malarkey.

They met in the conservatory. Since the New Year, the ceiling had been spray painted a light blue with gold sparkles. The wainscoting was a mahogany brown. The walls were papered in a jungle motif. The room was furnished with wrought-iron benches and rattan chairs upholstered in wild, colorful prints. Eventually, it would house a fish pond and a small waterfall. Plants of every size and variety adorned the once empty room. Vienna pointed out magnolias, hibiscus, begonias, and many species of cactus and ferns.

Rainey asked if she would help him decorate his buildings when the time arose. "I hope that we will still be together then, Vienna."

"Don't put the cart before the horse, Rainey. We are not even together right now."

"Ahh, but the day is not over yet and I plan to win you over with my charms."

She hit him with the paintbrush she was holding. "Let's get to work."

They painted until dusk and went in to clean up while Joe went to the diner to retrieve the supper that Lily had made for them. They dined on cabbage rolls, fresh bread, fruit, and ice cream. At 8:30, they all walked down to meet Lily and Sissy. Vienna thanked her for working her shift and said that she would make it up to her by treating her and Addy to the movies later in the week. Addy was holding hands with her and Rainey and wanted to know why he couldn't come with them.

"Sorry, Addy, I have to go back to the coast tomorrow to finish up at school and pack up my stuff. We will have many other nights to go to the movies together, right, Vienna?"

She didn't answer, but Addy did. "I'm glad you are coming back."

"Wild horses couldn't keep me away!"

"Hey, that is what V always says."

"And that is probably where I got it from."

When they reached the house, Rainey said that he hoped no one would mind if he and Vienna went for a little ride. After they drove away, Addy said, "Why does Rainey get to call her Vienna and we have to call her V?"

"That's just the way she wants it, honey," Lily offered in the way of an explanation.

"Well then, I want to be called Adelaide! Do you want to be called Sicily, Sissy?"

"No!" Sissy answered vehemently.

Rainey drove up to the Lookout and parked. Vienna was not happy.

"Why did you bring me here?" she demanded.

"To make amends. I made a big mistake last year. I have told you a few times that I am no good for you and that you would be better off without me, but now, I want to convince you otherwise. I want to be the man you deserve. I hate who I am when I'm away from you. I am beginning to believe that I should never have left the farm."

"Stop that, Rainey Quinn! You are going to be the best architect in the world! You are going to do what you were born to do. Your destiny was already in place long before you met me. At this point in time, I don't know if there are plans for me in your future or even if you want me in it. We have a long row to hoe. No one knows where the path is going to lead us. If we were meant to be together, then we will be…time will tell."

"There you go, being the voice of reason again. I am quite sure that I want you in my future. The question is: do you want me in yours?"

"Sometimes, I can't think of my life without you in it, and other times, I wish that I had never met you. I am quite convinced that I am a little crazy when it comes to you."

"I'm going to make this the best summer of our lives. Now get over here. I'm lonely without you in my arms."

This time, it was different. Rainey called Vienna every night that he was away. He never had contact with anyone outside the university except his housemates, Bev and John.

May was almost over when he returned. He helped Vienna study for her exams but didn't think that he was much help, as she was not interested in math at all. He hadn't realized that she had such a stubborn streak in her. When it came to math, she was adamant that she was going to fail it yet again. To her surprise, she passed all her exams and could enter grade twelve without having to repeat anything. She credited Rainey for the results. He was pleased to think that she thought he had helped.

Most of their time together was spent in Bridge Falls. Rainey was helping her father when she was at work and he was not haying at the farm. He thought it was time that his parents got to know her better and asked her to come to Hawthorne for the day at the end of June. They spent the day horseback riding. He was pleasantly surprised to find out that not only did she know how to ride but also insisted on saddling her own horse. When she was thirteen, she had spent the summer with an older girlfriend at Emerald Lake, working at the resort tending to the horses and taking tourists on trail rides. He wondered what else he was going to discover about her. He gave her the choice of the gentle mares and she chose Lady…no kidding, a lady for Lady V.

They rode up to his favorite spot, a lush hillside that stood watch over the fields and the ranch. The meandering river could be seen in the distance. They tethered their horses and stretched out in the daisy and lupine filled meadow.

"I could live here," Vienna commented.

"Do you think that you could be a farmer's wife?" Rainey asked. "It is a very hard life. They are up before the chickens and to bed whenever the work is done."

"I bet your mother wouldn't want any other life."

"You're probably right. Claudia, on the other hand, couldn't wait to get out of here. I know that I do not want to be a farmer neither."

"You're all about the big city, aren't you? I don't think that is the life for me."

"How would you know? You haven't tried it yet. But, you are wrong, I am perfectly happy being here in the sticks with you. I want you to spend the night at the ranch tonight. Would your parents be all right with that?"

"Well, they might be, but I don't know if I am. What do you expect from me, Mister?"

"Nothing, my dear. I thought that we could have supper with Mom and Dad and then visit with the boys. You will have your own room. What do you say?"

"Let's see what your mother has to say. Do we trust you to stay in your own room?"

Rainey smiled and told her he would be a gentleman. She laughed.

Patsy was delighted. Her son had a girlfriend, one that he cared enough to bring home. She knew that other women existed, but none whom he would talk about or bring to the farm. He was almost twenty-two and wasn't in any hurry to settle down. She and Paul were happy about that, but then last year, he had met V and he had become a different person—happier and content. She liked V and was looking forward to getting to know her better. They had a lovely dinner and V was more help to her in the kitchen than her own daughter had ever been. V related stories about her family and their many moves before coming to Bridge.

Chapter Six

Priscilla

Patsy noticed how her son hung on every word that V said. He was constantly smiling.

"I love living here in the valley. It is the most beautiful place I have ever been." She winked at Rainey in her funny little half wink. "Oh yeah, and I met this simply gorgeous man whom I am extremely fond of." V laughed, and Pasty and Paul laughed with her. Rainey was only slightly embarrassed.

Yes, Patsy had thought, *I like this girl very much.*

Vienna did spend the night and it passed without incident, although Rainey had a difficult time sleeping, knowing that she was in the room next to him. It took all of his willpower not to go to her.

They had gone to Jimmy's and Zane and Marley had come over. They shared laughs and drinks, and promised Zane that they would come to his first of July party next Saturday. It would mean another sleepover for Vienna. She didn't know that it would all lead up to the turning point in her relationship with Rainey.

The phone rang, at least Zane thought he had heard it. "Pipe done, everyone, it might be the fuzz." He said into the mouthpiece, "Zane's Mortuary, you stab 'em, we stab 'em, some go to heaven, some go to hellooo there."

"I'm looking for Rainey Quinn. Is he there please?"

Zane was sure that he had never heard that voice before. "He's here somewhere. Let's see if I can track him down. Who should I say is calling?"

"Priscilla."

Who the hell is Priscilla? Surely isn't anyone from around here. "Hey, Rain, phone call for you!"

"Take a message," Rainey replied. "I'm busy."

"Okay, but it's some strange woman."

Vienna laughed. "Yes, that would be for Rainey then."

"Very funny," Rainey told her. "Christ, who is it, Zane?"

"Some chick who calls herself Priscilla."

If looks could kill, Zane would be dead. Rainey said, "This won't take a minute, be right back." He left Vienna knowing he was in trouble. How had that bitch found him? "Geez, Zane, could you be a little discreet? Give me that damn phone. Priscilla, this is a surprise." He waved to Vienna and blew her a kiss. She had an amused smile on her face.

"A pleasant one I hope," Priscilla replied. "I haven't heard from you since you left and I was beginning to worry about you. Are you all right?"

"No need to worry. I told you that I was going to be very busy on the farm. Not much time for anything else. How did you get this number?"

"Your mother was kind enough to give it to me. Rainey, I am coming through your way this coming week and I am hoping that we can get together. Is that a possibility?"

"Look, Priscilla, this is not a good time. How about if I call you another day?"

"Sure. I'll let you get back to your party then. I'll see you when I see you, Rainey."

Thank goodness she had hung up. Not only was he going to have to explain her to Vienna, but she had called his mother. Damn that woman!

He could read her lips. "Who is Priscilla?" How much was he willing to tell her? He knew that she would understand a girl from his past calling him, but perhaps not as recent as the spring. He had first met Priscilla at some sorority event. She had latched on to him almost immediately and he had foolishly thought, *What the hell? What could one night hurt?* Only the one night turned into a three-month affair. He had no genuine feelings for her; it was just sex. He had attended some charity event with her that was boring him to tears. He had wandered out into the foyer, found a telephone, and dialed Vienna's number. He hadn't talked to her for months because he was too ashamed of himself. Without meaning to, he had broken down at the sound of her voice and confessed to her. He just hadn't mentioned Priscilla's name. Was this woman going to be the end of his tranquil life? *Please God, don't let her come. She's trouble with a capital T.*

He pulled Vienna up from the sofa. "Let's get out of here. Want to go for a ride to the Quarry?"

On the way out, he glanced at Zane, who mouthed, "Sorry."

They ran hand in hand to the Olds. The clouds had opened up and sent down the first rain in over a month. Once inside, Vienna said. "I'm cold, Rainey. Start Ole Betsy and get some heat in here."

"I renamed her you know. Get over here." He pulled her into his arms and kissed her until she couldn't breathe. "I've been wanting to do that all evening."

"As if that is the first time that we have kissed today." She was laughing. "Now, tell me, Sir, what did you rename her?"

"Gypsy Lady. What do you think?"

"Did you just make up that name in the spur of the moment? Do you think that naming your car after me would get you out of explaining that phone call? You can drive and talk at the same time, can't you? And, yes, I do like the name. It sounds intriguing."

"As you are, my dear. What do you want me to tell you? You want to know who Priscilla was to me. She is someone I used to see, that is all. She means nothing to me. She is coming up this way, though. Why? I don't know. I want nothing to do with her and I told her so before, but I guess I didn't paint a clear enough picture. Anyhow, I told her that I was busy so don't bother coming."

"No, you must let her come and you can introduce me as your betrothed. Surely, she will get the picture then. It will be fun to compare notes with her."

Well, at least she doesn't appear to be mad at me. But, was she kidding? He couldn't tell. She wasn't laughing, just smiling in a conniving way. Lordy, those two could never meet. He had no intention of ever calling Priscilla. He had all he wanted and needed right here. They went back to the party and nothing more was said, but deep down, Rainey had the sinking feeling that Vienna was not satisfied with his story. The "betrothed" word stumped him a little, though. They had never even talked about marriage. He had asked her in a roundabout way if she would come and live with him at the coast in the fall, and she had told him to get serious because they both knew that wasn't going to happen. Suppose if he asked her to marry him, what would she say? What was going to happen when he went to Italy in the fall? *Whoa*, he told himself, *one hurdle at a time. Let's make sure this Priscilla thing goes away…she could be the straw that breaks the camel's back.*

She did not call him and he certainly had no intention of contacting her. She hoped the element of surprise would be on her side. She pulled into the ranch on Saturday, at 2 P.M.

Priscilla had inquired at the general store in Hawthorne for directions to the Quinn ranch. She parked in the middle of a long driveway and, seeing no one in sight, walked up to the house. She climbed the few steps to a screened porch and knocked on the door, which was also screened. An old dog looked at her lackadaisically from his sofa bed and decided that she was no harm, wagged his tail, and went back to sleep. From somewhere inside, she heard a female voice call out that she would be right there.

She hoped that it was Rainey's mother.

A middle-aged woman came to the door. She was wearing a large apron over a checkered blouse and faded jeans. She had flour all over her face and hands. "Sorry," she apologized, wiping her hands on the hem of the apron. "I was just finishing with the baking. How can I help you?"

"I'm looking for Rainey," Priscilla said. "Is he here?"

"He is out riding right now, but I do expect them back anytime. Can I be of any help?"

Priscilla assumed he was with his father. "No, but thanks. I'll just wait for him, if you don't mind."

Patsy wondered who this pale, slender woman was. She definitely wasn't from around here. "Oh, of course, please come in. Would you care for some iced tea while you wait?"

"Thank you. That would be lovely." She followed the woman into the house. Noticing that the walls were filled with family pictures, she asked if it would be all right if she looked at them.

Patsy said that she wouldn't mind at all. She returned with the tea and told the stranger to make herself at home while she checked on the baby chicks. "I'm sorry. I didn't catch your name. I'm Patsy Quinn, Rainey's mother."

"Yes, I was sure you were. Nice to meet you. I'm Priscilla Ward, a friend of Rainey's from the city. May I come with you? I have never seen baby chicks before."

"I'm afraid that you might get those high heels of yours dirty, but you are welcome to come." Patsy wondered how she could drive with those things on.

"I'll be careful. The girl in the photos with Rainey, is it his sister? And the man must be his father or brother; they look so much alike."

"Yes, the girl is Claudia and the man is his father." Patsy held the door open for her and thought this couldn't be a very close friend, or she would have known that Rainey didn't have a brother. In the barn, Patsy showed her the new foal. "She doesn't have a name yet. Rainey wants V to name her."

Who the hell is V? Just as she was about to inquire, Patsy called out, "Here they are!"

Priscilla backed away so as not to be seen and peaked out the barn door. She could see the two riders coming in; one was definitely Rainey and the other was a young girl. Probably relative or neighbor, she thought. She watched him dismount and went to help the girl off her horse. She slid effortlessly into his arms and they stood there looking at each other as if they were lost in time. She watched them kiss; she could not look away.

Patsy shouted to her son, "Someone to see you, Rain."

"Be right there, Mom." He sauntered over to the barn hand in hand with his young filly.

He hadn't seen her or her car yet. Priscilla stepped out of the shadows. "Hello, Rainey."

She was the last person he expected to see. No hello, just, "What are you doing here?"

"I told you that I was coming…did you forget?" She was staring at Vienna.

"I thought you were kidding," he replied. Vienna was tugging at his arm. "Sorry, sweetie. This is Priscilla Ward. Priscilla, meet V." Rainey tried to sound normal.

"V?" Priscilla said.

Vienna stepped forward, offering her hand. "Lovely to meet you, I am sure."

Reluctantly, Priscilla took the hand that was outstretched and thought if felt cold. Sweetie, he had called this little farm girl "sweetie." How old was she, fifteen? Was he out of his mind? This V person was jailbait.

"Are you on your way to Alberta to your sisters?" Rainey hoped she would say yes.

Priscilla turned away from V and said that she was too tired to travel any further today and asked if there was a decent motel nearby.

"We won't hear of such a thing, will we, Rain? Patsy, can Priscilla have the room next to mine? And perhaps she would like to come to the party with us tonight? We can't have a friend of Rainey's staying in some lonely motel." Vienna smiled all too satisfactorily.

"Of course, dear. You think of everything. Will you see her settled then?" Patsy asked.

"Let me help you with the luggage," Rainey offered.

Vienna smiled at him and said, "Don't be silly. We can manage, can't we, Priscilla? You need to tend to the horses."

He said, "Are you sure, Vienna?" He really didn't want to leave them alone.

"I'm sure."

Priscilla thought that she had no other choice and so followed V to her car to retrieve her bags. "Vienna, is that your name?"

"My name is V. Only Rainey calls me Vienna." Her voice was sweet as honey…honey dipped in vinegar.

They entered the house through the kitchen door. There must have been a dozen pies on the counter. The room smelled of spices and fruit. V almost ran up the stairs, stopping at the top to see how Priscilla was making out with her luggage. Why she had brought so much was a mystery. She dropped the vanity case and went back down to help with the rest of the bags. Priscilla thanked her and trudged up the remaining steps. V pointed out Paul and Patsy's room at the end of the hall.

"This one is yours for the *night*, right next to mine," V said. "You have your own bathroom. I will share with Rainey."

Priscilla was well aware that V had emphasized "tonight." "I don't mind sharing the bath with you, V."

"That's okay. Rainey and I are used to sharing. Will you be all right? I have to go and fix us something to eat. We have been on a very long ride and are starving. Can I bring something up for you? Supper isn't until 6ish. Just whistle if you need anything."

"No, thank you. I'm okay." *What a little twerp! She acts as if she owns the place. She is probably somebody's welfare child.* She opened a window and lit a cigarette.

Rainey found Vienna with her head in the refrigerator. "What are you doing in there?"

She peeked around the door and said, "Cooling off. What do you want to eat?"

Good, she wasn't angry. He told her anything would do. He sat down at the table and watched as she slapped devilled egg (maybe a little too vehemently) on homemade bread. She added lettuce and handed him a sandwich.

She sat opposite him, took a bite of hers, and calmly said, "How do you feel with your old love upstairs and your little schoolgirl downstairs?"

He didn't have the stomach to eat anymore. He wanted to say, "Well, you invited her." Instead, he said, "I am not happy, and please don't ever refer to her as 'my love.' She never was and she has no business being here. She was not invited."

"Oh, she told you she was coming all right. Don't tell me that you didn't think she would show up. You didn't end it very well with her, did you? Or did you even end it?"

"Vienna, I didn't lie to you. She means nothing to me, as you will soon see."

"She's the one, isn't she, Rainey? How can I compete with the likes of her?"

"What the hell do you mean? Compete? Do you really think that I prefer some skinny socialite over you? There is no comparison! Next to you, she is Drusilla. I am so happy to tell you that she was never the one, *you are*, and you know it."

To his amazement, Vienna broke out laughing. "So your mother did read you fairy tales. I can't believe that you pulled that name out of your hat. You're right, she isn't so attractive. Whatever did you see in her anyway? Oh yeah, I remember."

"Come over here, you little tease!"

"You're going to have to catch me first!"

Priscilla heard a ruckus and went to the edge of the stairs to see what was happening downstairs. Rainey and V were chasing each other around the butcher block, laughing and squealing like children. She watched silently as V suddenly stopped and let Rainey catch her. They fell into each other's arms and kissed. She was green with envy. Mrs. Quinn came in the back door and told them to behave themselves, though she was laughing, too. She shooed them out and told them to go get cleaned up. They both kissed her on the cheek and grabbed a tart as they fled.

Priscilla ran back to her room and quietly closed the door. She heard them pass by her room, still whispering and giggling. Again, she thought, *He's off his rocker.* She waited until they were in their rooms and crept down to the kitchen. "Mrs. Quinn, what sort of affair is this tonight? What shall I wear? I don't want to overdress."

"It is just a farmers' get-together. Actually, all of Hawthorne and the surrounding areas will be there. Its potluck and live music follows the supper. We have three or four such events every year. Just dress casually, slacks or a light dress. Rainey prefers V in a dress."

As if I would take any advice from a teenager. "Do you mind if I ask you a question about their relationship? Are they romantically involved? She seems so young?"

"Where matters of the heart are concerned, there is no age difference. Rainey is crazy about her. She is the first girl he has ever brought home. They are very happy together."

Priscilla felt as though she had been slapped in the face. She returned to her room to shower and change. She chose creamy linen slacks and a pale, lemon silk blouse. She tapped on V's door and asked her if she could help her for a minute. V was dressed in a simple, light-green full-skirted dress. It came just above her knees, making her look plump.

"Sure." V followed her, wondering what was up.

Priscilla handed V a string of pearls, asking if she would mind fastening them for her.

"Yes, I think I can manage that. They are lovely. Were they a gift from an admirer?"

Priscilla thought of lying and telling her that they were a gift from Rainey, but thought better of it. "V, can I talk to you for a minute? Please sit down."

V sat on the edge of the bed, wondering what this woman had in mind.

"You seem like a lovely girl. Would you mind some advice from someone who has been around the block once or twice?" V didn't answer, so she went on. "How long have you known Rainey? I can't help but notice that you seem to have a crush on him. This can't be healthy for you if he is leading you on. He is much too old for you and I hope he doesn't end up hurting you."

Well, she was right about one thing, she certainly had been around the block a few times. "Do you really think that he is too old for me, Priscilla? Gee, I never even gave it any thought. We met last June." Her attitude toward Priscilla was very cool.

"Have you been seeing him all this time?"

"I think you know the answer to that." *Why is the woman beating around the bush?*

"What do you mean?"

"You want to tell me that Rainey was with you last spring, but I already know that."

"He told you?"

"Yes, he did. I don't need to know all the sordid details, but you should know that if you are here to get him back, you made the trip for nothing. Rainey will not be leaving me." Vienna arose and smiled sardonically. "Rainey and I have something very special. We are what they call 'star-crossed lovers.' We knew it from the first minute we met. We will always be connected no matter what. Now I hope that we can make your little visit a pleasant one…thanks for the talk."

Priscilla thought, *You arrogant bitch. What could she possibly know about life or love? She probably had been born in this hick town and would probably die here.* It was time to take the blinders off Rainey's eyes. She would wait for the right moment.

Half an hour later, they knocked on Priscilla's door and asked if she was ready.

V commented, "You look nice, Priscilla. Don't you think so, Rain? I'm glad that you chose shorter heels. You're so lucky that you can tolerate them. Being short, I could use the height, but they kill me."

"Speaking of shoes, Vienna, where are yours?" Rainey asked. "You are going to wear them, right?"

She pulled them out from behind her back. "Only if I have to."

I am going to be sick, Priscilla thought. *I have to get through to Rainey, I just have to.*

They met the Quinns in the kitchen, where she was introduced to Rainey's dad. They were taking two vehicles, as Patsy said they needed the room for the pies and they would be coming home long before the young people.

"Don't count on it, Mom," Rainey said. "V and I have had a very long day and are tired. We may not last too long. I'm sure that Priscilla is tired after her long drive also and will want to get an early start tomorrow."

I bet they are tired. It's just an excuse so that they can get home to their love nest. Ah, but I am here to put a stop to that, Priscilla thought.

The party was in a large, barnlike building called Hawthorne Grange. It was remarkably neat and clean inside, to Priscilla's amazement. The tables were overflowing with farmers' produce that included fried chicken, barbecued ribs and beans, hams, roast beef, and colorful salads. There were steaming biscuits and freshly baked breads, pitchers of iced teas and lemonade. The dessert table consisted of Patsy's pies, cakes, and squares, watermelons, and other fresh fruits.

Rainey led them to a table that was filled with people his age and an older couple whom he introduced as his aunt and uncle. Rainey held V's chair for her as she sat down. He didn't make a move to help Priscilla, but his friend, Yates, did and introduced himself.

The fellow across the table said, "Lady V, who is your friend?"

V scolded him. "Jimmy, you know better. Actually, she is a friend of Rainey's from the city. Meet Priscilla everyone. These are Rainey's friends, and now mine, I am pleased to say. Here we have the infamous Jimmy and Zane, Marley, and Yates, whom you already met."

V did most of the talking and Rainey seemed content to just sit and listen. She was definitely flirting with all his friends, but he didn't mind at all. She had made sure that she seated herself between him and Priscilla. Suddenly, V jumped up and ran to greet some people at the door. She brought them back to the table and introduced the girl as her best friend, Lara, and her mother, Anne, who was also Rainey's aunt. Jimmy got up and held the chair for the young girl who seemed to be about V's age.

"Why, Jimmy, I am impressed!" V said.

He laughed and winked at V. "You're not the only one learning good manners."

Some private joke, Priscilla thought and glanced at Rainey, who seemed to be amused at everything V did or said. Again, she thought, *I must get him alone.*

The dinner prayer had been said and there was a mass exodus to the food tables.

V nudged Priscilla and said, "Stay behind me so that you don't get trampled." Rainey grabbed her as she got up and gave her a quick kiss, but he did not join them in the line. She found out why. V filled two plates, one for her and the other for Rainey.

Well, isn't that sweet? Priscilla returned to the table with a plate of food that a bird would find inadequate. She had taken green salad and chicken, and a minute amount of potato salad and all on a paper plate.

Yates looked at her and said, "Is that all you city folks eat?"

On the other hand, V's plates were heaped with food. She passed one to Rainey, who said, "Remember the first night we met V and she told us that she didn't eat?"

Jimmy laughed. "As if I could forget that night! I know you never will."

Rainey squeezed V's hand. "You're right about that, Jimbo."

Priscilla thought she might choke on her chicken.

V told Rainey that he was up for desserts and to bring enough for the whole table. Yates offered to help, returning with a whole apple pie to share.

Priscilla had never known Rainey to eat sweets and mentioned it.

"I reserve my sweet tooth for when I am at home," he replied. "And now it does double duty because Vienna makes the most luscious desserts, and so does her mother."

"I'll vouch for that," Jimmy agreed, explaining to Priscilla that V's mom ran a diner in Bridge Falls and that Lara and V both worked there.

Soon the meal was over and the ladies and some of the men started the clean up. Patsy insisted that the young people sit and visit, which they all did, except Rainey and V. Priscilla soon lost sight of Rainey and assumed that he was out smooching with V. They weren't seen again until the band had started playing. They were the first ones on the dance floor. Yates asked her to dance and she thought, *What the heck? Why not?*

After the first set, Jimmy and Lara said they were going out for a cig and asked Priscilla if she wanted to join them. Yes, she certainly did, and she asked V if she was coming.

Rainey answered for her. "Vienna doesn't smoke. She gave it up for me. But we will join you all outside for some fresh air."

The guys all got drinks from the bar and Yates asked Priscilla what she would like.

She asked Rainey if he was upset with her and he said, "Why do you ask?"

"You have barely spoken to me and you haven't even asked me to dance."

"I never invited you here. If you had phoned, I would have told you not to come. I think that you can tell that I am totally involved with Vienna."

In a hushed voice, she said, "Oh, I can see that you are infatuated with her and she is all you think about! What is she, fifteen? You don't seriously think that you can have a lasting relationship with her, do you? Please tell me that she is not sharing your bed, which, I am certain, she is…or worse yet, has her naïveté gotten her pregnant?"

Rainey spoke in a very controlled manner, although he wanted to tell her where to go and that he would gladly take her to her car so that she could leave immediately. Vienna wouldn't like it if he was cruel. "Priscilla, listen very carefully. Vienna is the light of my life. She is the reason I get out of bed and the reason my heart sings. She has a vibrancy that is contagious. She is not intimidated by anyone and has a knowledge way beyond her seventeen years. Yes, I am enchanted with her, and not that it is any of your business, she is not sharing my bed. There is more to our relationship than sex. I hope this sets you straight, and by the way, I don't dance with anyone except her."

Vienna returned from her waltz with Jimmy, and Rainey got up, took her in his arms, and whisked her away. Priscilla had gotten the message and she couldn't wait for the night to be over. This public display of foolishness was making her nauseated.

The next morning, as she was leaving, she warned Rainey again. "You know that you are flirting with disaster. You have worked so hard to get where you are and I am afraid that you are going to abandon your dreams for a teenage vixen. You're not thinking with the brain God gave you. This isn't a fairy tale that is going to have a happy ending!" With that, she was gone.

He heard Vienna calling out his name. He turned and found her waving a broom. "Rainey, has she left? Drats, she forgot her broom!"

Rainey picked her up and swung her around. *Leave it to her to bring laughter into a depressing moment.* "Well, I do know that she is indeed a witch, so you must be…who?"

"Anyone you want me to be."

"I just want you to be you. Do you know how hard it was for me to stay in my own room last night? I wanted so much to come to you and hold you in my arms all night."

"It was for me, too, Rainey…except, I did sneak into your room."

"What? Why didn't you wake me?"

"I wouldn't have dared to wake you…not with your parents down the hall."

"You mean that you wanted to?"

"Oh, most assuredly, my lord; what do you think of that?" Her eyes were laughing.

"I think it is time that we did something about the way we feel. Will you come away with me next weekend?"

"Yes, where shall we go?"

"You leave that up to me, my lady. Wait a second, I do remember something about last night. Maybe I heard you leave or maybe I was dreaming. I did wake up, and you know what? It was 4:44. Did you notice the time?"

"No, I didn't. I can't for the life of me understand why you are waking up at the same time. Perhaps it is just your internal clock, or maybe you really are dreaming. Quit fretting over it. Let's go find your parents so that I can say thanks. I need to get home."

Chapter Seven

Summer/Fall, 1961

V ienna needed a new wardrobe. She took all of her meager savings out of the bank. She wanted to look perfect for Rainey. She found a red, lightweight jumper with a low neckline that wouldn't require a blouse. To her delight, she discovered a three-quarter length white summer frock made of waffle-weave cotton. It fit her perfectly, and with its ruffled petticoat, she felt like a Victorian damsel. She wished she hadn't cut her long hair. She found nothing that she cared for in the way of night attire; the black made her look too sultry and the white was too angelic. She left the store with her dresses. She decided to try the East Bridge Boutique. She had never ventured into it before as she heard that it was quite pricey. She found it to be a delightfully charming place. There were open trunks and cupboards where lacey articles peeked out from. The shelves housed large straw and fabric hats, and baskets of candles and soaps sat on the floor. There were pillow-laden settees, antique sewing machines, and writing tables all draped in embroidered needlework cloths. Frilly ferns and geraniums spilled from earthenware pots. Tables were set with tea sets and the cushioned white wicker chairs were an invitation to sit a spell. *Someday*, she thought, *I am going to decorate a room like this*. She made herself focus on the task at hand. She recognized the salesgirl as someone who frequented the diner and explained to her what she was searching for. She followed her to the back of the shop, and lo and behold was the perfect gown. There in front of her hung a pale, blue-green satin negligee and matching robe. She held it to her bosom and twirled. She knew that it would fit her and she still had enough money to pay for it. All she needed now was Rainey.

When Rainey picked V up the next morning, she was wearing the white frock. In her hands were her sandals, a pale, yellow shawl, and a wide-rimmed, floppy hat. She was already tanned a beautiful bronze and never wore anything on her legs except at work. Rainey placed her small satchel and the lunch that she prepared in the backseat.

"Vienna, you look as if you just stepped out of a seventeenth-century novel…a lady from another century. I never know if I am dreaming when I see you. I thank my lucky stars that I found you before you had the chance to work your charms on someone else. I have never met anyone like you. I know I have told you that before, but I can't say it enough. Vienna LaFontaine…even your name evokes romance."

"Rainey Quinn, I love it when you talk like that. When I am with you, I forget about my fantasies with castles and white knights because I am living my own real-life fairy tale."

"Now get over here and give me a kiss for the road."

"Happily, my lord." She laughed heartily. "Now, where are you taking me?"

"To Avastavalley."

"That sounds very mystical."

"As are you, my dear."

The day was very warm; they drove with the windows down and listened to WZPJ radio. The station played all the hits from the '50s and '60s. They stopped by a stream off the highway and shared the picnic lunch of sandwiches, raw vegetables, and fruit. Vienna was on her health kick again, Rainey was pleased to see. He noticed that she wasn't eating much but seemed to be concentrating on him. She was drinking in his debonair good looks. His hair was thick and a perfect shade of sand. He didn't have sideburns, but a little curl always fell onto his forehead. Then there were his eyes. She was sure they could put her into a trance if she looked into them long enough.

The only accessory that he ever wore was a watch. He seemed to always wear a white shirt with two or three buttons left undone and the sleeves rolled up to his elbows. He never wore tee shirts or shorts. She asked if there was time for her to put her feet in the water, and he assured her that there was.

He watched her as she waded into the stream, hiking her skirt up to her waist. He had an eerie feeling that the angels were about to descend and steal her away. The "Tips of My Fingers" was playing on the radio; he listened to the words for a while and suddenly remembered the nightmares that he had experienced where she was falling out of his reach. He jumped up and called her name, perhaps a little too exuberantly. She turned and waved to him that she was coming. He snapped out of the weird sensation that he had been experiencing and carried her shoes to the shore of the creek.

She leaned on him as he did up the straps on her sandals. He cradled her in his arms. She sighed. "I'm so happy."

He kissed her and shared her sentiments.

At 4 o'clock, they turned off the main road and followed the signs that brought them to the resort at Avastavalley. It was situated on Avasta Lake, in a remote valley and miles from the nearest small town. It was modern and rustic at the same time. Rainey checked in and watched from the inside of the office as Vienna wandered toward a huge fountain. There was no doubt in his mind that she was going to go wading and wondered if it was permissible when a large, brown dog ran up to greet her. She sat down in the grass with her new friend and was soon joined by two smaller dogs. The lady who was checking him in started to the door to call the dogs, but Rainey stopped her, saying there was no need as Vienna was obviously enjoying their attention.

Rainey had requested the last cabin on the shore of the lake. He handed the key to Vienna as he retrieved the luggage. She waited for him on the porch, where two green cane chairs sat waiting for the next arrivals. She turned and smiled at him, and slowly unlocked the door, wondering what the inside was going to look like. She wasn't disappointed. The floor was rough planking with oval, braided rugs scattered everywhere. A wooden table and chairs sat by the open window. The sizeable bed was covered by a patchwork quilt and a multitude of colorful throw pillows. There was no television. The artwork, which hung on the walls, was of the outdoors and wildlife. A small bookcase stood in one corner, housing an assortment of old and well-read novels. She was already sorry that they would only be staying the one night. She asked Rainey how he had found such a delightful place, hoping that he had not been here before with another woman.

"My mother suggested I bring you here. She and dad were here for their twenty-fifth anniversary and she thought that we might like it. Do you?"

"I do. I can't believe that you asked your mother for advice. How charming. What does she think that we are up to?" she teased.

"Oh, I think everyone knows, including your parents. Are you sure you like it?"

"Yes, I am more than sure. I love it, but I would be happy anywhere as long as I was with you. Shall we go exploring for a while? Silly me, I didn't even bring jeans or shorts."

"You'll be just fine. I am afraid the dogs and the grass have already soiled your beautiful dress. You are going to have to wear shoes you know."

The dogs joined them on their walk; he couldn't tell who was having more fun, the dogs or Vienna. Rainey wondered why there were no pets at the LaFontaine residence.

Maybe he would buy her one someday. Hell, he would buy her a whole menagerie!

Vienna had to change into her red jumper for dinner, as the white one was no longer presentable. She felt the electrifying tension between them intensifying and she thought that if they didn't leave right away, they would miss dinner altogether. Rainey was well aware of it, too, and didn't dare take her in his arms.

They enjoyed a tasty fare of brook trout and local produce followed by peach flan and coffee. The jukebox was playing an array of love songs. Vienna felt a lump in her throat when Skeeter Davis's "Will You Still Love Me

Tomorrow?" came on. Rainey hadn't noticed that she was uncomfortable. He purchased a bottle of fruity wine to take back to the cabin. They took their time strolling back. There was no one else around; the dogs had even gone to bed. He unlocked the door and placed the wine on the table.

Vienna came up behind him and put her arms around him. He pulled her hands up to his face and kissed them tenderly. He turned to face her and said, "Vienna…"

She pulled away and, with her fingertips still touching his, walked away until their hands could no longer reach. She blew him a kiss and retreated into the small bathroom to change into the green satin. It felt so cool on her skin that she shivered. She glanced in the mirror and wondered who was looking back at her. Surely, it wasn't the little schoolgirl who had left home this morning. She ran her fingers through her hair. She had never come this far before, and though she was anxious, she was also exhilarated. She found the man she loved standing at the window with his back to her, looking out into the night.

He turned when he heard her. His shirt was open to the waist. He put his glass down and walked toward her. His heart was beating rapidly at the sight of this ravishing young woman. "I am not worthy of you, Vienna. I cannot take your innocence. I fear that I would never be able to leave you again or that we might lose what we have."

"Shhh, such silliness. Will you not take me in your arms and make me yours, my lord?"

She started to kiss him and would not stop until she led him to the bed, and he succumbed to the passion that had been building all day. He whispered her name and drank in the pure smell of her and the softness of her skin against his. He caressed the smallness of her back, her deeply tanned shoulders, and kissed her neck and the hollow between her breasts. He reveled in every shiver that she expelled at her awareness of her sexuality. He had never experienced these feelings before with anyone and it scared him.

She lay in his arms and he never wanted to let her go. Tears were streaming down her face and he wiped them away with his kisses. No one had ever cried for him like this before. He had taken it too far. "Nothing will ever be the same for us, Vienna."

She smiled and said this time would stay with her forever. He held on to her as if his life depended on these moments and wondered what was going to happen to them when he went to Italy in September. He had put off telling her but knew he couldn't delay the inevitable much longer. It wasn't fair that he should find someone like her when so much was at stake for his future. He had not been one to worry but found that he no longer had control over his emotions. Was he in love with Vienna? Was this what love did to people? He had no other explanation. He didn't like being so vulnerable. He was going to have to come to terms with his newfound feelings, but not tonight…no, not tonight.

Vienna asked him what he was thinking so seriously about, and he answered, "Only you, my darling…only you." He was in over his head and he knew it.

Vienna awoke to find Rainey propped up on a pillow, staring at her. "And where have you been, Sir? You are all dressed already."

"Not very far. Here, I have a little something for you." He presented her with a small box tied with green ribbons.

She looked at him inquisitively. "For me?"

He looked around the room. "Do you see anyone else here? Open it please."

"Oh, Rainey, it is beautiful! Wherever did you find it?" In her hand she held a tiny turquoise-green teardrop on a delicate silver chain. It sparkled and danced as the light reflected off it. He offered to put it on her as she read the card that came with it.

"'Green is the color of the Earth and blue is the color of the sky. May this soothe and refresh you and bring you physical and inner peace of mind and body.' I shall never take this off, Rainey! Thank you." She kissed him.

"You are all the thanks I need. Whatever have I done to deserve you?"

It was well into the afternoon when they checked out. They had a quick lunch and Vienna said good-bye to the dogs. The owner said that she hoped that he and his wife had enjoyed their short stay and would come back again. He smiled sheepishly at the notion.

Vienna amused him with her tales as usual. She wanted to tell him about Maveryn and Scotland, but her inner voice cautioned her not to. "Would you like to hear of my strange visit to a Gypsy fortune-teller?" she asked.

He grinned and said, "This should be interesting."

"We were living close to Edmonton and a carnival had come to the area. It was spring. I was twelve, Sissy was eight, and Addy four. Mother wanted to have her fortune told and so dragged me off with her while Father kept the girls occupied on the rides. A barker directed us to a tent that had a sign that read: 'Minerva knows all. Sees all. Fortunes $1.'

"She was exactly as I thought that a Gypsy would look like: long, black, coarse hair wrapped up in a red kerchief, big hoop earrings, red, red lips, and dark, piercing eyes. She was wearing a long, purple skirt, a bright, yellow blouse, and a multicolored shawl. I swear she had men's boots on her feet. Around her neck hung amulets with the moon, sun, the stars, and other strange symbols decorating them. Drapes and scarves in heavy materials hung from the ceiling and walls. They were dancing as if there was a fan behind them. There were big old and ratty sofa chairs to sit in, and on the table was a cloth covered in the signs of the zodiac. A globe sat on it and there were strange cards strewn all over it. I know them now as tarot cards. Would you believe me if I told you that a big, black cat with piercing yellow eyes sat on a stool and watched us?"

"Vienna, I would believe anything you told me. Please go on."

"She told me to sit in the brown chair while she told Mother's fortune. She read her palms first and told her that she had a long health line and a strong love line. She would live to a ripe old age. She had her glide her hands over the orb that now was glowing blue and said she saw a future that would have Mother living by water and that she was getting the image of lots and lots of dirty dishes. Then she said she must read me. Mother told her no, that I was too young. She told my mother to hush and said, 'Come on, girlie. No charge. Don't be afraid. What is your name?'

"I told her V. She said that wasn't a real name and asked what it was. I told her Vienna. 'Ahh, that is more like it! Vienna, eh? Do you know what the meaning of the name is?'"

Mother told her that it meant nothing and that she had named all her girls after places that she wanted to visit.

"'You think that names have no meaning? Silly woman,' the fortune-teller said. 'I will tell you what Vienna means. It has warmth like warm red wine. It means friendship. You will impress and be admired by many. You will have great wealth. Now, let me see your palms. You, too, have a long life line. Some breaks in your health lines and your love line is broken. Come, let's see what the ball will say.' The orb was glowing beautiful greens and blues, just like this teardrop. I can still see it today.

"'Yes,' she said, 'beauty and good fortune will be yours and you will walk in foreign lands. You will know a great love but suffer deeply because of it. He will betray you. He will call you Vienna. That's all. That's all.' She quickly covered up the crystal ball that had suddenly turned dark and grey. Mother rushed me out, scolding Minerva for frightening me. But she had some last words for me. 'Tread lightly, child. Tread oh so lightly.'

"What do you think, Rainey? Are you the person she was talking about who is going to betray me? Are you going to break my heart? After all, you are the one who calls me Vienna."

He squeezed her hand and said, "I am amazed how you remember complete conversations that took place years ago. I have told you that many times before, or else, you are just a really good storyteller."

"Well, that is what I remember. Who is to say if it is accurate? We could ask my mother. Sometimes I wonder if I let you call me Vienna because Minerva said that I would find a great love and I felt such a strong attraction to you the moment that we met. But you haven't answered my questions yet."

"Vienna, I pray that I will not willingly do those things to you. I wouldn't take her words too seriously. They make things up you know, and you were so young and vulnerable that she probably was having fun with you and you didn't even know it. I am glad that you allow me to call you, Vienna. I cannot imagine having to call you V."

"All in all, though, Rainey, you have to admit that Mother's fortune was pretty boring compared to mine. Why would she want to scare me off, love? Anyhow, that is that and now it is your turn to tell me a story."

"I am not a very good storyteller, sweetie, and, in fact, I think that you have already heard all about my misspent youth, thanks to my so-called friends."

"Rainey, you are so lucky to have had the same friends all your life. I have never had any for more than a year until I moved here, and now I have Lara and I am very fond of all yours. I think that I will close my eyes for a few minutes. I didn't have much sleep last night."

"I wonder why. Put your head on my shoulder."

She did; he put his arm around her and kissed her on the forehead.

"Hands and eyes on the road, Mister, or I will do the driving."

"You're kidding, right? This from a girl who closes her eyes when we cross over bridges? I don't think so." He laughed and tried to concentrate on the road.

It was past nine when we arrived in Bridge Falls. Rainey was tired and I left him on the porch divan while I fixed us something to eat. The family must be off visiting, as the car was not in the garage. I poured two glasses of milk to go along with the cold roast beef and salads that I had found in the fridge. Rainey was almost asleep, but I told him to eat and that he should spend the night here. He looked at me as if I were crazy.

"Not *with me*," I said. "You can sleep on the couch."

I met mother and father at the door, asking them to be quiet as Rainey was sound asleep in the living room. The girls were spending the night at friends. If I had known then that Rainey could have slept in one of their beds…but maybe that was a little too close to my room. Mother asked me how the weekend went and I told her that it was very pleasant. She could read into it whatever she wanted.

And so, another summer was coming to an end. I would be back to school soon and Rainey would be back in Vancouver…or so I thought. Several times over the next few weeks, we had gone to the "line shack" at the ranch. The cupboards were loaded with staples and we would bring fresh produce with us. It consisted of two beds, a table, chairs, and an old chesterfield. It had a propane fridge and stove. We would ride the horses up and stay for the night. It was solitude and I loved it.

The last week of August, we were at a bonfire with everyone at the quarry. I figured that it was going to be the last night that we would all be together for a while. Rainey probably wouldn't be home until Thanksgiving. I was sitting with Ruth and Marley while the guys were cooking hot dogs. I was very surprised when Ruth asked me how I felt about Rainey going to Italy. I think that I was able to hide my shock and replied that I was not happy about it at all. The guys all joined us and Rainey asked if I would like to share a beer. I declined and said that I felt like I was coming down with the flu and should go home. Rainey knew that something other than illness was bothering me and asked what it was.

"Were you going to tell me that you were going to Europe as you were waving good-bye? Apparently, everyone is more important than me because they all know."

Lucky for us, there was a wide turn off as Rainey reacted and braked hard. The car came to an abrupt halt. "I'm sorry that you didn't hear it from me first. I was putting off telling you because I didn't want anything to spoil our last few weeks together. I'm a coward."

"It's a good thing for you that I am fast on my feet and didn't react too strenuously when Ruth told me the astonishing news. Did you think that I was going to go off the deep end? I am hurt that you felt you couldn't discuss your plans with me."

"I couldn't find the right words to tell you. I'm sorry. I never meant to hurt you."

"How long have you known that you would be going?"

"Too long. I knew last spring after school was out. It's only for four months. I'll be home at Christmas."

"Well, that makes everything all right then," I said sarcastically.

"Will you miss me? Please tell me that you will. I'll write you every day."

"I don't know. I am too angry with you right now, Rainey Quinn! Ask me tomorrow."

I was silent for the rest of the way home. I was still stewing over the fact that he hadn't let me in on his plans. Maybe I wasn't as important to him as I had thought. He asked me if I was going to invite him in and I said, "Suit yourself."

"I don't know if I should go where I am not wanted." It was his turn to be hurt.

I looked back at him and motioned for him to follow me. We stopped to say hello to the family, who were watching *The Wonderful World of Disney* on the television. Rainey sat down at the kitchen table and I asked him if he would like some decaf coffee. I kept puttering around until he asked me if I was ever going to sit down and talk to him.

"I thought that we had a simply wonderful summer. Was I wrong?" I asked him.

"No, you weren't wrong. It was the best summer of my life. That's the reason I put off telling you that I was going to Italy. I'm sorry. I won't make that mistake again."

"It's done. You can quit apologizing. I hope this isn't the beginning of the end. Do you want lemon meringue pie, apple pie, or chocolate cake?"

"Whichever one you made. What do you mean 'the beginning of the end'?"

"I made them all with Addy's help."

"Lemon then. Would you quit fussing and sit down?"

Addy had wandered into the kitchen and sat down beside Rainey. She stared at him.

"Addy," I said. "What are you doing?"

"Nothing, just wondering what Rainey did to make you so mad."

"The word is angry. It is nothing that you need to concern yourself with. Now go and ask Mother and Father if they would like cake or pie please."

"What kind?"

"Jumpin' Jehoshaphat, Addy, you helped me make them: lemon, apple, or chocolate."

"Oh yeah, I'll have chocolate cake and milk."

"I don't think that you should have chocolate this late in the evening."

"Then why did you ask me? Is she this bossy to you, too, Rainey?"

She ran out before I could hit her with the dish towel. I put a slice of lemon pie in front of Rainey and sat opposite while waiting for the coffee to quit perking.

"It's a good thing that I saw you first or you would have your hands full with that one. You do know that she considers you her hero?"

"What about you, Vienna? Am I your hero? Are you ever going to answer my question?"

I didn't have to ask him what question he was referring to, as I knew very well. I sighed. "I don't know. I have this sick feeling that the curtain is about to fall on us."

"Vienna, nothing is going to happen to us. Surely, four months isn't going to be our demise. Apparently, I have more faith in our relationship than you do."

Addy returned with her order and I helped her take the trays into the living room. Mother asked me if everything was okay and I told her, "Of course. What could be wrong?"

I sat beside Rainey and put my head on his shoulder. He kissed my brow and asked me if I had forgiven him. I told him that I wasn't angry but was missing him already. "I'll be here all alone and you will be in romantic Italy doing God knows what."

"Do you trust me, Vienna?" he asked.

"To be perfectly honest, I don't think that you can go that long without someone to keep you company."

"I'm going to prove you wrong."

"And how will I know that you will be faithful?"

"Because I am telling you so. You must have faith in me. I won't jeopardize us."

I wanted to believe every word that he said because where would I be if I didn't have him in my life? He then asked me if I would come to the coast with him for a week. He wanted to show me where he lived and the campus at UBC. He said we could go to the island, the Pacific National Exhibition, the museums, Stanley Park, and anything else that I wanted to do. I reminded him that I used to live there and had seen everything, but not with him as my guide, so, yes, I would go, but only for three days, and then I would come home by bus while he prepared for his overseas trip.

"No damn way am I putting you on any bus!" he argued.

"Well, Mister, that is the condition. Take it or leave it."

"Addy's right, you are bossy. I told you before that I would take you anyway that I can get you. I suppose that I will have to be satisfied with three days."

"All right then."

"Will your parents be all right with you coming with me?"

"It's not the first time, is it? Do you think they don't know what is going on with us? One would have to be blind and dumb, wouldn't he?"

On August 25, father drove me to Hawthorne. I visited with Rainey's parents for a few minutes before we set off for the six-hour journey.

After half an hour, Rainey said to me, "I don't think I can wait to be with you. We may have to get a motel room."

"Do you see what I mean, Rain? You won't last four months without someone in your bed."

"Easy, I won't have you to entice me."

"How am I enticing you? I'm only sitting here, listening to the radio."

"Maybe you are not even aware, but you sing or hum along with the radio, and that stirs me. Plus, I can feel the warmth of your body and smell your freshly washed hair. Need I say more?"

"Okay," I said moving away from him. "I won't sing anymore. Sorry about the hair."

"Oh no, you don't, get back over here! I have to get enough of you to last me four months, and don't you ever stop singing. It amazes me how you know all the words."

"I have a knack for remembering unimportant things, as you well know."

We arrived at his house in a nice, quiet district not far from the university. The place was clean and neat. His housemates, Bev and John, who had the basement suite, were on holidays. For the next three days and nights, we played house and I was sorry that I hadn't come for a week. One morning, we went to a shopping mall so that I could buy some new clothes for school. Rainey insisted on buying me a pink Banlon sweater set. I didn't have the heart to tell him that pink was not my color. While he was off buying some "men things," I wandered into a jewelry store where I purchased a Saint Christopher talisman for him. I hoped that he would wear it and that it would keep him safe for me. To my amazement, he loved it and insisted that I put it on him right away. He said that he would never take it off.

The day had come and I had to leave for home. Rainey still didn't want me going home on the bus, but he would be leaving for Europe in two days and still had lots of things to do, so he had no choice. At the bus depot, I pulled away from him with tears in my eyes. The trip home was very long and I felt like my heart was going to break.

The next evening, when we talked on the phone, I tried to be brave. He said that he would miss me something awful and would write as often as he could.

"I'll love you until the day I die, Rainey Quinn." I hung up while I still had some composure. The future did not bode well for me. I could feel it in my bones.

I didn't join in the Labor Day festivities. My heart wasn't up to any celebrations. The next weekend, I went to an engagement party for Zane and Marley. Lara was coming home from nursing school in Potsdam, so we went together. How nice for her that she was where her boyfriend lived. I was envious. She was so happy for Rainey and I, and she practically guaranteed that he would be faithful to me. She said that his mother had never known him to be so happy. That lifted my spirits and the Hawthorne gang told me that I was always welcome in their circles. I wouldn't snub them like I had last year.

That was true for September and October. I went to the movies with them whenever they came down, and sometimes, we would meet at the diner. I usually always accepted even though I felt like a fifth wheel. I had received a postcard from Rainey several weeks after he had left and a letter two weeks later. He was settled with his host family, the Perillies. He said that he felt right at home with them as they had three daughters, just like the LaFontaines. There was Sophia, who was twenty (I didn't like that); Magda, who was twelve; and Theresa, who was eight. He was immersed into the language program that he had told me about and living with an Italian family would be a big benefit to him. He hoped that he would be able to grasp it sufficiently in the short period that he would be there. He needed a working knowledge of the language for his architectural studies. He had already visited the Sistine Chapel in Rome and could not wait to return.

> *Vienna, I can't believe that Michelangelo painted the image of God in one day! I have like millions of others looked into the eyes of God as he depicted Him. What other wonders await me I can only dream about; that is when I am not dreaming about you. I haven't had any more nightmares and take that as a good sign. I hope that you will visit here one day. Please give my regards to your family. I am looking forward to hearing from you.*
> *Your humble servant,*
> *Rainey*

Wasn't he poetic? He hadn't said that he missed me. I wrote back, telling him of the news back home. I said that I missed him every single day and night.

October had come and gone and I had not heard from Rainey again. Jimmy asked me how our boy was doing, and I replied that I had no idea.

"Haven't you heard from him lately?" Jimmy inquired.

"No, I haven't. I am sure that he is doing just fine, living with four gorgeous Italian women. One, her name is Sophia, wants to come to Canada to be a model. I am sure that he will find a way to accommodate her." I feared I sounded bitter.

"Are you reading something into his words that isn't even an issue? Don't be making a mountain out of a molehill. You'll hear from him soon. Chin up."

"Thanks, Jimmy, but I have this terrible sinking feeling in the pit of my stomach." Of course I did, I just hadn't addressed it yet. Time was running out and I had yet to come up with a solution to my dilemma.

I checked the mail every day, but there was still no word from Rainey. I had sent him another two letters but had not heard back. Perhaps it was for the best. I stopped hanging around with Jimmy and the rest in November. I was sad all of the time and didn't want their pity. Zane and Marley had set a date to be married in the summer, Yates and June were planning their future together, and Jimmy was seeing someone, too. Jack had come back to town and wanted to take up with me again. I made it clear that it would only be a platonic relationship, and he said that he would agree to that for now.

I didn't even know why anyone would want to be around me. The light had gone out of my life. I was sick all of the time. There was little food that didn't make me ill, but I knew that I had to eat. Whatever was I to do?

It was a slow Friday, December 15. I told Mother that I was going to the mail as usual. I didn't think she was aware that I hadn't had a letter from Rainey for months. To my surprise, there was an envelope addressed to me from Italy. It was Rainey's handwriting. I went outside, cleared the snow from a bench, and, with trembling hands, opened it. I was already crying as I knew that he wasn't coming home to me. That would be for the best because then, I wouldn't have to feel guilty about what I was going to do. I thought the letter smelled of cherry blossoms. I read through my tears.

My dear Vienna,

I am becoming increasingly worried about you. Why haven't you answered my letters? I have phoned you several times and can't believe that I never catch anyone at home. I did manage to get through to my mom and she assured me that you were all right. Please don't give up on us, Vienna. We'll be together soon.

I am truly living my dreams. I cannot begin to describe all of the wonders that I have seen. I know that I will be returning here just as soon as possible. There is a possibility that I may find employment here. Wish me luck with my interviews. Of course, I still have to finish my year back home.

Life is very laid back here in the village and I do have a little time to relax with my adopted family. The food is good, though not as good as yours! Lots of wine. It is official now: Sophia will be coming home with me. I will have company on the flight.

They ask me if you are as lovely as in your picture, and I tell them "yes." I only have the one photo of us together that Aunt Mavis took last New Year's Eve. Why didn't we take more? I wonder. I am homesick for my raven-haired beauty.

I can now see the light at the end of the tunnel. The last four years of my life have not been in vain. The hard, grueling work is almost behind me and I can't see anything that would stand in the way of my achieving the long-awaited pot of gold.

I am so looking forward to seeing you. I will be arriving on the 22nd and will drive straight through to the farm, so I will see you on the 23rd. I am leaving right now to post this. I pray you are well.

Until I see you,
Rainey

The letter was dated November 29 and it was now December the 15. I didn't have much time. I crumpled it in my half-frozen hands and stuffed it in my pocket. I went straight home and told Father that I was ill and he best inform Mother that I was not returning to work. I went to bed with all my clothes on and straightened Rainey's letter out so that I could read it over and over again. Maybe I was being paranoid, but I was sure that I knew what had happened to the other letters that he said he had sent. He had entrusted Sophia to mail them and she hadn't. I imagined that she was in love with him. None of that mattered anyhow; he had not mentioned me in his future plans. He still had not said that he loved me. We could not interfere with his dreams. I knew what I had to do but just needed the courage to carry out my plans. Rainey came first and I would do nothing to jeopardize his career. I stayed in my room for three days and three nights. I was not getting any stronger. I was falling deeper and deeper into despair. I needed to take my leave for Scotland. Yes, it was Scotland. There had never been any Wales.

Chapter Eight

Scotland

I was eight years old the first time I saw Castle Avanloch. Father had been sent to a northern site in Alberta and Mother did not want to go, so she took me and four-year-old Sissy to her sister's in Scotland. We would be staying with Aunt Jannie and Uncle John for six weeks at Brackenshire Manor. They were employed by Lord Jeremy McAllister. John was his best friend and solicitor, and Jannie was mistress to the entire staff at Avanloch. They had no children between them, but Uncle John had two grown sons from a previous marriage and they both worked for Lord Jeremy in London in the family shipping business.

The manor house was a child's delight. It had two staircases and little alcoves that we could hide in. It was a gigantic playground. There was a cook, Mrs. Sharpe, and two maids, Millie and Emma, who tended to the twelve-roomed home. They all lived in the neighboring village in cottages, with names like Lavender and Heather. I wondered why we didn't name our homes in Canada. Sissy and I shared a bedroom and we could see the castle from our window. At the time, I thought castles only existed in fairy tales. I was too young to appreciate its magnificence and had very few memories. Jannie would invite us to tea in the afternoons in the drawing room. We would be served tea with sugar lumps and lemon in dainty little cups. There would be tiny cucumber and cheese sandwiches, and small iced cakes. We sat in velvet chairs near the fireplace, which usually had a small fire burning in it. Visitors often dropped in to visit with the Canadian guests.

We helped with chores at the manor and then were free to roam the grounds. It was like a zoo. There were chickens, geese, ducks, and lots and lots of bunnies. We would collect eggs in big straw baskets and get chased by the geese. In the meadows were horses, cows, and pigs. Sissy and I did not like the stinky pigs. Children would come from the village to play with us. That's about all I remembered of my first trip to Avanloch.

In June of 1956, Mother received a telegram from Uncle John. Aunt Jannie had been recovering from a bout of pneumonia when she slipped and fell down the stairs. She had broken her collar bone, a hip, and an arm. He requested that Mother and I come to help with her care and to lift her spirits. He sent us the fare and we left as soon as Father's leave of absence was granted. He would be staying behind to care for Sissy and Addy, who was only four. I was very excited to be returning to Scotland, except I hated the long and tedious airplane ride. Once we were safely on the ground in Glasgow, we traveled by train to Waverly and were picked up by Henry, who was Lord McAllister's chauffeur.

We found Jannie in great pain, but she put her happy face on for our benefit. Mother cried when she saw her lying so still in bed. She required complete care and Mother and I did our best to help the nurse, who came every day. Millie and Emma had been constant vigils at her bedside but could rest a little easier now that we were there. I took my role as part-time nurse seriously and even helped with her physical therapy. Doctor Williams said that our being there had definitely lifted Jannie's spirits, and thus, her recovery was coming along better than he had expected. Lord Jeremy had a device installed on one of the staircases that enabled Jannie to go downstairs in her wheelchair. How perky she became then, and as soon as the rains subsided, we took her outdoors every day for walks.

It had been stormy for almost a week. As soon as the skies cleared and my duties were completed, I ventured up the stone steps that led to the rose gardens at Avanloch.

Two huge, yellowish dogs came bounding down the path toward me. They were well behaved and didn't jump on me. A tall woman in riding apparel came around the corner. She was completely out of breath. She had the dogs' leashes in her hand.

"Shelley, Keats, mind your manners! I'm sorry if they startled you."

"Oh no," I assured her. "They didn't…well, maybe for a second. They are so gorgeous. You named them after poets?"

She was still scolding them but they were only interested in me. "These scoundrels do not belong to me, heaven forbid! They belong to Maveryn, Jeremy's fiancée. I am Ash and you must be Jannie's niece, V. Is that short for some other name?"

"Yes, but I do not use my full name. Is Ash your full name?"

"I was named after my grandmother, Audrey Ash. I prefer to be called Ash. Here, let me take the mutts back to their kennels. I need to get back to that monstrosity of a house. I do not know how your aunt ran it so easily. Thank God, Maveryn will be arriving soon." She tried to put the leashes on the dogs but they were not eager to go with her.

"Could they stay with me? I want to visit the ponds and they will be good company."

"Are you sure? The kennels are down by the horse stables. Do you know where that is?

"Yes, I remember. Thank you."

"I should be thanking you. I am sure that we will be seeing each other again."

Two days later, I met Maveryn in the same rose garden. She was simply the most beautiful person I had ever seen. She was removing the dead roses and storing their petals in her apron. She was wearing a long, full-skirted dress made of a lovely, soft, green material. Her skin was dotted with freckles and was the color of alabaster. A huge, floppy hat hid her magnificent red hair. Her eyes were green and they seemed to sparkle. Shelley and Keats came running to greet me.

She put her basket down and extended her hand to me. "Hello there. You must be the dogs' new love. Thank you for taking care of them for me. I am Maveryn."

"I am Vienna." I told her my full name, as I wanted to have one as lovely as hers.

"I thought that Ash told me that your name was V. Is that short for Vienna? It is such a charming name. Do you not like it?"

"Someday, I will be called Vienna. A Gypsy told me that when I am older, a man will win my heart and he will call me Vienna. Now, I am just plain V."

"A Gypsy, is that so? Do you like Gypsies?"

I told her that I had only met the one so really didn't know.

"Now you have met two," she said. "I come from a family of Gypsies. I am almost sure that the one you met was not a real Gypsy, just one masquerading as one to accrue money by pretending to tell fortunes. The carnival people are quite convincing."

I couldn't believe that she was a real Gypsy and told her so.

She laughed. "Most of us are ordinary people. Believe me, luv, there is Gypsy blood flowing through my veins. My family originally came from Romania and migrated to Wales a long, long time ago."

That was where my fantasy with Wales and Gypsies began. The summer with the lovely Maveryn took hold of my life. It was like living in a storybook. She had decided to call me Vela and I was to call her Mave. We would meet in the rose garden every day and wander with the dogs over the many paths and through the fields of wild flowers.

We always carried baskets with us to pick bouquets of white daisies, purple and yellow iris, bluebells, and the many hues of lavender. There were acres and acres of flowers. I was told that in the spring, the fields were alive with daffodils, crocus, tulips, and fruit trees in blossom. Thistle is the national plant of Scotland, and it was starting to bloom everywhere. Maveryn told me to be careful when I picked it because the stalks of the beautiful purple and pink flowers were quite prickly. I had asked Lord Jeremy why he measured his land in hectares and not acres. He told me that most of the world used the metric system and that someday, Canada would catch up.

Our walks would nearly always end at one of the three large waterways. Two were large enough for small watercraft and we often paddled around for hours, enjoying the wildlife feeding on the banks. There were deer, foxes, and the occasional coyote. The dogs were never happy with us, as we had to leave them in a pen on the shore. We would sit on the benches and feed the water fowl with scraps that we would bring from the kitchens.

We were expected back at the castle at 4 o'clock for tea. Maveryn was the hostess and the village ladies liked to come and meet the next Lady of Avanloch. Mother would usually join us and Jannie was also able to come via her wheelchair. She never complained, as she was so happy to be out and about.

One day, Mave took me into Waverly to do some shopping. She drove a little blue car. It was hard for me to get used to people driving on the wrong side of the road. I was sure we were going to have an accident at every turn. She would laugh heartily at my animated antics. We had a delightful luncheon in a quaint tea room. I learned my good manners from her. She was always courteous and friendly to all. She bought me my first long dress. It was blue and white with a sleeveless pinafore over it. I likened it to the one that Alice in *Alice in Wonderland* had worn. Maveryn must have been thinking the same thing, because when I emerged from the dressing room, she said, "Oh, there you are, Alice! I was afraid that you fell down the rabbit hole!"

All the salesgirls had a chuckle.

A pair of white flats completed the outfit. I thanked her over and over, and then she told me something astonishing. We were going to have a pre-engagement party so that I could attend, as I would not be here for the real one or the wedding. I was to help her with the arrangements. She asked if I would like that. How I kept from crying, "I do not know," but her next words did bring tears to both our eyes. She said that she always wanted a little sister and asked if I would be hers. That was just the silliest thing I had ever heard and I told her so, because I already considered her my big sister.

We had so much fun planning the party and I would remember the actual evening as the highlight of my young life. Soon after, we had to leave for Canada. I did not want to leave Jannie or Mave. They both assured me that I would always have a home here. I was happy that Jeremy would be home from now until October, so that Mave wouldn't miss me too much. Jannie had improved so much that we didn't feel guilty leaving her. Mother missed Dad and the girls, and I had to admit, so did I.

Mave came with Henry to the train station to see us off. We promised to write every week. It was a very tearful good-bye. I had never felt so sad in all my life. I had learned so much from Mave and I hoped that I could be the kind of person that she was. She said something very strange to me as she hugged and kissed me good-bye. "Vienna, you are going to be loved by a prince of a man and you will be his lady for all time."

Now years had passed and I could still see Maveryn smiling and waving as the train left the depot. That was to be the last time that I would ever see her alive. I had indeed found my prince and he called me his lady, but that had all come to an end. Oh, if I could only turn back the hands of time. I knew that we couldn't alter the past, but what if we could?

It was time for me to quit wallowing in "what-ifs." I had a few things to dispose of before I could leave. There must be nothing that would give my whereabouts away. Rainey must never know where I had gone. I was so glad that I had used Wales as my fail-safe, though at the time, I had no idea that I would ever need one. There was too much in my letters from Maveryn that would give away my location, so I bundled them up and put them in the bottom of my suitcase. Now I had to convince my parents to go along with my outrageous plan. As I was finishing up my packing, Mother knocked and came in.

"Oh good, you're up. We were just about to call the doctor, but I decided to check on you first... What are you doing with those suitcases?"

"I was on my way down to talk to you and Dad," I said. "I only want to have to say this once."

"Vienna Emerald, what are you up to?"

I stepped in front of her. "You will know soon enough. Let's go and find Dad."

I could hear her talking behind me but kept on going. Good, the girls were playing monopoly in their room. We found Father at his desk in the library. I closed the door behind Mother. This was going to require all of my strength and I didn't have very much. I was doing it all for love. Rainey could never know that I was carrying his child, for surely, he would do what he thought was right and I didn't want him that way. I didn't really think that he would come looking for me, but I had to try and make sure he didn't.

Father said that they were seriously thinking of sending for the doctor. I told him that I wasn't ill, at least not the way they thought. I told them that I needed to be on the first plane to Scotland. They stared at me in astonishment.

"Please listen to me very carefully and hear me out. There is no easy way to say this except I must leave town—and the sooner the better. I am going to have a baby and I can't have it here. No one is to know except you. I want to go to Jannie's. You know she will take me in. She said I always had a home with her no matter what."

Mother was hyperventilating. "My God, Vienna, a baby? Does Rainey know?"

"Don't be silly, Mother! Rainey has been gone for four months. He has nothing to do with this. To be perfectly honest, I have no idea who the father is."

Father was visibly upset and cursed. "Are you telling me that you have been promiscuous? I don't believe it! What aren't you telling us? Is that Jack the father?"

"No, I don't know." It hurt me that I had to lie to them. "I don't blame you for being disappointed in me, but that is the way it is. Now, will you help me and get me out of here? I can feel myself slipping further and further into despair. I am sorry to involve you in my situation, but I need your help. If you refuse, then I have no choice but to run away."

Mother was sobbing and Father, as usual, was the voice of reason. "Of course we will help you. What else do you require of us except seeing that you get to Scotland?"

"I am sorry, but you are going to have to lie for me. You will need to tell everyone that I ran away. No one can know where I am—not the girls, not even Lara, and especially not Rainey. I would surely die if he was ever to know. This is the last thing that I ever expected could happen to me and I am truly sorry for the heartache I am causing you."

After much discussion, they agreed that my plan was the best one, but worried how it would affect the girls. Of course, I was, too, and told them it would only complicate matters if they knew about the baby. I told my parents that I didn't care how they embellished my story, as long as they didn't disclose where I was. I called the girls to come down and told them that I had to go away for a while because of my health and that I had to go away to get better. I told them I would phone them every week, but they could not tell anyone where I was, especially Rainey. I asked them if they could do this for me, that it was very important that he didn't know. I didn't think they understood, but they promised me they wouldn't tell a soul. How could they understand? I didn't myself. They were the most upset over the fact that I would not be home for Christmas and that they would never see me again. I promised them that that was not going to happen. I told them I loved them and would miss them very much.

Jannie was called and readily agreed to my coming to live with her and Uncle John. I felt absolutely ill at what I had demanded of my family, but was praying that they could keep my secret. Two days later, on December the 20, I was on a plane to Scotland. My life as I knew it was gone. The die had been cast. I had taken the first step to my destiny.

The trip was a complete blur to me. I sat huddled in my seat on the plane, wrapped in a blanket. I couldn't get warm. Thank goodness, the kind people at the airlines helped me to make connections. I was relying on the kindness of strangers and hoped that someday, I could do the same for someone in need. Once I was safely on the train to Waverly, I began to relax a little, though all I could think of was Rainey and how he would react when he came home and found me gone. It might stun him for a while, but he would deal with it and move on to someone else. For me, there would never be anyone else.

The scene outside the window was grey and dismal, as if it were mimicking my feelings. I could see Jannie waiting on the platform for me. I nearly fell running to meet her. It was the first time I cried since reading Rainey's letter. She comforted me as no one else could; my own mother was not as understanding. I knew in the days to come it would take all my strength not to confide in her, but at all costs, I must keep the identity of the baby's father a mystery. The somber atmosphere at the manor only added to my despair. Apparently, there had been a death in the village that had affected everyone. Mrs. Sharpe, Millie and Emma welcomed me with open arms. I knew they would take care of me and my baby-to-be. Uncle John was still on assignment with Lord Jeremy.

I went directly to my room, as I was exhausted. I had my old room and tried to see Avanloch, but the rain and the fog were hindering the view. The night was closing in and it felt like a bleak house indeed. I didn't even have Maveryn. I had thought that all of my problems would not seem so insurmountable once I was here, but I was only fooling myself...nothing had changed. The man I loved may have been a million miles away. What had I brought upon myself and my unborn child? Perhaps I had acted too hastily; I should have waited for Rainey to come home. No, no, no, I had done the right thing. His life would be better for it and I would forget him in time. I took to my bed once more and let myself be carried away into oblivion.

Chapter Nine

Rainey, Winter, 1961

Rainey had never been so glad to touch down as he had today. The plane ride had been pure hell. Sophia talked nonstop, and even when he closed his eyes, she didn't take the hint to tone it down. Lordy, she was so insensibly boring. She may be hedging on twenty-one but acted more like thirteen. Thankfully, friends of the family picked her up and he took his leave from her. Sure enough, she fawned all over him and made him promise to call her as soon as he got back from his holiday. It was half past three. He took a taxi back to the house and thought of spending the night, but decided to drive straight through to Hawthorne. He hoped his all-season tires would be sufficient for the winter roads. By the time he got out of the city, another hour had past. The rain was coming down in buckets. He was sure to encounter snow on the passes, a stark contrast to the weather that he had left behind in Italy. He had been thinking of Vienna on the long flight whenever Sophia hadn't drowned out his thoughts. He found a radio station that played all of Vienna's favorites, and he imagined her singing along and his heart was happy. The roads were reasonably good and he arrived at the ranch shortly after 11. His parents heard him come in and that meant sleep didn't happen until almost 1 A.M. He awoke at 8 and waited until 9 to dial the LaFontaine residence. Coffee in hand, he waited for someone to answer.

A little voice came on the line. "Hello."

"Addy, is that you, honey? How are you? It's Rainey. Can I speak to Vienna?"

"You mean V?"

He had forgotten again. He said, laughing, "Yeah, V."

"She's not here."

"Is she at work? School is out for the holidays, right?"

"No—I mean, yes. V's not here, Rainey."

"Do you know where she is?"

"No, I am not supposed to say anything."

What a strange thing to say, he thought. "Addy, is your mom home?"

"No, Daddy took her to work."

"Is Sissy home?"

"Yes."

"Do you think that you can put her on the phone for me, honey?"

He heard her yell for her sister and a full two minutes passed before she came on the line. "Sissy, it's Rainey. Addy says that V isn't home. Do you know where I can reach her?"

"She's not here anymore, Rainey."

"What do you mean? Has she gone somewhere?"

"You had better talk to Mom. Bye, Rainey." She hung up.

What the hell? He grabbed the phone book and rifled through it until he found the number for the diner. Lily answered. "Lily, it's Rainey. Where the hell is Vienna? The girls said that she is not here anymore. What does that mean anyway?"

"She's gone, Rainey. She left home days ago. We don't even know where she is."

He could hear the trembling in her voice. "Are you trying to tell me that she has run away? That's just plain crazy! She's the most sensible person I know. That is not Vienna. She wouldn't do such a thing. What are you not telling me, Lily?" He was panicking.

"I'm sorry, Rainey. We are devastated. I wish I could tell you more. I have to go."

Jesus H. Christ! What is going on? He grabbed his coat and ran out of the house. Fifteen minutes later, he was at the LaFontaine house. Joe greeted him at the front door.

"Rainey, it's good to see you, Son. How are you?"

"Until I find out what has happened to Vienna, I can't answer that question. Please tell me that you have some answers for me. How can she be gone...what does that mean? She knew that I was going to be here today. Is that it, she doesn't want to see me?"

"I wish that it was that simple. Believe me, as far as we know, you had nothing to do with her leaving. She's just gone, Son...run off."

"How could she? Christmas is in a few days. Is she with Lara in Potsdam?"

"She is not with Lara. She's with Jack." Joe did not like lying and it came too easily.

"Jack? Who the hell is Jack?"

"I think his last name is Lord. We really don't know him very well."

This was making no sense. "You let her run off with a stranger? I don't mean to place blame on you, Joe, but...what about school? God, she is only seventeen!" He had to sit down.

"We didn't know she was leaving." Joe opened a desk drawer and pulled out a piece of paper. "This is how we found out that she was gone." He handed the paper to Rainey.

There, in bold letters, he read:

> *Mother, Father, don't be alarmed, but I am leaving Bridge. Please don't try to find me. I am old enough to make my own decisions. There is nothing here for me anymore. Just know that I will be safe and I will return someday. Please respect my decision. I love you all.*
>
>   *V*

"That's it?" Rainey said. "You call this an explanation? She doesn't even mention a Jack. She didn't even sign it. How do you know that she even wrote it?"

"She wrote it, Son," Joe replied. "Believe me, we are just as mystified as you are."

"I want to see her room, Joe. Will you grant me that courtesy?"

Joe got up, called Sissy, and asked her to take Rainey to V's room. Addy joined them, taking his hand as they followed Sissy up the stairs. The room was cold. He went straight to her closet, not having any idea what he was looking for. He asked Sissy what was missing.

"All that we can figure out are some jeans and sweaters, you know, winter things. And her white dress and yellow shawl are missing."

Rainey could see Vienna wading in the creek with her dress hiked up to her waist. She was laughing. He shook himself to bring the present back into focus. "Why would she take a summer dress in the middle of winter? Is anything else missing that you can tell?"

The girls had both started to cry. He put his arms around them. "I'm sorry, girls. This must be really hard on you and I am not helping. Did you ever see any of the letters that I wrote to her while I was in Italy?"

"No, but the little green teardrop that you gave her is gone," replied Sissy.

"Thank you," he said. "Do you know this Jack fellow?"

She looked puzzled but said she didn't. Then she went over to her sister's bed, lifted the pillow up, and handed another note to him. This one was in her handwriting:

> *When you're running away from your life, don't look over your shoulder to see where you have been, but keep looking forward and keep your life free from strife, and remember that someday, you can go home again.*

He was mystified by the words staring at him. Did that sound like something Vienna would say? At this point, he wasn't sure that he had ever known her at all. What would make a perfectly sound and logical person with a loving family run away? She was known to have visions of fantasy, but this was way beyond his comprehension. There was nothing more to say or do, so he left, asking Joe to let him know as soon as he heard from her. They shook hands and he hugged the girls again.

Joe said as he was closing the door, "Pray for her well-being, Rainey."

Surely Lara could shed some light on Vienna's disappearance. Just his luck, no one was home. With a heavy heart, he left Bridge Falls. Where was his raven-haired beauty? Did they not belong together? The first time that they had made love at Avastavalley, he knew then that he never wanted to be with anyone else and he would have sworn that she felt the same way, too. She told him over and over that she loved him. He hadn't said the actual words, but surely she knew. He had been faithful to her, but apparently, she hadn't been. He should be drinking in her beauty, touching her soft skin, kissing her cherry lips, and holding her in his arms. Instead, he was alone, driving through a blinding snowstorm, misty eyed and asking God what had gone wrong.

Without even planning to, he found himself at Jimmy's house. Alvira Douglas answered the door to a disheveled-looking man. He asked if Jimmy was home; she said that he was at Ruth's and offered to call him there.

"Don't bother, Alvira. I'll catch him tomorrow."

"He would never forgive me. Now sit and have some coffee. Stuart, come see who's here."

Rainey was having coffee with his best friend's parents when Jimmy came bounding in the door. "Rain, ole boy, I didn't think I would be seeing you until tomorrow. I thought that you would be so busy with V that you wouldn't be home until late."

"That's why I am here, Jimmy. What do you know about Vienna's disappearance?"

Jimmy's parents took that as their cue to leave the two alone.

"What on earth are you talking about?" Jimmy was stunned.

"You don't know? Apparently, she has run off with some guy named Jack Lord."

"Do you mean Jack Jennings?"

"So, you do know?"

"Hell no. I just know that she had a bit of a relationship with him, but that was last year. I saw her talking with him a few times last month, but she is in love with you, buddy. Why did you quit writing to her? She figured that you had found an Italian sweetheart and—"

"What are you talking about, Jimmy? I wrote to her every week; it was her who quit writing to me. And there never was any Italian woman. Where did she ever get that idea from? I couldn't wait to get home to her, but she's not here waiting for me. She's gone."

"That doesn't make any sense. I know that she changed drastically in the last few months. We tried to look after her for you, buddy, but suddenly, she was too busy for any of us. I don't think that any of us have seen her for at least a month. She changed and I thought it was because you told her that you had found somebody else. Her exact words when I asked how you were doing were, 'How would I know? He is too busy with his Italian women to write to me.'"

"Christ, Jimmy, that is so not true. I want to know what happened to all my letters."

"Can't help you with that, buddy. Blame it on the postal service, I guess."

"Tell me what you know about this Jack character."

"I honestly don't know him. He hangs around with the Southerly Gang when he is in town. I think that he works at some mine in Alberta and only comes home in the winter. He may have done time in the big house a few years ago."

"She's with a felon?"

"How do you know that she is with him?"

"Joe told me. I have spent an agonizing few hours trying to get information out of the family. According to them, she just up and left. They found a note saying not to come after her. I am not sure if they know more than they are telling me. The girls are terribly upset and my questions didn't help any."

"The note said that she had run off with Jack?"

"No. I think they just assumed that. Jimmy, how do you mean that Vienna changed?"

"You may not want to hear this, but I think you broke her heart. You quit writing to her and so what else was she to think except that you had moved on? We thought so, too."

"Christ, how many times do I have to say it? There was NO one else and I never stopped writing to her."

Jimmy got up. "I think you need something stronger than coffee. Rye or beer?"

"It's a little early, but I'll take a rye with a little ice. Tell me what you know, Jimmy."

"That's just it, I don't know a thing except, I told you, that she changed. She missed you, but she was dealing with it. Then one day, the light seemed to go out of her eyes. It was like she was struggling with something, but we never figured out what it was. I think she thought that you were living your dream and that there was no room for her in your world. She became very quiet and sullen, and you know that is not the V that we all know. Marley, Ruth, and I would call her, but she cut us out of her life; she was too busy for us. Sorry we didn't look after her for you, buddy."

"Hey, it's not your fault. I think the blame lies squarely in my hands."

"Rain, you did what you had to do and I think that she understood that, but did you ever ask her what she wanted out of life? I think that she would have said that she only wanted you. She loved you, she really did. I'm sorry for the both of you. I've seen you together and you were the happiest that you had ever been. You couldn't make a commitment, could you? And yet you thought she would always be waiting for you, didn't you?"

"You're right. I thought she would be here waiting for me, but we know how that turned out, don't we? I told her many times that I was no good for her, but she made me want to be. She lost her trust in me and I don't know why."

"Well, you got one thing right: she may have been too good for you. Did you love her? And if you didn't, why did you lead her on? No one else had a chance with her. She was out of bounds to the rest of us because she was always Rainey's girl."

"Are you telling me that you were interested in her romantically?"

"You bet, and so was half the town. You don't know what a gem you had, buddy."

"Yes, I do know, Jimmy. Does Ruth know you had feelings for her?"

"Sure she does. Last winter, after we all thought that the two of you had broken up, I tried to convince her that you were bad news. Sorry, but you had let her go. Have you forgotten that? Well, not to worry, she would have no part of me except as a friend."

"Ruth is a pretty amazing woman if she knew how you felt about Vienna and took up with you anyhow."

"There was nothing to be concerned about, as I told you, V was only interested in you. I'm beginning to think that one really can die from a broken heart. In V's case, she didn't die, thank God. She just slipped away and we were powerless to help her."

"She'll be back, Jimmy. She has to, so that I can make amends. She was my one and a million and I let her fall down the rabbit hole. I'm a pompous ass. You know what the really sad thing is, beside the fact that she is gone? I did love her. No, damn it, I do love her. I have never been in love before and I should have known that it was different with her. But, no, I let my precious career take priority as always. Well, I can live without it but I don't want to live without her. So, it is true, you don't know what you've got until you don't have it anymore. A lesson learned too late for me. You know, I think that I always knew that I would lose her."

"What do you mean?"

"I have had numerous dreams about her, and in them, I always let her slip away from me. I can't hold on to her. She disappears into thin air and all I have left of her is some red lace. In reality, that is basically what happened, except I don't even have the lace."

"Rain, they are just dreams. I think you are too hard on yourself."

"I could have stopped this from happening. I could have told her that I was in love with her. I never told her, Jimmy. Not once did I ever tell her that I loved her. What the hell is wrong with me? Three little words and I only said them to myself. If I never see her again, it will haunt me for the rest of my life. I am going to look for her, and when I do find her, I am going to ask her to marry me. I will make it my life's mission to find my life, my Vienna."

Rainey slouched into his parents' house and told them that Vienna was gone.

"V's gone? Oh my God, what happened?" Patsy would have dropped the tray she was carrying with their afternoon tea and cake on if Rainey hadn't reached out to steady her.

"She's not dead, Mom, just gone, left town. I'm sorry I scared you." He then told them an abbreviated version of the story, excused himself, and stumbled up to his room. Later, Patsy called him to come down to supper, but he couldn't stomach the thought of food. He only wanted to be alone. He found his luggage on the floor where he had left it in the morning when he had dashed off to find Vienna. Was that only this morning? It already seemed like a lifetime ago. He picked up one of the bags and rifled through it until he came upon the trinkets he had brought back from Italy for everyone. He found what he was looking for: a small floral box. With shaking hands, he opened it and lovingly touched the three silver bracelets that he had brought home for Vienna. He had found them in an antique shop in Rome and knew immediately they were for her. They were from Austria…how fitting…Vienna, Austria. He had smiled when he purchased them. Well, he wasn't smiling now. *Is this how it feels to have a broken heart?* he thought. He slammed the lid down on the box and hurled it across the room.

"Damn you, Vienna LaFontaine! Damn you!" he cried.

Across the great expanse of sea, Vienna lay in her bed, hugging her ever-growing body. Tears ran down her face like rain. "I will forget you, Rainey Quinn. I promise myself that I will forget you if it is the last thing I ever do. Damn me for loving you."

Bridge Falls

Lily phoned Joe and told him she was on her way home. She needed the fresh air and time to clear her head. She bummed a cigarette from one of her employees, whom she left to fill in for her. She had quit smoking a long time go but hoped that it would calm her nerves after talking with Rainey this morning and having to lie to him. Joe met her at the door and helped her off with her coat. They went into her sanctuary: the conservatory. She sank into one of the padded wicker chairs and Joe put her feet up on a hassock, then handed her a glass of vodka and orange.

"Did we do it, Joe? Did we pull it off? I'm glad I wasn't here to see Rainey's face. It was bad enough when I had to talk to him on the phone. How was he?"

"Just as we expected, heartbroken and down trodden. I wanted to tell him the truth, Lily, and damn what Vienna wanted! There was no question that he would forgive her, but would she ever forgive us? What a bloody dilemma! We have not seen the last of him. I only hope that he will go on with his life without her, and that someday, we will have our daughter back. He wanted to see her room but found nothing, just as we hadn't."

Lily put her head back and recalled how V brooded when Rainey had gone to Italy. She had snapped out of it eventually and went back to being her sweet, happy self for a while. One day in late November, she had found her daughter in the conservatory with a letter in her hands and tears streaming down her face. She gave no explanation, just that she was sad, but Lily knew that something else was going on besides the fact that V missed Rainey. She quit taking calls from Jimmy and anyone else who would call. Lara was at nursing school, and so it seemed as if V was all alone. She knew that V had taken up with Jack again but didn't call her on it. Christmas was coming and there was no baking or decorating going on. That had always been V's domain and the girls kept asking their sister when they were going to start, and she would answer, "Maybe tomorrow."

Now she wondered how she could have missed all the signs—the mood swings, the sickness, and the lack of energy. *What kind of a mother am I?* she asked herself. She blamed everything on Rainey being gone, but he would be home at Christmas so… She had wondered at the time of finding V with the letter if Rainey was not coming home, but V refused to talk about it. She didn't think for one minute that V didn't know who the father of her baby was, but Lily was afraid that it was Jack's. Had her daughter been so lonely that she had sought solace with him? Had Rainey broke up with her? That theory went straight to hell when he had shown up today. He was heartbroken and, like them, left wondering why.

Christmas Day, they spoke with Jannie and she said that V was very depressed. Right after the holiday, she was taking her into Waverly to see a doctor. She and the staff were doing everything they could to ensure that V had proper nutrition, but it wasn't easy, and hopefully, a professional could help. They talked briefly with their daughter but were not happy with what they were hearing in her voice. The girls cried when they spoke with her. Lily resented that they had all been blackmailed into keeping V's secret, but more than that, she was basically concerned for her daughter's state of mind.

The next time they heard from Jannie, they were much encouraged. The doctor had somehow convinced V to look after herself for the baby's sake and she was cooperating. The best thing that had happened was that Lord Jeremy's daughter and V had bonded. V was taking her role as a new mother seriously and was almost happy again. They let Rainey know that she was well but had to continue lying as to her whereabouts.

Christmas was not a happy place at the Quinn house. Rainey didn't even have the spirit to wrap the gifts that he had brought back from Italy. He just handed them to his parents and wished them a Merry Christmas. They understood that he was still upset about V's sudden departure and said nothing. Jimmy came by before dinner to see how his old friend was coping. He had never seen Rainey in such a state. The always groomed man looked like he had slept in his clothes—if he had been sleeping at all. He was unshaven and his eyes were bloodshot, as though he had been on a two-day bender. He told Jimmy that he had been phoning Vienna's parents every day and they still told him that they had not heard from her. Lara also knew nothing and was just as surprised at her leaving as was everyone else. He asked Jimmy if he could deliver some gifts to Vienna's family. He would not be going back to Bridge again. Jimmy promised that he would and asked Rainey if he would be joining them for New Year's Eve.

"Do you really think that I could go to the Grange, Jimmy? How could I without Vienna? Last year with her was one of the happiest times of my life."

"Sorry, Rain. That was really insensitive of me."

"You wouldn't want me there anyhow, Jimbo. I would probably get fall down drunk and go home with some married woman or pick a fight with you or Yates. The possibilities are endless."

"This has to be resolved soon. Surely V will be contacting her parents any day now."

"Truth is, Jimmy, I think they know exactly where she is, but for some unknown reason, she doesn't want me to know. I've gone through everything in my mind a thousand times and the outcome is always the same. The only thing that makes any sense at all is what you said. She thinks that I found somebody else and that I broke her heart. Well, now, I'm the one with the broken heart. Does that make us even? Bloody hell no!"

Jimmy left his best friend and assured him that he would keep him posted if he were to hear anything.

December 31, New Year's Eve

Rainey decided not to subject his misery on his parents any longer and left for Vancouver at noon. He had no one to celebrate with anyhow and so may as well be driving. He had plenty of time to think on the monotonous trip. He analyzed his life up until now and felt that he had been reasonably happy, and more since Vienna had come into his life. Then, in the blink of an eye, that had all come crashing down. He played the scenario of the past week over and over again, and the answer was always the same: Vienna was gone. Would the old saying, "out of sight, out of mind" apply to him? He doubted it, but on the other hand, she might return and he would forgive her for leaving, and they could get on with their life together.

January 8

Classes resumed. Nothing had changed. Everyone wanted to know about his Italian adventures. He was giving a detailed account before his class and professors later in the week. No one inquired about Vienna. Did any of them know that she even existed? He had kept his personal life to himself. He was still making weekly phone calls to the LaFontaine residence. The answer was always the same. She was well but was not coming home. He was somewhat consoled with the fact that she was keeping in touch with them but wondered why he didn't receive the same courtesy. If only she would call him, they could resolve anything…anything.

Chapter Ten

Brackenshire Manor

It was the eve of Christmas; Millie had left the door ajar as she exited with an armful of linens. She insisted on making my bed afresh every day although it was not necessary. I could hear faint voices echoing up the stairs from the kitchen. I wrapped my shawl around me and went to close the door, but instead stopped and listened to the conversation between Jannie and Mrs. Sharpe, as I seemed to be the subject of their discussion.

"It has been nigh three days, Miss Jane. We must get Miss V out of that room. It is no good she be alone all the time. After all, it be Christmas tomoreee. She refuses most of the meals I send. Millie has taken to sittin' with her 'til she eats the porridge. She likes it with a little cream and syrup, imagine that. No need, she eats most of it. She likes her bread and bannock to be toasted with jam. She will not touch the colcannon or the boiled vegetables. She does not like any meat. She sends the warm milk back, but I put a pinch of the whiskey in it last night and she did have some. I think the heather honey hid the taste. Me and the girls all had hot toddies when we was with child and it did not seem to harm our bairns. You ask the doctor when you go."

"I am sure that one little toddy will not hurt, but let's not make a habit of it. You know, Mrs. Sharpe, the food is much different in Canada and V is still fighting the sickness. Have you asked her what she would like?"

"Oh yes, ma'am. She says not to bother with anything special, bit I dunna mind. Tea with milk and sugar, crackers, and a weak broth she says, though she not like me broth much. Should I send Henry to Waverly for some fresh greens and fruit? I think I will make her some chicken soup."

"Sounds good. Now I must be off up the hill. I want to make sure that all is ready for little Rosalyn's Christmas morning. I shall see to V when I return."

"Is the Lord Jeremy to be home tomoreee?"

"One can only hope so. Nevertheless, I will be bringing her here tomorrow for the festivities. I cannot bear that she be alone with that witch of a governess!"

True to her word, Jannie came up to visit with me when she returned. She made me feel like a spoiled child, which I suppose I was. Millie, Emma, and Mrs. Sharpe were doing their best to appease me, as they were only concerned for my health. They would all be here for Christmas morning and the least I could do was to come down for the traditional breakfast and gift opening. Rosalyn would be joining us. I had not met her yet.

The next morning, I bathed and dressed. I had no nice clothes but my three-fourth-length white dress, so I donned it with a long, cream-colored sweater that Mrs. Sharpe had given me. I peered into the mirror and wondered who that ashen face was that was looking back at me. Why did my dress from last summer hang on me? Shouldn't I be gaining weight? I could very well be endangering the life of my unborn child. It was no fault of hers. She had been conceived in love, at least on my part. I was sure that I was carrying a baby girl. I couldn't bear it if it were a boy who looked like Rainey. There, I had said his name and the sky hadn't fallen. It was time for me to take control of my life and stop bemoaning my predicament. Unwed mothers raised children on their own all the time in much worse circumstances than mine. I had crossed the Rubicon and I must face the future that I had chosen for me and my child.

I dabbed a little corral lipstick on and pinched my cheeks hard, hoping to bring a little color to my pallid complexion. I entered the living room to find everyone gathered around the beautifully decorated tree. There were at least a dozen excited children madly unwrapping gifts. Paper, string, and colorful ribbons were strewn everywhere. A wave of nostalgia washed over me as I thought of Christmas back home without me, and a little tear trickled down my cheek. Jannie spotted me and came over to usher me in. She told me how happy she was that I had decided to join the festivities. I shared hugs, kisses, and Christmas wishes with everyone. One little red-haired child came over to me and asked me to help her unwrap her gift. I asked her what her name was, although I already knew that it had to be Maveryn's daughter.

"Rosy," she answered.

"Hello, Rosalyn, I am Vela."

"Are you my new mama?" she asked me.

I was startled by her bold question. I found my way to a large, overstuffed chair and sat down. Rosalyn had taken hold of my skirt and followed after me. She crawled right up, squeezed in beside me, all the while holding on to her present. I was most curious about her actions. Jannie had been watching us and presented me with a brightly wrapped gift with Rosalyn's name on it. She whispered for me to give it to the child, which I did. Together, we unwrapped the parcel and found a small, red-haired doll inside.

"She is just like me, Mama! Thank you."

I looked at Jannie, who only shrugged her shoulders as if to say, "I don't know."

"Rosy, honey, this is not your mama," Jannie said. "Do you remember that your mama had to go to Heaven?"

"That mama. This is my new mama. She told me to find her in a dress just like she went to Heaven in."

That was a little unnerving. Why had I chosen to wear this white frock this morning? Here was this three-year-old child who had found me in a dress just like her mother's and thought that I must be her replacement. What was I to say? I had enough problems of my own. For now, I would do nothing, for surely she would be off to play with the other children and forget about the lady in white. How wrong was I?

Just minutes before we were to be seated for breakfast, Lord Jeremy made his appearance. If I looked like death warmed over, then he looked like a man who had been to hell and came back unwillingly. He was greeted warmly by one and all. Minutes later, he spotted me with his daughter on my lap. His face registered no emotion whatsoever.

"Your father is here, Rosalyn." I pointed him out to her. "Don't you want to say hello?"

She kept playing with her new dolly. She didn't even blink an eyelash as she said, "Papa not like me. Dolly need name. What should we name her, Mama?"

That sparked something in me and I wondered how this wee child could feel that her father didn't like her. Was it because she reminded him so much of her mother? Jannie had told me that he was seldom at the castle and that her care was left to a stern governess. He made his way over toward us.

"Good morning and Merry Christmas, Rosalyn," Lord Jeremy said. "Are you having a happy day?"

She completely ignored him and looked at me. "What should we call her, Mama?"

Well, that brought the Lord of Avanloch out of his stuffy and haughty demeanor. "Rosalyn, this is not your mother! You know that she is gone. Now come with me and I shall take you home."

"No, no! She is mean. I want to stay here with Mama and Jannie."

She was clinging to me, tears streaming from her little green eyes. The whole room was staring in our direction. Jannie came over to try and calm Rosy down, but she wouldn't budge from me. Jeremy was at a complete loss and was visually upset.

I finally found my voice. "Surely no one has to go anywhere right now, do they, Sir? Why don't we all sit down and enjoy this marvelous breakfast that the ladies have prepared? What say we take our places at the table and you can sit between your father and I...would you like that, Rosy?"

She agreed through her tears but never relinquished her hold on me. Her father looked at me strangely. I do not believe that he had intended to stay for the meal, but I guess I hadn't given him much choice. These words came to mind: "And a little child shall lead them." I was about to find out how true those words were.

Two more places settings were quickly added to the festive table. Mrs. Sharpe and Mrs. McDuff, along with other ladies from the village, had prepared a scrumptious brunch. There were several types of sizzling sausages and maple bacon, honey roasted ham, and salmon patties. There were eggs Benedict, fried potatoes, breads and cheeses, scones and jams, and shortcakes and fruitcakes. Of course there was the traditional porridge, strong tea and coffee, and hot cocoa. A lovely grace was spoken by Uncle John. I had seen very little of him since coming to the manor, and he would be leaving with Lord Jeremy again soon after a brief holiday. I surprised myself and ate a hearty meal. Rosalyn had a good appetite and liked to help herself from my plate. Lord Jeremy was going to scold her but decided to let it go when I shook my head. After everyone had their fill, the men retired to the sitting room to partake in some good old-fashioned Scottish whisky. The ladies cleaned up as usual, laughing and apparently enjoying the work. Millie and I were designated to take the children back to the living room so that they could play with each other and their new presents.

Lord Jeremy pulled me aside and said, "I want to thank you for the kind way in which you dealt with Rosalyn. You are very compassionate and I do apologize for her thinking that you are her mother. Would it be too much for me to ask you if you could check in on her periodically while I am away?"

I assured him that it would be my pleasure and he thanked me again. He then informed me that I was not to want for anything and that all my doctor's bills would be taken care of. I was not offended but told him that I was not derelict.

"It is what Maveryn wants. It is settled then." He did an about-face and somehow convinced Rosalyn to return with him to Avanloch. I stayed out of her sight but was sure she was searching for me as her father carried her off.

Later, I recalled my conversation with him to Jannie.

"Yes, he still talks like Lady Maveryn is still with us," my aunt said. "He cannot face the fact that she is gone. I guess when you wait most of your life to find the love you so desperately need and then it is taken from you in the blink of an eye, it would be hard for anyone to accept. He is currently receiving counseling from a therapist in London. Now get yourself up to bed for a rest. The Christmas supper will be upon us before we know it."

We hugged and I went upstairs.

I was glad that I had joined in the celebration but was most curious about Rosalyn.

I was just settling down in the rocking chair beside the window when Millie poked her head in. "Will you be coming down for the Queen's Speech at 3, Miss V?"

I had no idea what she was talking about, so I just told her that I would think about it.

"Well then, I must be on with me packing."

"Packing?" I inquired. "Whatever for?"

"Why, for St. Stephen's Day… Do you not share it in Canada?"

"We have Boxing Day. Is that the same? What do you do? We just relax and visit."

"We gather up clothes and foodstuffs that we do not need or want, box it all, and give to the less fortunate. It goes far back, this custom."

"What a lovely tradition. I am sure I will learn of many others in this enchanting country. May I contribute? I have clothes that no longer fit me. When do you have time to spend with your family, Millie?"

"After this evening, I will be on my holiday for several days, but all will be here for the supper tonight. I will return for your contribution later. Thank you, Ma'am."

"Please do not call me ma'am. I am younger than you. Just call me V or Vela."

"Vela?"

"Yes, that is what Maveryn used to call me and Lord Jeremy calls me that also."

Millie returned half an hour later and I presented her with a few articles. As she was leaving, a thought crossed my mind. "Millie, are Shelley and Keats still alive?"

"Yes, they are, but are mostly in their kennels these days. Lord Jeremy could not part with them but has no time for them when he is home. Duffy takes them out on walks."

"I was most fond of them when last I was here. Maveryn and I spent many a day roaming the grounds with them."

"Yes, I remember. She spoke of you often with affection."

"By the way, where is her grave site? Is there a family plot?"

"She is in the family crypt."

"There's a mausoleum on the property? Where? Will you take me there one day?"

"Yes, of course, just as soon as the weather turns."

I was not anxious anymore, and when I closed my eyes and saw Rainey, I did not cry. I tried to focus on what I remembered about Avanloch. It was hard to imagine the splendor of the gardens, as all were barren and under a cover of snow. Spring was still two months away and the roses were still resting. It was the time of rebirth and it would also be the birth of my love child. I wiped the tears from my eyes and wondered if there would ever come a time when there would be no more tears to shed.

A little chickadee came and sat on my windowsill, and serenaded me for a few short moments until he was called away by his lady friend. Even in the dull December light, there was a flicker of more promising days. How depressing it must have been in the centuries before, when there was no electricity or radios or telephones. Perhaps life was much simpler then, and there was no time to sit and bemoan one's situation because they simply knew no other life. The maidens were left alone while their menfolk were off to fight some war of the times with no way to communicate, and so they never knew what fate had befallen them. Perhaps I would pretend that my love was off fighting some cause and would return someday. But in truth, it was I who crossed the sea to a battle all my own.

Avanloch may have had a romantic history; I did not know. If I remembered correctly, it was once a stronghold, but from what century was unclear. It had been pretty much been destroyed in the Scottish wars. It had once been called The King's...something; I couldn't remember. By the late 1800s, the younger McAllisters took up the plight of restoration. It was still undergoing constant renovations, thanks to Jeremy and his father before him. It was not the huge monstrosity like some medieval ones, even though it boasted towers, turrets, great halls, and manor houses and was constructed of stone and brick. It was quite comfortable with modern heating and conveniences. I could not recall all of the rooms and was looking forward to renewing my acquaintance with the structure. It would give me something to do on these long winter days and Jeremy had asked me to check in on Rosalyn. I heard Millie out in the hall again and asked if I could bend her ear again.

"Millie," I asked, "how bad was it when Maveryn became ill?"

She sat down on a chair beside me. "Oh terrible, just terrible. She had been so full of life. She had everything to live for…Mr. Jeremy and little Rosy. Oh how she did love that child, as we all did love her. The horrible disease could not be controlled. Lord Jeremy had her to doctors all over England and France, and who knows where else. She knew there was no cure and begged him to bring her home to Avanloch and her daughter. Her room was brought down into the cozy sitting room, where she could be part of the household. I hear that Mr. Jeremy still looks for her there. Thanks that little Rosy was too young to know what was happening to her mama. The winter was terribly bad and long, but Miss Maveryn made it through to see the crocus and daffodils in bloom. She passed away the first day of spring."

I let Millie continue with her work and tried to resume my rest, a little sadder than before my revelation of Mave's last days. The day was darkening and the rain mixed with snow had started to fall again. I wondered what the weather was like at home. I closed my eyes again and there was Rainey. I thought, *Doesn't he get tired of living in my head?*

The last day of 1961 was here and Millie and Emma were leaving to attend the New Year's Eve celebrations at the Horn and Loch Pub outside of Waverly. I asked what the festivities consisted of.

"There is much celebrating to oust the old year and welcome the new. Some are sad to see it go, as it was a good year for them, and others are glad to kick it in the rear. We play darts and shuffle board, drink, eat, and be merry. There are always musicians and dancing, and of course, the bagpipes at the midnight and the singing of 'Auld Lang Syne.' What are the customs in your country, V?" Emma asked.

"Pretty much the same, I guess. I have only been to one New Year's Eve party and that was to a dance last year. I will always remember it."

"Were you with your young man, Miss V?" Millie inquired.

"Millie!" Emma scolded.

"That is quite all right, Millie. I know that you have all been curious as to the reason why I came here to have my child. He is the reason and I can say no more. I wish that you all have a joyous night. I shall be thinking of you and the bagpipes at midnight. I have always loved them, especially when the pipers are playing the haunting 'Danny Boy.'"

"V, why do you not come with us?" Emma asked.

I laughed. "You do know that I am not of legal age to enter a pub, don't you?"

They laughed with me, and I told them to run off, have a good time with their hubbies, and to have a cheer for me. They said that they didn't like to leave me alone, but I assured them that I wouldn't be alone, as I was going to the church service with Jannie. They left and I returned to my room, wishing that it was the eve of 1960 and I was preparing for my date with Rainey.

It had been a very long time since I had been in a house of worship, but I found myself thoroughly entranced in the sermon. The Reverend Peters spoke of forgiveness and everlasting love and renewal. A feeling of peace came over me as I listened to his comforting voice. I vowed that I would return to this little sanctuary often. I had the first undisturbed sleep that night since coming to Brackenshire Manor.

On January 2, Jannie sent word down from Avanloch that Ash and all her guests had left, and asked if I would care to come for a visit. I certainly did, and Duffy, as he preferred to be called, drove me up. He ushered me into the vast kitchen where his wife, Mary McDuff, the head cook, was having tea with her assistant, Reita.

"Speak of the devil! 'Tis about time that you came to visit us, child. We been awaitin' to see you. Come, let me have a gander at you." She pulled herself up from her chair with great effort, I noticed. "Darn rheumatism." She grumbled as she embraced me in one of her warm hugs that I remembered from childhood. "You barely have the color to you. We must see to that and put some meat on your bones…have you been starving yourself then? 'Tis not good for the bairn. Miss Jannie says that little Rosy has taken a likin' to you, poor little tyke. Let's go and find the rest of the house. Did Emma tell you that her sister, Amma, is still here and will wed this summer?"

"For the love of Mary, will you let the girl get a word in edgewise?" Duffy scolded.

I smiled and said, "Yes, Emma informed me. I am looking forward to seeing her again."

We found Amma, Jannie, and a new girl, Shalla, in the great hall, attempting to hang a newly cleaned tapestry. I couldn't remember if I had ever been in this part of the castle before; the hallway was very long and wide, and the main entrance and staircase were breathtaking. Amma had been so kind to me when last I was here; she greeted me as if I was her long-lost sister. I was introduced to Shalla, who was the same age as me. They both addressed me as Miss V.

"Please, everyone, I am V, just V, all right?"

"We are so very pleased to have you living right down the hill. It is finally quiet again now that Miss Ash and her strange friends have vacated the premises," Amma exclaimed.

"Amen to that!'" Mary McDuff agreed.

From overhead came a stern voice reverberating down the stairs. "What, pray tell, what is going on down there? I thought the dogs had entered the premises! Do you not know that Rosalyn is doing her studies and must not be distracted?"

I looked up, as did everyone. There, at the top of the staircase, stood a woman of great stature. She was dressed all in grey and her hair, which was the same drab color, was piled up on her head in a knot. Was this harsh Amazon of a woman Rosy's governess? Heaven forbid. No wonder the child didn't want to come home. We heard the patter of little feet.

"Now look what you have done! Back to your room, child!" Miss whoever-she-was ordered, but it was too late.

Rosalyn had spotted me and cried out, "Mama, Mama."

She started down the stairs but the governess grabbed hold of her arm and stopped her.

"Your mother is not here. She's dead, you know that. Stop squirming!"

"Unhand that child!" I ordered.

She looked at me with the eyes of a mad woman but kept her firm grip on Rosalyn, who was crying and trying to pull free. "And who might you be?" she demanded of me.

I had started up the stairs with Jannie close behind.

She sneered at me. "Aha, you must be that trollop who has come here to take refuge and hide her shame."

There were gasps of horror behind me but her words did not faze me. "That would be me, and you must be the spinster poor excuse for a governess! Leave hold of the child."

At that precise moment, Rosalyn bit the hand that held her and kicked her in the shin. That was enough for the woman to release her hold and I reached up and pulled Rosalyn into my arms. She held on to me tightly but turned and cried, "I hate you! I hate you!"

We backed slowly down the stairs and Jannie spoke in a very authoritative voice. "This is the final straw, Ms. Downey. You best pack your bags and be gone. Henry will see you to the train."

Ms. Downey defied the advice. She started down toward us. "Ha! You have not the authority to release me from my position. Now hand over that hellion. She must be disciplined."

Rosy was clinging to me and I had no attention of handing her over to a mad woman. The rest of the household, including Duffy, who had heard the commotion, stepped in front of me to halt the old biddy from coming any farther down the stairs.

"You have no authority over me, do you hear?" Ms. Downey said. "Only Lord Jeremy can quit my contract."

"Or me."

We all turned to find Ash standing in the doorway. Where had she come from?

"I don't know what is going on here, but it appears you have done something to offend the entire staff, Ms. Downey. If you are threatening my niece in any way, then they have every right to be ousting you. Do you need any help in packing? I am sure we could oblige you."

The old woman turned on her heel and, with a huff, said to Ash, "We'll see who has the last say. Surely not you, you royal pain in the ass!"

Ash smiled at the reference. "I guess it's a good thing I forgot my portfolio…good for Ms. Downey, as Lord knows what you all would have done to her. Nice to see you, V. You do know how to stir up a hornets' nest, don't you?"

I had completely forgotten about the actual hornets' nest that I had unearthed during my last visit, which had sent us all scattering to escape their wrath.

Jannie thanked Ash for showing up at the right moment. "She was always so sickeningly sweet whenever Jeremy was here. He couldn't understand why we disliked her. I am sure that she did more harm to poor Rosy than good. Imagine making a child study?"

"She certainly has taken to you, V," Ash said. "Why do you think that is? Jannie told me what transpired at the manor on Christmas Day. Are you all right, Rosalyn?"

"Yes, Annie. Mama came for me." She was still trembling and held tightly to me.

"V?"

"I don't know, Ash. We just have to go with it. If I am her refuge, then so be it. She needs me right now and perhaps I need her, too. Perhaps she is the reason I am here."

"I really don't have a say in her care, but I must say that you are a healthy alternative. If you feel that you are up to taking on the burden of another child…" She looked at my expanding stomach and smiled.

I was sure that she was as curious as everyone else as to why I had come to Scotland in my condition. I told her that I would do my best.

"Okay then, my friends will be wondering what is taking me so long." Ash turned to Jannie and said, "Can I count on you to relay to Jeremy what has happened here? I will be out of the country for several months, as you know, but will try and keep in touch. As yet, I don't know what the services are like in Ceylon. I bid you farewell again and good luck. I believe that Rosy is in good hands with you, V."

I thanked her and carried Rosalyn into the small drawing room, where there was a warm fire burning in the hearth. So there I was, with my own child inside of me and another one on my lap, whom I seemed to have inherited. Was it too much to ask of someone not eighteen yet?

Jannie came and sat down bedside me. She was exhausted. "Well, good riddance, the old biddy is gone! I sent her off with a few meager possessions and told her I would forward the rest along with her severance pay…not that she deserves any. I am so very glad that you are here, V. I fear I could not have gone through with her eviction without you."

"I am sure that you could have, Jannie. Whatever possessed Mr. Jeremy to hire such a crotchety old woman? Surely there are qualified young women out there who would fit the position better than she. Who cared for her after Maveryn's passing? Was it you?"

"Two of Maveryn's sisters came over from Wales and stayed on for a couple of weeks, but they had their own families to tend to and had to return to them. They wanted to take Rosy with them, but Jeremy would not hear of it. He said that Maveryn needed her here. Now I suppose I shall go to the manor and pack up a few things to tide me over until we figure out what to do."

"You will do no such thing!" I said. Rosy was sitting at my feet, busily coloring, and every few minutes, she would look up at me and smile. I knew that I was making the right decision. "We will have her room packed up and take her to the manor to live with us there. You have your duties here and can't be looking after her, whereas I have nothing much to do."

"Yes, V, that sounds like the best plan. Are you going to let her keep calling you mama?"

"Just until she needs to no more," I answered.

Jannie and I returned to Brackenshire Manor with Rosalyn between us. Amma brought up the rear, carrying some of Rosalyn's favorite things. Shalla and Duffy were bringing the rest of her room down as soon as we were ready for it all. As soon as we reached the gate, Rosalyn broke free from us and ran down the road, shouting something we couldn't understand. She banged on the door until a surprised Emma opened the door. She threw her little arms around Emma's legs and said, "Emmma, I coming to live here."

She looked at us over the clinging child and we nodded and smiled. Amma told her sister that it was so and explained what had happened.

"How wonderful. Where will be bedding her Miss Jannie? *Ah dinnae ken*."

Every once in a while, people would lapse into their Scottish dialect and I found that I could usually understand what they were saying. Generally, it was only the older folks who spoke it, but they needed to pass it on to the next generation before it was lost.

Chapter Eleven

Rosalyn and Ava

J annie suggested that Rosalyn would be most happy close to me, and that meant that she had the little room across from mine. It had been closed up to preserve heat and had not been used since Uncle John's mother had used it as her sewing room. I agreed and the preparations began. Walls and windows were scrubbed and the closets cleared out of miscellaneous things. The floor was washed and a remnant of carpet was laid down. Duffy was called to bring down the bed, dressers, and toy box. He arrived within minutes and, in no time at all, we had the room looking like a little girl's should. This was all under the watchful eyes of Rosalyn. She would amuse us all by running back and forth between her room and mine, each time exclaiming, "Look how fast I am, Mama. I get bad dreams, I can come fast. Look, Jannie. Look, Emmma!"

I assured her that she could come to my room anytime and wondered what a child so small could possibly dream about that would scare her. Perhaps she would not anymore now that she was away from that dreadful woman.

The whole household was delighted that Rosy had come to live with us. I felt sad for Amma, as she was tearful when she left, telling Rosy that she would miss her. I told her that she wouldn't have the chance to miss her, as we would be visiting Avanloch every day. I seemed to be able to make promises quite easily, but the one I made to myself had not materialized...I had not forgotten Rainey. Every night, I went to bed with him in my head, and my heart and I prayed that it would be the last time I would think of him.

The first night passed quietly with my new roommate across the hall. I had asked her if she would like me to tell her a bedtime story and she asked what that was. Of course, the old biddy wouldn't have told her any. I could hear her telling Rosy to close her eyes and get to sleep or the boogeyman would get her.

I shivered. I started to tell her Addy's favorite story of *Cinderella* but didn't get very far before the two little green eyes had closed and she was fast asleep. I hoped that every night would be the same but decided that I had better refresh my memory of fairy tales.

Jannie had made an appointment with a doctor in Waverly for me the next day. I supposed that it was time. Soon, everyone would know that my baby would be arriving sooner than expected.

I knew that she was there before I opened my eyes. I could hear her breathing.

"Mama, you sleepin'? She shook me ever so lightly on my shoulder, and when I didn't flinch, she tried to peel my right eye open.

"Rosalyn, what are you doing up so early?" I pretended to scold her.

"Look, Mama, the sky is open. It not early."

I lifted the quilt up for her to crawl into bed with me.

Just then, Emma appeared at the door. "Rosalyn Anne McAllister, what are you doing waking Miss V?"

She hid under the blankets, giggling all the while.

"Hold still, Miss V, there is a big mouse in your bed. I will get the broom and chase him out! I hope he doesn't bite."

"Look, Emmma, it's me, Rosy." She poked her head out so Emma could see her.

"My word, it's not a big mouse but a little monkey! Now get ye up. It's time for your breaky or do you ladies wish to have it in bed?"

"Can we, Mama? Can we?"

"I think not. We will go to the kitchen and have breakfast like proper ladies." Was this how my mornings were going to be from now on? The only thing better would be to wake up and find Rainey sleeping next to me. Stop it! Stop it!

Rosalyn wanted to come to Waverly with Jannie and me, but Emma promised that she would take her to tea at Avanloch and she could visit with Amma; that seemed to appease her. Henry drove us into town for my appointment with Dr. Lancaster. In a way, I was dreading it because the exam would reveal that I was further along in my pregnancy than I had told Jannie that I was. I had limited experiences with doctors and didn't know what to expect. Would he be crotchety and scold me for neglecting the baby's health? Instead, he was very kind and fatherly, and instructed me to call him "Doc." He asked how he should address me, and I told him V or Vela.

"Vela it is then. Now, young lady, I want you to go with the nurse and she will get you ready. Do you wish Jannie to be with you?"

I told him it was not necessary.

When he rejoined me, he asked how far along I thought I was. I told him four months or more.

"Hmm, I thought your aunt said less than that."

I didn't say anything else until the exam was over.

He left me to get dressed and returned a few minutes later. "Well, Miss Vela, I find you to be in fairly good physical health. All of your vital signs are tip-top. The baby has a healthy heartbeat and all seems to be well with him or her. I find that you are indeed into your second trimester. The only thing I am a bit concerned with is your weight. You are much too slim for your condition. Have you been unable to keep food down or do you not have an appetite? Jannie informed me that you are much slimmer than the last time she saw you."

I asked him how much I weighed and he converted it from kilograms to pounds for me. That meant I had lost over 20 pounds. "I did have morning sickness, or should I say, all-day sickness, for a few months, but I am pretty much done with that. I am afraid that I have been in a state of melancholy for some time now and perhaps it was contributing to my loss of weight. My appetite has picked up some these last few days."

"I can see how you must be feeling homesick, but this should be a joyous time for you, is it not? May I ask why you came to Scotland to have your child?"

"I am not homesick. Everyone here is so kind and I am kept very busy, especially since Lord Jeremy's daughter has come to live with us at the manor. No, that is not it, Doc. I may as well tell you sooner than later, as I am sure you will keep my confidence. I left home because I did not want the father of my child to know that I was pregnant. My family has promised to keep my whereabouts and pregnancy a secret until I am ready to tell him, and that may very well be never. No, he is not married and is a very honorable man, but I don't want us to be the reason that he gives up his career. Yes, he does have the right to know, but this is the path that I have chosen to take and I will not stray from it. Is there any way that I can have two sets of birth records, one for when she arrives and one for two months later?"

"You have handed me quite a dilemma, young lady. Your secret is safe with me and perhaps we will dwell into it on further visits. Two birth records would be illegal on my part, but I am sure the matter can be resolved later. My immediate concern is to keep you and the baby healthy. We are going to set you up with a vitamin protocol and I want you to try and put a little weight on, okay?"

I promised him that I would try. He said that he would not treat my melancholy at this time, but if it persisted, he would refer me to another doctor. I knew that he meant, a "shrink." I was hoping to deal with the problem on my own. We made an appointed for the next month and had Henry drive us to the pharmacy.

Jannie took me to a quaint little shop where I purchased several long dresses and smocks, nightgowns, and comfortable shoes. We went to a market where I found all sorts of healthy foods that were not served at the manor. I hoped Mrs. Sharpe would not be offended when I returned with such items as cold cereals, salad fixings, and fresh fruit, which were rare in her kitchen during these winter months. I would soon have the courage to venture into her kitchen and prepare my own soup and rice dishes. We rounded off the trip with a nice luncheon at a fancy restaurant. I picked up a treat for Rosy and we headed back to Brackenshire. I confessed to Jannie that I was further along in my pregnancy and told her why I had left home. She was not surprised.

"My dear, I have thought as much and knew that you would tell me when the time was right for you. I respect your privacy, but I am always available if ever you feel you want to talk. We must prepare the household for your new delivery date, however."

January turned into February, and then suddenly, it was March. Winter had overstayed its visit and spring was warmly welcomed. The sun was ushering in more daylight, and though the winds were brisk, no one seemed to mind as the rains had subsided. I discovered that "Now sun, now rain" was known as a Scottish shower.

Every day, Rosy and I would walk up to the castle on the hill to take tea with Jannie and whoever else was visiting. Once a month, several ladies from the village would join us and keep us updated as to the comings and goings of the local folk and any gossip that they felt was pertinent. I was sure that I was also a big topic for them to discuss. No one had made up any far-flung story as to why I was here and why there was no father on the horizon. Occasionally, an unexpected visitor would arrive, hoping to catch Lord Jeremy in attendance; he seldom was. He had made an appearance at the beginning of February and was very pleased to find that Rosalyn was happy and in good health. I had prepared her for his visit and asked her if she could be kind to him; she said she would if I didn't send her to live with him in the big house again.

Jeremy conveyed his deepest thanks to me. "I do not know what to make of her affection for you, Vela, but you are truly a godsend. Is she any bother to you? You are looking so well. I don't want her to be a burden on you. I hesitate to think what will happen when your own child arrives. I have neglected her terribly and, someday, I know I will have to make arrangements for her care. Can you bear with her until then?"

"I realize that she reminds you of Maveryn and it is hard for you to look at her sometimes, but someday, I hope that you will see her as a blessing and a lasting memory of her mother. Free yourself from any thought that she is a burden. On the contrary, she is a delight and we all love her here and at the castle. There are no arrangements to be made as long as I am around."

"I will hatch a plan to repay you, Vela. For now, you have my undying gratitude."

Rosalyn and I could now maneuver the rugged stone steps to Avanloch. The mosses were still slippery, but we took our time and she always held on to me in case I tripped.

"I will catch you if you fall, Mama, don't be scared." Such reassuring words from a bonnie lass. The ivies were creeping up the slopes and the crocus and daffodils were peeking out from their hiding places. Some of the trees were in bud. I wondered if there was a cherry tree among the midst. The birds were busy setting up housekeeping, and the bees had come out of their winter hives and were buzzing around the newly opened flowers. Rosalyn wanted to know the name of every creature, be it bird or bug. I had found various books on the flora and fauna of the area in the castle library and carried them in a rucksack on my back. Thankfully, there were many benches along the climb and we took advantage of them. I had put on 10 pounds, all in my stomach, and was becoming more and more cumbersome. I was in good health, and by the way, the baby was kicking, and I knew that she was, too. Rosalyn was very aware of what was going on inside of me and would often lay her head on my tummy to talk with her sister.

One day, she asked me what we would do if the baby came out a "gummy boy." I wondered what she meant by "gummy" but told her that we would have to keep him anyhow. She had answered with, "Let's get a girl name then and it will have to be a girl then, right, Mama?"

"I don't think that it works that way, sweetie, but we can try. How about Ava? Do you like that for a name?"

"Ava. What more, Mama? I have tree names."

"Ava Lane LaFontaine," I answered, and thus had chosen my baby's name. I silently wished that someday, I could add Quinn to that name.

The first day of spring, I left Rosy with Amma and Jannie in the tea room, and Emma and Millie took me to Maveryn's resting place. Of all the times that I had roamed the grounds when I was younger, I had never come across the entrance to the family crypt. Just as well, as I would not have known what the huge stone, windowless building was. The entrance was nearly hidden from view. We had to squeeze between fully grown ewe trees, which had not been trimmed for some time, to continue on the path. Emma unlocked the door with a huge key that she retrieved from its hiding place among the bricks. I shivered as we entered. She led me to the one bright spot in the whole of the building, an alcove that housed a beautifully decorated stained-glass window. There on a small ledge sat an exquisite rose-flowered urn that contained Maveryn's ashes. The plaque beneath it read:

Maveryn Rosa De La Mare McAllister
Beloved wife of Jeremy
Devoted mother to Rosalyn
Taken from us before her time
May the angels keep her
Until we meet again

I laid the bouquet of spring upon the window and we left with tears in our eyes.

Jannie remembered my birthday and left orders for Mrs. Sharpe to prepare all my favorites. One day, I approached her and asked if I might help out in her kitchen from time to time. She had answered, "To be sure, I would appreciate the help whenere ye feelin' up to it, luv, and to be sure, these hands could use the help."

I had a craving for chocolate and decided to make my own birthday cake. Mrs. Sharpe offered to find me a recipe, but I assured her that I did not need one. She was impressed that I had all the ingredients in my head and passed me everything I needed from the pantry. Layer cakes were not all that common here. They had lots of tarts and fruity cakes, and some very strange puddings. Rosalyn had joined us after her nap and insisted on many candles. Henry joined us for supper, as he usually did several times a week. He was a widower and Mrs. Sharpe a widow. They had known each other a very long time and carried on as if they were an old married couple. I asked him how he liked my cake.

"Don't know. Needs more tasting." He passed his plate to me for another slice.

We all laughed and Jannie said that he had paid me a very huge compliment. Rosy asked if she could have the same cake for her birthday.

Sleep did not come easy for me that night and I blamed it on the chocolate. I had cut my caffeine intake down to one small cup of coffee in the morning, but was working on eliminating it altogether. I had replaced my love of the beverage with herbal teas. I had finally managed to tolerate the milk that came from the dairy in the village. It was very rich, and so I diluted Rosy's and mine. No one seemed to think I was daft.

I was recalling the party that Lara and Jimmy had thrown for me last year. How I missed them. The movie theatre was in Waverly and that was over an hour's drive, and who would I go with anyhow? It wouldn't be the same without my friends from home. My parents had phoned earlier to wish me a happy birthday and inquire about my health. I told them that all was well. They didn't volunteer any information regarding Rainey and I didn't ask. If I were too curious, they would be suspicious.

Rosalyn had fallen asleep during my storytelling, as usual. It had taken weeks to get through *Cinderella* and we were working on *Snow White* now. The hour was late and I gave up trying to sleep. I got out of bed and sat and rocked in my chair. Rainey was with me again. I was remembering the horrifying revelation of his misdoings last year. That should have been the end of my fixation for him, realizing that he could not be faithful to me, but of course, it hadn't. I could no more stay away from him than the sun could keep from rising every day. I was sure that he had already moved on and was in the arms of some dazzling beauty. I tried to erase the image from my mind, but to no avail.

I yearned to have contact with Lara but knew that I must not. Perhaps I could write her and have Uncle John post it for me the next time he would be in a foreign country. What an idea! I would not leave a return address, and that way, if she talked to Rainey, she wouldn't be lying as to knowing my whereabouts. On the other hand, it wouldn't make me feel any better, as I couldn't receive mail from her. Better to leave it alone for now. Mother talked to Lara regularly and told me that she wasn't happy that I chose to stay in hiding. I often wondered what the outcome would have been if she had been home when I was going through hell, trying to decide what to do about my pregnancy. Would she have been able to convince me to confess to Rainey? *Don't go there, don't go there!* I thought. I needed to quit torturing myself. I had made my bed and now I must lie in it…alone.

March left us and with April came warmer days and nights. We celebrated Rosalyn's third birthday on the thirteenth. Jannie had gone to Edinburgh with Uncle John for a short holiday. I had sent money with her to purchase gifts and novelties for Rosy's party. All the children close to her age from the village were guests, and because the day was warm and sunny, we were able to play games and have cake and ice cream outside. She was most pleased with a red tartan outfit that I gave her. Lord Jeremy was not in attendance, but we gave her a present from him just so that she wouldn't think he had forgotten her. It was tossed aside while she went on to open up something new.

Easter Sunday was soon upon us and again the day reined sunshine. We put on an egg hunt for the children and attended church in the evening. Lord Jeremy sent word home that he would be arriving within the week. I had a little chat with Rosalyn and told her that she must be nicer to her father. She said that she would as long as she didn't have to move back to the "ugly castle."

Lily and Joe had been sending me money every month so that I could insure that I had a proper offering of things for the baby. They need not worry. All the ladies had been knitting and crocheting up a storm. They taught me the basic stitches so that I could knit a blanket. I soon learned that it was not my forte but persevered anyhow. Jeremy had left word with Amma that I was to have full access to Rosalyn's baby furniture, so I did not have to worry about a crib or bassinette or pram. I certainly was not above taking charity from him. I was a little surprised that he had not already sent it all off to the local Sally Anne. Anyhow, it was much appreciated and I would be sure to thank him when next I saw him.

Uncle John had hinted that Jeremy was going to curtail some of his overseas involvement and spend more time at the estate. I hoped that meant more time with his daughter.

Jannie tried to have me moved to a downstairs bedroom, as she was concerned that I might have an accident on the stairs. I assured her that I would take extra caution and not venture down unless someone was with me, if that would ease her mind. I did not want to move away from Rosalyn, who had offered me great advice on how to descend the stairs. "Do like me, Mama. Sit on your rump and go down." I told her that if I did that, I would never get up again. I was becoming very bulky. I had gained 15 pounds, which had made Dr. Lancaster very happy. I could not maneuver the garden steps, as they were slippery with all of the mosses and so had to go on the road to Avanloch for teatime. Henry had taken to giving us a ride in the golf cart, which always brought delighted whops from Rosalyn. I was looking forward to resuming my walks through the rose gardens soon.

My due date was for the middle of May. Preparations had been in place for some time now. If the doctor did not arrive in time for the delivery, then I would be in the capable hands of Jannie, Emma, Mrs. Sharpe, and Mary McDuff. From the village would come Sallie, the local midwife. I was nervous, to say the least.

At 12:30 A.M. on May the 13, I was awakened by a presence standing over me—I should say floating over me. I felt a peace and calmness enfold me. It was time and I reached out for the cow bell to alert the household, but before I could ring it, Jannie was at my door. "Something awoke me, V. Are you in labor?"

I told her that I thought I was, and she called out to John, who summoned everyone else and called the doctor.

When what seemed like an eon had passed, the ladies all said in unison, "Now!"

With my last ounce of strength, I pushed and cried, "Rainey! Rainey, help me!"

"Mary Queen of Scots, Miss V, you have delivered us a bonnie bairn," I heard Mrs. Sharpe exclaim and a tiny whimper was expelled from my newborn baby. I asked if she was all right and they placed her on my stomach for me to see for myself. She was this tiny, quivering, pinkish doll who was cooing and stretching. I was crying and laughing at the same time, so happy that she had finally arrived.

"Is she cold?" I asked and Jannie placed a thin blanket over her just as we heard a booming voice from the doorway.

"Well, well, well. You couldn't wait for the ole doc to arrive, I see. Whatever shall I do with you ladies? Part the way, girls, and let's have a look-see. Yes, indeedy, you got your baby girl, Vela. Nurse Mason will take her and weigh her, clean her up, administer the drops, and check her vitals. As far as I can make out, though, she appears in fine form. Now, how about you, Vela? Any pain or discomfort?"

I told him that I felt fine, just a little tired.

"And that is to be expected. A little nap and you will be tip-top. Now, I don't suppose that anyone noticed the time the wee one was born?"

"I did, Sir. It was 4:44," Emma announced.

"4:44, not 4:45?" the doctor asked.

I assured him that the time was correct.

"And," he said to me, "you weren't so busy that you were watching the clock?"

"It was revealed in a dream a long time ago. I didn't know what it meant at the time but it makes sense now."

"All right then, 4:44 it is."

"Help me, help me, Mama. I can't get out!"

"'Tis, Rosy. I shut her door so as not to wake her. I best go and get her." Emma let go of my hand, which she had been holding throughout the delivery, but not before she asked me why I had been calling out for rain during the final delivery. I said I didn't know.

Rosy came into my room, rubbing her sleep-filled eyes. "Why are all these peoples here, Mama? God hasn't opened up the light yet?"

The nurse brought Ava back into the room and placed her in my arms. Rosy's eyes lit up.

"Mama, oh, Mama, is it our baby? Is it Ava Lane?" Rosy climbed into the bed with me despite everyone cautioning her to wait a while. Together, we examined our new miracle. Everything was perfect. Rosalyn gently touched Ava's chubby little cheeks and counted her fingers and toes, as only a three-year-old could. "She's pink, Mama. And look, she has yellow hair and blue eyes."

The doctor told her that she wouldn't stay pink and that even her hair and eyes might change color. He told us that Ava weighed 7 pounds and 3 ounces.

"Will she get red hair like me?" Rosy asked the doctor.

He laughed. "Well, we will just have to wait and see. Now, I think we should all clear out and let this new mother have a little rest. I want to see you and Ava in my office as soon as you are up to travelling…say in four or five days, unless you want to come and spend a few days in the hospital right now?"

I certainly did not!

After all had left, the nurse showed me how to nurse and told me not to worry if Ava was not too keen on it right away. Perseverance would win out.

I closed my eyes and whispered, "You have a bonnie daughter, Rainey Quinn."

Jannie waited until it was 8 A.M. in Bridge Falls before placing the call. Lily picked the phone up on the first ring, almost as if she had been waiting.

"Lily, V has had her baby," Jannie said.

"What?" Lily was hyperventilating. "It's too soon! Are they all right? Jannie, tell me, is V all right?"

"They are both just fine, Lily. The baby is full term. It's a girl and she is beautiful!"

"What? I don't understand. The baby isn't due until July; it's only May. How can she be full term?"

"That is one more thing that V kept from us, Lily. For reasons of her own, she did not want us to know how far along she was when she came over here. Do you have any idea why?"

"Maybe, I am not sure. How is she really? And the baby is a girl?"

"Her delivery was relatively easy. She went into labor about midnight and the baby was born shortly after 4:30 this morning our time. She weighs 7 pounds 3 ounces. Her name is Ava Lane."

Lily was crying now. "When can I talk to her, Jannie? Do you know that it is Mother's Day here? Is it there, too?"

"No, ours is much earlier. She is still resting, but I am sure that she will call you tomorrow. And, Lily, she does not want it to be known that she had the baby. As far as anyone is concerned, she is still due in July. Do you think that you should tell the girls? I know it will be a difficult decision for you."

"They have already had to keep her whereabouts a secret. I doubt that I can ask them to keep this quiet also. Joe and I will decide what is best. Thank you, Jannie. And tell V that we love her."

Lily found Joe in the study, working on plans for the new dining room. "Joe, that was Jannie on the phone. V has had the baby. It's a little girl and she called her Ava Lane. Isn't that just beautiful?"

"Isn't this too early? I thought the baby wasn't due until July?"

"That's right, Joe, that is what she wanted us to believe. You do know what this means, don't you?" And she answered her own question. "It means she knew very well who the father was. She wasn't the tramp she made herself out to be. Rainey is indeed the father! Thank God! But why doesn't she want him to know?"

"Do you really think so, Lily? I thought she was in love with him, and he certainly is with her, I am sure. He is still calling about her. Something is not right here."

"Do you think that we should tell him, Joe? And what about the girls? How can we keep this from them? Jannie said that V doesn't want anyone to know yet."

"We have kept her secret this long, Lily, and I think that we have to keep going on with it. It is not our decision to make. There may be far more to this than we are privy to. Let's not complicate matters. She and the baby are healthy, then that is all that matters right now."

Chapter Twelve

Rainey, Summer, 1962

Rainey had not talked to Vienna's parents since January and decided to give them a call. Yes, she still called them now and then, and, no, she was not coming home. She had not asked about him. *C'est la vie!* He resumed his relationship with a full bottle of rye.

For several months, he kept in touch with Jimmy and Lara. No one had any word of Vienna's whereabouts, so there didn't seem to be any sense to keep bothering them. He had limited interchange with Bev and John, his downstairs friends. They knew about Vienna's disappearance and did not push Rainey for day-to-day details. They were worried about his drinking and lack of socializing, however.

March 17

This was Vienna's birthday month. He scolded himself because he didn't even know the exact date. Vienna had said that some actor or something had died on her birthday. Who that was, he couldn't remember. She would be eighteen now. He had made himself a sandwich for dinner and sat down in front of the television with it and a glass of his usual, ice and rye. He reminded himself to go to the market tomorrow for groceries and booze.

That night, he had the dream. He hadn't had it since Christmas. Now, he knew why: the alcohol numbed his brain, and he surmised that one couldn't dream if he was soused. Tonight, he had run out of liquor. He wouldn't make that mistake again. The clock read 4:44 when he awoke. He threw his pillow at it and sent it crashing to the floor.

April 20

Rainey's parents came down to spend Easter with him. They had not told him that they were coming. He found them in his kitchen when he got home from a market run. It was Good Friday, but he couldn't see any good in it. His mother had brought dinner with her and was warming it up. She had made all his favorites and even brought a turkey for Easter. They voiced their concern over Rainey's weight loss and pale complexion. His father took him into the living room, sat him down, and proceeded to talk to him about his drinking. They knew he had a problem because every time they talked to him over the phone, they could hear it in his slurred voice.

Rainey put his head in his hands. "I know, Dad. But it is the only way that I can numb the pain."

"Son, do you think that you will see V again? I believe that she will come back someday, and whether it be tomorrow or next year or ten years from now, your life will have gone on because time doesn't stop for anything or anyone. It's up to you how you choose to live. I've never known you to be a defeatist, but you are throwing five years of hard work down the drain. It's time that you took stock in what you have worked for and dreamt of for so long. And if and when V does show up, do you want her to find you in the bottom of a whiskey bottle?"

Rainey promised that he would curb his drinking. He told his dad about the dreams and how the alcohol seemed to keep him from the nightmares.

His dad said the same thing that Jimmy and Vienna had both said: "They are only dreams, Son. Try to find something positive in them and maybe they will fade away."

The rest of the visit was spent pleasantly and he was glad that they had come. The dreams continued until May the 12, when he had the last unnerving one.

May 12

Rainey had joined his friends Bev and John for dinner. They had gone to a local Chinese restaurant. He was home by eight. He felt groggy, blaming it on the MSG (monosodium glutamate), and laid down on the couch. He fell into a deep sleep almost immediately. When he awoke, he realized that he had been dreaming. He thought, *Damn it, I had the dream again!* Something was definitely different. His watch read 8:45. *Okay then.* He tried to piece together what he had dreamt but he could not bring it into focus. Vienna was in it, of course, but he could hardly make her out. She was not in the usual meadow or on the cliff, but on a purple cloud. He thought, *I guess we do dream in color.* She was holding something that he could not make out. What was she saying? *"Let me go Rainey, let me go."* or was it *"Help me, Rainey"*? She blew him a kiss and evaporated. He had a strange feeling of finality. He tried to shake the feeling off and again blamed the Chinese food.

The next day, he phoned his mother, as it was Mother's Day. No, they hadn't heard anything about V. Not satisfied, he put a call through to Bridge. Yes, Joe had said they had heard from V just a while ago. She was all right. He did manage to get out of Joe her whereabouts: "overseas." Well, that certainly cleared that up. He hung up the phone, disgusted as usual.

June 25

There was rain in the air as Rainey made his way home from Hawthorne. He had spent the weekend with his parents before he accepted a job offer at Billings Architectural. Despite all of his drinking and depression, he had graduated in the top ten of his class. He had applied at several other companies and chose the Billings one, as it was only a half-hour drive from his house. By the time he arrived in Hope, he was fatigued. The relentless rain did not help any. He thought of pulling over and taking a room for the night, but drove on, hoping the rain would stop. It didn't. He turned off at a junction and followed the signs to a flashing neon sign advertising food and drink. He parked and ran into Scotties Bar. He ordered a burger, coffee, and a beer. The place was quiet except for two fellows playing pool and a table occupied by three women. He was almost through with his meal when he heard a loud voice, which he was sure he recognized.

"What a f…in night! Do you gals have any idea how f…in long it took me to find this little shit hole? Who picked this frigin' dive anyhow? I hope you've ordered for me. It's going to take me a while to catch up."

Rainey could hear her plainly and so could everyone else. He thought about sneaking out the back door as she was the last person on Earth he wanted to see, but he was too late, she had spotted him.

"Girls, do you see who I see? Lord, do you not have any mercy?" She plunked herself down on a stool next to him. He did not look up. "Rainey Quinn! As I live and breathe. What the hell are you doing in this classy joint?"

"Well, I was minding my own business until this brassy broad interrupted me." He waved his hand around the room. "Isn't this a little upscale for you, Priscilla?"

She laughed. "Buy a lady a drink?"

"I would if I saw one."

"Ouch, that stung. What's got your shorts in a knot? Love life not going so well? Oh, puh…lease tell me you are not still pining over that schoolgirl?"

Rainey stood up. "Not that it is any of your beeswax, but, yes, I am still in love with Vienna. I always will be." He tossed a twenty on the counter and flipped her a quarter. "For old time's sake. This is what you were worth to me."

"Don't let the door hit you in the ass!"

He gave her the finger.

He didn't even notice if it was raining when he walked to his car. He felt energized. Funny how the banter had made him aware of what he had to do. "I'm going to go to Wales. I am going to find Vienna and bring her home." He turned the radio on and smiled as he sang along with Elvis to "It's Now or Never."

Ten minutes after arriving home, he found a colleague's phone number and was on the phone to London. "Stu, Rainey Quinn."

"Rainey, ole chap, how are you and to what do I owe the pleasure?"

"Is it a good time? Hell, I forgot the time difference."

"Not to worry. I've been up a while."

"Stu, I am wondering if you can help me. I have to go to Wales on some personal business and hear that you practically have to sign your life away to rent a car over there. Would it be better for me to fly into Heathrow and get a car there?"

"You may be in luck. As it is, I am on my way to Bangor, which is in northern Wales, this weekend. Is this anywhere close to where you want to go?"

"I'm looking at the atlas and I see that it looks close to Anglesey Island. I need to go there and do you know of any Gypsy settlements in the area?"

"Sounds intriguing. I don't know what you are up to, but I would be happy to tour you around if you can be here by Friday, and I wouldn't be interfering."

"Thanks ever so much, but I couldn't ask you to interrupt your life for me."

"What life? Daisy is on a cruise with her family, and as I said, I am going to Bangor anyhow. It is my Aunt Maddie's sixtieth birthday. She is practically my only living relative, so I never miss a special occasion to visit. She could be a big help to you in locating who or what you are looking for."

"Since you put it that way, I would be delighted to have the company, as I know nothing of the area. All expenses are on me. And, Stu, I am looking for a woman. She disappeared last winter and she always talked of Wales, her aunt, a castle, and gypsies. I need to try and find her. I hope I can make arrangements tonight. If not, I will call you soon as I do. Time difference is about eight hours, right? And, Stu, thanks."

"Waiting to hear from you, buddy."

Rainey was able to get a flight to London arriving at noon British time on Friday, June 29. He informed Stu, who told him that he had spoken to his aunt, and she wanted to join in the quest with them and was going to find out what she could about any Gypsy settlements. Rainey hoped that it would be a successful venture and was looking forward to doing something constructive in his hunt for the woman he loved.

The week dragged on. Rainey wanted to get going now that his plans were in motion. He called his parents and told them that he had decided to take a little trip and would be away for a week or so. Secretly, he hoped that it wouldn't take that long.

Finally, he was on the flight to London. He had not hesitated to call Stu for advice, which turned out to be better than he had expected. They had met in a museum in Florence, Italy, last autumn on one of Rainey's sightseeing tours. They had both been admiring paintings of Monet's "Garden at Giverny" and had started up a conversation. One thing led to another and soon they were at a little café sharing stories. Stu was a scholar of English literature and was in the country gathering information for an article that he was writing. He had rented a cottage in a Tuscan villa and did all of his traveling from there. He invited Rainey to spend the evening with him and take a trip through the wine country the next day. Rainey accepted, as he had not made other arrangements yet. Over the weeks that Stu was in the country, they met many times and discovered Italy's wonders together. They became good friends and promised to keep in touch. He was sure that he had told Stu about Vienna but hadn't mentioned that she was the one he was searching for when they talked on the phone last week. There would be plenty of time for that.

Stu was waiting for him at the luggage carousel. They greeted each other with handshakes and the usual unimportant things like, "How are you?" and "How was your trip?" Stu jokingly asked Rainey if he had brought the rain with him. Once they were in the 1950s Austin Healy that was Stu's pride and joy, Rainey thanked him again for picking him up and arranging the trip to Wales.

"That is one huge airport. I would probably be wondering around all night if it wasn't for you."

"No problem. I am pleased to be of service. I can hardly wait to hear the details of your lost lady," Stu said in his impeccable British accent.

Rainey asked Stu if he had told him about Vienna last year.

"Aha, the Lady Vienna. It would be hard to forget that lovely, enchanting name. Indeed I do, Sir! Is she the object of your discontent?"

"Yes. I have been in quite a state since returning home from Italy last winter. I arrived at her house in Bridge Falls, which is just a dozen miles from my hometown of Hawthorne, to find her gone."

"Gone? Do tell."

Rainey related his story to Stu. He didn't leave anything out. He told him of his heavy drinking, the self-pity, and his inability to accept the fact that he might never see Vienna again. It felt good to talk to Stu again.

Soon, they arrived at Stu's flat, which was a walk-up in the heart of a busy downtown London. It was comprised of long hallways that led to the bedrooms, the living room, and kitchen. Rainey couldn't help thinking that those hallways were a complete waste of space, the architect in him musing over ways to improve the lay out.

The room he was to have overnight was sparsely decorated and free of clutter, which did not prepare him for what he was to encounter in the rest of the flat.

Rainey followed Stu into the library, aka, the living room. He had never seen so many books in one place except a public library. He knew that Stu was a fanatic when it came to collecting works of words, but this was excessive. Two entire walls consisted of shelves that reached up to the ceiling. Every square inch of the floor, the shelves, the cupboards, and even the T.V. were overflowing with volumes of every size and color. Books spilled out from under the chesterfield and the coffee table. No light from the windows could enter, as there wasn't an opening big enough to let any in. Rainey let out a low whistle.

"Sorry," Stu apologized as he threw newspapers and magazines to the floor so that they could sit down.

"Hey, no need to apologize. I completely understand about obsession. How do you keep it all looking relatively neat? I suppose that you know where you can lay your hands on anything you want at any time. I seem to recall that you have a photographic memory."

"It is not that perfect, but it helps, plus the fact that most everything has been categorized and is color coded on how important they are to me."

"Really? Where have you got your typewriter hidden?"

"It's in my bedroom. I'm glad that the bathroom is between us so that I won't keep you awake tonight."

"I don't think that I will be getting much sleep anyhow. Do you do most of your writing at night? What does Daisy think about you burning the midnight oil?"

"I only require three to four hours of sleep. Believe it or not, I have been de-cluttering. The kitchen and the room you are in are completely free of books, except Daisy's cookbooks. I am now working in clearing the dining room, which you probably didn't know even existed."

Rainey looked behind him and realized that was indeed a table. Jokingly, he asked how the bathroom was and if there was any reading material in it.

"That's not as funny as you may think. That was Daisy's final turning point. She was sick and tired of having to remove books from the tub every time she wanted to take a bath. She gave me an ultimatum: either clear the place out or we move, and there would be no wedding until she can see that she means more to me than 600,000 books."

"Sorry, Stu, I have to side with her on this one."

"Do you have any idea how difficult this is for me? It's a bloody nightmare! Do you know that I have manuscripts dating back to the beginning of the written word? I have first editions, original handwritten narrative poems, and plays of the seventeenth century. I have complete works of prose from the masters—Lord Byron, Shelley, and Keats, just to mention a few. I have the Canterbury Tales in long hand, which I paid a small fortune for. There are volumes on every war in history. Shakespeare himself would envy my collections of his works, if he did indeed pen them. Sir Arthur Conan Doyle, Virginia Woolf, Agatha Christie, Dickens, Kipling, Coleridge, Wordsworth, *Beowulf*, *The Faerie Queen*; they all live here. And, of course, every first printing of the Bible that I could lay my hands on. Should I go on?"

"I think I get the picture. Now, what can I do to help you?"

"I guess you could help me with some sorting if you like. How about we have a little toddy and work for a few hours and then hit the pub down the street? You haven't gone cold turkey, have you?"

"Sounds good to me. I have a drink now and then, just try not to when I am alone. I don't doubt that the task of ridding oneself of his collections is a daunting one. How do you decide what to keep and what to get rid of, and where does it all go?"

"Other collectors from near and abroad, schools and libraries. Some even goes in the trash."

They worked until 8 P.M. and then made their way to Sheridan's Pub, where Rainey was treated to a good fare of English fish and chips, and hospitality.

The next morning, they were up and off at 7 A.M. Stu informed Rainey that the trip to Bangor would take about five hours, depending on how often they stopped. Rainey assured Stu that he wasn't here for a sightseeing trip, so they could skip any off-highway sites. He learned from his colleague that Wales was known as the "Land of Castles." He wondered how many and would this make his task even harder. Apparently, it was a country of magic, mystery, and enchantment. This was right up Vienna's alley, so no wonder she wanted to come here.

As they drove through small towns and hamlets on the way to Bangor, Rainey couldn't help but be impressed with the verdant fields and magnificent views of the mountains. They were the Cambrian Mountains, Stu informed him. As they drove through Clwydian Hills, the Irish Sea came into view. Bangor was located in northeast Wales with Caemarfon Bay on its doorstep. The Isle of Anglesey was across the waters, accessed by the Menai Suspension Bridge.

Maddie met them at the door. She lived in one of those cottages that you read about in fairy tales—white picket, rundown fence, ivy-clad thatched roof; the house itself was white with blue doors, trim, and shutters. The worn stone walkway and yard was covered in masses of colorful flowers. There were tall rosebushes, white, pinks, and pale oranges. There was no grass to speak of. Maddie was dressed in long, grey slacks, a bright, flowered blouse, and grey vest. She had a moccasin—like high boot on her feet—and she carried a huge sun hat and sunglasses.

I think I am looking at the original fairy godmother, Rainey thought.

Her eyes sparkled when she spoke. Her smile was contagious.

If this is how one can look when she is sixty, bring it on, he thought again.

She hugged Rainey like she was his long-lost grandmother. He wished her a happy birthday and thanked her for wanting to help him.

"This is going to be one happy day. It is a long time since I have been of much use to anyone. 'Tis to be an adventure and I have made arrangements with an old friend who will have information for us to visit a gentleman in Bhor, who may be able to shed some light on where your dear Vienna is. I hope I do not hold you back, as I am a tad bit slow. Now, Stu, let's get this young man to the isle and see what we can discover. I do not want you to be too disappointed, as very few castles are occupied. Tell me about your affairs, Rainey Quinn. I am a teensy bit curious of your plight."

He liked her. It had been a long time since anyone had called him by his full name. Only Vienna did. He had no problem relating his love story to Aunt Maddie.

Rainey held the car door open for Maddie.

"Don't be daft, lad." She nudged him with her walking stick, pointing to the back door. "Would ye expect me to put myself into that little seat? This puddle jumper was made for the wee leprechauns."

Stu laughed. "Don't argue with her, my friend. You would never win. Besides, she likes to do her driving from the backseat."

"Tut, tut. Now, do ye fancy a quick tour of the area before we hit the bridge?"

"Sounds good to me," Rainey agreed. He was still trying to think of who she reminded him of—one of his pals' grandmother, the old lady in the shoe? He chuckled to himself. No, he was sticking to the fairy godmother look-alike. He would never have thought these things if it hadn't of been for Vienna's influence.

"What's tickled your funny bone?" Stu wanted to know.

"Just reminiscing." He turned around to face Maddie. "You know, if I didn't know better, I would place your accent from somewhere in the South—Southern United States, that is."

"Well, Rainey, you're absolutely correct. I spent over twenty years in Savannah, Georgia, with my husband, God rest his soul. He was employed by an engineering company. I am afraid I picked up the Southern drawl and never got my own completely back."

Rainey expressed his sympathy for the loss of her husband.

"Thank you, lad. I do miss him, but we had a good life and I've no regrets. Now get back to Vienna."

They drove by the university to Caernarfon Castle. Now, this was a castle! It was at the south end of Menai Strait, 8 miles southwest of Bangor. Even at this early hour, it was flooded with tourists. Stu informed him that it had the reputation of being the mightiest in the land. Rainey could understand why; it was magnificently massive. They walked to a viewing platform so that he could get the full effect of the towers and clusters of turrets, which boasted stone eagles. The town site of Caernarfon was behind the castle walls. They didn't have time for the grand tour and struck out for Anglesey via the Menai Suspension Bridge, which was a great achievement for its time. Maddie gave Rainey a detailed account of the construction of the seven-year project. She told him that the man responsible for this acclaimed structure was Thomas Telford, who began life as a shepherd in his native Scotland. He was amazed to learn that the bridge was completed in 1826 and was the first iron suspension bridge in the world. He would have liked to meet the genius behind the marvel.

Rainey received no answers regarding Vienna's whereabouts on the isle. There were no such occupied castles as she had described to him anywhere. They asked in marketplaces, seaside inns, people they encountered on the roadsides, and finally at the information center. It didn't help that Rainey didn't know Jannie's last name. The trip was not a total failure, as the countryside was awash with interesting places. The white peaks of the Snowdonia Mountains were in view as they journeyed through colorful waterfront villages. It was a land of rugged cliffs, beaches, and fertile fields. They encountered the ruins of forlorn castles, burial sites, and stone walls that once housed small farmsteads. They visited the seaport of Holyhead, which Maddie told Rainey was only 24 miles from Bangor. Their last stop before supper was the historic town of Beaumaris, which was the site of the renowned Beaumaris Castle. This was an unfinished masterpiece of military architecture, which Rainey and Stu explored. Maddie told them to take their time. She had been in the castle more times than she cared to remember. Although Stu had also toured it many times, he said that he never got tired of it and seemed to always find something that he had missed before. He led Rainey to the top of the inner wall for a view of the castle layout and the breathtaking scenery that surrounded it. They walked through the wall passages that linked the towers, the domestic chambers, and the semi-octagonal chapel. An hour passed unnoticed by the pair but their hunger forced them to return to the main entrance, where they found Maddie deep in conversation with several tourists or perhaps locals.

"Time to find us a fine establishment for supper, Maddie," Stu said. "Do you have a favorite?"

"As a matter of fact, I do, Stu. It is just down the road from here."

The inn was called the Seaside Country Inn and Pub. It had a romantic charm about it and reminded Maddie of one she and her husband had frequented in New Orleans. She mentioned that she thought there was a similarity between some of the buildings and homes in Wales and in the South in the USA. There was a fire burning in the cozy dining room and they were welcomed by a spirited young lass dressed in red and green tartan. She ushered them to a table overlooking the harbor and presented them with menus that heralded a poem by John Masefield about the sea. Everything appealed to their appetites but they all settled on a meal suggestion for four. It consisted of rack of lamb, roasted beets and potatoes, and local salad greens. They enjoyed a pint of ale while waiting. Stu mentioned to the waitress that it was his aunt's birthday and asked what she could suggest for a dessert. She wished Maddie a happy birthday in Welsh and she would not leave until Stu and Rainey had it down pat. They must have said it fifty times before she was satisfied with their rendition of *Penblwydd Hapus*. They all had a good laugh. The meal was delicious and the sea-salted caramel chocolate cakes were superb. Maddie blew out the candle that been thoughtfully placed on her portion and thanked the boys profusely. Rainey assured her that it was his pleasure and would have a hard time repaying the both of them for their hospitality.

They returned to the mainland via the Britannia Bridge. Maddie apologized for not coming up with any answers for Rainey.

"I knew that it was a long shot, Maddie," he said. "I want to thank you for the effort. You have nothing to be sorry for. I had a wonderful day."

They had a night cap of sherry before turning in. Maddie's hospitality also included a bed for the night. She said before they went to their respective rooms, "I hope that tomorrow will prove to be more informative when we visit Mr. Louis De La Mare. He is the person my friend, Sara, has contacted for us. Apparently, if there is anything to find out about Vienna and her family relationship with a Gypsy settlement, he is the go-to man. We must get you and Vienna reunited. Any man who would go to this extreme to find the woman he loves should not and cannot be denied. Once we have your love life settled, we will have to work on Stu's and that little Scottish heifer."

"Aunt Maddie, did you just call Daisy a cow?" Stu asked.

"I didn't say that exactly, did I, Rainey?" With that, they all retired for the night.

Rainey awoke to the sweet aroma of coffee the next morning. Thank heavens Aunt Maddie was also a fan of his morning fix of caffeine. Stu preferred strong tea but would drink what everyone else was having. They ate a quick breakfast of warm rolls and jam, then left to wind their way to the south of Wales. The destination was Bhdor, southeast Wales. They passed fields of grazing sheep and running horses. Rainey liked to think that the horses were wild Welsh ponies. The riverbeds were lined with lush foliage and wild flowers. He lost count of the castles that they could see from the roadways. Numerous signs pointed the way to others or other attractions. Maddie had given him a map so that he could follow as she gave her running commentary on the area. The only medieval castle they visited was at Usk. From there they found the small township of Bhdor and Stu followed the directions that Sara had given Maddie. They found the home of Louis De La Mare 10 kilometers down a worn, grassy, and gravel road. He was in his yard, tending to his vegetable garden, and looked up when he heard the vehicle. He was a gentle-looking man with fairly long, white hair. Rainey guessed that he was in his seventies. He welcomed them and invited them into his humble home. The interior was as polished as the outside was and offered comforting seating, which was rich in color and texture. He apologized for the condition, as it was not the same without a woman's touch. He beckoned them to sit while he retrieved the refreshments. He returned with a warm pot of coffee and small cakes. He also produced a bottle of "home-brewed" wine. He asked them if they would join him in a wee drink and, without waiting for an answer, poured them a healthy portion into amber glasses. He proposed a toast and said, "*Croeso*." He translated it: "Welcome."

Maddie said, "*Salute!* Thank you for agreeing to see us. I understand there has been great sadness in your life in the past few years and we are sorry for that."

Mr. De La Mare rose and showed them pictures of his departed wife, Rosa, and the daughter that he lost only a year and a half ago. "Thanks be to the God that Rosa was spared the earthly crossover of her beloved Maveryn. They are together now in the Holy One's graces and I shall join them one day. But here is the future, Maveryn's daughter, Rosalyn. See how she favors her mother?"

Looking at them from a mass of unkempt red hair was a beautiful, mischievous, green-eyed small child. Maddie said, "I bet this one is a handful. Where is she, Mr. De La Mare?"

"Please, call me Louie. Rosalyn is with her father in Scotland. We tried to bring her here to live with the family, but he would have none of it. I have not seen the child since our Maveryn's memorial. It is too far to travel for me. The other daughters have been to visit. They are not happy with her care. They say that Rosalyn's father is so forlorn with grief he can barely stand to see her likeness to her mother. What can we do? We are paupers and he is a powerful lord of the country. But that is not what you came to see this old man about. Who is to speak?"

Maddie looked over to Rainey, who then put his glass down and said, "Sir, I have already led these two fine people on a wild goose chase and I am afraid that it will not end here neither. I had reason to believe that the woman I love came to Wales. We are both from small towns in Canada. She told me tales of her aunt living on the Isle of Anglesey, in a castle, which, apparently, was a tale all right—a fairy tale." He paused and took a deep breath. "She also said that her mother's family had relatives of Gypsy descent in Wales, which has led us to you. We were told that you are the premier expert on the subject."

"Sir, you give me too much credit," Louie replied. "What be the names of all involved?"

"Her name is Vienna Emerald Lane LaFontaine. She is called V by everyone but myself. Her mother's name is Lily Lane. I believe that Lane is her maiden name. Her father is of French heritage, as are you, Sir. I am sorry, that is all I have, which is nothing, but I had to come anyway."

"Of course you did, Son. I would go to the ends of the earth for my lost Rosa also. There is still hope for you, however. I must say up front that I do not know any of these names, except LaFontaine, which, of course, I have knowledge of, but not here. I have not heard that name here in Wales, nor do I recollect the name Lane. I do not believe that it is a Romani tribe. However, our descendants come from many places and have been discriminated against for many years, so who is to say that Lane was not from an original tribe? Certainly, I do not pretend to know all the history. I am going to my files and make a few calls. Please help yourselves to more wine or the coffee."

Rainey was not hopeful and with good reason, for the little information he had supplied were sketchy to say the least.

A half an hour passed before Louie returned. He expressed his deepest regret that he was not able to come up with anything. He had his daughters make phone calls to people they thought may know the name Vienna, but to no avail. It was not a name that would go unnoticed. His files also revealed nothing. The trio thanked him for his trouble and hospitality, and bade him good day, but not before leaving him with their phone numbers and addresses. His last words were: "*Pub loc* and Godspeed."

Maddie said it meant "good luck."

It was a somber, quiet trip to Newtown, where they dropped Maddie off to visit with her friend, Sara. They declined tea after giving Sara a brief account of what had transpired. They would leave the rest up to Maddie. Rainey felt a deep sadness upon saying good-bye to Maddie. In the brief time he had known her, he had come to think of her as his own aunt. He promised to keep in touch.

Stu made good time on the 200 k trip back to London. Rainey was able to get a flight out to Toronto, but not to Vancouver, the next day, so he decided to take it and visit with his sister and family for a few days before heading home. He knew that he would not be seeing them for a long time, as he had made up his mind what he was going to do with his life and hopefully end his addiction to finding Vienna.

Rainey arrived home on July 6, and after a call overseas, he phoned his best friend. "Jimmy, I'm done. It's over. My trip to Wales revealed nothing of Vienna's whereabouts. I knew it wouldn't, but it was just something I felt that I had to do."

"Hold the fort, Rain. You've lost me, bro. Wales? Wales in Great Britain? You mean you were there looking for V?"

"Sorry, bud, I thought I told you. Anyhow, I turned up nothing."

"You're telling me that you went to a foreign country to hunt her down? Whatever gave you the idea that she may be there?"

"She used to talk a lot about Wales and Anglesey, so I took the chance and went."

Jimmy was not sure that he had heard Rainey right and said, "Take it from the start. Are you telling me that just because V talked about Wales, you figured that was where she went? Did you take into consideration that she was a great storyteller and that Wales and this isle of whatever were imaginary?"

"I am not sure that I reasoned anything out. She always sounded so sincere when she spoke of castles, gypsies, and mystic lands that I convinced myself that she had indeed been there and maybe went back. What can I say, Jimmy? I haven't had all cylinders firing. Anyhow, I went but I wasn't alone. Did I ever mention my friend in London to you? Well, he and his aunt were my guides. We turned up a fat nothing. Anyhow, why I am phoning is that I am going back to Italy. It is time to end my obsession with Vienna. I cannot stay here. There are memories of her everywhere and I need to go where she has never been. I have been in contact with an architectural firm in Milan. I had been offered a position with them upon graduation and I have decided to accept. I will try and keep in touch, and thanks for your support."

"You're leaving right now? Did you forget Zane's wedding next weekend?"

"Give my apologies to the happy couple. A wedding is the last thing I need. I hope the next time that I talk to you, I will be a different man. Thanks again, Jimmy. Bye."

He hung up before Jimmy could say anything else or even wish him luck.

Chapter Thirteen

Vienna—Avanloch

Ava was asleep and would be for several hours, and Rosalyn was with Emma and Amma in the village for their final dress fittings. Rosalyn was to be the flower girl at Amma's wedding. She was very excited. Her dress was orange taffeta and decorated with pale yellow daisies. Before she left, she told me to keep an eye on her sister. Rosalyn had taken it upon herself to be at Ava's bedside whenever she was awake. She would sit in a big chair near to the crib and talk constantly of the goings-on around the house. She would pretend to read as she recited the stories that I had told her every night Ava was a very good baby. She slept from ten at night to early morning, having many naps throughout the day. She seldom cried, and when she did, Rosalyn would rush to find me and say that Ava was unhappy. I allowed her to hold Ava when she was supervised. She did not like to be far from her baby sister, and some nights, she would fall asleep in my bed, trying to keep her eyes open while I read to them. Later, I would carry her to her own room.

I left Ava in her bassinette in the kitchen with Mrs. Sharpe, as I had decided to have some time to myself roaming the gardens. It was June 29. Amma's and Johnny's wedding was tomorrow at noon, in the pavilion behind Avanloch. I thought that I would end up there to see if there were any last-minute preparations that I could help the family with. However, I never made it there. I had hiked up the embankment behind Brakenshire Manor and crossed over Miller's Creek on the footbridge that would take me to the rose gardens. Shelley and Keats surprised me, as they were seldom out of their kennels. They nearly knocked me down as usual. I followed them up the path and encountered Lord Jeremy and Duffy.

"Vela, how nice to see you out and about," Lord Jeremy said. "We could use a woman's opinion of where to plant this latest unnamed tea rose. What do you think, should it be in front of Rosa De La Mare or Lady Audrey Ash? I am going to call it Lady Maveryn. It is supposed to be a creamy apricot color."

I knew that the nursery in Waverly sold roses at a discount every year that came from a major distributer in England that only tagged them with color but no name. Maveryn had purchased the first two, naming them for her mother and Jeremy's. I gathered that this was to be a tradition every year. I suggested the planting to be between the two and that next year one could be next to Maveryn and be called Rosalyn. Jeremy agreed and said that Ava also would have a rose named for her—after all, they were sisters. He then asked if he could have a few minutes of my time. I said, "Certainly."

We left the planting in Duffy's capable hands and wandered up the path. Half of the roses were in full or partial bloom, with the later ones just reaching bud stage. It was indeed a sight to behold! Lord Jeremy beckoned me to take a seat on the wrought-iron bench as we neared the end of the magnificent garden. We were seated overlooking the wild flower fields and ponds. In the distance, we could see Millerfloss River, winding its way through the valley, with snow-capped Widow's Range completing the breathtaking picture.

Lord Jeremy sat down beside me and said, "I have been doing some serious soul searching and have decided to spend more time here at Avanloch and get to know my daughter better. I know that she is not fond of me, but with your help, I hope that I will be able to change her opinion of me."

"Just how can I help you, sir?" I asked.

"I would like for you and the girls to come and live at Avanloch."

"I am not trained to be a governess, if that is what you are suggesting, Sir."

"You do not need any training. You have more compassion and knowledge than a person twice your age. No, I would like you to make it your home and to be in charge of the household. You know that Jannie will be completely retired soon and I do not wish to replace her with an unknown. The staff already love and respect you and I have all the confidence in you that you will make an excellent mistress."

"You cannot suggest that I be a replacement for my aunt. She has had years and years of experience and I have no idea of how to run a household. I thank you for your confidence, but believe me, you will be better off served by someone with the proper qualifications."

"Do you not think that Jannie was a novice when she first came to us? I am not just suggesting that you come to work for me, I would like to propose that we marry and make a home for the girls."

At that moment, I thought that he had lost his mind and I was sure that my expression conveyed how perplexed and astonished I was. I stood up and said to him, "Sir, I could no longer marry you than I could the man in the moon! Someone else has my heart and I am afraid he always will have it."

He was not offended by my comment. "The father of Ava, I am sure. And my heart will always be with Maveryn. I am not suggesting that we be man and wife but only parents to the girls. I would like you to become Rosalyn's adopted mother and I, in turn, would adopt Ava. Heavens, I am old enough to be your father! Please sit down. You would have the east wing as your own or the south tower, and I will remain in the north wing. I need to know that Avanloch will continue to thrive while I am away or after my demise. I believe that you will always have the good sense to see to its needs. Maveryn will be so happy if you accept."

I let the remark about Maveryn go for now. "Sir, you hardly know me or what I am capable off. I do not think that you have given this matter careful thought. Are you ill? Is that why you are grasping at straws?"

He did not understand what I had said and I realized that it was not a phrase that was in use in Scotland, but he answered me anyhow. "I have given the proposal a lot of thought and it is the conclusion that I have decided upon. I hope that you will realize that I am serious. You love and care for Rosalyn as if she were your very own. Have you not wondered what would become of her if you should leave?"

"Yes, I have, Sir. I have been contemplating about my situation and know that I cannot stay at the manor for much longer. I must find employment. Never in my wildest dreams did I ever think that the way for me to stay and keep the girls together would come in the form of a proposal from you."

"So you can see that what I am suggesting makes sense for all of us? I do not expect you to make a decision right away, but would hope that it might be soon. Maveryn will be delighted by your acceptance."

There it was again, the "Maveryn will be" phrase. I replied, "I am not so sure that she would approve of your choice."

"Nonsense, she became very fond of you that summer you spent here. She thought of you as a younger version of herself."

I laughed. "Oh, if she could only see me now. Here I am, dressed in my drab maternity dress and army boots. I am but a peasant compared to her elegance. My hair must have branches imbedded in it." I shook my head, hoping to dislodge any foreign materials.

He commented on the new color of my hair, saying that he liked it.

"I have let it go back to its natural shade. Rosalyn calls it burnt sugar taffy. Where she got that from, I do not know. I used to color it black." He did not ask why and I did not tell him that I had dyed it on a whim. I had met Rainey several days later and he commented on my raven hair, so I kept it. It would never be dark again.

I was fiddling with the straps on my hat, not sure of what I should say. "Sir, I ask you again, are you ill? Is that the reason why you have made such an offer?"

"My health is perfectly fine. I am convinced that this a logical answer to both our plights. In time, you will come to agree, I can only hope."

"Not many men, and especially one of nobility, would consider taking a single mother and her child into their home. Have you thought of the consequences?"

"Consequences? Do you mean what others will think? Balderdash! My family is John and Jannie, and my employees, Rosalyn, and I hope to include you and Ava in that circle. I have no close friends. And, my dear, I am certainly not noble. Now, I will pose a question to you. How many young ladies would take it upon themselves to take over mothering duties to an unknown child?"

"Probably a lot more than you would imagine, and she certainly was not unknown. She was the daughter of my dear departed friend."

"Speaking of that, I would like to thank you for your kind and comforting words that you conveyed at Maveryn's passing. She treasured the correspondence she received from you and commented that your writings reminded her of the way the Bronte sisters wrote. I, too, have noticed that you speak with a knowledge that most young people do not possess."

"I do not know about that. Perhaps I am just an old soul. Have we strayed from the question in point?"

"Yes, I believe we have. As I told you before, Vela…you do not mind me calling Maveryn's name for you, do you? I know everyone else calls you V. Anyhow, I do not require an immediate answer. I am not going anywhere."

"Have you seen the wheels turning in my head? All the time we have been talking, I have been contemplating how I shall answer you and I think that I have come to an answer. I hope you will not think less of me if I accept your kind offer of marriage here and now. The more I think about things, the more I make wrong decisions, and so, I shall say yes and it will be done."

"I do so admire people who can think on their feet. You will not regret your decision. I have no doubt that there would have been a steady stream of young men coming to court you, and for the love of me, I do not understand how your young man let you get away."

"He did not let me go, Sir. And that is all that I will say on the matter for now."

"I think the first thing that we have to do here is to get you to quit calling me, Sir."

"It may take some getting used to for me to call you by your given name. I am sure that is not the only thing that I will have to get used to."

"There is lots of time and there is no hurry. Are you in agreement with me that we should ask the Reverend Peters to marry us?"

"Oh yes."

"Then it shall be. The sooner that we can get all of the legalities settled with the girls, the better. Shall we confer with Reverend Peters this evening then? Would July 6 be to your liking? I thought that we could just have Jannie and John stand up for us."

"Yes, I am not one to change my mind, but never have I had to make such a big decision. I am afraid that if left to give the matter too much thought, I may have a change of heart. Jeremy, are you positive that there will never be another in your life to love as you did Maveryn? I can comprehend that somewhere down the road, you may find another, and when and if that day happens, please know that I will not hold you to our agreement."

"The future is not for us to see, but as of today, I can say that love has come and gone for me. I respect your decision to keep your past life private, but if the time ever comes and you wish to reunite with Ava's father, I will do everything in my power to assist you. I am a firm believer that true love happens only once and you cannot and should not deny it. I would give up my kingdom if I could have Maveryn back."

"Thank you, Sir, but that will not be happening anytime soon. I must leave you now, as Ava will be wakening soon."

"Thank you, Vela."

I found Mrs. Sharpe, Amma, and Emma having tea at the manor's kitchen table.

Rosalyn ran up to me. "Where were you, Mama?"

"I went for a little walk. How was your dress fitting?"

"I am good in it, Mama. And tomorrow is Amma's wedding."

"I know, darling. You will be beautiful. I see that Ava is still sleeping. Do you think that you can go back to your drawings while I have tea with the ladies?"

She whispered in my ear, "I am drawing a picture for Amma. Shhh."

I removed my boots and washed my hands at the big sink. "I am glad that you are all here. I have something to tell you."

Jannie arrived and asked how my outing was.

"It was interesting, to say the least. I ran into Lord Jeremy in the rose garden. He approached me with a very unexpected proposal. Please do not think less of me. He offered a solution to my situation, that of being an unwed mother with no means to support herself and her child. He suggested that the girls and I move into Avanloch and become parents to them. He asked if I would consider marriage, and after some thought, I agreed."

There were gasps all around except from Jannie, whom, I surmised, already knew about Jeremy's plans.

"Oh, Miss Vela, that is quite the offer I say, but you do not love him and he is so much older than you," Emma lamented.

"You are right, Emma. I do not love him, nor does he love me. Our hearts belong to others, one still alive and one departed. This is for the girls."

Jannie took my hand in hers and encouraged me to go on.

"We all know that this dear woman here will be retiring from her duties at Avanloch soon," I continued. "Jeremy does not wish to replace her with an unknown and is under the misguided assumption that I am up to the task. I do not think that anyone could take your place, Jannie, but perhaps with your guidance, I may one day be a poor substitute."

"I know that you will be a valuable asset to Avanloch and Mr. Jeremy, V. You will learn as you go, my dear, just as I did. I think that we are all in agreement that the important thing here is the children. Rosy should be in her father's house, though we will miss her dearly, as we will you and baby Ava. I shall do everything in my power to make your transition uneventful for you. You have my blessings."

"You will be Lady Vela of Avanloch!" Amma exclaimed.

"Oh my, I never thought of it that way," I said. "This is all too much! Perhaps I was too hasty in my acceptance. What was I thinking? I cannot be in charge of a household!"

"Nonsense," Jannie told me. "No one is expecting you to take over completely. Amma, Shalla, and the McDuffs will be there to steer you. Jeremy would not expect anything from you that you cannot handle."

"I will be so happy to be working for you, Ma'am," Amma said.

"No one will be working for me, Amma, and please never call me anything but V or Vela."

"Mama, Ava's up," said Rosalyn.

After I fed Ava and handed her over to Emma, I asked Rosalyn to come and sit with me in the sitting room. I asked, "How would you like to move back to the castle?"

She jumped off my lap and stood in front of me. Her lips were trembling and there were tears in her eyes. "Why, you mad at me, Mama? You don't want me now that Ava is your little girl?"

I gathered her stiff, sobbing body into my arms. "I am so sorry, Rosy. I said that all wrong. I am going to Avanloch with you, and so is Ava. We will all live there together with your father. I would never leave you, my darling."

"Promise, Mama?"

"I promise. Now what do you say?"

"Does my father want me to come?"

"Yes, he does, darling. And we are going to be yours and Ava's mother and father. We are going to get married, just like Amma and Johnny. Would you like to come to the church with us?"

"Can Ava come, too?"

"Of course she can. It is a very big house so I am going to need a lot of help. Do you think that you will be able to keep looking after Ava? It is a very big job for a little girl."

"I not so little, Mama. I got lost and scared in that house one day."

"Well, we will have to make sure that you never get lost again. I will tie a ribbon around your neck with bells on it . What do you think of that?"

"Just like the bells in Tinkerbelle?"

"Yes. That way, I will always know where you are when you ring them."

"Okay, Mama. When shall we go?"

"Tomorrow."

We had visited Reverend Peters and were to be married a week from today, which would be July 6. At first, he was very uncertain about our sudden decision to wed, but once he heard our reasoning, he agreed to perform the ceremony and offered his guidance.

Jeremy and I had walked the short distance to the chapel, and on our way home, he asked me if I had any misgivings. I told him that I was still apprehensive and scared, as I had always thought that I would marry for love. His words to me were, "Someday, I hope you will marry the man of your dreams.

As I told you before, I will not stand in your way. Until then, we will make a home for the girls and you will have all the security for your future that you require."

How could I argue with that?

I went to bed as soon as I had the girls settled. I soon found myself in the castle—at least that was where I thought I was. I was in a room I did not recognize. There were no furnishings in it; there was nothing that I could make out from the pale light coming in the window from the fading moon. I fled and found myself in another room….this one was in complete darkness. I could not see but felt that someone or something was watching me. Was I being chased or was I the pursuer? I had no control over my movements. I was being drawn by some unknown force. I heard my name being called, "Vienna, Vienna, come back, come home." I tried to move toward the voice but could not. Coldness had enveloped my body and yet I had the sensation of being on fire. I was panicking. I felt that I was surely going to die. The chilling fog was consuming me and drawing me down into some unknown abyss. The darkness was swallowing me and I was slipping into oblivion. Something was grabbing at me…

There was a bright light shining in my face. Little hands were shaking me.

"Mama, Mama, wake up. Ava is crying." Rosalyn was shining her Peter Pan flashlight on my eyes.

"It's okay, Rosy, Mama is awake now. I am sorry if I scared you."

"You had a bad dream, Mama. Ava is scared."

I crawled out of bed still in a stupor and picked Ava up. I asked Rosy if I had been screaming, and she said no, just calling out, and it woke her up. I thanked her for waking me and was sorry that I frightened her and Ava.

"It okay, Mama. I am going to wait for you in your bed and rest."

The moment her little head hit the pillow, she was fast asleep. This darling three-year-old was not only Ava's guardian, but now it appeared that she was also mine. I closed my heavy eyes while Ava nursed and I tried to relieve my nightmare. Before I had fallen asleep, I remembered that I was thinking I was making a huge mistake by marrying Jeremy. Would I live to regret it, just as I regretted fleeing from Rainey? Should I give up, go home, and beg Rainey to take me back? A thousand scenarios were running through my head and I resolved nothing before I fell into the gloom of the dream.

Yes, I would marry Jeremy and I would make a home for these two precious girls. Perhaps down the unknown road, I would find my love again, God willing.

Jannie woke us the next morning. "Are you ladies planning on sleeping all day? Have you forgotten what today is?"

Rosalyn poked her head out from under the quilt. "Auntie, is it Amma's wedding? Mama had a bad dream. I had to sleep here so she wouldn't be scared."

"Is that so? Thank heavens you were here."

I asked Jannie if we had overslept, and she said no, but we had better get a move on. It was already 9:30 and the ceremony was to begin at one. I sent Rosy into the tub and fed and dressed Ava, hoping that I would not have to redress her before we left. Rosy went down for breakfast, saying that she was too "cited to eat." By the time I had bathed and dressed in the new frock that I bought several weeks ago, Rosy was back and eager to put on her new dress. I divided her natural curly hair into strands of ringlets and fastened with yellow and white daisies that matched her dress. Amma had given her a gold locket as a gift, and as I tried to do up the clasp, she twirled around, doing a little jig.

"Keep still, you silly goose," I said. "You will have lots of time for dancing at the wedding."

"What's silly goose, Mama?" Rosy asked. "Do I look good?"

"You are beautiful, darling. Now let's collect Ava and make sure that those men have picked all of the flowers for your basket. You will remember to toss the petals as you walk down the aisle, right?"

"Of course, just like you showed me how. Let's go, let's go. Duffy is coming in his cart. Can Ava come with me?"

"We will walk up with Jannie and Uncle John. I will see you up there. Come here and give me a big hug. I love you, Rosy."

"I love you, Mama."

It was a beautitiful day for a wedding. The sun shone brightly on the happy couple. Rosy did flower girls everywhere proud. Her friend from the village, Edward, was the ring bearer. He was also the groom's nephew. He and Rosy held hands afterward and were partners for practically all the dances. Her father was allotted one waltz and, with Ava in my arms, so was I.

After the wedding feast, Jeremy asked me to join him in a proposal for the newlyweds. Johnny had been apprenticing in Waverly as a carpenter. Jeremy asked him if he would like to come to work for him, as there were to be many changes to the estate and we could definitely use his expertise. He was hopeful that Amma would be taking on the role as my assistant and perhaps they would like to have the Willowisp Manor as their new home. They were both too surprised to speak. I also had no knowledge of the generous offer. Willowisp was a smaller manor house than Brackenshire and had not been occupied for twenty years or more. I knew little of its interior and had only passed by it the day that I had visited Maveryn's resting place.

"The place will take some work to make it livable again, but I am sure that you two will rise to the task," said Jeremy. "Meanwhile, you may have rooms in the castle if you like. I am sure that Vela would like to have Amma close by, as she has been used to having Emma near."

"Thank you, Sir. Your offer is very generous, and if Amma is agreeable, we would be forever beholden to you," said Johnny.

He looked at Amma, who could no longer contain her excitement and burst out, "I love that house, Sir Jeremy! Every time I pass near it, I think what a shame that no one is living in it. It is not in so much disrepair as you think."

Johnny was laughing. "I think that she is in agreement to be sure, Sir. I think that perhaps we will take a gander up there now before we leave and just see how much work is required to make it livable. What do you say, honey?"

Amma had already changed into her traveling clothes and the two of them ran off hand in hand to check out their new home. I told Jeremy that he had truly given them a fine wedding gift and I was looking forward to having them as neighbors. I made my excuses as I left to find the girls. I was very happy for the bride and groom, but on the other hand, I wish that it was me and my love who were running off to start a new life together. I could not stop the flow of tears.

We all slept soundly that night. In less than a week, I would be the newlywed, but it would certainly not be the wedding of my dreams.

The next day after church, Rosalyn and I walked up to Avanloch to see what had to be done for our arrival. Jeremy met us at the front entrance and welcomed us. I had never entered through the huge doors before, so I had not had this view of the grand hallway and staircase before. I had always used the "servants' entrance" and the back stairs that led into the kitchen from upstairs. It was truly a remarkable room. It was referred to as the reception hall. In the center of the room was a colossal, round oak table with an extremely large vase of seasonal flowers in the center. Several maroon velveteen settees were situated throughout the room. The ceiling was at least 40 feet in height, but I was a very poor judge of height and length, so it could have been less or more. Dropping from the elaborate ornamental ceiling was a massive chandelier. A worn Heirloom rug was centered on the hardwood floor beneath the table. Bronze and marble busts stood on their own or sat on small mantels. I recognized Mozart, Julius Caesar, and Aphrodite. On the flocked walls were portraits of family, and queens and kings. Several ornamental plants sat in corners. That would be one of my first duties as lady of the house, to replace them with real ones, I told myself. All of the doors that led to the various other rooms were closed, giving the hall a cold, enclosed feeling. I thought that I would like to have most of them open. The *pièce de résistance*, however, was the grand staircase. It wound its way through 5 landings, each with eight steps separating them. The original staircase had been torn down after the end of World War I and had been replaced with this elaborate structure. The design had been copied from a mansion in Savannah, Georgia, that Jeremy's grandfather had envied. The walls had been plastered and papered with specialty scenes taken from Scotland's past, which included castles, pastoral fields, fauna, and hunters and foxes, birds, and many breeds of dogs. A textile company in London had been commissioned to bring the whole wall to life, and indeed they had. The stairs were made of a local marble stone in shades of greens and blues. The delicate banister curved around and around, and was ten times the one that was at the Palace in Bridge. Jeremy informed me that the wood was teak and had been carved by a master craftsman from Rome. Apparently, it had taken him several years. The copper scroll work on the grill appeared to be done in hieroglyphics. Jeremy said he knew nothing about it, but it would surely be in the history of the house papers if ever I decided that I wanted to explore them. I already knew that I did. I also knew that the girls and I would not be using these stairs regularly. I confessed my misgivings of having Rosalyn playing on them and Jeremy suggested that we could have them cordoned off for the time being.

"Yes," I agreed. "We will need to barricade the bottom of the stairwell also. Rosy is a very obedient child, but I do not want to risk her falling. We won't have to worry over Ava for a year or so. I am glad that the banister at the top is high and that it would be impossible to get through the railings. Now, where has that girl got to?"

Jeremy asked me if I wanted to familiarize myself with the rest of the house.

"No, not today," I said. "There is plenty of time for that. It is all too overwhelming for me. Just take me to the east wing, if that is to be ours. There you are, Rosalyn. Have you been bothering Mrs. McDuff for one of her treats?"

Shalla and Rosy were making their way down the long corridor from the kitchen. How she had snuck away so quickly was beyond me.

Jeremy nodded at me. "Yes, I will have Duffy work on the barricades immediately. Rosalyn, you must listen to your mother and the rest of the household as to where you are allowed to go. Do you remember the time we lost you?"

"I listen to Mama and Amma and Shalla," she replied. "I not get lost anymore."

"Good." I took her little hand and told her that we were going to go up the "big stairs" today, but she was not to use them when she was alone and we were going to put a door on them just in case she forgot. We would mostly be using the lift to go up and down. It was very easy to operate and safe.

"My legs are still dancing. Don't go fast."

Laughing, I said to her, "Do you mean you are still tired from all the dancing at the wedding?"

She nodded. "Will there be dancing when you marry Father?"

"No, we are going to have a very quiet wedding. Only Jannie, Uncle John, you, and Ava will be there. Then we will come back here and have a nice supper."

Jeremy agreed and said he would talk to Mary about preparing a celebration, and perhaps she, Duffy, Henry, Mrs. Sharpe Emma, and Shalla could sit down with us. I told him that I thought that was a wonderful idea, and Millie would probably like to come, too.

The second floor consisted of twelve bedrooms. Jeremy had a suite in the north wing and I was to have the two in the south wing. Rosy's room was connected by a door next to mine and a shared bathroom. I had decided that I would keep Ava in my room for the time being, but that she could also have a crib in Rosy's room, as it was very large and had also been used as a schoolroom. There would be no schooling going on here for a long time. In between the north and south wings were eight other rooms; Ash had a two-room suite in the east wing. She had her own private bath, as did Jeremy and I. The other six shared three common baths. The northwest wing housed eight rooms plus the lift and the southeast wing had only five rooms plus the small foyer. My bedroom had windows facing to the west. It consisted of a large, four-poster canopy bed that had what appeared to be mosquito netting wrapped around each post, or perhaps it was just for affect. There was a huge wardrobe and a silk screen decorated with a Chinese motif for privacy. Several dressers, one with a mirror and settee, made up the remainder. It did not appear that the lower windows could be opened. A crank was in place for the top panes of glass to be slightly released. Jeremy asked me if it was to my liking and I said that it certainly was. Then he led me into what he called "my sitting room," which had south- and east-facing windows. I loved it immediately.

My eyes scanned the walls that were papered in pastel-flowered patterns. Above the wainscoting were portraits of Jeremy's family. He told me that I may remove them and place them in other parts of the house. I thought that I might just take him up on that idea. Here, the windows had been modernized, I was pleased to discover, as I swung two of them open. The breeze that came in was a warm welcome to the stuffiness of the bedroom. A writing desk occupied the space between the windows. Two overstuffed easy chairs sat on either side of a small table. A chaise lounge sat under a gold-gilded floor lamp. All of the upholstery was pale yellows and oranges, which matched the wallpaper, with red rose pillows enhancing the look. Colorful throws added to the inviting atmosphere. Jeremy opened two wooden doors and showed me where the ledgers were kept. They also housed a library of time-worn books of which I would be eager to peruse. I approached a door that was locked and asked Jeremy what was behind it. He said that Uncle John was going to be going over the finances with me and that he would explain the locked door. Curious.

"What do you mean finances? I do not want anything to do with the assets of this house or especially your business."

"Well, my dear, you have no choice. You are to know everything regarding the maintenance, the staff, and the day-to-day operations, and I am afraid that includes monetary measures. You will have several working accounts and, of course, cash, but that will all be explained to you, perhaps as soon as tomorrow."

"I thought that I was to be in charge of the house? You said nothing about being involved with money matters. What else are you keeping from me?"

He smiled, but it was not amusing to me. "I believe that you are getting yourself all worked up about nothing. You are not required to be an accountant; that is John's job. I want you informed about certain aspects, that is all. You will not be required to do any banking, just to keep track of your expenditures. I think that we had agreed that you would be modernizing Avanloch and bringing her into the twentieth century. Did you think that you would be accomplishing that on your good looks alone?"

I was shocked at what he was insinuating. "I am not dumb, Sir. Of course I knew that there would be money passing hands, but you make it sound as if I am going to have a say in all the expenditures. How could you trust me with that kind of information? Are you not afraid that I could abscond with all your inheritance?"

Now he was out and out laughing. "Oh, Vela, what a breath of fresh air you are! This ole house will never be sad again. And, of course, I do not think you are stupid; I would never make that mistake. I am sorry if I was rude. The thought of you robbing me blind never even occurred to me. You are the least likely of anyone whom I have ever known who would do such a thing. Now, can we call a truce for today? I look forward to many lively discussions with you. Look, Rosalyn has fallen asleep on the divan."

"Yes, I will take my leave now. I am just saying, though, that you really do not know me or what I may be capable of. Still waters run deep. Now pick up that sleepyhead and we'll be on our way." I felt like I had just scolded my father.

Avanloch had not been reconstructed as a military fortress, although it had been rebuilt on the ruins of the sixteenth-century Kings Down Castle. Upon the end of the Scottish wars, the original lands and buildings were left in total disrepair. Jeremy's great ancestors had left the ruins to rot and had taken up residences in other more hospitable lands. Around about the year 1840, Jeremy's great-great grandfather started to rebuild on the Kings Down site. Upon his passing in 1855, his son, Stewart, took up the challenge. He renamed it Avanloch in honor of his wife, Avaleena, who was the daughter of a Spanish count. Little progress was made in the years leading up to World War I. However, by 1920, construction had begun again with funds that the family had accrued from the shipping business they had started in the early 1900s. It would seem that war was profitable to some. Robert Bruce McAllister, Jeremy's grandfather, saw the castle rise to his expectations before his death in 1942. He was ninety and his wife, Mary, had passed away three years earlier. They lived in residence with their son, Donavan Bruce, and his wife, Lady Audrey Ash, who remained to complete the interior to its pre-1950s standards. Jeremy and his sister, Ash, had been born in the castle and began remodeling upon the death of their parents. Ceilings were lowered, cold, hard, stone floors were replaced with six different types of hardwood, and most of the windows had been replaced and could now be opened but were still covered in heavy fabric. The plumbing had received the biggest upgrade and had seen ten more bathrooms installed. The kitchen had undergone a major improvement and boasted all of the latest technology. It had two commercial-sized electric ranges with two additional wall ovens. The coal-burning stove still stood and was used in cool weather for keeping kettles hot and providing extra heat. There was a still an oversized fireplace in use. It and others like it were part of the heritage and ambiance of the castle. Jeremy preferred to call it Avanloch and not a castle. Ash called it a monstrosity but seemed to be very fond of her old home and boasted about its charm to her friends. When she wasn't traipsing around the world with her acting troupe, she lived in a small flat in London.

Entrance into Avanloch's grounds was through a large iron gate at the bottom of the property. It was usually open, as there was no fear that an invasion was going to take place. Seven-foot high rock walls had once surrounded the castle, the manor houses, and a great portion of the acreage. They had not been maintained, as the need was not there except for 50 feet on each side of the entrance. The rock work was covered in ivies, blackberries, and anything else that chose to grow on it. The Village of Domne was a short distance from the gates. Residents did not like the name, so it was just referred to as the village. A paved, circular road led to the entrance of the castle. At the gates, a road veered off to Brackenshire Manor. Avanloch was situated on a hill and overlooked the valley and the village to the east. The landscape was made up of rolling lawns with hedges of yew or boxwood that circled the drive. Large native trees lined the paths that led to the garages and other buildings. The barns were between Avanloch and Brackenshire. In the center of the curved drive was a huge, four-tiered fountain with a water nymph perching on top, pouring out water. She seemed to be mistress to a host of fairies playing in the pools. Rosalyn had asked me what her name was and, off the top of my head, I had replied Laralei. She liked the name and then wanted to give all of her friends names also. I told her that we would have to think on that.

We had spent Monday packing, and on Tuesday morning, Rosalyn and I made the walk to get settled in before Jannie arrived with Ava. The children's furniture had already been delivered and set up by Duffy and Henry. There were twelve rounded steps circling the main entrance. They were flanked on each side by two very statuesque stone lions reclining on marble platforms with stately Roman columns surrounding them. I thought that they looked a little threatening, but they were friends of Rosy's. She called them Zeus and Zoar. I admitted to her that I did not know who Zoar was, and she said she didn't either but that he had to have a name. She climbed the steps to where she could talk to them and gave each one a hug. She knew that I wanted to go in the back door, so she joined me as we made our way around the mansion. I said as we passed the family dining room that we must have French doors installed here. Of course, she wanted to know what French doors were.

We were greeted warmly by Mrs. D and Shalla, who said they had been anxiously awaiting our coming. I refused tea for the time being, saying that I must see that Ava's room was all ready, as she would be here any minute. They followed us upstairs to be sure that I would be pleased with the way they had set up the furnishings.

"I am very pleased," I said. "You didn't leave anything for me to do now, did you?"

"It is my job to see that you have very little work to do, Ma'am," replied Shalla. "You will have enough with the children."

"Shalla, do I look like a ma'am to you? That makes me feel very old. What do I have to do to convince you to call me, Vela?"

"Nothing, I will try my best."

"Thank you. What do you call Jannie?"

"Miss Jannie."

"I will be Mrs. McAllister in a few days, but I do not wish to be miss or missis, okay? Just Vela or V."

"What will the mister think?"

"He will be happy if I am happy. Now, soon, we must talk about a replacement for Amma. Do either of you have anyone in mind? I prefer to have someone who is very conscientious and could really use the work. She does not have to be trained, as she will learn just as I have to learn the ways of this big house."

"Ma'am…I mean, Vela, I did not know that we were losing Amma. Is she moving far away with her new husband?"

"Oh no, she is to be my assistant. She and Johnny are going to be living at Willowisp just as soon as it is livable. So, we will need someone to help you with your duties. In fact, I am not too sure that we won't be hiring temporary staff if Mr. Jeremy wants to start entertaining. I just hope that won't be for a long time. I am very happy with the way things are right now."

Jannie arrived with Ava, who was fast asleep, so we decided to have tea in the drawing room. We let her sleep in her carriage while Rosalyn made herself comfortable on the floor with her crayons and books. First, she informed Ava that this was her new home and Mama's, too.

Ava woke up just as Uncle John walked in. He asked me if I was ready to have a look at the books. He sat down to enjoy a cup of tea while I protested.

"I do not see any reason for my being involved with the finances. That is your job, is it not? Jannie, how much were you involved?"

"I only kept track of the household's expenditures, but you are to be Jeremy's wife and heir, so you will have a bigger responsibility. It won't be as difficult as you may think, dear."

John agreed with her. "Yes, you have nothing to fear, V. Jeremy wants you to have a working knowledge of the affairs of the estate and the shipping company. Be assured that you will not be required to participate in enormous projects unless you choose to be. Mrs. McDuff has her own monthly allowance for the provisions of the kitchen and storage cupboards. The maids report to her as to what is needed, but she would prefer it if they reported to you from now on. You and she can haggle that out. Now, if you are ready, we should get a move on."

Jannie said that she would take Rosalyn and Ava for a walk around the grounds.

I followed Uncle John upstairs to the sitting room where Jeremy and I had left off yesterday. First, he went over the household ledger with me. Everything seemed simple enough. Mrs. D's accounts, Duffy's accounts, which included maintenance of the grounds, feed and fodder for the farm animals, and miscellaneous things like petrol and coal. At least, I didn't have to have a hand in that. I was to have access to all if I desired, and I assured him that I wouldn't, but he said to give myself time and I might just take an interest in everything.

There, we were done, that wasn't so bad. I thanked him and thought that we could now get on with other things.

He took my hand and said, "Hold on there, Missy, we haven't finished. There is the matter of your allowances." He opened up another ledger and there, in bold letters, were the headings: "Vela, Rosalyn, and Ava for the month of July." The sum of $1,000 was entered into each account.

"What is this?" I questioned, stunned.

"Your monthly stipends. As you can see, I am translating the monies into dollars so that you will not be confused."

"Monthly! You must be kidding? How could we possibly spend that much every month? Is there insanity in the family or are they just spendthrifts?"

"There is no insanity." Uncle John was laughing. "There is plenty of money, thanks to the shipping business, and the farm is also turning a profit. You do know that the dairy and the flour mill in the village are owned by Avanloch, don't you?"

"No, of course not. How would I know that? Does Jeremy own the people, too?"

"He pays them all a very decent wage and he would object highly to your suggestion that he owns them."

"I am sure that he would. I didn't mean it quite like that. I know him to be a very decent and honorable man. But you haven't answered me yet. Why the big sum of money for me and the girls?"

"It is there if needed. What is not used will go into their college accounts. They will require day-to-day things like clothes, books, and toys. You may spend yours however you desire, or just bank it. Jeremy does not want you to have to ask for a thing."

"I am sorry, but I find the whole thing ludicrous. There is no way in hell that I could even spend that much money, or would even want to. I suppose that once I get started on doing some upgrades to the castle, I will be needing funds."

"Oh no, this is your own personal money. You have an unlimited account for whatever you chose to do to Avanloch."

"I give up! I am going to have to think a long time on this. If I am going to have free range with infinite dollars, who is to say that I won't go crazy and bring unimaginable changes to the house, castle, whatever?"

"Go for it! We could use some upgrades to the manor also and, of course, you will be overseeing the improvements to Willowisp."

"What? Do you and Jeremy think that I know anything about construction?"

"Just kidding, dear. You and I will see that Johnny and Amma don't go overboard. The reason that everything has to be accounted for is for the government you know."

"Yes, I am well aware that no matter what country one is from, the authorities want their share of the rewards. What say does Ash have in all of this?"

"She wants nothing to do with any aspects of Avanloch. She is partner in the business and so she has to contribute her share of the profits to its upkeep. Not really, but that is just to keep her honest. After all, she does use the place as a vacation home for herself and appointed friends. I am sorry, but you will have to put up with her whenever she chooses to show up."

"I am sure Ash and I can come to some civil understanding regarding her visits. I will not tolerate her taking advantage of the help, however. They are not here for her and her friends' convenience. Now, are we done? I am sure that I will be calling on you for help very soon. I only hope that I do not have nightmares revolving around numbers. What is with this locked door? I have visions of a crazy family member being held hostage in there."

Again, I had made John smile. He produced a large skeleton key from the ring that was in the desk. "Nothing as sinister as that, V, but I think you will find what it is housing intriguing."

There was nothing behind the doors except another door, which he opened with a switch on the side of it. To my amazement, it slid to one side and there appeared a dumbwaiter. "Well, so this is what has to be kept under lock and key, and where does it come out on the main floor?"

"One of Rosalyn's nannies, I forget which one, asked that the door be locked in case the child got curious and climbed into it. The exit point is in the hallway between the formal dining room and the large drawing room. Are you ready to see what lies behind the wall?"

"The wall? Whatever do you mean?"

Uncle John told me to stay put and went back into the sitting room, and in seconds, the wall to my right opened up to reveal a black void. He rejoined me, reached inside the emptiness, and found a switch that illuminated a stairwell.

"A secret passageway!" I exclaimed in delight. "Of course, it is a castle after all. Can I explore? I am dying to see where it goes. This is just like in the movies." I felt like a little child.

"Do you have the time to go exploring, V, or should we leave it for another day? I am sure that Jeremy would like to be your guide. You see, there are two other hidden stairwells, one in the north tower and one on the main floor. They all meet up at a point in a secret room in the cellar. There is also another dumbwaiter that starts in the tower and has a stop at Jeremy's quarters. He will be home on Thursday and will acquaint you with all the idiosyncrasies of Avanloch."

"Oh, all right. I suppose I should rescue Jannie from the girls."

Back in my sitting room, John showed me how to activate the opening of the wall to the stairs. There was a button hidden in the wallpaper, which was almost impossible to detect.

"As if I am ever going to need an escape route," I said.

"Here's hoping that we will never be invaded. I doubt that they were ever used in days gone by, but in case of fire or some unforeseen event, you know that they are there. I believe that it is mandatory for all castles to have certain features."

"You mean there is a criterion that has to be met in order to have castle ranking?"

"Not sure, and certainly, it is not important to the McAllisters. If it wasn't for the stone and rock that is the backbone of Avanloch—oh, and the turrets and towers—it could be just an ordinary residence."

"I don't think anyone would ever call Avanloch a run-of-the-mill dwelling. After all, how many homes have manors, carriage houses, and a small town in their description of their property?"

We returned to the main floor via the elevator, which, I was pleased to see, was in good working condition. Rosalyn ran over and hugged me, and informed that Ava was asleep. I thanked Jannie for taking care of the girls. She answered that it was her pleasure and would do so at a moment's notice.

"I think that Uncle John has a few plans for you and him coming up soon. You both deserve a long vacation."

"Oh, we won't be going far. Once you are all settled in here and I feel that you will be able to handle it all on your own, we may venture a trip to Canada."

"You mean that you would visit Mother and Father? They would be so thrilled to see you. I hope you will go and soon."

"Oh, not that soon, dear. Perhaps in the spring. We should be going, John. I have to run some errands for Mrs. Sharpe in the village. Do you need anything, V? Will you be all right here alone this evening?"

"Of course I will be…we will be. And we will hardly be alone. The Duffys are here. I am sure Rosalyn will keep me very busy. We have some putting away to do in our rooms. Thank you again and we will see you tomorrow."

I felt like I hadn't held Ava all day, and yet it had only been a few hours. I picked her up and sat in the big green chair that had room for us all. Rosalyn cuddled up and said she hoped that we would be having supper soon, as her tummy was grumbling. No sooner had she spoken when Mrs. D entered and asked us if we would be ready to dine in fifteen minutes. I said I would feed Ava and then we would be down. Shalla had gone home, so it would be the Duffys and us. I had expressed my desire to have our meals in the kitchen when Mr. Jeremy wasn't home. It was so warm and inviting there, and reminded me of home.

My tour of Avanloch started in the kitchen, which led to the family dining room through swinging doors, and to the sitting room, library and the small drawing room where guests were received and informal teas were held. I called this side of the castle "the right-north wing." It was much smaller than its counterpart. These were the only five rooms that I was at all familiar with. We entered into the reception hall from the drawing room, and walked down the long corridor to the pantries, storage, and closets that were outside of the kitchen. The staircase started in the far northwest corner of the kitchen . We had now done an about-turn and were heading back up the corridor. The Duffys' suite was next to the second back door and was hardly ever used by anyone except them. I believed that the second secret underground stairway was here somewhere, but I didn't question Jeremy as to its whereabouts. There was a large, unused room complete with bedroom furnishings next to the elevator and dumbwaiter. I was told that it was used occasionally by staff who would sometimes spend the night. Next was a small room that had a linen closet and serving carts that was adjacent to the formal dining room. Jeremy informed me that the table, china cabinet, and sideboards had been in the family since the reconstruction. The hardwood floor was carpeted in a rich, dark, blue pattern, which seemed to match the dinnerware that was visible through the glass cabinet. Silver settings rested on the sideboards with gold-trimmed stemware. The table was draped with a lace cloth, embroidered napkins, and a beautiful blue-flowered tureen sat in the center. A candelabra with at least fifty glowing lamps hung from the lowered gold-decorated ceiling. Large, oval glitz-trimmed mirrors adorned the walls, as did famous prints from Rembrandt and Renoir. French doors opened onto a veranda on the west wall. All in all, the room was very pleasant. I looked forward to entertaining friends here.

We exited through a south-facing door and found ourselves in the games room. A large billiards table, several card tables, and reading chairs with their own lamps inhabited this space. Two comfortable-looking chesterfields sat in front of the largest television that I had ever seen. Across the hall was an empty room. It was bright, clean, and naturally lighted from the windows that were uncovered. Jeremy told me that it had once been known as the smoking room. He had it fumigated, repainted, and carpeted, and not a hint of smoke lingered. I asked him if we might turn it into a downstairs playroom for the girls, and he thought it was a wonderful idea. So, I guess this would be my first project. The music room was next. It housed a grand piano and a magnificent harp among other nondescript instruments. I asked Jeremy about the harp and he said that it belonged to Maveryn. I did not question him further, as I could tell that he did not want to discuss the matter. Next was a small den, and in between it and Jeremy's office was a boarded-up door that seemed to lead outside. I asked him what was behind the boards and he said nonchalantly, "The conservatory is what used to be there."

"Use to be? What's in there now?"

"It's still there, just boarded up."

"May I inquire why?"

"Of course. It is to be your house, too, after all. After my grandmother fell through one of the windows and was mortally wounded, my grandfather had it closed up, and there it sits, untouched since 1939."

"How tragic for your family. I would dearly love to have seen it. Do you think that it will ever be restored? I only ask because I helped my father restore the conservatory in the house my family owns in Bridge Falls. We spent months working on it to have it ready for a Christmas present for my mother."

And there, I had, without wanting to, brought Rainey back into the picture, remembering all the evenings that we had spent sitting hand in hand, listening to quiet music, the soothing sounds of the small fountain, and the songs of the love birds. I sighed and opened the double doors to the grand drawing room.

If I didn't know better, I would have thought that I had entered into a Roman theater or a Sheik's harem or a 1920s dance hall. I guess it was a combination of all three. There were stairs leading up to a small balcony that overlooked a stage, heavy-drapery-enclosed small rooms, and Gothic columns appeared to be holding the ornate ceiling from falling down. There was a red grand piano with enormous candelabra adorning it. Elaborate chandeliers and strange-colored garlands boasting foreign-looking insignias hung from the detailed ceiling. I immediately thought that Liberace must have designed this Hollywood extravaganza. The whole room was red and gold—walls, sofas, chairs from every period in time, fabrics, trimmings, pillows…everything with hints of black here and there. It was mind-boggling. I could not absorb it all, nor did I want to. I turned to exit the way we had come in. Jeremy noticed how perplexed I was and asked if I had enough for one day.

"Yes, enough. I now understand why Avanloch looks so lopsided. That room is as large as the whole right wing. Who designed and decorated it? And is it ever used?"

Jeremy laughed. "Not by me. Ash and her troupe make use of it occasionally, I am told. I am afraid that the honor of its structure and contents goes to my great ancestors. We were never allowed in it when we were growing up. Of course, that never stopped Ash. I think that maybe that room is responsible for her career choices."

"Who would ever think that the interior of this place could be so stunning when the outside is cold stone and grey? There are rooms within rooms, probably a mile of corridors, and things I have yet to discover. One thing is missing, though: where is the moat and wasn't there something known as a 'keep'?"

"Oh, there was a moat complete with draw bridge and chains—no alligators, though. That was a long, long time ago. The 'keep' is actually what the castle or fortress is referred to by some. I am afraid we have come into the twentieth century. In a way, it is sad, and I am mostly to blame for that, but I choose to live in the present. Well, most of the time anyhow." He walked me to the lift and presented me with a ring that held about a dozen keys. "They are all numbered with the various upstairs rooms. This one," and he separated the key that was for room seven, "may prove to be of particular interest to you. It is always locked. Everything in there is at your disposal. You may even find a suitable outfit that will save you from venturing into Waverly. I believe I am not wrong when I say that you like vintage clothing."

"Yes, I do, but whatever are you talking about? Is the room a closet? And whose is it?"

"My grandmother's. No one else has ever been her size, but you are. Ash pointed that out to me. I hope you will enjoy the rest of your day. Until supper then."

I said to Rosalyn, "You know your numbers, don't you, sweetie?"

"Yes, Mama," she replied. "I can count 1, 2, 4 6, 7, 9, 10. Is that good?"

"Pretty good, dear. Can you help Mama find number seven room?" It will soon be supper but I have to see what is in number seven." The upstairs rooms encircled the stairway. I had never paid any attention to the numbers before, but surely must have noticed that our rooms were 10, 11, and 12. My sitting room was the last of the south loop. On the immediate east wall was a small alcove that adjoined the two wings. There were no windows in it, just settees and a small library. I thought that it was a complete waste of space, but then it did separate my quarters from the east wing that contained Ash's suite and several other bedrooms, which, I now noticed across the wide expanse, were rooms one to four.

Rosalyn ran ahead of Ava and me and shouted, "Here are seven, Mama."

I unlocked the door and we entered into a large boudoir.

"Who sleeps here, Mama?" Rosalyn wanted to know.

"No one anymore. Your great-grandmother used to. Do you know what a grandmother is, Rosy?"

She shook her head no.

I explained as best I could. Poor child was just like me, no grandmothers. She asked if she could sit at the mirrored dresser and comb her hair with the pretty brush. I checked it out to make sure that it was clean, for as far as I knew, nothing had been touched in almost twenty-five years. That was not the case. Everything was immaculate, as if Miss Mary was still in attendance. I proceeded to open the closet doors, not knowing what to expect.

"Oh my, oh my," I stammered.

"What's 'ohmy,' Mama?"

"Come and look, Rosy."

"Is this a store, Mama?"

"No, honey, it is not a store. These clothes all belonged to your great-grandmother and your daddy says that I should wear some of them. What do you think?"

"I like the red dress and the purple hat and shoes."

"Hand me one of those shoes. Thank you. Oh, I won't be wearing any of these shoes. Look how small. Maybe someday they will fit you," I said, laughing as she put them on and went clopping across the room.

I found a light, cream-colored, linen a-line dress that would be suitable for the wedding but was sure that it would be too small. I found a suitable petticoat and tried them on with Rosalyn giving me instructions. I looked in the full-length mirror and could not believe my eyes. I had not wanted to see myself since shortly after Ava was born. I only looked at my reflection when I combed my hair, which was not in good condition, so I usually just pinned it up. But who was this waif peering back at me. I turned to Rosy and said, "Is this me? Is this your mama?"

"You silly," she answered. "Here are some necklaces." She had opened one of the drawers to find an array of colorful trinkets.

I was still in dismay over my wretched body. The dress hung on me. Where was the once robust girl with the laughing eyes and the raven hair? Where was Vienna?

Mrs. D and Shalla were sitting at the oversized table, playing a game of cards.

"What's the matter with you, child?" Mrs. D asked. "You look out of sorts."

"I need to weigh myself," I replied. "Where is there a scale?"

"In the far corner of the pantry. Shall I fetch it for you, Miss Vela?"

"No thanks, Shalla. I will find it. Rosalyn, mind the ladies. I will be right back."

I returned and asked how to transfer pounds from kilograms. They hadn't a clue.

"Why didn't somebody tell me how skinny I am? I look like death warmed over."

"Oh, Missy, you're not that bad. A few extra pounds wouldn't hurt any, though. You are probably just run ragged, what with the bairns and the move is all," Mrs. D said. "Now, come along to supper then. Duffy and the mister are waiting."

"Will you help me to put some weight on, Mrs. D?" I asked.

"To be sure, luv. Bring the vittles, Shalla."

We all sat down at the table and helped ourselves. Jeremy asked Rosalyn how her day had gone. She said, "Fine. Mama and Ava and I found the clothes room. Mama said she is too skinny. She wants to look like somebody named…what name, Mama?"

I hadn't realized that I had spoken aloud. "Oh, nobody, honey. I want to look healthy, is all. I need to get fatter."

She found that amusing. "You mean like Bully the cow?"

We all laughed.

"Sort of, dear. Jeremy, you can help me perhaps. I need to know how to transfer kilograms into pounds." He told me how and I did the math. "Oh dear, no wonder I look so frail. I am only 107 pounds! I use to weigh 140 and I was very healthy! Hand me the potatoes please, Duffy."

"Some people would give their eye teeth to be slim, Vela. You can't do it all in one sitting you know," Jeremy said, trying to convince me.

"But it is not me," I countered. "Even your grandmother's dress was loose on me."

"You found something to your liking then for tomorrow?"

"It will do. I will find a nice shawl to cover up my slenderness."

"You will be lovely, Miss Vela. Will you let me do your hair?"

"Yes, Miss Shalla, I would love for you to fix my hair."

She blushed, but I was hoping to make a point and to get her to quit calling me "miss." The eve of my so-called wedding was spent in the drawing room, sitting quietly and listening to music on the radio. When it was time for the girls' bedtime, we said good night to Jeremy. He escorted us to the lift, saying that he hoped we would have a good night's sleep. I didn't think that would be possible.

When we alighted from the elevator, I took stock of the rest of the west wing. To my right was number five, Jeremy's rooms. On the other side of the elevator was the locked number six. I had inquired of Uncle John why the room was locked and he had told me that the ceiling was caving in and was not safe. I wondered why there were only four rooms in the east wing. Most curious, when there were eight on the west.

Tomorrow, I would be getting married. I was sure that I would not sleep. However, after the made-up fairy tale that I composed for Rosalyn every night, I found that I was indeed sleepy, retired to my bed with a novel, and soon fell into a deep slumber. Ava's crying awoke me at 4 A.M. I was surprised to find that I had slept without dreaming of Rainey, which would have been a nightmare.

Chapter Fourteen

Life as Lady Vela McAllister

*S*o *this is what it feels like to be married. No different than yesterday, except I now had a Mrs. in front of my name*, I thought. The ceremony went smooth as silk. Ava slept through it and even Rosalyn was still. When Reverend Peters told Jeremy that he could kiss the bride (which was customary, but in our case, it should not have been), he kissed my forehead. That was as far as anything would ever go in this relationship. Rosy insisted upon throwing rose petals at us, which, I must say, released the pent-up tension that I was experiencing. Henry had driven us to the chapel in the sedan, and was waiting to take us to Avanloch and the supper that was waiting for us.

Along with Jannie and Uncle John, Henry, Emma and Millie, Mrs. Sharpe, Amma, the McDuffs, and Reita, the part-time cook, we sat down to a delicious meal that had been prepared. Mrs. D and Reita had cooked a turkey with all the trimmings, as they knew that it was one of my favorite dinners. A small wedding cake that Mrs. Sharpe had made was a delightful surprise. Rosalyn asked why there were no candles on it. Somehow, she also said the right things to amuse us, though in her mind, she was dead serious. We spent the rest of the evening in the parlor, where we were presented with a lovely photograph album that had been assembled by Emma. It contained pictures of Jeremy when he was young and a few of me that Jannie had taken on my previous visits to Scotland, as well as Rosalyn's and Ava's. There was plenty of room for many years to come. John was the photographer for the night and I insisted that everyone be included, as they were all our family. The photo of Jeremy and me was not the wedding picture of my dreams. I went to bed with a heavy heart. Knowing that the girls would always be taken care of was little consolation, but as I had told myself many times before, I was the only one who made the bed that I must lie in.

My daily routine consisted of breakfast with Jeremy (when he was home) and Rosalyn. After Ava was fed, bathed, and put down for her morning nap, Rosy and I would venture outside to do some exploring. Shelley and Keats always attended us with their usual playfulness. Rosy asked if they could come and live in the castle, and I told her that I thought that was a splendid idea but that we must consult her father. He was agreeable, as long as they would act respectably. We promised that they would and that they could sleep in the alcove next to the elevator. It might take a little time to train them, though. Afterward, Jeremy told me that he had been a little worried about the security when he was away but would feel better now that the dogs would be our protectors. He thanked me for coming up with the idea and I promptly told him that it was his daughter's idea.

He didn't seem surprised and said, "Maveryn has been worried also, but now she will be able to rest, knowing that you and her beloved dogs are all under one roof." He quickly excused himself and left me wondering once more.

I knew that he had been seeing an analyst, as he called her, in Waverly and wondered if it was because he could not let go of Maveryn and that was why he still talked about her in the present.

I could probably use some of her counsel myself. I believed that I held my depressing moods from everyone sufficiently, as I really had become good at faking my feelings. No one had a clue as to how I felt when I was alone. The trick was to concentrate on the tasks of everyday life and keep active so that my mind wouldn't wander back to 1961.

The summer was unreasonably hot. Our jaunts through the gardens were limited to the morning hours. By one o'clock, we were seeking the cool shelter of the castle, which stayed at a moderate temperature thanks to the overhead fans and the stone structure. One night in late August, we received our first threat of rain in two months. It came on us suddenly in the form of an electric storm. For hours, the sky was racked with discharges of lightning and the rumbling of distant thunder followed close behind. I loved the dynamic energy that accompanied the storm, and yet it made my hair stand on end. When I was a young girl living in the prairies, I used to hide under the bed during such storms, covering my ears and crying. Mother could do nothing to coax me to come out. The thunderstorms that we had in Bridge Falls were less intense but still electrifying. Rainey had relayed his love of the weather phenomenon to me one evening as we sat on the front porch and watched the impending storm gather momentum. He had held me and comforted me every time there was a loud clap, slightly amused by my trepidation. Slowly, I came to appreciate the magnificence of the light and sound show, and now I had no fear of lightning and the loud clamor that accompanied it.

I had closed the drapes in the bedrooms and sat huddled with Rosalyn on my bed.

"Rosy scared, Mama. Will it hurt me?"

"No, darling, we are quite safe here. Your father is keeping watch. How about another chapter in my fairy tale?"

"Yes, please. I think that Shelley and Keateys are 'fraid, too."

"Do you want me to take them downstairs?"

"No, they better stay here. Tell me some more about Emerald and Laddy, Mama."

Ava was asleep as usual in her crib that I had moved beside the bed, so I continued on with the story that I was making up as I went along. The storm had lost some of its intensity by 10 P.M., and between the peaceful sound of the rain that was streaming down the windows and my voice, Rosalyn fell asleep. I gently released my arm from around her and tiptoed to the door, calling the dogs quietly. I led them to their sleeping quarters, which they had accepted readily when we first brought them to the house. If they wanted out during the night, they could go down the kitchen stairs, which we left open at night. Johnny had installed a doggie door as one of his first duties when he and Amma had arrived home.

I waited until they had settled in their beds before returning to the girls. Just as I reached the grand staircase, I heard sobbing coming from below. Curious, I undid the latch and silently descended slowly. As I reached the second landing, a streak of lightning lit up the foyer and a hazy apparition seemed to float across the room. I held my breath as I watched it evaporate into thin air, but for a second, I swear it turned and held up its hands, wings, whatever, toward me. I was not frightened, as I wasn't sure if I had really seen a specter or if the night was playing tricks with my imagination. I listened and felt that the weeping was coming from Jeremy's office. I crept toward the door and, sure enough, he was in there, sitting in his armchair, holding his head in his hands.

Hearing me, he said as he looked up, "Maveryn? Have you returned?"

"I am sorry, Jeremy. It is Vela."

"Oh. I am sorry. Did I awaken you?"

"No, I was not asleep. Can I do anything for you? Has Maveryn been to visit you?"

He looked at me and, with a whisper, asked me if I knew about Maveryn's ghost. I told him that I now understood why he still referred to her as if she were still alive, because she had been appearing to him.

"You don't think that I am crazy because I see her?" Jeremy asked.

"No, of course not," I replied. "Does she upset you when she comes?"

"No, only when she leaves."

"How do you feel when she is visiting you?"

"She gives me hope and reassurance, and I feel this overwhelming peace. Then she goes and I have to face the fact that I have been talking to a ghost."

"I prefer to think of her as a spirit or an angel. If she gives you comfort, I think that you should be thankful for the time that you spend with her and not to be so sad when she leaves. I believe that angels only have so many moments to visit the ones they love at a time. I have never had the opportunity to be blessed this way, but for a second, I thought I saw her as she left you. Perhaps she was on her way to visit Rosalyn."

"Perhaps I no longer need my therapist. You have the answers that I am seeking. Thank you. And, yes, she does leave me to check on the girls. Not just Rosalyn but Ava also. She is the reason you are here in Avanloch you know."

"I suspected as much."

"She is very wise, is she not?"

"Maveryn is a lovely and caring soul, and I promise that I will always love her daughter and take care of her. It appears as though another storm is coming. I best return to the girls. Will you be all right?"

"Yes, I will be now. Thank you for understanding."

We did not talk of the incident at breakfast the next morning, but as usual, Rosy made the meal interesting as she relayed her version of the storm to her dad, using her hands to convey how big the lightning was and her voice to mimic the thunder. Jeremy left for London shortly after.

In the middle of September, I was outside of the main entrance, sizing up the driveway, pondering what we could do to improve its stark appearance. Except for the fountain, it was pretty uninviting. I had not done a thing on the inside as I didn't know where to begin. A snazzy yellow convertible sped into the drive and stopped just short of where I was standing. It was Ash and her companion, Stephanie. She had not called to say that she was coming, which was typical Ash.

She jumped out and ran around to greet me. I had not known her to be affectionate, but she seemed genuinely pleased to see me as I gathered by her long hug.

"How lovely to see you, Ash," I said. "Did Jeremy know that you were coming? He is in London you know."

"Yes, I saw him yesterday. Have you met Steffie?"

"Nice to meet you; any friend of Ash's is welcome here. You will be staying a while, won't you? We do not get much company and Rosy will be so glad that you are here. Let me help you with your bags."

"Here, Vela, this is your wedding gift," Ash said, handing me a heavy package.

"Whatever have you done?"

"I hope you will be pleased. Jeremy gave me a hint."

They followed me into the grand hall and down toward the kitchen. I suggested that they leave their bags by the elevator while I fixed them something to eat.

"Mrs. Duffy can do that. Where is Rosalyn?"

"Amma has taken her and Ava for a visit to her mother's in the village. They will be back shortly. I am afraid you are stuck with my cooking, as Mrs. D is at her sisters."

"Where is Reita?"

"She is away also. It won't be so bad, Ash. After all, I have been preparing meals since I was twelve. You're in luck today, as we have cold fried chicken and salads, and of course, freshly baked bread. Will that suit your palette?"

"Definitely, sounds delicious. What do you say, Steffie?"

"Wonderful! I am famished. How old are you, Vela?"

"Going on nineteen. Why do you ask?"

"This all seems like such a big responsibility, this huge expanse of a house and you have two children, and now you are cooking. Do you ever have any time for yourself?"

"Well, I do not do much housework or cooking usually. We do have help. Amma helps me with the girls and running the castle. Shalla and a new hire, Cyan, do the entire grunt work. Once a month, several others come in to do the deep cleaning, if it seems necessary. I think that Jeremy wants to start entertaining in the New Year, so I suppose that we will make use of the other rooms."

"You mean you are not using the left wing?" Ash asked.

"Not much," I said. "We really do not need all that space. Johnny is just about finished with the old smoking room that we are turning into a playroom for the girls. Sometimes, Rosy and I plunk away in the music room and watch a Disney movie on the big T.V."

"I can hardly wait to show Steffie the grand parlor! She is an actress you know, and is the lead in my new production. V, are you going to open the present?"

I undid the ribbon and opened the heavy box. Inside I found three volumes of poetry. The authors were no less than Curer, Ellis, and Acton Bell. "Oh my," I said.

"You do know who they are, don't you?"

"Of course, Ash! They are the pen names of the Bronte sisters, Charlotte, Emily, and Anne. These books are in pristine condition. Are they original? And where on earth did you find them?"

"According to my friend, they are. He has tomes and tomes of manuscripts and first editions of every and any book you are looking for. Though I must say his collection is dwindling since his fiancée gave him the ultimatum: it was either her or his overstocked library. He chose her. And so, I was able to get my hands on these. I can probably swindle some of their novels for you if you like. I am sure I can strike up a bargain with him."

"Thank you, Ash. This is quite enough for now. Please thank your friend, whose name is…?"

"His name is Stu and he resides in London just a few blocks from us. The luncheon was delicious. Can we expect more at dinner?"

"I hope you like pot roast. It is all ready to go into the oven shortly. Are you going to get settled?"

"Yes. Will you join us in the grand parlor in half an hour?"

I agreed and went to answer the doorbell as they retreated to Ash's suite. I wasn't sure of their relationship but had a pretty good idea. I once had a female friend who preferred women over men, and I suspected that was the case here. Anyhow, it was none of my business. Everyone had to make his or her own happiness.

"Yes, young lady, what can I do for you?" I asked.

Rosalyn had run ahead of Amma and Ava and was waiting for me to let her in. She was barely tall enough to reach the doorbell. "Mama, 'tis me," she said. "I fool you again."

I hugged her. "Yes, you did. Did you have a nice time at Granny Keys?"

"Yup. Who is in the yellow car?"

"It's a surprise. How did you get so far ahead of Amma?"

"I run fast. You know I can, Mama."

We sat down on the marble steps to wait for them and I listened to the tales of the day as only Rosy could tell. It was Ava's feeding time, so I sat in the small parlor and nursed her while waiting on Ash. I had asked Rosalyn to wait and watch in the main hall for our guests. I definitely knew when they had arrived. With a hoop and a holler, Rosy greeted her auntie calling to me, "Mama, Mama, Annie Ash is here!"

I settled Ava back in her carriage and we all went into the "big room." I had not ventured in it since my discovery of it with Jeremy. Steffie had almost the same reaction as I had. She stood in the doorway, I believed, a little flabbergasted.

Rosy said, "Wow! Who lives here?"

"Have you never been in here before, sweetie?" Ash asked.

"I don't think so. Have I, Mama?"

"Well, not with me," I said. "Maybe with your father, I don't know."

"I am not to come in here, he told me." She started to back away.

Ash grabbed her and told her that it was okay as long as she was with an adult. There were so many really, really old treasures in there that they all had to be careful so as not to break anything. She picked her up in her arms and beckoned for Steffie to follow her to the stage where she sat Rosy down in one of the oversized chairs. "This used to belong to Louis XVI, who lived a long, long time ago, so it is very old, so we never want to get jam or anything on it, okay?"

Rosy nodded. "Yes, Annie."

Ava had started to cry and Rosy was rubbing her eyes, so we left our guests to themselves so that we could take our naps. Supper would be at 6, I informed them, and stopped by the kitchen to throw the roast into the oven.

Ash and Steffie stayed for three days. I thoroughly enjoyed their visit, especially when we took Steffie horseback riding. She had never been on a horse before so we gave her the gentlest mare, Lady Grey. It all was too amusing. She went up one side of the horse and down the other. We tried not to laugh, but she was a good sport and encouraged our amusement at her expense. The ride did not go quite as planned and we were back at the stables within an hour. Dismounting was not a feat that went well, but we did manage to get her down, thanks to the patience of Lady Grey. When they left, I asked when they would be back, and Ash asked if they could come for Christmas. Steffie wanted to know if there would be horseback riding. I told her no, but if there was snow, we could go on a sleigh ride. She liked that. I kissed them both and thanked them for coming.

The Christmas season was fast approaching. We all had a hand in decorating Avanloch. Mrs. D said there hadn't been such joviality in the house for years. I knew that she meant: since Maveryn's passing. I had no idea if she had made any further visits to Jeremy, as he did not talk about it again. His plans for spending more time at the estate did not materialize. He managed to make an appearance every three weeks or so, which was fine with me. He was not my husband in the way that it mattered.

The tree was up and all the baking and purchasing of the girls were completed. We had spent endless hours wrapping and decorating. Care packages were tied with frilly ribbons to present to the families in the village. They contained specialty cakes and jars of mincemeat and jams, and a ham and a turkey. There were toiletries for the women and toques and socks for the men, and of course, toys for the children. Reverend Peters had helped us with special needs. Jannie and the staff from Brackenshire had also pitched in to help us with this new tradition. It was something that Maveryn had the chance to do only once, so I was pleased that I could carry on for her.

How and why it happened, I did not really know. I lost almost three days of my life. I did not remember much except going to bed one evening, feeling terribly sad. I suppose I was remembering my life back in Bridge Falls. It was now one year since I had left home. There was a knock at my bedroom door. I sat up to discover that it was still light outside and wondered what I was doing in bed at such an early hour. The children were not with me.

"Come in," I called.

A middle-aged woman, whom I had never seen before, entered and came over to my bedside. "Hello, Vela. I am Dr. Jai Behimma. Everyone calls me Jai. Jeremy asked me if I could check in on you." She extended her hand to me and I took it.

I noticed at once that she had very kind eyes and her voice was very low and soothing. "I'm not sick, am I? I don't feel ill."

"No, you are not physically ill, but I think that perhaps you have been under great stress and that has caused you to escape into another world for a little while."

I sat straight up. "What do you mean? Where did I go? I don't remember going anywhere. Where are my girls?"

"It is all right, Vela. Your girls are just fine. They are with the family downstairs. I didn't mean to suggest that you had gone on a trip away from them. Have you been having feelings of anxiety and sadness, Vela?"

"I have them sometimes, yes. I don't let anyone see me that way, though."

"I think that it is time that you started to let others help you with your emotions. That is why I am here. Will you tell me what has brought you to this point?"

"I don't know what you mean. What point? All I know is that it is early and I am in bed. Has something happened that I am not aware of?"

"Do you know what the date is?"

"Of course, it is December 20!"

"I am sorry to tell you, but it is the 23rd; you have lost some time, haven't you?"

"Oh dear; this has never happened before. When I have had feelings of overwhelming sadness, I have always been able to deal with it. Are you suggesting that I went away somewhere in my mind for three days?"

"Yes, I believe that is one way of explaining your lapse in time. Do you agree with me that we must do something so that doesn't happen again?"

"How are we going to accomplish that?"

"If you will be agreeable to have some sessions with me, I believe that we will be able to find the root of your depression."

"You think that I am depressed?"

"Depression is a real condition, and if left untreated, it can lead to serious health problems. It is not only a disease of the mind but of the physical body and the soul. If you will let me, I hope to help you to be healthy again."

"What will I have to do?"

"You will need to be honest with me and with yourself. There is a reason for your sadness and we need to research the cause. I would also like to give you some medication that should help to alleviate the despondency."

"I am still nursing. Will I have to wean Ava completely?"

"No, you can just keep doing it gradually. I understand that she is taking a bottle and eating quite well, is that right?"

"Yes. I will agree to see you professionally, as the children are the only reason for my living. I want to see them first."

"Of course, and they want to see you. Jeremy has asked me to spend the night, so I see no reason to continue our conversation tonight. Tomorrow will be fine. I will tell Jannie that you are ready to visit with the girls."

She was just about to open the adjoining door when I asked her if she was Jeremy's psychologist. She said that she was.

"You know that he is not crazy, don't you? Maveryn really does exist."

"Crazy is not a term we use. But, yes, I do believe that, somehow, she is still here. Have you had any encounters with her spirit? If so, we can talk about that another time."

"I need five minutes to wash my face and comb my hair."

I looked dreadful and was sure that I must smell the same, but the girls did not care.

Rosalyn ran up to me and threw her arms around me. "Are you better now, Mama? I was lonely when you were sick. Ava lonely, too."

I cradled Ava in my arms and sat on the bed so that I could hold Rosy, too. "Yes, my darlings, Mama is better. I missed you, too."

Jannie asked if I thought that I would be up to having dinner downstairs, and I told her that I was, but that I would need to bathe and dress. She collected the girls and said that she would send Amma up to help me. I appreciated the help.

Everyone was delighted that I was feeling better, and I thanked them all for their roles in helping with Ava and Rosalyn. Dr. Jai smiled at me and I felt that I had taken a step in the right direction by joining them all for dinner.

I started on the medication that night. I had no memory of the last few days but had to do everything in my power to make sure that I never went there ever again. How much of my despair I was willing to tell the doctor, I did not know. Would I confess my feelings of loneliness and desperation? Would I, without meaning to, bring Rainey into the picture? I must guard against that... It was not time.

I had my first session with Dr. Jai the next morning. She asked me how I had slept, and I told her that I had slept peacefully.

"Are you subject to dreams, Vela?" the doctor asked.

"Yes, I have always been a dreamer," I replied. "Does that have anything to do with the way I have been feeling?"

"That depends. Do you have dreams of recent events, the past, or just things that make no sense? Can you remember them in great detail or in fragments? Mostly, how do you feel when you are reconstructing them, are you sad or happy or noncommittal?"

"I have strange dreams. Sometimes, I am on great adventures with faceless people, and other times, I dream of home and the people I love. Usually, though, my dreams make no sense and when I recall them, I try to analyze them. I have dreams of birth and death, but the most common one is that I am lost and cannot find my way. I seem to be searching for something that I never find. A dear friend of mine used to have a recurring dream that upset him, and I kept telling him that it was only a dream. However, the dream came true. He doesn't know it, but I do."

"I don't understand. How would you know this and he doesn't?"

"Because the dream was about something that was going to happen to me; we just didn't know it then."

"Does this person have a name? And why haven't you told him?"

"I no longer have any contact with him. Anyhow, are my dreams any more different from anyone else's?"

"Vela, I feel that there is something in your past that you are not ready to reveal to me. And that is fine. We are going to go slowly, one day at a time. I am only here to help you with your well-being. Do not think that I am prying when I ask you certain things. We cannot go forward if there is a huge impediment in the way. Do you understand?"

"Yes, I do, but I am going to tell you out right that there is a part of me that I will probably never reveal. If that is to be a barrier, then so be it."

"Vela, I will try and earn your trust. Now, tell me about your family and friends back home in Canada. I love your country and once thought that perhaps I would set up a practice there. However, a colleague of mine had to take a leave from his practice in Edinburgh due to illness and asked me if I would consider taking over for him. I thought it would be for a year or so, but that was five years ago and I am still here."

"What happened to your friend?"

"Oh, he returned and the need was such that I agreed to stay and to cover all the surrounding towns like Waverly. It means that I travel a great deal, but I wouldn't give it up for anything. The Scottish people are a delight, and where else would I have the chance to lodge in a castle?"

I laughed when I asked her if any ghosts had visited her.

"I am pleased to say no, but then maybe, I wouldn't be such a skeptic. What do you think? Is the castle haunted? Do you ever have any misgivings living here?"

"I am never afraid, if that is what you are asking. If Avanloch is haunted, I am sure the spirits are friendly."

"How much contact do you have with your family and friends?"

"I talk to my parents and sisters almost every week. Unfortunately, I have no contact with any of my friends. Actually, there is only one and I miss her very much."

"What is stopping you from having contact with her?"

"Perhaps you do not know the reason why I came here to give birth. The father is not in the picture and I do not want him to ever know that I had his child. My family is keeping my whereabouts a secret, but I cannot expect to lay that burden on Lara."

"Lara, what a lovely name. You do so want to hear from her, don't you? Well, let's come up with a way that you can and keep your address anonymous."

"How can I do that?"

"I think that it is important that you converse with her and keep tabs on what is happening in her life, and I am sure that she is worried about you. Hearing from you will also ease her mind. Our friends are of great importance, and do not underestimate what she will do for you. Now, suppose you compose a note to her and we have Jeremy mail it from one of the port cities that he visits. I am sure that he will be agreeable."

"What a marvelous idea! I must admit that I have thought of just a thing, and now, hearing it voiced, I can see that it will work. But how is she going to answer me without an address?"

"I am sure that we can set up a forwarding box somewhere. Shall I approach Jeremy with the suggestion, or would you like to?"

"Thank you. I will. I am sure that you know why he and I married. He is a wonderful and kind man and has already offered to help me in any way that he can."

"Very well. I will take my leave now, as I do not want to miss the last train to Edinburgh. Shall we make an appointment for two weeks from now? I can come here if you like, but I think that you should get out more. I have an office on Front Street in Waverly."

"I will come there. Thank you and Merry Christmas. I shall look forward to seeing you again."

She wished me well and presented me with her card that contained phone numbers at which she could be reached night or day…just in case.

Christmas came and went but was much more enjoyable than the previous one. I now had two darling children and dear friends to share it with. I called the family back in Bridge. According to them, all was fine. I inquired about Lara and Mother said that she asked about me every week. I told her to tell Lara that I would be sending her a letter soon. Addy and Sissy had been told about Ava's birth. There were no secrets there anymore, unless you counted the one that gave her birth date as July and not May.

I had follow-up sessions with Dr. Jai every week but had no idea if I was making any progress. Perhaps the visits with her and the medication were helping, as I had no further lapses into despair.

Rosalyn was four years old in April and Ava turned one, though we would not be celebrating her birthday until July 13. That was the day she would come to know as the day she was born. Heaven only knew when I would tell her all the truths regarding her birth. I finally sent a letter off to Lara, whom Jeremy was mailing for me. We had yet to set up a fake address. I was taking driving lessons from Henry. I feared that I was not a good pupil. Jeremy surprised me one day, suggesting that I bring the conservatory back to life. In May, I discovered something about the McAllisters that no one had bothered to tell me.

Chapter Fifteen

Rainey, Italy, 1963

"How do I look, Rainey?" She proceeded to twirl around in her new Palo De Near original. She was 5 feet 7 inches, and in her 4-inch heels, she was taller than he was. Despite her very lean model body, she was not very graceful in ordinary circumstances. This being one, as she almost tripped showing off.

"You look fabulous as always, Zeta," Rainey said. "How much did it set you back?"

"That is not important. There are going to be many big fashion names at the gala and so many beautiful girls. I must look better than any of them!"

Vanity, your name is Zeta, Rainey thought. He had met her at an Italian festival last October. She was a looker—longish black tresses, brown eyes, and red, red lips. She looked nothing like Vienna despite their resemblance in coloring. He thought that she was on the verge of becoming anemic. Her 102-pound frame was greatly assisted by heavy lacquered hair, long, fake eyelashes, and 2-inch imitation nails. He had never seen her eat a carbohydrate in all the time that he had known her. Lettuce, chicken, and fish were her diet, but she sure could put away the wine.

There was a fairly simple relationship. She never made any demands of him and didn't seem to have any prior baggage, unlike him. Her only desire was to take her modeling career to America. Marriage and children were not in her immediate plans. He was lonely when they met, and within two months, he had invited her to move in with him. He had a comfortable two-bedroom apartment in Milan, close to his job. Zeta was always on location somewhere and was usually only home three nights a week. Rainey did all of the cooking and had a cleaning lady come in once a week. He had joined a gym and played soccer for fun. He attended Zeta's fancy functions only because it was better than being alone. Tonight, they were going to a charity ball. How was this any different than the life he used to lead in Vancouver?"

"Oh, Rainey, I forgot to tell you that your mother sent another parcel. It is on the table. Why don't you open it while I finish getting ready? The taxi will be here in ten minutes."

He put down his drink and went to retrieve the mail. Every two or three weeks, his mother sent a letter and the newspaper from Bridge and the local monthly circular. He was sure there was nothing that couldn't wait until he got home later but started to untie it anyhow. Two letters fell out of the wrappings. He bent down to pick them up and noticed that one was addressed to his cousin, Lara. "What the hell? Why would there be a letter to her?" Something was very familiar about the handwriting. "Shit!" He turned the envelope over but there was no return address, just a note from his mother, saying that Lara had wanted her to forward this to him. There was no mistaking the writing— it was in Vienna's immaculate hand. He could not bring himself to open it. Surely nothing good was going to come from that letter. The best thing for him to do was just to put it aside until later. He hadn't thought of her in such a long time that another few hours wouldn't make any difference. Why should he put himself in a mood before the party?

"We best go down to wait for the taxi, Rainey," Zeta said. "What's wrong? Not bad news from home I hope."

"No, no. I haven't even opened Mom's letter yet. Here, let me help you with your wrap." He turned at the door and looked at the letter as if he were leaving Vienna behind.

They were early, as usual. The bar was open and that was Rainey's savoir all evening. After the preliminary speeches by the governing heads of the Orphans Aid Organization, a silent auction was held. As it was, the evening had already cost Rainey a month's pay, so he wasn't going to indebt himself any further. He didn't even pretend to make a bid on items that had no interest to him at all. The dinner was a potpourri of Italian cuisine. Zeta ate salad and shrimp. Two hours later, a popular local band appeared on the scene. Rainey only listened to a foreign language music station. He did not want to hear anymore heartbreaking songs. He figured that if he couldn't understand the lyrics, he wouldn't be haunted so much by the melody. Before he left Canada, he could have sworn that every songwriter knew his misery and was composing especially for him.

They shared a table with three other couples who Rainey had met several times before. He had nothing whatsoever in common with any of the men and the women were all rivals of Zeta's. What was there to talk about…the weather, politics and the state of the world, and sports? None of which was his topic of choice. Zeta wanted to dance and he didn't. She didn't beg him or pout, but found herself someone who was willing to trip the light fantastic with her. He was smiling to himself, wondering how a woman who could walk down a steep runway in 4-inch heels without ever looking down and never falter, and then get out on the dance floor and flounder like a fish out of water.

"She's not a very good dancer, is she, Rainey?" A so-called model friend of Zeta's had sat down beside him. "Care to dance?"

"Not tonight, Stella. Sorry."

"How about a walk on the promenade? It is so stuffy in here."

He declined again. It wasn't the first time that she had flirted with him. In fact, he had found himself in this situation many times before while attending these galas. There were plenty of eligible men around from all corners of Europe and probably even America. He had met several who were descendants of royalty. There certainly wasn't anything special about him except that he was "taken," and that seemed to be the turn on. He asked, "Stella, where are you from? I don't recognize the accent. Someplace exotic?"

"I was born in Borneo, in a town called Kennedale, which is in Malaysia. Have you heard of it? The rain forests are the best in the entire world. I miss home very much but must pursue my career. Do you know what that is like, Rainey?"

"I do. I suppose that is why I am here." Vienna was with him again. As soon as Stella had mentioned Borneo, he had heard her voice. They got caught in a sudden downpour while they were at the line shack in Hawthorne. They had raced back to take shelter, with her crying, "Don't look at me, Rainey! I must look like the wild woman from Borneo!" Would he have remembered that if there was not a letter in her handwriting awaiting him in the apartment?

Zeta returned and shot daggers at Stella. The night couldn't end soon enough for him and, secretly, he was telling himself that this was going to be the last affair. He was getting pretty good at making up excuses like the one he had made at Christmas. Zeta had wanted him to go home with her to meet the family in Portugal, but he had told her that he already had plans to spend the holidays with his friend in London. As it turned out, the very next day, he had received an invitation from Stu, so it hadn't even been a lie. Zeta was disappointed but accepted it.

They were both shivering from the cool, early morning rain that had descended upon them as they had stood waiting for the valet to call them a taxi. They had not warmed up on the short ride home and found the apartment to be as chilly as the temperature was outside. It was 3 A.M. on Sunday, March 30. The thermometer read 15 degrees Celsius. Rainey cranked up the heat and sat down to read the letter. He had sent Zeta to bed without him saying that he would join her shortly, but in fact had no intention of doing so. He sighed and tore open the envelope that had been resealed with tape.

My dear Lara,

Oh, how I miss you! I hope that someday you will forgive me for disappearing without a word. I have yet not even begun to forgive myself.

I have a very busy life but I am not always happy. However, I am well and I pray that you are, too.

I think of you and all the friends I left behind. Did Zane and Marley get married? How is Yates's relationship with June progressing? And how is that scoundrel, Jimmy? I hope you have someone special in your life! I cannot help but mention Rainey. I hope that he has found the answers to all his dreams. It hurts me to admit that I was not to be one of them. Someday, I will dance again, but know not when.

Soon, I will have an address at which you may write me. I look forward to that. Please remember me with fondness.

You still remain my dearest friend,

V

So that was it. There was no return address except that it bore a New Zealand postage stamp. What the hell was she doing there? Why and when had she taken it upon herself to think that she was not part of his dreams? He had escaped to Italy to be free of her memory, and now here she was, smack dab in the middle of his life again. He put the letter up to his lips and smelled the scent of cherry blossoms.

If the guys from home could see him, they would say he was crazy. He could be living every man's fantasy. He had a decent job doing what he had always wanted to in a country that he loved, surrounded by beautiful women who, for some reason, found him attractive. Maybe he was off his rocker, as he realized *again* that he was still carrying a torch for his teenage sweetheart. *Thank you very much for the letter, Lara*, he thought vehemently.

He gathered up some blankets and a pillow from the linen closet and settled in on the couch to read the letter over again. Vienna would be nineteen now. He couldn't believe that he hadn't seen her in more than a year, and the mere suggestion of her made him wish that it was 1961 and that they were back together. What kind of a hold did she have on him anyhow? He hoped that he was too inebriated to dream.

It was never the same between him and Zeta. She was constantly on shoots throughout the country even though Milan was the fashion center of the day. It was also experiencing an economic rebound with rebuilding and new construction of homes and factories that had taken their toll during the war. Rainey could see that he had a future here for many years to come. There was a big demand for skyscrapers and high-rise apartments.

He was pretty much on his own, with Zeta only coming home for a few days a week. He didn't mind visiting the museums and theatres on his own, and even attended a few operas with his boss and his wife. All of them seemed to depict love lost and nearly always ended sadly. He didn't need that. He had gone to an open-air concert where a beautiful French songstress had been the headliner. He hadn't been able to make out all the words in one song that she was performing, but it was of a woman named Vienna, or maybe it was just the city. It didn't matter. Vienna was here again.

He was glad to get away again to London in early May. Stu and Daisy were to be married on the fourth. Zeta was away on assignment. Rainey was just as glad to be going solo. When he returned to Milan several days later, he found a very enamored woman waiting for him. Zeta greeted him with open arms, kissing him over and over.

"I missed you so! I love you, Rainey! Do you love me?" She hadn't waited for an answer but said, "Let's get married."

He held her away from him. "Whoa, girl... where is this coming from? I thought you liked our relationship the way it is. I am not ready for marriage, Zeta." He added to himself, "Especially with you."

"But, do you love me, Rainey?"

"I don't want to hurt you, Zeta, but I am not a man who falls in love easily, and what would marriage be without love?"

"So, you do not love me."

"I care for you, but I am not in love with you."

"How do you know if you have never been in love before?"

"That's just it, Zeta. I have been in love before and what I feel for you is not the same. I am sorry if I led you to think that we had a long future together."

"No, you haven't. Are you still in love with her, Rainey?"

"Sometimes, I think I am."

"Is she the one you call Vienna?"

He was shocked that she knew her name. "Why would you ask me that?"

"Why? I will tell you why. You call out for her when you are sleeping!"

"I am truly sorry about that. How long has this been going on? I certainly am not aware that I am talking in my sleep."

"For a while. I think it became more prevalent a few months back. You are not talking, though. You are almost crying when you say her name. You are begging her not to go. Who is she, Rainey?"

"No one that you need to concern yourself about. Will you please leave it at that?" He left her standing there and knew that he was going to have to end things with her. At the moment, he didn't know how or when. However, as usual, the situation took care of itself. Two days later, he received a phone call from his mother, saying that his father was in Vancouver General Hospital after having suffered a heart attack.

The earliest flight that he could get would see him arrive in Vancouver in two days. He would have to endure a six-hour layover in Chicago. He arrived at 3 P.M. and took a taxi directly to the hospital. He found his mother and sister at his father's bedside. He was very pleased to see him sitting up and rushed over to give him a hug.

"Rainey, you're here," his father said. "I told your mother not to worry you."

"Really, Dad?"

His mother answered, "You know your father, doesn't want to bother anyone. Thank heavens Claudia was already in Hawthorne, and Saul and Mavis were only a shout away. The four of us had him into Bridge in record time and he was air-lifted here four hours later. Thank heavens for modern medicine and Dr. Johnson."

Rainey questioned them as to what had been done to prevent another attack and why had this happened in the first place, knowing that his father had been in perfect health when he had left for Italy.

"Son, I guess these things can happen to anyone," his dad said. "As it turned out, I had three blocked arteries. I guess, if I am honest, I was having some minor chest pains all that week but chalked it up to preparing the equipment for the haying season."

"I want to talk with his surgeon, Mom," Rainey said. "Who was it?"

A nurse had two of his dad's doctors paged, and within half an hour, they had answered all of Rainey's questions. His arteries had been cleared and stents were inserted. He was to follow a special diet for a while, and with the medications and frequent checkups, Rainey was assured that his dad could go on living the same as before. He was cautioned that his dad should not resume hard labor for a while. It was going to be a task to keep his father from assuming farming chores this summer, but that was what he was there for.

"How long are you on leave from your job, Rainey?" Paul asked his son.

"I won't be going back to it, Dad. When the haying season is done with, I plan on taking a job much closer to home."

"I told you, Patsy, that this was going to happen. I wish that you had waited until I was home and fully recovered before informing him. Now look, he has left a perfectly good job to—"

Rainey didn't let him finish. "Thank God Mother has more sense than you, Dad. You know perfectly well that I would not have forgiven her if she had listened to you. I think that you shouldn't be upsetting yourself and just be grateful that we are all here."

"You're right, Son. It will be good to have you home. Sorry, Patsy. I suppose I am going to be a little difficult for a while. Do you think that you will be able to put up with me?"

"Well, dear, I can't say that it will be a hardship. After all, I have been doing it for thirty years already."

Patsy and Claudia had been staying in a hotel close to the hospital, as they hadn't wanted to drive the distance from Rainey's place. He insisted that they now move into his house, as when his dad was released, he could rest there until he felt like making the trip home. His dad said that he was ready to go right now but would listen to his doctors.

Three days later, they were back in Hawthorne to everyone's delight. Claudia had flown back to Toronto, promising to come later in the summer with the boys. As soon as Rainey had his dad settled, he was on the phone to Lara. When they were through discussing his father's surgery and recovery, he asked her if she had heard from Vienna again.

"Sorry, I haven't Rain. I have been waiting and praying that she would contact me again, but I guess she is still not ready."

"Do you still get word from her parents?"

"Yes, every month. They say that she is recovering slowly. Don't ask me what that means, Rainey, as I do not know."

"What could she possibly be recovering from? Was she sick? Do you think that she is in some sort of facility somewhere? The letter you sent sounded perfectly normal."

"I know, I know. I made a copy of it and have read it over and over, looking for some clue, believe me. So we are no closer than we were a year and a half ago."

"Lily and Joe are hiding something. I felt it from the first. Many times I have thought of questioning the girls again but couldn't bring myself to bring any more sadness into their lives. They idolized their big sister."

"I know. You may be happy to know that Jack Jennings was back in town last winter. He had no idea where V was. He was just as surprised as the rest of us to discover that she was gone."

"Do you believe him, Lara?"

"Do you think that I am the only one who gave him the third degree? Jimmy and Yates had their day with him and came up empty also. I had asked Paddy if he knew anything about her and Jack when she went missing. He had told me then that Jack had no idea where she was. He said that V was the only girl who Jack had ever cared about, and if they were together, Jack would have been a happy man, and he certainly wasn't."

"None of that makes me feel any better, Lara. I thought I was finally getting over her until you sent me her letter. Now, I am at a crossroad again."

"Did I make a mistake, Rain? Should I have kept it to myself?"

"No, I am glad that you did. Someday, I will face reality. Right now, Dad's health is the only issue. See you in a few days?"

"Yes, Mom and I will be over. Chin up, Rain. I am really glad that you are home."

Next call was to Jimmy. Rainey said, "What's this I hear that you're tying the knot?"

"Thank God your home, buddy," Jimmy replied. "I was beginning to wonder who could fill your shoes as my best man! You're up to the task, aren't you?"

"You've heard that phrase 'always a bridesmaid, never a bride'? Well, it applies to me, too. Three times a best man, but never a groom."

"What's up with that, Rain?"

"Have you spoken to Lara in the last few months? She has heard from Vienna and forwarded the letter to me. No answers. She asked about all you guys, though; said she misses everyone."

"Did that include you?"

"Well, she said that she was sorry that she wasn't in my future plans and that she wasn't always happy. I'm right back where I was before I went to Italy. What do you think I should do, Jimmy? Should I try to find her again? Did I not pursue it enough last year? I am not happy either. Why the hell can't I get on with my life?"

"I don't think that you have any choice. She will find you when the time is right."

Chapter Sixteen

Avanloch, 1963–69

Interesting times were upon us all. Ash had been home for the Christmas holiday and, with Steff, had given us a preview of their spring play. Ash had written it and Steff had the leading role. It was titled "The War Mother." It was about a woman who found nine orphaned children in war-torn Germany and brought them home to England to try and find new families for them. The play was premiering on May 4 in London and Ash was expecting Jeremy and I to attend. I was very apprehensive about leaving Ava, but Amma and Shalla insisted that I go and that they were already second mothers to the girls, so what did I have to worry about?

The play was excellent and, of course, I cried most of the way through it. Steff was brilliant. They all received a standing ovation from the packed theatre. It had been especially harrowing for Ash, as she had to attend a wedding ceremony for her friend, Stu, only hours before the curtain dropped. I was hoping to meet Stu, who had sent me further volumes of the Bronte sisters' early years. There was no time and I couldn't very well intrude on a man during his wedding. Perhaps another opportunity would arise.

On May 23, Amma, Emma, Shalla, and Millie were at Avanloch with me. Their hubbies, and in Shalala's case, beau, were all attending a stag in the village. Mrs. Sharpe and Jannie were in Waverly for the night and Mrs. D was at her sister's, or so we thought. We had prepared supper for Duffy and Henry, and when they had retired, us girls decided to play a game of cards. The wee ones were sleeping in the downstairs playroom. Ava had a crib and there was a day bed for Rosy.

We settled into the games room which was right next to where the girls were sleeping. Amma was in charge of deciding what we would play.

"Look what I found, ladies!" she announced as she climbed down from the ladder.

"What have you there, Amma?" Emma asked. "Oh no, you wouldn't!"

"What is it?" I was curious.

"It's the forbidden Ouija board," Emma said. She scolded her younger sister for bringing it down from the shelf. "There is a reason that it was put up on the highest shelf. Do you not remember?"

"I know what an Ouija board is," I said. "What could be the harm in asking a few questions?"

"You don't know this one," Millie answered.

"What? It's only a game."

"This one has a name," Millie said seriously.

"Oh, and just what does it call itself?" I asked.

"Mama. It won't answer you unless you address it that way."

"Well, I am the mama here and I for one would like to ask a few questions."

"Yeah, Emma, me, too. How about you Shalla? Millie?" Amma asked.

"All right then, but don't say I didn't warn you. If Mrs. McDuff knew—"

We reminded her that Mrs. D was at her sister's.

For half an hour or so, we had some fun with "Mama," asking silly questions. It was Shalala's turn and she asked if she was going to receive a ring this year. The board ignored her and spelled out *Liz Beth*.

Emma and Millie simultaneously took their hands off the pointer and sat back from the table. They looked at each other; their eyes were as big as saucers.

"Did you do that Millie?" Emma asked.

"No, did you?"

They lapsed into their Scottish dialect, which I could not understand, but it sounded as if they were blaming each other for tampering with the movement of the pointer.

Finally, I said, "Are you two finished? The rest of us would like to know who Liz Beth is."

Reluctantly, Emma spoke. "She was Jeremy's and Ash's little sister."

"And…I was hoping for a bit more information than that."

Millie, who was the eldest, decided to be the spokesperson. "It was in the late spring of '38. I remember because I had just turned twenty-two a day before and Liz Beth had brought me a present. The next day, she had an argument with her mother, Lady Audrey. Liz Beth was a spoiled little child, and whenever she didn't get her own way, she would say that they would all be sorry one day. Well, her threats came true. She had run out of the house and down to the lake. Whatever possessed her to take the canoe out is anyone's guess. She hated the water and had refused to learn how to swim. She fell out of the boat while trying to reach an oar. Jeremy was the first to get to her, having been summoned by his mother that his sister was acting up again. He saw the whole thing from the top of the hill. By the time he found her in the murky water and performed rescue breathing, she was already gone. Some say that she was still alive when he brought her here and that she died in her mother's arms. I think that it scarred Mr. Jeremy for life and poor Lady Audrey was never the same and died prematurely, never fully recovering from the loss."

"Oh, how horrible," I said. "No one has ever mentioned her to me. Are there not any portraits of her in the house?"

"There may be one in the foyer. Have you seen one of a young girl, Amma? I can't remember," her sister asked.

Amma wasn't sure.

"Were one of you thinking about her and the Ouija board picked up on that?" I said. "I have heard that it is very sensitive and reflects unconscious thoughts."

They both said no. Amma was too young to remember the dreadful incident and Shalla wasn't even born then. Apparently, the matter was never discussed in respect for Jeremy and Ash.

"I think we have to try the board again," I suggested. "We may have summoned her spirit. Maybe she wants to tell us something."

After much discussion, Emma and Millie agreed. We asked "Mama" if she was going to talk to us again and the pointer quickly traveled to "yes." We had agreed that Millie should do the talking.

Tentatively, she asked, "Are you here, Liz Beth? How can we help you?"

The pointer moved at once and spelled out "help me." It started to move again but we were halted by a voice from the doorway. I think that we all thought if we turned, we would see the child standing there. But it wasn't her; it was Mrs. D, and she scared the living daylights out of us all.

"What are you ladies doing? That witch board is the work of the devil! No good can come from it. Emma, Millie, what were you thinking? Give it to me. I am going to get rid of it once and for all. Thank God I came home before you conjured up any spirits."

"Mary, you 'bout bloody scared the bejesus out of us. Don't go getting your knickers in a knot. We was just having some fun," said Emma.

I had never heard Emma talk like that before.

"Fun? Was it fun? I don't hear anyone laughing," Mrs. D countered.

"Please sit down and join us, Mary. You look plum tuckered out. What happened with your sister? We weren't expecting you until tomorrow. Can we get you a cuppa tea?" Now I was starting to talk like them.

"I could use one. Shelia was called away to her son's, so I said I may as well come home. I will not take part in your ghost hunt, though."

"We did not conjure up any ghosts, but one came to us," Millie told her.

"I don't believe it! Who was here?"

"No one was here. We think that Liz Beth tried to make contact with us."

Mary crossed herself and whispered to herself, "Keep the head."

"What is she saying?" I asked Millie.

"She is just telling herself to stay calm and not to get upset." She turned to Mary and said, "She asked for help."

"Do ye all think that I am daft? I know how this thing works…someone pushed it to say those things."

"Honest, we didn't Mary. We need to go back and find out how to help Liz Beth." Emma was serious, but so was Mary when she told us that we needed something else. "We need to have a séance. Yes, only a séance will do."

We were all shocked to hear her suggestion. I asked her why.

"Because we need someone who knows what he is doing and not just playing around with this board that can be maneuvered."

"Why do you think that one of us may have spelled out her name? What would there be in it for anyone?"

"Not you, Vela, or even Shalla and Amma, but these two…" she pointed to Emma and Millie, "…they knew her."

"So what if we did? You still haven't explained why you want to hold a séance. Are you saying that you believe in the occult, Mary?" Emma asked.

"I don't, but it must be done. Liz Beth has to rest. We have to put her to rest."

"She has been gone for twenty-five years. Why would she suddenly appear after all this time?" I wanted to know. "And why do you think that she needs help?"

"Because the playing field has changed. There are things happening here and she may not be comfortable with the changes."

"Do you think that it is me, Mary? Am I a threat to her and her resting place?"

"No, no, child. She hasn't been at peace ever since she pushed the Black Russian down the stairs."

I was so confused that I was about to question her sobriety when Amma gasped.

"What do you mean?" Amma asked. "I was here that day. I saw her fall, all on her own, down the stairs. We all testified that it was a horrible accident."

"Reita and I both, we did see a specter push her," Mary replied. "We decided not to speak of it ever again. But we knew…we knew that it was Liz Beth, because if it wasn't her, then we had another ghost at Avanloch."

I didn't use profanity, but I did then. "Who the *hell* is the Black Russian?"

I guess my sudden outburst broke the tension, as the three of them started to laugh. Shalla and Amma looked at me, shrugged their shoulders, and rolled their eyes.

"First, there is Liz Beth, is her full name Elizabeth? And now, the Black Russian. Is there anyone else that I should know about? Mary, do you truly believe that Avanloch is haunted? I haven't seen anything or heard anything unless—"

"Unless what, Miss Vela?" Mary asked.

"Never mind for now. I want to hear more of the Black Russian. How did she get that name?"

"Her real name was Tatylyanna Stroganoff."

Emma corrected her. "Mary, her name was not Stroganoff, it was Speshiloff or something."

Mary went on. "Stroganoff, Rasputin, Tolstoy, Spleshoff, what's the difference? Miss Maveryn named her that."

"Oh, so Maveryn knew her?" I asked

"No, she was gone long before Miss Maveryn was on the scene."

"I don't understand. If they've never met—"

Millie spoke up. "No one ever heard of Taty again after her death was deemed an accident. Her family was not happy with the police report and tried to make trouble, but it never came to anything. As it turned out, the family didn't even have the funds to have her body shipped back to Russia, let alone to hire a lawyer. Mr. Jeremy obliged them that way. The once aristocratic dynasty had squandered all their assets and was bankrupt. So their hopes were with the two daughters marrying into money. Unbeknownst to Mr. J, he was one of the flies in the trap."

"How did he meet her and why was she here?" I asked.

"Now, that is another story. To be short, he met her in some Russian port near the Black Sea. Three months later, they were engaged. Jannie caught Taty in some unscrupulous acts and told Mr. John, and he had Taty investigated and that was the end of that. Mr. Jeremy broke it off with her by post, telling her that he knew what the family was up to, but she may as well keep the ring as he did not want it back. I think it was probably worth several thousand pounds. Well, lo and behold, if the woman didn't show up here unannounced and, of course, the Lord Jeremy was not here. You tell her the rest, Amma, because you know it best." Mary nodded to Amma.

She sighed. "Well, I guess I bore the brunt of her wrath. She never approved of the way I made her bed or pressed her clothes. That particular day, I was in the foyer, arranging flowers, when she appeared at the top of the grand staircase. She started in yelling at me that her tea and porridge were cold, and I was to fetch her a hot meal, and while I was at it, I needed to remake her bed—"

Mary interrupted. "Reita and I had come down from the kitchen to see what the ruckus was all about and Jannie popped her head out of the study. You go on, Amma."

"I guess that I had enough of her insults. She had already driven two of our part-time girls off so I just blasted off and told her that she could damn well make her own bed, and that if she wanted a new meal, well, that was going to be when Hell froze over!"

Mary put her arm around Amma, as she could see that she was getting herself in a state by reliving that dreadful day over again. "We was so proud of you, child," she stated.

Amma continued on with her narration. "She started to curse me in her native tongue, and now and then, she would throw in some choice English expletives. The last thing she said before she took the fateful steps forward and tumbled to her death was, 'You will all be sorry, you poor excuses for servants.

I shall have you all booted out the door.' Then there was nothing but a blood-curdling scream and the thumping as she hit the railing and came to a stop at the first landing. There was only a spot of blood from her head wound. No one pushed her that I could see."

"That's right, deary, you could not a seen from where ye was standing. But, Reita and I, and Miss Jannie, we done see. If it wasn't Liz Beth, then it must be Lady Mary."

"Ladies," I pleaded, "are you now telling me that there is another ghost here? How many of you have actually seen something? You didn't mention that Jannie was here that day before."

"Now, don't ye be worrying yourself about the ghosts. They are all friendly, except that Russian."

"Are you now telling me that Taty also haunts Avanloch?"

"To be sure, Vela, wees never seen her, only Miss Maveryn has."

"She told you that, Mary?"

Amma answered for her. "On her deathbed, she warned us to beware of the Black Russian. That was the first time we ever heard her referred to as that and the name just stuck. But, no, we had not come upon her or anyone else's spirits, contrary to what some believe."

Mary only smiled and said, "You are all skeptics, but one day, you will see."

"I hope for the children's sakes there are no evil phantoms roaming these halls," I said.

"To be sure, Miss Vela, the good, they outnumber the bad. The children's, they be protected."

I started to shiver. "All this talk has made me cold. Perhaps we should call it a night. Not that I will get any sleep."

"But what about the séance?" Shalla asked.

"Do you really want to hold one?" I looked around for everyone's reaction and was not too surprised that they were all in agreement. "All right then. Does anyone know where we can find a medium?"

Emma looked at Mary. "Let's see, humm, does anyone know a medium?"

"Mary McDuff, I thought that you were not a superstitious woman."

"We Scottish all be a wee that way. I get me rheumatism herbs from Mollie Magan and she can bring forth the spirits."

"Have you witnessed this?"

"No, not me, but I have heard, right, Millie?"

Millie agreed. "There be a problem, though, as Missy Molly be laid up with some serious injuries from falling from her wagon. She is in the hospital at Waverly."

"You don't say? I never heard. Is she going to be all right? Millie doesn't like to be associated with her, though they both share a last name."

"I am over that Mary, as it seems that she does a lot of good for people with her roots and potions and salves. I suppose if one believes, anything will work. We will just have to wait until she recovers before we can conduct our séance."

"I surely did not expect to step in this when I walked in the door tonight," Mary said.

There was a hundred and one questions that I wanted to ask, but they were going to have to wait until another day. As soon as Jeremy returned home, I was going to have to tell him that I had found out about Liz Beth. That was her actual name; it was not short for Elizabeth or anything else. Meanwhile, I kept up with my driving lessons and had decided that it was time that I wrote Lara again. Uncle John had finally set me up with a postal box in London that would forward my letters here. He said that it was very discreet and I took the plunge. I told Lara that it was not a true address and that she must keep it to herself. She responded to me right away, saying that she was so happy that we could finally correspond. She said that she would keep my address a secret. I hoped that I would never have to ask anyone to lie for me ever again.

Jeremy was home for our anniversary. I had been in Scotland for eighteen months and had been married to the wrong man for one year. He bought me and the girls a brand new jeep. He knew that was what I wanted, as I expected to take the girls on many jaunts throughout the summer and good weather. I passed my driver's test and started to plan short trips.

I confessed to Jeremy that I knew about his little sister. I just didn't tell him how I had found out. I didn't want him to know that we had used a Ouija and wanted to protect the others. The story that I told him was that I had inquired about the portrait and reluctantly, Mrs. D and Millie told me the sad story. He said that he was glad that I knew. So, that was that and I had no idea if I would ever tell him that we were planning a séance. That is, if it ever took place. Apparently, Molly Magan was not making great progress. We had no sightings of anything abnormal. I visited the mausoleum and placed flowers on both Maveryn's and Liz Beth's final resting places. Nothing had been disturbed.

It was a glorious summer for me and the girls. Every day that we were home, we took long walks through the blossoming gardens and meadows. We tossed grain and bread to the foul and watched the baby deer frolic on the other side of the lake. Of course, Keats and Shelley were always with us. Ava was walking but tired easily. That didn't hinder us, as Johnny had rigged up a cart that could travel easily over the rough terrain that she could sit in. Several times, she tumbled out of it but with no lasting injuries. Rosalyn was the one who cried, as she had been the one pulling the wagon. She apologized to Ava over and over again. Ava thought it was part of the game.

I finally braved the road, and the girls, Amma, Shalla, and I ventured out on day trips to the surrounding sites. Mrs. D always packed us enough food for several days…just in case, she would say. We explored faerie pools, waterfalls, and abandoned homes. We would leave home at 5 A.M. to travel to the coastline, where we would romp in the sands, build castles, and sometimes stay until the sun set way out at sea. On those days, we were lucky to be back by midnight, but it was well worth the long days. We visited landmarks and saw from a distance landmarks such as The Old Man of Storrs. We saw boats out at sea, shipwrecks, and experienced many a weather phenomenon such as dramatic hailstorms in the middle of a sunny day. These trips would be repeated year after year and we would always discover something new.

In Lara's first letter to me, she had informed me of Rainey's dad's heart attack and that Rainey had returned from Italy and was not going back. She confessed that she had forwarded my letter of last year to him, just so that he knew I was all right.

I wish that she hadn't sent the letter to Rainey, but I guess she was only following her heart. From now on, she would only tell him that I was well. She was not to know that I suffered bouts of melancholy. Yes, I still preferred to call it that. I had wondered at the time why Rainey had returned to Italy but supposed that I might never know. I wondered if he had found a woman over there that he could love. If so, Lara had not said so. I wanted him to, yet I didn't. How fickle was that?

I was hardly seeing Dr. Jai anymore, as I seemed to be handling my emotions on my own. Johnny had hired a crew to dismantle what was left of the conservatory. Apparently, after Miss Mary's demise, her husband had wrecked havoc with the room, destroying everything, even the Greek columns that held the ceiling up. I entered the room only once and thought that it was useless to bring it back to life. The few remaining windows were blackened from the weather, the walls were rotted with mold, and the ceiling had all but collapsed. The plant life had been left to decompose and the whole place smelled rancid. Crockery had been smashed into smithereens and lay scattered across the floor. Johnny suggested that I not return until the clutter and debris had been dealt with. I asked him if he thought that it would be worth renovating, and he said that once the mess was cleaned up, it would be like starting from scratch. By the end of the summer and countless trips to the landfill, the old room was once again empty. It was left open for weeks for a full airing before the new windows were put in place. New columns were on order to my specifications and plastering of the ceiling and walls had begun. The rest would be up to me to decide how I wanted to create my Eden. It would be my winter project, when the days were long and dismal.

At the beginning of October, we were all told that Mollie Magan was prepared to conduct us in a séance. I wasn't entirely sure that we should go ahead with it, but the others convinced me that we should. We set a date for October 11. Jeremy would be in New Zealand.

Mollie had sent her instructions ahead for us. I hadn't realized that there were rules.

First: We must all genuinely want to be there. We must be positive and not frivolous.

Second: We must be patient, so as not to rob the medium of energy.

Third: We must be able to convey love, as it was the presence that enabled communication.

Fourth: We must not be cynical or fearful.

Fifth: We must not have any hate or envy toward one another, as that would defeat the purpose.

Sixth: Faith was good, but we best not to bring our religious beliefs to the table.

We all knew why we would be conducting the séance, and that was for Liz Beth.

Now, the room should be a comfortable one with a table and chairs, perhaps one that the subject was familiar with. We would be sitting in a circle, close enough to hold hands. Our knees should not be touching. The lights should be dim, or else we could use candles. Some soft, meditative music in the background would be nice. Once she had started, we would need to remain seated, keep our eyes closed, and think only loving thoughts. We must not call out or even whisper any communication that we felt but remember them to share later. We should not expect to see an apparition or to hear a voice emanating from the corner of the room. Above all, we must be open to anything.

The storm season was upon us. Sure enough, the skies were threatening to burst open the evening of October 11. There were five of us awaiting Millie, who had volunteered to bring Mollie Magan to Avanloch. Shalla had decided to decline the séance, and so there was Jannie, Mrs. D, the sisters, Emma and Amma, and myself. We would be a gathering of seven with Millie and Mollie. I need not worry about the children, as Shalla was keeping them occupied. Duffy was visiting in the village. We were watching at the window for Millie's truck. When it came to a halt in the driveway, the others sent me out to greet them as I should as Lady of Avanloch. I scowled but went anyway.

Mollie Magan was the oldest person I ever met. I discovered later that she was ninety one. I couldn't decide if she reminded me of a garden gnome or an elf or a witch. Indeed, she seemed to have characteristics of all three. She walked with the proverbial gnarled cane. She had been injured in a previous fall from her wagon many years past and could no longer stand erect. I wouldn't have expected anything less from a woman her age. Her fingers were curled around her walking stick. I couldn't but help notice the nodules protruding from her knuckles. Her face was weathered and wrinkled, and I feared that if touched, she would fall to pieces. Her eyes were sunk deep into their sockets, but I believed that they were black. I was glad that she didn't appear to have any visible warts. On her head, she donned a thick, grey toque. She had on a long-sleeved, dark, woolen dress, and a threadbare shawl covered her shoulders. Around her neck were a dozen amulets that must have weighed 5 pounds, with some of them hanging down to her waist. She wore rubber boots, which she removed when she entered the foyer and asked us to excuse her bare feet. I presented her with a pair of red slippers, telling her that the floors were very cold and I wished that she would keep them, as they had been newly knitted and had not yet found an owner.

She bowed to me, which was totally unexpected. "Ah, the Grand Lady of Avanloch. We meet at long last. I have heard many a good word about thee. Your kindness is known by all. The Christmas package was greatly appreciated. It is an honor to have you invite me into your palace to assist ye."

"Ms. Magan, I am but a naïve young girl who has come to your country to live. I have been welcomed by all I have met and now I welcome a woman who is somewhat of a legend into this castle, which, by some strange circumstance, I call home. I, as are we all, am indebted to you for agreeing to perform this service. Please call me Vela, as I assure you, I am no lady."

She let out a deep cackle. "A sense of humor, I like. And these ruby slippers must be that ye think I be the good witch. I hope my appearance does not frighten you, child."

"I assure you that Vela does not frighten easily, Mollie. I can attest to that. She is not a bit apprehensive that this huge mansion may harbor ghosts. She has gumption, as we use to say in the old days," Jannie told her.

"I say she comes from good Scottish stock. Now what we say we get this show on the road? I fear that there is a storm brewing in the wind. What would a séance be without some special effects? A tempest in a teapot, so to speak."

I took her arm gently and led her into the room we had made ready.

"You don't know worry, Missy, I am not as fragile as I look. 'Tis thee I am concerned about. A big undertaking for such a young lady. Ah, right, you no lady."

"That's right, Mollie, I am no lady."

We all had a chuckle, which relieved some of the pent-up tension that we were experiencing. Everyone but Amma and I had sat in on a séance before. I had discussed the proceedings with Jannie prior to tonight and had asked her if she had ever had an encounter with any of Avanloch's former residents. She said that she wasn't at all sure. Sometimes, she had the feeling that there was a presence in a room with her. She never felt threatened or frightened from the experiences but thought that the feelings had intensified since Maveryn's passing. I did not volunteer that Jeremy had numerous visits from her. We had chosen the tea room to hold our session in, as it was the coziest and had a round table that we could all sit around in comfortably. We chose to light candles. Amma had brought her portable cassette player and chose a soft, meditative tape to enhance our mood.

We sat holding hands with our eyes closed while Mollie gave us a few instructions. She did not go into a trance but sent her energy to us through body and mind. After twenty minutes, we were told to open our eyes and, one by one, to relay any information that we may have gathered during our sitting. Unfortunately, not one of us had felt that we had experienced a visit from Liz Beth.

I was last to portray my thoughts. "I am sorry, perhaps it was my fault. As hard as I tried to concentrate on her portrait and what little I knew about her short life, the only image that came to me was that of Maveryn."

A hush came over the room, as one by one the ladies all revealed that they, too, had felt the presence of the former Lady McAllister.

Mollie Magan was delighted. "Aha, I thought as much, as I was feeling that she, too, was in the room with us. Her spirit is the stronger force." She asked us what the feeling that we received from her was, and we all answered, "A sense of peace." Mollie clapped her frail hands and said, "We are all in agreement. The affair has been a success. Perhaps it wasn't the result that we were looking for, but I deem it to be significant."

We agreed with her and voiced that we might try to conjure Liz Beth up another time.

Mrs. D provided refreshments and we discussed our undertaking further. By the time we saw Millie and Mollie to the door, it was 10 P.M. The sky was still overcast. I took Mollie's hands again and thanked her, telling her that she was welcome anytime.

She thanked me as she looked at the dark clouds. "See? No thunderous bolts or tornado-like winds descended upon us. We did not anger the heavenly God. This was a good sitting. I am not surprised that there are entities here; after all, 'tis an ancient castle. There are bound to be many restless souls roaming about these halls. They will manifest themselves in one way or another if they wish to be disturbed. Sleep peacefully, my friends."

I asked her why, after all this time, was something happening. She said the same thing as Mrs. D had…that the playing field had changed. That meant me. Apparently, I was more sensitive to the spirits.

I did sleep well, however, and was refreshed the next morning, knowing that I was not the only one who had felt Maveryn's presence. I had not shared with anyone the night that I had witnessed her apparition.

For the time being, we all agreed not to pursue the spirits any further. If one of us experienced a presence again, we would be sure to share it.

Not only was Johnny at work preparing the conservatory, I also had him install lampposts to the driveway. When lit at night, they definitely brought a homier atmosphere to the stark bleakness of the castle. I had wanted them working by Halloween, so that the trick-or-treaters from the village would have an illuminated walkway. Rosalyn dressed up as Tinkerbelle and greeted the children with bags of goodies. She insisted that I wear a costume also, and I chose something from Miss Mary's closet, a 1920s cha-cha dress.

I had gained 6 pounds, but some of her clothes were still too big for me. I made full use of her attire, as there certainly was an outfit for every occasion. I had taken the girls into Waverly on a spending spree. They each came home with ten new fall outfits, sleepwear, and several pairs of shoes. For myself, I only purchased walking shoes and riding boots. I was still hesitant on spending money on myself. Weather permitting, I had taken to horseback riding every afternoon while the girls were resting. I tried not to remember my days with Rainey when we rode the fields and meadows of the Quinn ranch. I am afraid I did not win over those recollections.

I was very slow with my plans for the conservatory. I had decided to name it Eden. I needed help and invited my parents and sisters to come for Christmas. They had not even met their granddaughters. Jeremy insisted on paying their fare. They accepted and I was thrilled to be seeing them again. They stayed for a week and we had a glorious time. We had not seen each other for two years, such a long time. I asked them countless questions about what was happening in Bridge, with the restaurant, and the never-ending re-modeling of the Palace. We never discussed Rainey. I believe that as soon as they saw Ava, they knew that he was her father, but they never questioned me. Rosalyn and Ava loved their new aunties and grandparents. It was very hard to see them leave. I promised that I would be home soon. Father gave me invaluable help with the plans for Eden. I only wish that he could be here to see them through. It was such a letdown after they left that I started my sessions again with Dr. Jai. She encouraged me to keep my promise to my family and plan a trip to Canada. I was sorry to say that I never followed through on those plans until five years later.

In the autumn of 1964, Rosalyn was five and it was time for her to enter kindergarten. She was quite adamant that she was not going. No way was she going to leave her sister. We finally reached an agreement that she would try it for two days, and if she still didn't like it, then I would not force her to go. She came home the first day brimming with enthusiasm and the subject of her attending school never came up again. In just two and a half years, Ava would be doing the same thing.

The school in the village had been closed down for a number of years, but with the rapid growth of new children entering the school year, it was reopened. Jeremy had a huge influence over the school board in their decision to reinstate it. He had paid for the complete remodeling of the two-room schoolhouse in the summer of '64, knowing that he didn't want his daughter to have to travel to Waverly for at least four years. For now, there would be K-grade three in the village. Maybe that would even change in time. The older children had a bus trip of an hour to and fro Waverly. It made for a long day, but what could one do? The village and the area had a population of less than 200. That number was growing rapidly, as more people were choosing to live in a small hamlet.

By the summer of 1964, my Eden was nearing completion. If I hadn't decided to have a Roman-like pool installed, it would have been finished earlier. The pool took up a fourth of the space, but I wanted it large and deep enough to swim in. It cost a small fortune, but Jeremy was totally agreeable to it. He wanted his girls to learn how to swim in a controlled environment. Of course, I was to be their teacher. I had a healthy respect for water and I hoped to instill the same in them. I realized that I would have to take certain precautions, like keeping the doors to Eden locked. Only with my permission would entrance be allowed, even to the staff. No accidents were going to take place on my watch.

Jeremy asked me well in advance if we might throw a costume party that October. I did not want to but could hardly deny him the first opportunity to entertain since our marriage. I had met a few of his acquaintances in London and the odd time that they would drop by. I had not been impressed with any of them, but I would make a conscientious effort to be a good hostess. The soiree was to be held in the grand drawing room; so much ado was made to ready it. Jeremy was home for the week prior to the ball, so he assumed the responsibility for the preparations. Extra staff was hired; even Mrs. D and Reita were to have six additional helpers. Invitations were in the mail in September to seventy-five people! My saving grace was that Jannie, John, Ash, and six of her friends would be attending. We would be "rooming" most of the guests. I could not imagine. The tower rooms were opened up to allow for further bedrooms. It sounded as if the whole affair was to be an orgy. I really thought that Jeremy had gone to extremes for his first social affair. As it was, I needed not to worry. Only fifty attended and the majority of them were in their later years. That was only forty new people that I would have to meet. I only took exception to one gentleman whose name I will not mention at this time. I hope that I mistook his intentions toward me. It had been a very long time since anyone had flirted with me, so I convinced myself that I was reading too much into his actions. After all, would a duke conduct himself that way? Little did I know.

The party was a huge success. I had donned as my costume another gem from Miss Mary's closet. It was a turn-of-the-century gown of black velvet that required several petticoats. Amma had pinned my hair on my head in the fashion of that day—a pompadour, I was told. For the first time in years, I wore a slender, black, 2-inch pump, or else I would be trampling on the dress hem. I was going to wear jewelry from Mary's vast collection, but Jeremy presented me with an emerald-stoned necklace and earrings for the occasion and said he hoped that I would do him the honor of wearing them, so I did. I prayed that it was only a kind gesture and nothing else.

The guests all left after a late brunch the next day. Even though I had enjoyed the party, I was glad to see their backs. Ash, Steff, and two other friends stayed on another day. That pleased me. We went riding without Steff, who declined, saying that she would rather stay with the children. Ash and I did not encourage her to join us.

Jeremy thanked me for being such a gracious hostess and promised that we would only entertain once or twice a year. I told him whatever he wanted was all right with me. That night, I had my first visit from Maveryn, and two days later, I received a letter from Lara, saying that Rainey had married.

I had been extremely exhausted in the days following the party. My sleep was constantly being interrupted by peculiar dreams. I had visions of a beggar coming to our door, asking for silver, and of my lover leaving me for another woman. I dreamt of the duke who had flirted with me. His name was Roberge Farradan. I didn't know if that was his real name or if I had made it up in my fantasy world of the night. When I was roused from my sleep several days later,

I truly believed that I was hallucinating. I had switched on the bedside lamp and was going to check on the children when I saw her. There, in the pale moonlight, was a woman dressed in a long, white gown. I knew at once that it was Maveryn. She floated on by me and I could tell that she was going to the girls' room. I followed her. She hovered over them like a hummingbird. Satisfied, she turned to me and, with a nod, was gone. I imagined that her next stop would be to find Jeremy. I wondered if this was a nightly occurrence for her. I felt the same feelings of peace and calmness that I had on the other occasions when I had felt her presence—the night of the séance and when I had seen the vision in the foyer. I now knew that it was she who had paid me a visit on the eve of Ava's birth. How many people could say that they had the privilege to see a loved one in her heavenly body? I returned to bed fully intending to discuss my visit from Maveryn with Jeremy and my friends the next day.

Something got in the way of my revelation. In midday, I received a letter from Lara, which I opened right away. It read:

Dear V,

I hope this finds you in good health and that you no longer suffer from melancholy. I have debated with myself as to whether I should relate to you recent events. I hope that I have read your feelings toward Rainey correctly. Am I right that you only wish him happiness?

He was married in September. Her name is Louise Morgan. She is from a wealthy family. Word has it that her father is financing Rainey's architectural firm. The wedding was a big f…in extravaganza. None of us were comfortable. Jimmy wasn't even asked to be the best man. Can you believe it? Some relative of the "bride" was. Jimmy pretended not to feel rejected, but I am sure that he was. I managed five minutes alone with Rain. I did not get the impression that he was altogether happy. You know me, I came right out and asked him if he is in love with Louise, and this is what he said, "Lara, she is not the love of my life. You, more than anyone else, knows that I crossed that bridge a long time ago. I guess that after all is said and done, I needed someone to share my life with. I can't say that I was entirely ready, but it was opportune for me, so I will try and make it work."

Does that sound like a man on the most important day of his life? V, I think that he is still in love with you. I know you don't believe that he ever was, but you didn't see how affected he was when he came home and found you gone. Have you waited too long, V? Anyhow, if it is any consolation, Louise did not make a good impression on any of us. I had the feeling that she thought we were all country bumpkins. I don't think this "arranged" marriage will last. Pessimistic much?

Oh, by the way, I caught the bouquet. Jimmy made me stand in line! Ha-ha-ha! I don't even have a prospect looming on the horizon.

When are you coming for a visit? I miss my old friend.

Love you,

Lara

Initially, I was not upset with the news. I put the letter in my pocket and went out to the potting shed to gather up the utensils that I would need for a final pruning and picking in the rose garden. Before too long, the tears were streaming down my face and I had to take a seat on the nearest bench. I reread Lara's words over and over, especially the ones where Rainey had said that the love of his life had been gone a long, long time. That was me, and I wondered how I could live with myself any longer. Had I expected him to wait forever for me? Was there ever a more red-blooded man? He could have his pick of the crop, and in a way, I was glad that he had chosen someone who he wasn't head-over-heels in love with. Did I dare to hope that his marriage was to be a placebo like mine? Yes, Lara, I had waited too long. Now, I must get on with the rest of my life until…

Was I still thinking that someday, I would be reunited with the only man who I would ever love? Bloody hell, I was.

I answered Lara in a few days and thanked her for the news. I told her that it did not make me happy, but I had no right to even consider the fact that Rainey might love me. We must no longer dwell in the past. I encouraged her to not give up on her love life. Someone wonderful would come along for her. I would try and come for a quick visit the next time that Jeremy was traveling to Canada.

Then I did something unfathomable: I penned a note to Rainey. I went to my private sitting room where I would not be disturbed. Rosalyn was in school and Amma had taken Ava for a visit with her mom, Granny Kay. Amma was expecting a baby in the spring and we were all excited about that.

I found the perfect blank notepaper that had belonged to Maveryn. It was a very thin vellum and there were trees in blossom on the front…perhaps they were cherry. I opened it up and wrote:

My dear Rainey,

Please excuse the intrusion into your life, but I feel that I must apologize for my foolhardiness. I do not want you to feel that you had anything to do with my selfish departure. This is to release you from any guilt that you may have felt. Please accept my apologies.

I want to convey my very best wishes to you and yours, and pray that you will live a long and prosperous life. Happiness is to hold the people you love in both hands and dance. I wish this for you.

Remember me with kindness,
Vienna

I sealed the envelope with an invisible kiss and addressed it to Rainey in care of his parents in Hawthorne. I printed the address in bold letters. I did not want Patsy to recognize my handwriting, for I was afraid that she would not forward my message. For all I knew, it might never find Rainey—and maybe that might be for the best.

I mailed the note to Rainey two days later, when I went to London with Jannie and John to see another play that Ash had written and produced. It was not nearly as good as her first play, but I did not tell her that.

The Christmas season came and went again. I was dealing with the gloomy, stormy weather, keeping myself occupied with my Eden. I was spending thousands of dollars on plants and furnishings. Jeremy would bring a new item home from wherever he traveled. So far, he had returned with exotic orchids and foliage. At Christmas, he presented me with an elaborate, Venetian stained-glass window. I was very happy when I was decorating. The girls and I would play in the pool after their lessons. They both loved the water.

In January, I received a scolding from Lara. It appeared that Rainey had indeed received my card. He had phoned Lara and relayed to her my words. He demanded to know if she was in contact with me. He told her that the postmark was from England and asked if she had my address. She had to lie for me again. Was that what I wanted her to do? She was sick of this farce. Rainey had said to her, "Tell your friend I said thank you for the well wishes, but just when I thought that I was putting her in my past, she opened up old wounds again." She finished by telling me to quit fooling with his heart and find someone else to play games with.

I did not have to read her words over again, as they were etched in my mind. I had made a mistake when I wrote to Rainey. I would not do that again.

The next months were not easy for me. I was having regular sessions with Dr. Jai but had still not confessed to her any of my past that I knew was the cause of my depression. I did not answer Lara, nor did I open any of her subsequent letters for a long time. Why she continued to write to me was beyond me. Finally, almost a year later, I opened her last letter. She said that she knew that I was upset with her but she was not giving up on me. She mentioned that Rainey and Louise had a son now. That would probably keep them together. She asked if I was, at long last, truly happy for him. She wanted to know if she should continue sending news of him. Rainey did not contact her anymore. Her exact words were: "He is still pissed with me for harboring you. He will never forgive me." I answered her, telling her how sorry I was to have caused dissention between her and her favorite cousin. The blame lay heavy on my shoulders. I told her that I would never contact him in any way, shape, or form again. Yes, I was happy for him on the birth of his son, as being a mother, I knew what joy children bring.

Ava started kindergarten in the autumn of 1967. Rosalyn was in grade three. The years had taken my babies. I was alone except for the staff half the day. Amma had given birth to a little girl in '66. She and Johnny were ecstatic. They named their daughter Alexandria. My girls had shortened her name to Alexa, which everyone soon adopted. She was my saving grace, this bundle of delight. She was walking and talking, and anything that I may have missed out on or forgotten with Ava and Rosalyn, I was showering on her. She was like my third daughter. She called me Tia.

I had several more encounters with the Duke of Hennessey, Roberge. We attended a celebration of his tenth wedding anniversary in London. There, for the first time, I met his wife, Lauren. Jeremy had informed me on the train ride that he had married her to save his family's status. She had all the money and he was destitute.

They lived in a palace called Calendria. Everything that was lacking in class at Avanloch was here, but the atmosphere was cold and inhospitable. They had no children and I felt that if I touched anything, it would crumble into dust. The Duchess Lauren was enamored with her title and approved of everyone addressing her as Lady. Roberge introduced me as Lady Vela of Avanloch. She took my hand and said that she was delighted to finally meet Jeremy's young wife. Her hand was ice cold and her eyes were colder. She held her head high, as if lowering it would put her in a different class. I smiled and said in my most regal voice that the honor was all mine and thanked her for inviting us into her stately domicile. I accepted Roberge's offer to dance and tasted acid in my mouth. Imagine sleeping next to that snow queen! I apologized to him if I had sounded rude, and he laughed and danced me away from the crowd. I found myself in a small vestibule with him. He sat me down on a tufted sofa and joined me. I told him that I was not at all comfortable being alone with him. He laughed again and said that this was the twentieth century and said, "Aren't you game for a little fun?"

I stood up and said, "Not under your roof."

"Well then, I guess we are just going to have to find another roof."

"That is not what I meant and you know it, Sir!"

"How I love some life in my women! I know you noticed that stone of a woman that I am married to and I also know that you share a loveless life—"

I cut him off in mid-sentence. "You know nothing of the sort. Please do not assume that I care to carry on a tryst with you." I left him laughing. I was not amused.

Unfortunately, I was to meet up with him again at the opera house in Edinburgh. He approached me at the intermission when I was left standing alone. I was sure that he had waited just for such an opportunity. He bowed and reached for my hand, smiling like the Cheshire cat. "My lady, how de-lighted I am to see you again."

I surprised myself by responding, "Oh Lordy, not you again."

That brought howls of laughter and an audience straining to hear our con-versation.

"You wound me to the bone, Madame. What must I do to assure you that my intensions toward you are serious?"

Thank goodness Jeremy was returning and that ended his flirtation. I excused myself, but not before he said, "Until we meet again, my dear."

I supposed that I would continuously be running into him, seeing that he was in the same circle as Jeremy. It wasn't that I found him unattractive, because he certainly had the looks of an Adonis, but he was a bit crude for my liking. I had no vows to uphold, but I wasn't about to become an adulteress.

I was still in love with Rainey. So suppose that he was Rainey, what then? There was no question; I would do whatever he wanted.

I went home and contemplated what I had been thinking. Was it time for me to go home and make amends? There was a little matter of a wife and son standing in my way. *Vienna, you silly, silly girl, your life with Rainey is over and you best get over it*, I thought. *And quit promising yourself things that are never going to happen.* There, I hoped that I had laid the notion to rest…again.

I did decide one thing though. I definitely was going home…home to Bridge. It had been several years since my family's last visit. In the summer, I would take the girls.

The girls kept asking me every day when we were going to go and see Lily, Papa Joe, and their aunts. It was like counting down the Christmas calendar. I was looking forward to the trip myself. I hoped that Maveryn would understand. I left that up to Jeremy, as it seemed that he was the only one she conversed with, if indeed she did. She was making an appearance more and more often. Her visitations were no longer limited to the bedrooms. The first time that Rosalyn had an encounter with her departed mother, she was eight. It didn't faze her at all. She came to me and said, "Mama, my mother in Heaven came and saw me last night. She looked so beautiful. She is watching over Ava and me. We must tell Ava that if she sees her, not to be afraid. I think I will keep it a secret from my friends. What do you think?"

I told her that I, too, had seen her mother many times, and so had her father. Yes, we should talk about it with her sister and that we should definitely just keep her visits within the family. No one else from outside Avanloch would understand, or else they might be afraid that it was haunted. Not everyone understood that there were kind and loving ghosts. Soon, Maveryn's presence was felt by Amma and Mrs. D. She was visiting less and less, as she herself seemed to be satisfied that all was well. Perhaps we had disturbed her when we held the séance. By the time we were leaving for Canada, she had quit making an appearance altogether. Even Jeremy felt that she was at peace and that she trusted us to keep the girls safe.

The day was finally here, when we would be leaving. The girls were beyond excited. I had plans to make the whole trip an adventure for them. They had been on the train to Edinburgh before and always enjoyed it. This time, they found it boring and long. It didn't help matters that our flight was delayed and we had to spend an extra hour at the airport. Once in the air, their enthusiasm returned. They had a big letdown again when we arrived in Toronto. Even though we had discussed it many times, they seemed to have forgotten that this was not our destination. Another plane ride, then the train, and then the car journey to Bridge. It was almost midnight when Father picked us up off the train. The girls slept all the way home. I decided that I would never do the trip in one day ever again.

I had written Lara that we were coming. I told her that I would dearly love to see the gang from Hawthorne, but it probably wasn't a good idea. She agreed with me. They still frequented Lily Lane's, so if I ran into them, so be it. There would be no chance that I would run into Rainey, as his newest son was only six months old, and she was sure that he would not be traveling with him. And he couldn't leave him alone with Louise, as she had postpartum depression.

We slept on and off all the next day, but I was able to squeeze in a quick visit with Lara. We both bawled like babies. She was the same old Lara. She couldn't get over how slender I was. Mother told her that they were going to have to do something about that. I said, "Please fatten me up. I have been trying for years but not getting very far. It's not that I don't eat, just that I wear it all off traipsing around forty rooms and a hundred acres. Not to mention my volunteer work or keeping track of two energetic children."

Mother said, "A few hamburgers and crullers every day and I promise that you will go home a few pounds heavier. Every woman's dream, right?"

We were to be in Bridge Falls for two weeks. When Lara wasn't working at the hospital, she was with us all the time. Sissy and Addy both worked at the diner. They were young ladies. Sissy was twenty-one and was engaged to be married next year. Addy, my baby sister, was seventeen. I had my twenty-fifth birthday this past year; I had not been home for seven and a half years. I wasn't entirely sure that I wanted to return to Scotland. I knew that there was no longer any chance for me with Rainey, so what was the use of hanging around and wishing that a bright-red 1956 Oldsmobile would come driving down the street and that a blue-eyed, sandy-haired man would be at its helm?

I took the girls exploring to all the old haunts. They swam at the falls in the cold river but never even noticed the temperature. One day, I donned a floppy hat and dark sunglasses and ventured into Hawthorne. The girls were at a neighbor's child's birthday party, so I had three hours all by myself. I sat in the car near the general store but didn't see a soul I knew. I drove around and out to the Quinn ranch but turned around before I got to their driveway. I cried for my teenage memories. I started for home, but something made me turn down 4th Street. I passed Jimmy's house and parked for a few seconds, knowing full well that I was flirting with disaster. I wanted to see him, but my little voice told me to get going. I checked my rearview mirror and there he was, coming toward my car. I swore.

"Can I help you, Ma'am?" Jimmy said. "I couldn't help but notice that you appear to be looking for something."

I threw caution to the wind and took my glasses off. "I swear if one more person calls me 'Ma'am,' I am going to take his head off!"

"Lord loves a duck! V! What a sight for sore eyes. Get out and let me see you."

I removed my hat and climbed out. "I see you are still using my superlatives. A lot better than that language you used to use."

He laughed and we hugged for a very long time. I asked him where Ruth was, and he said she was out of town with their daughter, Constance, who was four years old. He wanted to know all about me and where I was living. I felt badly that I couldn't tell him the truth, but I told him what I could.

"I guess you know that I am married and have two daughters," I said. "My husband is quite wealthy and we travel a lot. Let's just say I live overseas."

"I know all of that, V, but where are you in life? Are you happy? Do you ever think of Rainey? We were all so worried about you when you left so suddenly. I thought that Rain was going to go out of his mind for a while. What happened?"

"Oh, don't tell me that. I truly thought that he had already let me go. I hate to admit it, but I was suffering from depression and I needed a change of scenery. Nothing is secret anymore, except I am not ready for anyone to know exactly where I am. Lara doesn't even know. Someday, I hope that I will have vanquished all my ghosts and will be able to be free from my guilt. Do you understand any of this, Jimmy? You know, I came here today on a whim. I shouldn't have."

"I think I know exactly where you are coming from, old friend. The heart is a fragile thing. I was on your side you know. I knew what Rainey did to you and I blamed him for your leaving."

"You shouldn't have, Jimmy. I hope that it didn't cause a riff in your friendship."

"Nah, we kissed and made up. You know that he is married and has two sons, right?"

"Yes, Lara informed me of that. I have asked her to keep me informed. Can you understand that I don't want him to know that I keep tabs on him? There is no way that I could face him, not in a thousand years. He is married and has kids. That makes me happy."

"If you met the battleaxe that he is with, you might change your mind."

"Why do you say that, Jimmy?"

"She is a society gal. Won't step foot in this hick town ever again; once was enough for her. Maybe I shouldn't say that because she may be coming for Patsy's and Paul's anniversary party, if Rainey has his say."

"When is that?"

"Not until October. Anyhow, I don't like her and she doesn't like me or anyone else. Whenever Yates or I go to the coast, we meet Rain away from his house. He's changed you know. Hey, we have known each other since time began and you notice things."

"How do you mean, Jimmy?"

"Not in a good way, V. He puts on an act when we are around, but you can see the coldness in his eyes, almost like he is lost. At least he stopped drinking after Morgan was born. I think that he is the main caregiver. Hey, enough about him. I want to know more about you. Why are you so skinny?"

"I am not skinny, Jimmy."

"Yes, you are. You are model thin."

"I had better get a move on. Can I ask you to keep this meeting just between you and me, or is that too much to ask? I don't care if you mention that you saw me, because, after all, I am here in Bridge. Please don't relay any of our conversation to Rainey. I don't think that would be a good idea."

"You're right. He has enough to deal with. I'm coming into town tomorrow. Can I buy you a coke at the diner, say at two?"

"I will be there. See you then."

I didn't know if I felt better or worse for seeing Jimmy. Lara was off the next day so she joined us. I left the girls with Father. I didn't think it was a good idea that Jimmy saw Ava. He was disappointed not to meet them and I told him there would be other times. He was happy to hear that I was going to be coming back to town in the future. Lara insisted on paying the bill and Mother said she would not take money from her. While they were arguing, I told Jimmy that I would drop him a note once in a while, but he was going to have to keep it to himself.

He smiled and said, "I like it…sort of a conspiracy. My lips are sealed wherever you are concerned, Ma'am." He held his hand over his head. "Please don't beat me to death."

"What are you two clowning around about?" Lara asked.

"She doesn't like to be called Ma'am is all. Why's that? Do you know, Lara?"

"She married into royalty, don't you know? And everybody calls her Ma'am or Lady. She wants to be just V."

"Get out of town!" Jimmy exclaimed. "Is this another secret?"

We all laughed and I was the happiest that I had been in a long, long time.

Two nights before we were to leave for home, there was a loud knock at the front door. Mother and Father were in the conservatory, where they still went after Mother returned from work to have their little cocktail. Addy and Sissy were giving Ava and Rosalyn pedicures, so that left me to answer the door. Jack Jennings stood there, handsome as ever. He hadn't changed at all.

"Jack?" Why I asked I didn't know, because it was obvious that it was him.

"Hello, V. You act as if you don't recognize me."

"I'm sorry. I am so surprised to see you. How are you?"

"About the same as the last time you saw me. Can you come out for a coffee, or is your husband here?"

I had a feeling that he knew Jeremy was not with me, or why else would he be here to ask me out. Well, not really, it was just for coffee. It didn't take me long to say yes. I told the girls that an old friend had stopped by and that I was going to visit with him at the Java House. He held the truck door open for me while I climbed in. I asked him if he was still working at the same mine, and he said that he was in a camp outside of Edmonton, driving a rig for an oil company. I imagined that he was making good money to afford this brand new, fancy vehicle. He said that the roads were washed out due to heavy rains and that was why he was home, visiting his parents.

The coffee shop was the same as I remembered it and I felt like I had never left town. We made small chitchat. I was soon to discover that Jack was married and his wife and son were in Edmonton. The marriage was not working out and I expressed my regrets.

"Nothing to be sorry about," he assured me. "Do you want to hear something strange? I married her because she looked like you."

"Oh, Jack," I lamented. "We were never going to amount to anything in our relationship, you knew that. I am sorry if I ever gave you the impression that there was hope for us. I was so young back then and I made a lot of mistakes."

"I don't blame you for anything, V. You can't blame a guy for hoping, can you?"

I was experiencing some pent-up emotions as I looked at Jack. God, he still had that brooding, electrifying way of talking. If I hadn't been so enamored with Rainey when I first met Jack, things might have turned out differently for us, but I certainly wasn't going to tell him that. I was struggling with my own emotions. I had been too long without a man's arms around me that I was imagining what it would be like with Jack. Thank heavens he broke the spell and asked if I had seen any of the old crowd. We talked a little while longer and then he said that he had better get me home, as he had to leave early tomorrow morning. He said he was sorry that he hadn't found out sooner that I was in town. For a second, I considered asking him if he couldn't stay another day but decided I should just leave things the way they were before I stirred anything up. It wasn't every day that you met somebody you used to care for and found out that he might still have feelings for you. If he had been Rainey, I would have been begging him to stay.

We shook hands at the door and then a quick hug. He wished me the best and I told him that I hoped his marriage would work out.

He shrugged his shoulders and said, "Whatever will be, will be."

I was a little sad to see him leave, and yet relieved. I hadn't realized just how vulnerable I was. I thought, *Now why did a picture of that flirtatious duke come into my mind?*

When Henry picked us up off the train in Waverly, I thought he was acting a little strange. When I asked him if everything was all right, he replied hesitantly, "Oh, things be a little off, Miss." He nodded to the girls in the back so I didn't question him any further until we dropped the girls off at the kennels to visit with their beloved dogs.

"All right, Henry, what gives?" I said.

"There be some trouble at the mansion, Miss Vela. I best to let the ladies fill you in."

He dropped me off at the main entrance instead of the kitchen door, as if I were a guest. The minute I walked in the door, I knew something was definitely wrong. We had long ago quit with the barriers on the grand staircase, but today, they were cordoned off and several panels were missing from the second landing. My first reaction was that one of the staff had fallen. I dropped my purse and headed for the kitchen just as Amma was coming out.

"Oh, thank God that you are home!" she said.

"What has happened here? I am almost afraid to find out."

We embraced and she said, "It is not as bad as it looks. No one was seriously hurt. Well, no one from the house. One of Johnny's men is in the hospital. Don't panic. He is going to be all right."

"What, are you telling me that a grown man fell through the railing? That is almost impossible. It is as sturdy as the Rock of Gibraltar. Whatever was he doing?"

"No one saw, Vela. We just heard a piercing scream and then the thud. When we got to him, he was lying in a crumpled heap but he was conscious. He said that he was pushed."

"Pushed? How could that be? Who else was working with him? If someone else was with him, then he must know what happened."

"That is just it, Vela, there was no one about. He had been working in room six—you know, the one next to Miss Mary's, the one no one ever goes in. Mr. Jeremy decided that he wanted to have it remodeled so that it could be used again."

"I wasn't aware that anything was amiss with it."

"Have you ever been in it? I think not. The room has not been broken into ever since…"

"Ever since what, Amma?"

She answered me in a whisper. "Ever since Tatylyanna was sent to her death."

I was still confused. "Are you trying to tell me something, Amma?"

Shalla and Mrs. D emerged from the kitchen and I went through the greetings again.

"How about a nice cuppa tea?" Mrs. D suggested.

We followed her, and once we were seated, the story started to unfold. They had their own versions and I listened, trying to piece it all together. Apparently, Sam, the one who had the "accident," had already been experiencing strange goings-on in number six. The door would slam when there wasn't even a breeze, the power would go off and on intermittently, and he always felt that he was being watched. On the day of the accident, he had left the room to retrieve some tools that he had left at the top of the stairs, and when he bent over, he was struck by an unknown force. He had seen nothing but swore that he heard a hissing and felt a hand on his back before he was sent careening down the stairs. Of course, Mr. Jeremy was not at home. He never was when anything happened.

"I'm feared that she is out, Miss Vela…the Black Russian, she be back." Mrs. D was convinced that it was she who had pushed Sam.

"Do the rest of you think the same thing?" I asked.

Amma said she hoped not and Shalla said that she never even knew her.

"The first thing that we must do then is to seal that room up."

"Johnny did so right away," Amma informed me.

"Then he believed that Sam was indeed pushed?" I asked Amma.

"He doesn't believe in ghosts, if that is what you are asking. He was very upset at what happened. He doesn't have an explanation. He remembered the accident of before but had never heard Mrs. D's and the others' version. I truly think that he thought that it was a lot of malarkey, but because his daughter was at the castle every day, he listened to the ladies and had the room sealed."

"Does everyone from the manor know?"

"Yes, it was Millie and Jannie who convinced him to do it."

"I have but one question—" Mrs. D was interrupted by the girls bursting in the door. "There are my girls, come and give ole Mary a big hug and let's hear all about your holiday. This house has been so empty without you two. I hope you not a planning on going away again anytime soon."

They both looked at me and Rosalyn asked, "Are we, Mom?"

I told them not until Sissy's wedding, which was not until next year.

Ava said that the dogs were so lonesome and asked if they could please come in. I told her to ask Mrs. D, who had probably just washed the floor.

She replied that she had not and added, "Don't you think that it be a good idea to have them big dogs on the premises so that they can be a looking out for these girls?"

I agreed, and off they ran to unpack and get the gifts that we had brought back for everyone, but not before they let Shelley and Keats in. Shalla offered to go with them and I thanked her and told them that I would be up shortly.

I asked if anyone felt threatened in light of what had happened here. They all said that they didn't, but that they were on their guard and stayed away from the head of the stairs.

"I think that we should call Mollie Magan in," Mrs. D suggested.

"And what do you think that she could do?" I asked

"Do ye not think that we need an exorcism?"

"Mary, that is for the living who are possessed, isn't it? And a priest performs those rites. I do not think this qualifies. But I am not against seeking her sage advice. Ask her to visit us. I think that it is also high time that Mr. Jeremy know that some of you think that it was Liz Beth who pushed Taty whatever downs the stairs. Or does he already?"

"No, I do not think so. I surely never told him. Maybe Miss Jannie did. He does know that Lady Maveryn knew something, or why else would she refer to her as the Black Russian on her deathbed?"

"We may never know, Mary. Does anyone know if Maveryn kept a dairy? I would have thought that I would have come across one by now, unless Jeremy has it."

"Can't help you there, but it does sound like something she would have done. But, I still have a question. How do we know that the Black Russian is at all in her room? Perhaps she did not get back before it was shut up."

Chapter Seventeen

1969–1972

What had I come home to? I liked it so much more before all this talk of ghosts, séances, and things that go bump in the night. Mrs. D had posed a valid question about whether that Russian lady had indeed been in her room (and why was it considered "her room"?) *Oh Lord, please take me back to Bridge, where life is so much simpler. My feelings regarding love, I think I can handle. At least they are tangible. Seeing a wispy image of Maveryn, I could take, but dealing with some unknown entity was not in any realm that I have ever pondered*, I thought. I had read and heard of many stories of ghostly encounters by reliable people that could not be explained. Surely, there were experts who were trained to deal with the paranormal. Perhaps it was time to call in a ghost hunter. There must be some in Scotland, as there were many castles, and I was equally sure many tales of haunting. I would have to get Jeremy's take on the matter.

For now, I, too, would be on guard. I was jet lagged and train weary, and needed to rest. *On guard? How does one guard against a force that is undetectable?* I prayed that I would not have nightmares.

I checked in on the girls and they were still relaying their adventures to Shalla. I said that I was going to try and take a little nap. I believed I fell asleep as soon as my head hit the satin pillow.

I soon found myself strolling through a rose garden. It wasn't Avanloch…that I was sure of. This garden was unkempt. I was struggling with the branches that were impeding my progress. At every step, they reached up and tried pulling me into their thorny grasp. The roses were all black and they appeared to be taunting me. They were all decaying and had a strong musky odor. There was someone on the other side of the rambling, prickly barbs. He was calling for me to come with him to his palace. I could barely make out his face, but I knew the voice; it was Roberge's. Someone else was there, and he was crying and saying that I must go with him. I knew that it was Jack. I reached out from underneath the brambles but they wouldn't let me go. They were ripping my hands and arms, and wrapping themselves around my legs. I felt like I was being torn to shreds and buried my head, succumbing to the pain, when I felt a strong arm around me pulling me free. I looked up into the azure eyes of my love. I reached up and heard Rainey's sweet voice. "Come home, Vela. Come home. It's time to come home." Something was wrong…Rainey didn't know Vela.

"Vela, are you awake? It is time for supper."

The dream was gone. Shalla was at my door.

We had spent last night in Edinburgh, as it was late when we landed. Jeremy had a small apartment there for just such occasions and we had arrived home at a decent hour of the day. Perhaps next time, we would fly into London and spend the night with Ash, if she was home. I didn't know how Jeremy could be on the fly all the time. Of course, he didn't have to worry about two children and keeping them occupied and safe. I might have had a nap, but I felt like I had been up for days. No, I didn't think that I had napped at all. I shivered as I remembered the dream.

"What's wrong, Mama? You look like you have seen a ghost."

Out of the mouth of babes. I assured Rosalyn that I was fine. I looked at Mrs. D and we started to laugh.

The next morning the barking of the dogs awoke me. I jumped out of bed and ran into the girls' room. Shelley and Keats were running around the bed, yelping at Ava and Rosalyn, who were jumping on the bed as if it were a trampoline.

"Hi, Mom," they called in unison. They had taken to addressing me as "mom" now and then.

"I think that you should quit jumping on that bed before you end up in the cellar. I'm going to grab a housecoat and then we will go down for breakfast."

"But, Mom, we have already eaten," Rosy informed me.

"What? I don't believe you."

"Yes, it's so, Mama. Ask Mrs. D. Can we go to the cellar? Will you take us?" Ava asked. "What is down there?"

"Why in the world would you want to go down into a dark and dismal basement? I am sure there is nothing there except canning and wine, and oh yeah, spiders."

"Oh, Mom, you're just saying that. Can we ask Duffy to take us? We just want to explore," Rosy begged.

"No, and I don't want to hear another word about it. I'll see you after coffee."

"Amma and Johnny asked if we could go with them to Waverly to help with Alexa. Can we go?"

"The word is 'may.' Yes, you may go."

"Thanks, Mom." They came over and hugged me.

I found Millie and Mrs. D in the kitchen. I helped myself to coffee and Mary asked what I wanted for breakfast. I said, "Toast is all. How are you, Millie? What is new and exciting at the manor?"

"Nothing. It is my day off. Jannie and I are off to deliver some groceries to Mollie Magan. Mary says that you are thinking about consulting her about the other day."

"Do you think that she may have some advice for us, and would she mind if I joined you on your visit?"

"Oh, do come. She will be delighted. Can you be ready in half an hour?"

"You bet ya."

We drove the 12 kilometers in Millie's old, beat-up truck. The road was rough but well worn. I commented on that and they informed me that Mollie had customers from as far away as Edinburgh. People swore by her herbs and roots that she made into salves and potions. Mrs. D said they controlled her rheumatism better than any doctor-prescribed medications. I had been envisioning a cabin in the woods, much like the one from *Hansel and Gretel* that the witch lived in. I was not disappointed, as it was so, without the sugar and gingerbread, however. The modest cottage was set in an opening in the forest. It was surrounded by hollyhocks and delphiniums. Ivy climbed clear up to the roof and mingled with the overgrown climbing roses. Smoke was spiraling from the chimney. Even though it was a warm summer day, it was cool here in the trees.

Mollie met us at the door. She was leaning on two canes. She was sporting a black eye and a bruised face. "Welcome, welcome to my humble abode," she greeted us.

"What has befallen you, Mollie? You're a sorry sight!" Millie exclaimed.

"Not to bother yourselves. I swear I donna know who will send me to the grave first, that stubborn mule of a horse or that belligerent cuss of a cow!"

We expressed concern over her painful-looking face, but she said that it was nothing. She motioned us to a well-worn chesterfield that was covered with a colorful afghan. The kettle was whistling and she rushed off to fetch us a pot of tea. Millie poured the steaming brown liquid into dainty little cups for us all. Then she opened a tin of biscuits that Mrs. Sharpe had sent. Millie also set to work unpacking the bags of supplies that she had brought.

"I *dinnae* know what I would do without this girl. Now what do I owe the pleasure, Miss Vela? I hear that there has been a little trouble at the castle. Be I right?"

"It happened while I was away in Canada. I must say that I am a little relieved that the girls were not there to witness the accident. I suppose that you have heard the speculation that the Black Russian may have been at work?"

"Yes, Millie has kept me posted. I trust that the young man is recuperating, and can he be trusted to be discreet?" Mollie asked.

Jannie said that Johnny had spoken to him and told him that if he valued his job, he would not mention that he had been pushed. Sam had said, "When Hell freezes over will be too soon for me to step foot back in that mausoleum."

Then she turned to me and said, "Sorry, dear, but I believe the constabulary will be calling at Avanloch."

I answered her, "Let them come. I am sure that they will discover nothing and leave thinking that a young man had taken an unfortunate fall while venturing too close to the head of the stairs. That, plus he was probably imagining that there must be ghosts and goblins roaming around, waiting to have a bit of fun with a newcomer. It makes for a good story to tell your grand-children, doesn't it? That an evil specter shoved you down a flight of stairs and that you lived to tell the tale?"

"I think you are right. Lord Jeremy, he is a powerful man and no one is going to mess with him and his castle. By the by, is he knowing of the mishap?"

"No, Mollie," I replied. "He will return home tomorrow. What I am wondering is, do you think that there's possibility that the soul of Tatylyanna is still at Avanloch? Could she truly have been locked in that room all this time and, once the door was opened, took her revenge out on poor Sam?" I hoped that she had an answer, and she did.

"I have heard of spirits being locked up or asleep for many a year and then suddenly appearing for no apparent reason. On the other side, do ya not think that they cannot transcend through walls? If she is really still at Avanloch, and according to Miss Maveryn, she is, there is no way to predict what she is capable of. Again, on the other side, perhaps she is quite content to be in her room and resented the intrusion into her private domain. Poor Sam, he was the one who interfered with her solitude, so he was the one to suffer. Can you see what I am saying? There is no way to know. And it may have truly been only an accident. However, if there be another incident, then steps must be taken."

"Yes, I understand all that you are saying. And if something does occur, are you suggesting that we contact a physic or a ghost hunter?"

"Perhaps." That was all that Mollie would say. She took us into a room behind her tiny kitchen, which was her workshop. I was amazed to see such an array of sprays of herbs and leaves hanging from the rafters. The shelves and countertops were overflowing with jars and vials that contained Lord knew what. The smells were overwhelming.

There was a roaring fire ablaze in the hearth. A black cauldron was sitting on the grates just above the flames. I tried to inspect the contents, as whatever was cooking was bubbling a frothy, white vapor. The steam kept me from getting close enough to peer in.

"Just frog legs, entrails, and a little eye of newt cooking there, Miss." Mollie looked at me and winked.

I guess she was fooling with me. I inquired about her garden and she opened the back door to reveal a large plot of tangled and overgrown wild vegetation. Most of it looked like weeds to me.

"There be nothing in there, Missy, ceptin me herbs, nettles, and roots. I learned long ago that the garden will look after itself and come back year after year if you treat it with respect and only take what you need from it. It just needs sun and water, and it likes to be talked to." She giggled again.

It was almost a cackle. I think that she liked to play the part and she played it well.

"Now, tell me, do ye young girlies like fairies?"

"They certainly do. I have a fondness for them myself. Why do you ask?"

"Well, if there be neither a cloud nor rain on the eve of August 13, there will be fairies. Mist does not bother them. If they are not afraid and the pixies take a likin' to them, there is sure to be a show. The elfin pools are just always down the path. Come by just before first dark."

"Thank you, Mollie, we will be here. I am rather concerned about your welfare, though. Suppose something worse than a kick from an ornery cow befalls you, how do you get word out?"

"Do not mind your pretty head about ole Mollie. I have been looking after myself for well unto ninety years. If the carrier pigeons fail me and the rain obliterates the smoke signals, then I may just have to use that big, black contraption over there on the wall."

I followed her outstretched hand to see a box that obviously held a telephone.

They all laughed. I hugged Mollie and called her a mischievous little devil. She sent packages home for Mrs. Sharpe and Mary McDuff. She also presented me with a small vial of colorless liquid.

Her eyes were full of impish delight and she said, "This works way worse than mace."

I asked her what it was for.

She stated matter-of-factly, "For the black lady. A whiff of this and she will turn tail and run."

Millie and Jannie were grinning when we walked back to the car. I told them I never knew if Mollie was serious or not, and they said, "Best that you heed as to not."

Jeremy arrived home that night after I had retired. As usual, the girls and I had played a game and read chapters in a Nancy Drew mystery before their bedtime. When we were in Bridge, I had collected all the Hardy Boys and Nancy Drew books that I had been saving and brought them home to share with Rosalyn and Ava, in hopes that they would enjoy them as much as I had. They did, and I, too, was reliving the tales over again.

I then went into my sitting room and rummaged through all the drawers and closets, hoping to find a journal that Maveryn may have stowed away. I found nothing and briefly considered exploring the hidden stairwell for a nook that may conceal such an item. I talked myself out of that nonsense quickly. I had only been down there once before and that was with Uncle John. To go down alone would be insane, especially with Tatylyanna on the loose. I laughed despite my uneasiness. Perhaps another time, when I had my ghost-busting vial with me.

After breakfast and the presentation of gifts from their father, the girls set out on one of their adventures with friends from the village. We need not worry, as the Reverend Peters's fiancée, Miss Betsy Burns, was at the helm of the summer program. Today, I believed that the children were to be visiting the Green Slough in search of creepy crawly things. The girls had left home decked out in rain gear and rubber boots, which told me that they were going to come home covered in mud. Better them than me.

Jeremy escaped to his study after presenting me with a yellow cockatiel for the aviary in the conservatory. We now had a collection of seventeen, which I considered to be twelve too many. They chatted, sang, and whistled all the time. Sometimes, I wanted solitude and preferred to listen to calming music. Of course, the birds liked the music, too, and it just stimulated them more. I was working on finding a cover that I could lower on the cages so that they would think it night.

I no longer listened to the type of music that I used to love. I had discovered a French songstress by the name of Gizelle Marchant. Her haunting voice seemed to soothe my soul. I preferred not to translate her works into English, as I could tell by the melody that they were all about love, which probably meant sadness and heartache. That seemed to be the way that I conceived love.

I knocked on Jeremy's door and asked if we could have a few minutes of his time. He said certainly and put his papers aside. I was sure he was wondering what Jannie, Mrs. Mrs. D, and myself could possibly want. I let Jannie and Mary take the chairs opposite his desk and I sank down into the cool leather of his rocker recliner, which was off to one side. He already knew about the unfortunate accident and had commented on it earlier as "a crying shame." He stated that he would be responsible for all of Sam's bills. Well, I would certainly hope so, as it had happened on his premises.

Jannie was the spokesperson. She started off by telling Jeremy that she was sorry that she had kept this from him for such a long time, but due to recent events, it must now be brought to his attention. "Have you never wondered why Maveryn, bless her soul, spoke of the Black Russian as she lay dying? You know that it was her who named Tatylyanna that, don't you?"

Jeremy nodded. He was definitely uncomfortable discussing his departed wife.

Jannie continued. "This isn't going to sit well with you, but she didn't want you to know. She was being taunted by Tatylyanna."

I thought that Jeremy was going to explode. His face turned beet red and said, "What are you saying?"

"Maveryn told me and Emma that she had visitations from Taty and that they were not pleasant. She was told to stay away from you or suffer the consequences. That is why she insisted that room six be sealed up. She hoped that it would keep the Black Russian from escaping, and it seemed to work until she became ill."

This was news to me. I had not known that it was Mave who had the room sealed.

"Why would she have kept this from me, Jannie?" Jeremy asked. "If I had of known that she was having delusions, I would have seen that she received help."

"They weren't delusions, Jeremy. She probably knew that you wouldn't take her seriously, just as you are not now. Whether you like it or not, Sir, there are ghosts in this house and I, too, have seen them."

"Jannie, Jannie, come now, you don't really believe in the undead now, do you?" he asked.

"They are not the undead; they are the spirits of the departed. Your own sister, Liz Beth, is one. She is the good force, as is Maveryn, who roams these halls. Taty is the evil entity that pushed poor Sam down the stairs almost to his death."

"Now, I have heard everything!" Jeremy was on his feet and fit to be tied.

Jannie had found her voice and was relentless. "No, you haven't! Liz Beth is responsible for Tatylyanna's fatal fall."

"Jannie, have you taken leave of your senses? You know perfectly well that Liz Beth wasn't even alive then."

"Exactly. Have you not heard anything that I have been saying? Your sister was protecting you and everyone else from that evil woman. She came out from her resting place to save the house from disaster. Don't just take my word for it, Mrs. D, Millie, and Emma saw Liz Beth also."

Jeremy looked pleadingly at me, but I had nothing to offer.

"'Tis true, Mr. Jeremy, I've seen poor little Liz Beth materialize out of nowhere and give that wicked woman a shove, and then she was gone on the cloud that she came on, but not before she looked in our direction. Of course, we were all so shocked that it dinna register on us what had just happened," Mary said to defend Jannie.

"That is exactly it, Mary, you were all in a state of shock. Later, when things had calmed down, one of you put the notion in the others' ears and, together, you created this wild story." Jeremy sat back down and smiled.

I did not care for the way he was making light of a very serious matter.

"I can definitely see where you ladies could get caught up in the moment," he said. "None of you cared for Tatylyanna, and with good reason, I might add. But as for Liz Beth manifesting herself is just plain fantasy."

"Jeremy, how long have I worked for you? Do you not trust my word? Why would I and the others make up ghost stories after all this time? Do you think me to be daft? Put it together. Sam was sent down those stairs after he started on changing *her* room. She didn't like it. Are you not concerned for your children's welfare?"

"Of course I am, but suggesting that there is an invisible presence that is waiting to do them harm is ludicrous."

Jannie got up and spoke in Jeremy's face. "Think about it. Think long and hard. We need to be prepared, though I know not how."

Before she and Mary reached the door, I took my turn at Jeremy. "Too bad that you have never had a visit from the spirit world. Oh right, you have. Why is it all right that you can see and talk with the departed but no one else can? Are you special? Even I and your daughters have been visited by Maveryn. Do you think that she is the only one who is able to return? I will tell you one thing, Jeremy. Until this matter has some resolutions, which would take for you to admit that something may be amiss, I will take the girls and leave. And, by the way, you may as well know that Liz Beth spoke to us from the Ouija board...she asked for help." I shut the door quietly and walked arm and arm with Jannie and Mary to the kitchen. Was this going to be my excuse for leaving Avanloch? I didn't need one...I wanted to go home. I wanted to see Rainey.

I donned my riding garb and lit out for the stables. I found our stable hand, Patrick, hard at work, trying to get our newest horse used to the bit and bridle. He had long ago quit trying to help me saddle up. As far as I was concerned, it was all part of the ride. I told Patrick that I would be out for several hours with Atlántida, so not to worry. This horse and I were of a kindred spirit. She seemed to sense my moods and today was our day to gallop. We covered the bridle path in record time, then I coaxed her into a gentle walk and we meandered home. The tension of the last few days seemed to have disappeared and I was a calmer person when I entered the house. My intensions were to head straight for my room, shower, and change, but Jeremy stopped me.

"Do you think we can have a talk, Vela?" he asked.

I answered yes, but first, I had to get Rosalyn to help me with my boots. He said that he would, so I followed him to his suite. I had never been in his rooms before and was a little surprised that he had asked me into his private domain. His den was definitely masculine. It was decorated in all shades of brown. There was only one window, and it faced west and was heavily draped; I supposed to keep the hot sun out. However, there was a fire smoldering in the hearth, which seemed contradictory. He motioned me to a chocolate chaise lounge while he took a seat in front of me on a hard-backed straight chair. He had my knee-high boots off in no time and I thanked him. He rubbed my feet for a few seconds, which I thought was completely out of character for him.

Jeremy sat back and said, "I suppose I owe you and Jannie an apology for the way I acted earlier. I do take the matter serious. You see, Vela, I do know about ghosts, and not just Maveryn's. As children, Ash and I both had en-counters with the previous inhabitants of the castle. I am not even sure if they were all relatives, as some of them appeared to be from the days of the Scottish wars. In our early years, we only had each other, so we pretended to be king and queen, and we invented our own loyal subjects. Pretty soon, those in-visible figures became real. We denied it at first, but when we could see we were in no danger from them, they became part of our lives. To this day, I do not know if it was pure fantasy or not. We've only seen them in the towers. They never manifested themselves to us anywhere else. Of course, we grew up and we put our childhood fancies to rest in the castle in the sky. Once I thought that Miss Mary came to visit me, but I put it off as a dream. I have not had any encounters with my dead sister. I believed that I was only imagining Maveryn's presence until you and the girls insisted that you had visits from her also. It is still hard for me to conceive that ghosts exist, childhood memories aside. Do we need help, Vela? You tell me what to do."

"It is obvious that you have had more experience in the matter than I. Should we consult a physic or a ghost hunter? I know not. I never allow the children upstairs without the dogs; speaking of which, Shelley and Keats are starting to show their age. I think that we had better be on the lookout for two new puppies that we can train before we are left with no protection for the girls."

"I, too, have had the same thought. I will put some calls in tomorrow to local dog breeders and we shall have new additions to our family soon. I have a call-in to a college friend who has had dealings with the paranormal. Hopefully, he will get back to me before the day is done. I must visit with Jannie and offer my apologies."

"I don't know of anything else that we can do. I hope that you are not upset with us. While we are in the confessional, I may as well inform you that we ladies also had Mollie Magan here to lead us in a séance. We were trying to reach Liz Beth, but were unsuccessful. We all received loving vibes from Maveryn, though."

"I already knew. John informed me and I decided not to say anything. It is your house, too, and I know you are only trying to protect the girls. Shall we wait until I hear from Allister Brown before we commence with any further shenanigans?"

I agreed. He informed me that he would be staying here at Avanloch until we had an answer one way or the other, and that his doors were always open.

Two days later, Jeremy's friend, Allister Brown, showed up at the castle. He was a tall, thin, scholarly-looking chap. He wore horn-rimmed glasses and had arched eyebrows that covered half of his forehead. He carried a satchel and an umbrella. He also brought with him several cameras and a suitcase, for he would be spending the night. His British accent was so strong that I could barely understand him. I hoped that I wouldn't require a translator. His suggestion was that Jeremy and two others accompany him into room six. It was hardly a suggestion, more like an order. He said one other thing: that I must be there, too, for it seemed likely that I was the catalyst! I was not agreeable, nor was Jeremy. He wanted to know who had put these proceedings into motion. I told him about the Ouija board and that had led to the telling of the story regarding Liz Beth and Tatylyanna. I made sure that I told him that I was not here when any of that happened or when Sam had the accident. He didn't care. He felt that I must be present when he did his observations in room six.

"I don't see what good I will be, but all right," I said.

Johnny was to be the other observer. Amma took the girls to her mother's, and the Duffys, Jannie, and the rest from Brackenshire would take up residence in the main hall, just in case Taty appeared at the stairs. I had no idea what this man was up to but made sure that I had my running shoes on.

Thank our lucky stars that there was not an electric storm brewing. We entered room six at precisely 9:30 P.M. on a moonless Wednesday night. Allister wanted it pitch dark, which it was. He and Jeremy went in first, and Johnny and I followed, quickly shutting the door behind us. I was holding on to Johnny with one arm and I had my concoction of Mollie's remedy for evil spirits in my other hand. With a tiny flashlight for illumination, Allister set up the cameras. I was expecting to feel an evil presence breathing down my neck, although I had no idea what that would feel like. I only knew that I would know it when I felt it. Instead, I only felt bitterly cold and I was shivering. Jeremy had told me that it would be chilly, so I thought that I had dressed sufficiently, but obviously, I hadn't prepared myself for this glacial temperature. We were supposed to keep together and be silent. That was pretty hard for me to do because my teeth were chattering.

"Hurry up, hurry up, Tatylyanna. Do something." I was silently intoning her to come forward so that I could get out of this deep freeze.

Suddenly, there was movement. Allister cautioned us to remain steady, or at least I thought that was what he said.

He spoke boldly and authoritatively. "Is that you Miss Speshiloff? We have been waiting for you. We mean no harm."

Silence. The next thing I remember was Johnny reaching down and picking something up. He grabbed my arm and ushered me out the door. Jeremy and Allister followed close behind. I peered down at the entourage waiting in the grand hall. I waved and shrugged my shoulders to signify that nothing had happened.

Allister said to me, "What was that all about? I thought that I had made it perfectly clear that you were not to speak."

"I never said a word," I replied.

The three of them looked at me peculiarly and Jeremy suggested that we go to his suite. Allister motioned for me to take a seat and asked me what I remembered after we entered the room.

"Nothing," I said, "except that it was bitterly cold in there and I couldn't wait to leave."

"You don't recall anything else?"

"No, should I? Did something happen?"

Jeremy sat down beside me. "You don't remember speaking?"

"I don't think I did. Why? Is it important?"

Allister instructed me to sit back, relax, and close my eyes. I asked him if he was going to hypnotize me, and he said, "No, please do as I ask."

I obliged him, though I knew not what he was expecting of me. I heard someone speaking.

"Leave my room at once! I only want to be left alone. Why are you here?"

"Are you a threat to the people in this house?" It was Allister.

"No. I have no ill will. Now leave and take that damn toolbox with you!"

I was told to open my eyes. "So, she made contact. It is a good thing you taped her. How come I didn't hear her when I was in the room, yet the rest of you did?"

"That was you on the tape," Allister said.

"No, it wasn't! That wasn't me."

"I'm afraid it was, Vela." Jeremy looked at me. "Even though the voice was quite stern...it was yours."

"Well, that is just crazy. Why would I say those things? It makes no sense."

"Think about it, Mrs. McAllister. It makes perfect sense. Tatylyanna was speaking through you."

That was the first time I realized that his name was the same as Jeremy's, except for the Mc. "Are you suggesting that I was acting as her 'familiar,' so to speak?"

"Well, we do not usually refer to spirits that inhabit someone else's body, or in your case, voice, as that. But, yes, in a way. She chose you to speak for her."

"As long as it is a one-time thing, I suppose that I can deal with it." I arose and headed for the door. "That's that then, isn't it? We can rest easy. We will never enter that room again. Is that what you picked up, Johnny, the toolkit?"

He nodded and got up to leave with me.

"It is not that simple, Madame. We have only begun to scratch the surface here . There is much more investigating to be done."

Allister was beginning to annoy me. I said, "Sometimes, Sir, things are really just that simple. I believe that we are done here. What do you say, Jeremy?"

"Yes, I believe we have accomplished what we wanted to. Taty is not a menace."

Allister said that he thought we were making a big mistake. Jeremy told him, "Sorry, old chap, but I think that there is no need to disturb the Black Russian anymore. The room is sealed again and it shall stay that way."

Johnny and I left the two of them still discussing the recent events. We joined the others in the kitchen and gave them a brief outline of what had transpired.

"Is that it then?" Mrs. D asked.

"Yup," I answered. "No more séances, no Ouija boards, no more ghost seekers. We are done." I offered to go with Johnny to pick up the girls, but he said that they were spending the night with him and Amma and were probably fast asleep. I thanked him for being my guardian.

He saluted me and grinned. "It was my pleasure, Lady V."

I smiled at him and wondered why I had never noticed before how much he resembled an older Rainey. And then I giggled. Aunt Jannie asked me if I was all right.

"I am," I replied. "I am just perfectly fine."

I had laughed because it had suddenly occurred to me that Rainey was no longer twenty-one, but thirty, the same age as Johnny. I had missed his birthday. On the way to my sitting room, I passed Tat's room and made a note to myself to put a "do not disturb—*ever*" sign on the door.

I found a suitable card for Rainey and penned him a few lines.

My beloved,

Another year has passed and still we are not reunited. I fear that perhaps that day will never come and it is I who is to blame.

My life has not changed drastically since the last time that I wrote. There have been some strange going ones here at Avanloch, but I am assured that all has been resolved. The "ghosts" have all been silenced…at least for now.

The girls are growing like weeds. Ava favors you more and more every day. Those beautiful azure eyes of hers remind me of you every day. She has a stubborn streak in her—much like her father. She is curious about everything and fears nothing. My gorgeous Rosalyn is as different from Ava as night and day, and yet, they are best friends. She looks nothing like me, of course, but has my personality and is fiercely protective of me and Ava. In a few days, I will be taking them to visit with a friend who is the local sage and expert on all things mystical. She has promised that there will be fairies! I am just as excited as they are.

I pray that you are in good health, my love. I miss you with a yearning as deep as the emerald sea. Forever, I am yours.

Vienna

I untied the yellow ribbon that was keeping all the letters and cards together that I had written to Rainey throughout the years and added the latest to the ever-growing pile.

The next morning, I found that Allister had left even before the birds were up. It was just as well, as I didn't want to talk to him. The girls were in the music room, practicing. Ava and Rosalyn were both becoming little musicians. I had tried many times with different instructors to play the piano, but found that I didn't have the patience to sit and practice the same pieces over and over again. So it was surprising to me that Ava had taken to the piano so readily. Her father was not musically inclined, either. Now Rosalyn, I could understand, as her mother had been an accomplished harpist, and that was the instrument she had chosen. Twice a week, I took them into Waverly for their lessons. I grabbed a cup of coffee and strolled down to say good morning to them. They called me a sleepyhead and asked me to listen to a piece that they were working on.

"It's already ten o'clock," I said as I sank into an armchair and gave them my full attention. I was usually up before anyone else, so it was a little strange that I had slept so late and without troublesome dreams also.

Jeremy poked his head in the door and commented on how good the girls were doing. He asked if he could have a word with me. I followed him out into the hall.

"Do you feel safer now that we have had our little encounter with you know who?" he said. "You were so brave and took the whole episode as if it were an everyday occurrence to you. I am very proud of the way you handled yourself, especially with that pigheaded Allister. Hopefully, we will never need another 'so-called expert.' But if we do, I will not be calling on him again. I did not care for the way he talked to you. You are all right with it all, are you not?"

"As I told you all last night, I have no memory of anything, so maybe it just hasn't had time to sink in," I replied. "You're wrong when you say that I was brave. I was shivering the whole time we were in that room and it wasn't just from the cold. Ask Johnny, who had a firm hold on me all the time. He'll tell you how I was shaking. I was scared and hope that I never have to be an intermediate ever again."

"As do I. I have a board of directors meeting in London day after tomorrow but do not need to attend if you would like me to stay."

"Heavens no. Please go to your meeting. We will all be fine, I am sure. The girls and I have a very busy week ahead of us."

As usual, he thanked me, gave me a kiss on the forehead, and went off to pack. I honestly never missed him when he was away and wasn't all too sure that he didn't have a lady friend somewhere. I hoped he did.

August 13 arrived and we were off to Mollie's. There was a half moon out and no storm clouds loomed. I had warned the girls that Mollie was a very old woman and not to be shocked at her appearance. Ava asked me if she was a witch. I told her no, but she had a similar appearance to the ones who were in the storybooks, though she was kind and not evil.

We arrived at 8:45 in the evening and Mollie was waiting for us, lantern in hand.

"Ah, at last, I am to meet the children of Avanloch. Such a delight that you have come to see me fairies. I am a hopeful they will come out to play tonight."

Rosalyn spoke for her and Ava. They were holding hands and moved toward Mollie. "Thank you for inviting us, Miss Mollie. Can we call you that? We have been waiting a very long time it seems for this day to come."

"Yes, yes. Follow me. We want to get a good seat before the dancing starts."

The path was wide enough to accompany two at a time. Rosy walked with Mollie and Ava held tightly to me. I could feel that she was a little apprehensive. We ambled on at a slow pace behind Rosy and Mollie, who was dependent on her two walking sticks. Rosy asked her if she could take the place of one of the canes. Mollie passed one of them back to me and crooked her arm through Rosy's. I was so proud of that girl I could have cried. After about ten minutes, we came to a babbling brook. All we could hear was the water tumbling over the rocks. Mollie held up a finger to caution us to be quiet. She motioned us to a mossy slope where we were to take up residence and wait. After maintaining complete silence for a few minutes, the show began. They came out of the forest and traveled up and down the stream, soaring toward the sky and then descending, dipping into the cool waters, and then up again, higher and higher. They illuminated the night with their tiny, luminescent wings. They darted in and out of the trees and came so close to us that we could almost touch them. They were here, there, and everywhere. The girls were in complete astonishment. They had never seen fireflies before, so I wouldn't spoil it for them, for they truly believed that they were seeing tiny fairies. I needn't have worried because Mollie explained in a hushed voice that fairies were indeed magical and could change shape and form to suit their needs. I didn't even know if the girls heard her because they were so engaged with the dance that they were in a trance, trying to follow every movement of the dozens of lights before them. Suddenly, one by one, they took their leave from us and flew in formation back to where they had come from. The girls clapped their hands, and Mollie and I joined in.

They were so boisterous on the trip back to the cottage that they probably awoke all the sleeping critters. As we thanked Mollie and were to take our leave, Rosy asked her if she could hug her. Mollie threw down her canes and welcomed them both into open arms. I knew there were tears in her eyes as there were in mine. That was the first of many visits to Molly Magan's for the girls.

Life returned to normalcy at Avanloch. The girls were getting ready to start a new school year. The schoolhouse in the village now accepted children up to grade four, so this would be the first year that Rosy would have to travel to Waverly every day, as she was entering grade five. The girls would be apart for the first time, and I was more worried about Rosy than Ava about the separation. However, they both accepted it fairly well.

There was so much to be done in the fall that we hired extra staff. While the cooks were busy in the kitchen, canning and freezing the rewards from the harvests, the house was being thoroughly cleaned. Drapes and tapestries were sent off to the professionals. Apparently, this was a ritual that happened every five or seven years and had not been done since Maveryn's death. Jannie was here to help me with the supervision, as I had no clue what a big undertaking it was. While the hundreds of windows were bared and washed, I decided to take stock and change a few things, starting in the grand dining room. It was there that Shalla found me and told me that I had a phone call. I asked her who was calling, as I hardly ever received calls, and she said, "A Mister Roberge Farradan."

I should have told Shalla to say that I wasn't available, but I decided that I was only postponing the inevitable, as I knew exactly why he was calling. "Hello."

"Lady Vela, how lovely to hear your voice. I trust that you are in good health." There was no mistaking his hint of a Spanish accent mingled with the British.

"Hello, Roberge. Yes, thank you, I am well. And you and your lovely wife?"

He laughed very vigorously, at the implication that his wife was lovely, I assumed.

"You have not answered my invitation to the soiree that is to take place in October at the palace. I sincerely hope that it doesn't mean you won't be attending."

"I am sorry that I have been lax in answering, please forgive me. I am afraid that it has been like a beehive of activity around here all summer. Now the girls are back in school and what with their music lessons and the house cleaning… I hope you can understand. But, to answer you, I must decline the invitation. I cannot speak for Jeremy, as he is away on business. May I have him call you when he returns?"

"Surely you know that it is only you that I am interested in. I believe that we have some unfinished business to attend to."

"To be certain, no, I do not."

"My lady, there is no need to play coy with me. I think you know exactly what I mean. There is a pent-up tension between us that I think we owe it to ourselves to explore further, do you not think?"

"Sir, I can assure you that there is nothing to explore. I thought that I made it perfectly clear. You will have to do your exploring with some other poor damsel, which, I am sure, there are many of." I disliked him referring to me as "my lady."

"You do amuse me, my dear, but I can guarantee you that I have not given up the cause to have you in my bed."

"That is one quest that you are never going to achieve. Good-bye, *Sir*." Before the words were completely out of my mouth, I heard him smirking. I hung up the phone with only a faint murmur of disgust. If this was a game, then I was becoming quite adept at playing. I found myself humming as I returned to the task at hand, the dining room.

Something was missing from this elegant room and I didn't mean the window dressings. The tables and sideboards were draped in delicate lace cloths, the crystal stemware, the blue-patterned century-old china, the porcelain statues of parrots and dogs, the golden chandelier, the glitzy mirrors—all of this was perfect, so what was wrong? It had too much of a formal atmosphere to it. The chairs were too stiff, the yellow wallpaper seemed old and drab, and there was no real warmth to the room. I called in Cyn, Marianne, and Gail and sent them on various errands for me. I found Johnny in the kitchen, repairing a cupboard door, and asked if he would assist me when he was done. He told me that he was finished and off we went to the conservatory. The girls returned with the items I had asked for and I started in to work. In less than an hour, I completed my task and stood back to see if I met with my own approval.

I substituted half of the straight-backed chairs with a more comfortable arrangement of colorful seating. Yellow, red, and blue Queen Anne and Louis XIV now occupied a space at the table. There was less seating, but I was fine with that.

I stepped back to see if the new arrangements met with my approval. I had ordered pale-blue sheers to accompany the royal blue toile drapery, which was being cleaned. The dining room's natural light was from four double French doors that opened up to a terraced portico. I planned on keeping the heavy chintz drapes clasped open with just the sheers filtering the afternoon sun in. With Johnny's help, I placed potted palm ferns to the sides of the doors, and on each side of the marble fireplace, we placed lacy ferns in wrought-iron urns. The red silk upholstered chairs had to go. There was no place for them in this room of delicate blues, whites, and golden hues. They could go back to the grand hall. I searched the breakfront for an oversized bowl that I could place lotus flowers in for the dinner party that I was hosting for Jeremy's business partners. I found the perfect crystal, oval, leaf-patterned dish, which was just deep enough to hold the petals and buds, and would go perfectly with the silver candlesticks. All in all, I was satisfied.

I wasn't looking forward to the party. I would rather be out riding or working in the garden but was resigned to the fact that I had certain obligations to Jeremy, which I must uphold. As usual, the evening came and went without incident. I had learned nothing from previous situations that the anticipation of such events was only threatening before they actually took place.

For Christmas that year, we had the usual celebrations with our Avanloch family and then Jeremy took the girls and me to the French Riviera for a week. The girls had a splendid holiday, but for some unknown reason, I kept searching every stranger's face for Rainey. I came home and started my sessions up with Dr. Jai again; winter was not a good time of year for me.

In the spring of '71, we went to Bridge for Sissy's wedding. Everything was lovely. The girls were in the wedding party and were absolutely delighted. I guess out of duty, Sissy had asked me to be her matron of honor. I tried to decline but was not successful. I did get the chance to call Jimmy, but he wasn't home. Lara and I had our usual wonderful reunion. She informed me that both Jimmy's and Yate's marriages were deteriorating. I was saddened to hear that.

The year went swiftly by. I was consumed with making changes to the few rooms that were left. Within a year, I had accomplished all that could be done with the family dining room, the sitting room, and the drawing room. Everything was as bright and cheerful as I could make it without tearing the whole place down and starting from scratch. My next project was to be the towers.

It was hard to believe, but Ava was ten and Rosalyn was thirteen. It was July and they were going to an adventure camp for two weeks. I had never been without them for more than two days and was feeling very apprehensive. Jeremy talked me into going on a trip to Vancouver and Seattle. He always tried to visit all the ports that he had headquarters in at least every other year and he was overdue for these two. The girls insisted I go.

"But suppose you get homesick and I am not here, what then?"

"Mother, quit worrying. We have each other and you deserve a holiday without us. Please go. Maybe Lily and Papa Joe can come and see you."

I went and it was almost the beginning of the end for me. I could not help myself. I looked up Quinn Enterprises in the phone book. I used the driver that Jeremy had made available to me and had him take me to the address.

I had the limousine driver, whose name was Manuel, park on the opposite side of the street from what I assumed were Rainey's offices. We made polite conversation while I was building up the nerve to venture inside. It was easier to confide in strangers. After listening to Manuel's woes of how he had to leave his family in Mexico to find work, I confessed to him that I was here to see an old flame but was not certain if I should pursue it any further.

He said to me, "Sometimes, the heart wants what it wants and there is no denying it. You should take the chance, Miss McAllister. I have learned a saying here in Canada. It is 'nothing ventured, nothing gained.' Yes, you have heard it?"

"Yes, I have. But I am not sure that it applies to me."

Half an hour later, I opened the car door. I took a deep breath and said to Manuel, "Wish me luck, but be ready to roll if I say go."

"Right."

I took a deep breath and took the longest walk of my life. I climbed the three floors to his office. My hand was on the doorknob but I couldn't open it. I was terrified at what I might find inside. I was startled by a young woman who had silently come up behind me. She apologized for scaring me and asked if she could be of some assistance. I told her that I was looking for Rainey Quinn. She opened the door.

"Well, let's ask Sylvie if he is in." She had her hand on my arm as if she knew that I was ready to run. She steered me in the direction of an older woman's desk. "Sylvie, this young lady is looking for Mr. Quinn. Is he in?"

Please Lord, let the answer be no.

"He should be back anytime," Sylvie replied. "Why don't you have a seat and wait for him?"

I was looking at his office door. I wanted to go over and rub my hands on the glass window that spelled out his name, Rainey L. Quinn. Instead, I backed away toward the door I had come in through and uttered, "I have a driver waiting; perhaps another time. Thank you."

"He really should be back momentarily, Miss... Who should I say...?"

I didn't hear the rest. I was gone, running down the stairs, praying I didn't run into him.

Manuel saw me coming, jumped out, and opened the car door for me. "Should I drive, Miss McAllister?"

I tried to compose myself. "Not just yet. Not just yet." I had come this far, I owed it to myself to see it through. A few minutes later, a yellow sports car drove into the parking lot across the street. He climbed out and momentarily looked across the street. Perhaps it was unusual to see a black limo parked in this area.

I couldn't take my eyes off him. He was the same striking Rainey, head of sandy hair, khaki pants, and a brown blazer. I was sure he had loafers on. He reached the entrance and turned once more in our direction.

Through tears, I said, "It's time to go, Manuel."

"Are you sure, Ma'am?"

"One more minute." I watched him enter the building, and after a few minutes, he emerged and I panicked. He glanced across the street in our direction. I couldn't bear the thought of his rejection, so I abandoned my mission.

"Now, Manuel, go. Go!"

Chapter Eighteen

Rainey, 1963–72

The summer was going to be a long one. He had been on a hiatus from hard work for almost a year. However, he was glad to be home and away from Zeta. She called him every week, inquiring about his father and asking when she could come over to be with him. All her papers were in order; she was trying to get a work visa. If they were to be married, things would be a lot easier for her. She was not listening to him. Finally, he was tired of it all and told her flatly that she was not to call him anymore. There was no future for them. He was still in love with Vienna and they were to be married. She never called him again. He didn't even feel shame at the lie. He wished it were true.

He stood up for his best friend and was happy that all his buddies had found someone to share their lives with, wondering if his turn would ever come.

In October, he left his parents' home once more to pursue his career. He was thankful that he hadn't sold his house, as prices had skyrocketed and he wouldn't be able to pay rent. He had refused to take money from his folks. It would be a while before they would have all the hay sold and he knew that he could manage somehow with what little he had put away.

He found a job almost immediately with the firm that had accepted his application the year before. He was not too humble to make apologies for his previous actions and guaranteed them that they would not regret their decision to give him another chance, as they soon found out he was a gifted architect and his services of designs were in great demand. He would be sure to make junior partner before long.

In December, he met Louise Morgan. It was a pre-Christmas party and was hosted by his boss, Howard Kline, for present and former clients. He was first introduced to her father, Calvin.

"Is this the young man you have been raving about, Howard?" Calvin asked. "I have heard good things about you, Son. What say we schedule a meeting for next week? I'll have my gal get in touch with your office. This is my wife, Bernice, and my daughter, Louise. Girls, this is the boy wonder you've heard Howard talking about, Rainey Quinn."

Rainey greeted them as he would anyone. Somehow, everyone wandered off and he was left alone with Louise. He offered to get her a drink, and before long, they were talking as if they had known each other for years. She wanted to know all about his adventures in Italy and France. He said he was sorry to disappoint her, but he was too busy working to have had any great stories to tell. She wasn't anyone who stood out in a crowd. She was rather plain, with short, blonde hair. She was tall and very fit. He soon found out that tennis and golf were her passions. She worked for her dad in a very minimal capacity. Apparently, she was too busy heading up funding for the arts and hosting charitable events. She was an only child and was expected to give her father an heir, and soon, before he had one foot in the grave. She laughed when she told him that.

"As if that is ever going to happen," Louise said. "I amuse him, though, with prospects whom he hates. He says I am getting long in the tooth and, before long, no will want me. What do you think, Rainey Quinn?"

He didn't like her calling him by his full name. That was reserved for Vienna. Perhaps it was time to put the dream to bed and opt for a plain Jane heiress.

He went home to Hawthorne for a week at Christmas. Paul was fully recovered from his surgery and had put some weight back on, but Patsy had changed her cooking habits. She had always been health conscious, but now, she realized they both needed to cut back on the fat and red meat. That was pretty hard to do when you raised your own beef, but she had incorporated more fish and chicken into their meals. Paul complained at first. He missed his thick, juicy steaks, but soon adapted to leaner cuts. The freezer was full of newly butchered beef and pork, and Rainey was the recipient of 100 pounds of meat. He didn't refuse it but wondered how he was ever going to eat it all. He usually ate out. It was easier than cooking for himself. He knew not to refuse his mom.

He had his meeting with Calvin Morgan in early January. Calvin had a fairly substantial project for Rainey. At first, he wondered why the man had not gone through Kline and partners to engage his services, but soon found out why.

"Son, I have not always been satisfied with some of the work from Kline," Calvin began. "His employees are a little too cocky for me. I want you for this small project to test the waters and see if we will be able to see eye to eye. Believe me when I say that there is a substantial development that I am in the midst of undertaking. The design is going to take an inventive mind and I hope that you have the fortitude to see it through with me."

"I can't in good conscience go against the firm I am working for," Rainey replied. "I thank you for your consideration, though. It does sound intriguing."

"You have no idea what a mega endeavor I am dabbling with. You will have work for many years to come, but don't be concerned with Kline. I fully intend to go through him for this mediocre remodel of the canneries offices. I want to request you to be the chief architect if you agree. If we work out well, then we will discuss the other venture. What do you say, Son?"

"That I can work with, and as it is, I have just completed my latest job, so I am available for the time being."

"I am taking a meet with Kline later but I am sure he already knows my plans. Are you free for dinner tonight, Rainey? There will be just the four of us. That is, if you don't mind Louise joining us? You two got along all right, didn't you?"

"I think so. I have not seen her since the party. Perhaps you should check with her. She may have other plans."

"Believe me, she doesn't. Shall we say 6:30 for cocktails then?"

"Thank you, Sir. I will be there."

The project of the remodel was his. Howard did caution him against Calvin, however. He told Rainey that he had known the man for twenty years and knew him to be ruthless and a cutthroat. He said that he would stop at nothing short of murder to get what he wanted, and it appeared that he wanted Rainey. For what purpose, he didn't know at the time.

That was a little disconcerting, but nothing that Rainey felt he couldn't handle.

There was always a beginning to everything, and that January evening was the start of Rainey's new life. He began seeing Louise on a regular basis, away from her parents. There hadn't been anyone in his life since Zeta and he had been experiencing feelings of loneliness again.

Louise kept him busy away from work while Calvin talked his ear off every chance he got about the "big one." It was happening; the project had been approved.

Rainey found out what had been approved by the city fathers. It was to be a multimillion-dollar complex in the heart of the city. It was to be called Centennial Plaza and would be a multifaceted structure. It would consist of high-rise apartments, specialty shops, restaurants, and clubs. Perhaps a bank and a theatre. The opportunities were unlimited . The ocean would be its window to the east and it would all be landscaped in a park-like setting.

Calvin said this was his biggest endeavor. He was extremely excited and wanted Rainey on board, and not through Kline Enterprises. He wanted to set Rainey up with his own firm. He already had offices picked out. They were near to the construction site of the plaza. He would finance it all, interest free.

Rainey wasn't sure that he liked someone else mapping out his life, yet how could he refuse? This was his dream of a lifetime. Once he had control of the project, Calvin would have to back off. He hoped. Another thing crossed his mind before he accepted. Was Louise part of the package? Needless to say, he didn't ask.

With mixed feelings, Rainey resigned from Kline. They had hired him and he gained experience at their expense. Howard bore him no ill will but cautioned him again to not let his integrity be compromised.

He was working ten to twelve hours a day on the plans for the complex. His office was temporarily workable. If the project was to meet the projected start date of October 10, he had no time to waste. That only gave him five months to come up with the bare bones. Louise was diligent and brought him lunch every day at 1. She was working four blocks from him at organizing a fund-raiser for a new library. Several evenings a week, she delivered dinner. She would stay and help him systematize his blueprints. Yes, she was very good at organizing.

It was late in July. They sat at a small table and shared the Chinese fare that was the entrée of the day. Rainey thanked her and went back to work. She cleaned up and was about to take her leave when thunder shook the building.

"Now where did that come from?" Rainey said. "There was no mention of a storm, was there?"

"I don't think so," replied Louise. "Do you mind if I stay until the rains let up? I had to park a few blocks away."

"Of course not. Stay as long as you like."

"I promise to be quiet. Rainey, do you like me?"

"What a crazy thing to ask. Of course I like you. I wouldn't be spending time with you if I didn't. Now what is this all about?" He didn't want to deal with her foolishness, nor did he have the time. It appeared that she had another question and it certainly wasn't one that he was expecting.

"Do you like me enough to marry me?"

"What? Did you just ask me to marry you? I kind of thought that I would be the one to do the asking."

"Well then, here is another question. Were you ever going to ask it?"

"To be perfectly honest, I hadn't given the matter any thought. I've been a little preoccupied. I thought that things between us were just fine the way they are. Call me old fashioned, but I always believed that love should be involved before two people take the plunge. We have never even talked about the L word or the M word, have we?"

"Perhaps my biological clock is ticking. I have never let Daddy's continuous nagging for a grandchild bother me before, but lately, he is scaring me. I don't think that his health is all that good. Have you noticed him slowing down?"

"Your dad? No. He is just as robust as ever. Have you tried to ask him if something is wrong?"

"Yes, and so has Mother, but he denies that anything is wrong."

"And your answer is to get married and give him an heir, am I right? And on top of it all, you are willing to compromise yourself and marry without love?"

"I never said that I didn't love you, Rainey. My feelings for you are as close as I have ever got. How does one know when she is in love, do you know?"

"As a matter of fact, I do. When you wake up in the morning and you can't wait to get your day over with because you know at the end, you're going to be with her. Her smile and her laughter are with you constantly. You think about her all the time. You eat, sleep, and breathe with her name on your lips. And when it's time to say good night, you are worried that she is not going to be there in the morning. Her touch is like a fire you can't extinguish. But do you want to know what the worst thing about being in love is? It's unpredictable. It's here one day and gone the next. The high that you experienced with your feelings of devotion is nothing in comparison to the numbness that you suffer when love dies. Yes, Louise, I have been in love before and it is not something that I want to encounter ever again."

"I am so sorry, Rainey. She really hurt you, didn't she?"

"No, I am the one who is sorry. Love is a high and I think everyone should experience it at least once. You deserve to have someone love you. Don't compromise yourself, Louise."

"Maybe I am not interested in that kind of love. I am a rather cold person, as you have witnessed. Perhaps I am not in love with you, but I do love you. I think that we could form a partnership and be relatively happy. I'm not getting any younger. Does it bother you that I am four years older than you?"

"No, of course not. You're really serious about this, aren't you?"

"Surprisingly, I am. I may not have much to offer in the looks department, but I am in good shape and I have good bones, and I can certainly pay my own way."

"You're a striking woman, Louise. Marriage is a partnership and should not be entered into lightly. Perhaps respect and tolerance are equally as important as love."

"Are you considering my proposal, Rainey?"

"You're thinking in a year or so down the line, right?"

"Oh no, I can't have you changing your mind or coming to your senses or even getting back together with 'her' again. I mean soon, say September."

"Whoa, that is not at all possible! Have you forgotten what I am doing here? I have a deadline to meet. But to set you straight on the other matter, it has been over for a very, very long time and I do mean *over*. She is so far out of the picture that she isn't even a memory."

Louise wasn't sure that she believed him, but she didn't care. Rainey was going to marry her. He father would be so happy.

What he told her about Vienna's memory was a lie, a big, fat lie. He still loved her.

"You can knock it off early for one night, can't you, Rainey? Let's go over to the Paramount and get a room for the night."

"Why there?"

"Because it is too far to go to your place and I certainly don't want to go to mine. I want to spend the night with you, isn't it obvious?"

"Well then, let's go to my room at the Rim. It's closer and it's already paid for."

"Why do you have a room there?"

"You're right, it's too far to go home, and on nights like tonight, I just bed down there. No driving involved, just a few short blocks. Are you still interested?"

She was. They donned their coats, grabbed an umbrella, and ran laughing into the street. This wasn't the first night that they would be spending together. There had been others; they just weren't very memorable. Louise wasn't a warm-blooded woman. He had the distinct impression that she did what she thought was expected of her in bed, and the sooner it was over with, the better. This was not going to be a romantic relationship, and it was just as well, because the one that he had could never be topped. He wondered if he could really commit himself to a loveless marriage.

Rainey had his arm around her and was about to tuck her hair behind her ear but stopped. He pulled himself away. That was a gesture that he always did with Vienna, and it drove her to "seventh heaven," she would say. The second he played with her hair, she was ecstatic. He shook himself out of her spell.

"Is everything all right, Rainey?" Louise asked. "I hope so. I am so very happy. You make me happy. I promise I will try my best to please you. Can you be patient with me?"

"You please me, Louise. Stop berating yourself."

She was getting out of bed to have a shower and he told her to take her time.

This wasn't going to go away anytime soon, was it? When had he started talking to himself? It didn't do any good because he never came up with a solution of how to rid himself of her. Now, he was remembering the day that she came running out of the house in Bridge, bursting with exuberance. He had opened the car door for her but she ran around to the passenger side. He asked her what she was doing and she said, "Shhh, don't touch me. Do as I say, okay?" He agreed. She had asked him to hold his hands up away from his body with fingers open. "Now close your eyes. Quit fooling around, Rainey. Close your eyes. Do you want to play or not?"

He had answered, "With you, of course."

She hushed him again. He closed his eyes. The next thing he felt were her fingertips mingling with his. "Don't speak," she whispered. After several minutes, she told him that he could open his eyes. "Did you feel anything?"

"Did I feel anything, are you kidding? I felt like a force was moving through me. I felt electrified. What did you do to me, you little imp?"

She had thrown her head back and laughed. "That's the power of us, Rainey. It's the rapture. I do believe that I own your soul." She tried making a quick exit, but he had grabbed her and held her until she quit laughing.

"Did you put a hex on me again?"

"I felt it, too, Rainey, a force pulsating through my body. We can never be free of one another . We are forever hopelessly and gloriously lost."

It was past time for this to be over. He was going to live his life for himself, to hell with love; he was going to marry an heiress. How bad could that be?

He left the wedding preparations entirely up to Louise. They set the date for September 5th. The sooner to get it over with, the better. He was too busy to have a hand in the preparations and left it all up to her. He submitted his guest list and that was it. Louise asked him who he wanted for his best man and he said Jimmy. She seemed surprised. Two weeks before the big day, Rainey realized that he hadn't even asked Jimmy to do the honors. He mentioned it to Louise and she said that it had all been taken care of.

"What?" Rainey said. "You don't even know him."

"Don't be silly, Rainey," Louise replied. "Of course I know my own cousin. It is you who hardly knows him, but he accepted readily."

Rainey couldn't believe that he had heard her right. "Excuse me, but did you say you asked your cousin to be my best man?"

"Well, you asked me to ask him."

"I don't think so, Louise. How could you possibly think that I meant your cousin? You're right, I don't know him. When I said Jimmy, I meant my best friend, Jimmy Douglas, from Hawthorne."

"You want me to tell my Jimmy that you have changed your mind? That would just be cruel. If you had taken any interest in our wedding, this wouldn't be happening! What do you want me to do?"

"You're right. I have been preoccupied with this damn job. It is just as well, I guess, as we haven't heard back from half the Hawthorne guests, have we?"

No one had been more shocked to hear of his upcoming nuptials than Jimmy, who heard it first from Patsy Quinn. He had phoned Rainey to congratulate him. Rainey felt guilty that he hadn't ask Jimmy to be his best man then and wondered how he was going to explain it to his oldest friend. He waited until Louise left and called him. Luckily, he found Jimmy at home.

"I want to apologize to you, buddy," Rainey said. "I left this bloody wedding in Louise's hands and she took it upon herself to ask her friggin' cousin to be my best man. Can you imagine? That job was supposed to be yours. Is it too late to ask you now?"

"No need to apologize, Rain," Jimmy answered. "It's better this way 'cause I may not even make it down. Ruth's due date has been moved up to the twenty-fourth, so she is definitely not going to make your wedding. I'll just have to play it by ear."

"No worry. God, you're really going to be a dad! I think my little buddy is all grown up.

Jimmy laughed. "Your turn is coming. Did I hear a little hesitance in your voice regarding the big day?"

"I'd be lying to you if I told you that I was looking forward to it. At this point, I just want the whole damn thing to be over with. She's not the right girl, you know that, Jimbo, but I have decided to settle. Doesn't sound like me, does it?"

"Well, if you are making a mistake, then it's yours to be making. I wish I could tell you that she was coming back to you, but I can't." He didn't have to mention any names because they both knew who he meant.

For the first three months, Rainey and Louise lived with her parents. After a brief three-day honeymoon, they moved into her parents mansion while they house hunted. Louise thought that she would like one of the penthouse suites that were to be built in Centennial Square. Rainey said no way were they waiting that long to find their own place and they were definitely going to buy a house. He hardly had the time to house hunt, but if he had left it up to her, they'd still be at her folks'.

He found a reliable realtor who found him the perfect house. It was an older three-storey Tudor overlooking the Pacific Ocean. Immediately, he had plans for remodeling, if he ever had the time. It would mean a twenty-minute commute downtown but would be worth it. Shopping and schools were close and the neighborhood was basically young families with a few seasoned older couples rounding it off. Louise was not impressed but warmed up to the idea when she found out there were tennis courts nearby. Having the Bay Golf Course ten minutes away sealed the deal. Everything she needed was here. He actually went furniture shopping with her because he didn't entirely trust her tastes. The interior of the house was being painted, and with a few small repairs, they expected to move in by Christmas. Rainey couldn't believe that it had all come together so quickly. He had already changed his mailing address to the new residence. One evening in early December, he made a trip out to the new house to see how things were progressing. He already had mail. It was an envelope addressed to his parents' address and forwarded to his new one in his mother's handwriting. There was no return address. He was going to put it away until later, but something made him open it immediately. He got the shock of his life. It was from Vienna. He walked into the living room and sat down; he was trembling. With trepidation, he read.

> My dear Rainey,
>
> Please excuse this intrusion into your life, but I feel that I must apologize for my foolhardiness. I do not want you to feel that you had anything to do with my selfish departure. This is to release you from any guilt that you may have felt. Please accept my apologies.
>
> I want to convey my very best wishes to you and yours, and pray that you will live a long and prosperous life. Happiness is to hold the people you love in both hands and dance. I wish this for you.
>
> Remember me with kindness,
> Vienna

This couldn't be happening. He had waited what seemed a lifetime to hear her say his name and she had. My dear Rainey...did that mean that she still considered him hers? Why, after all this time, had she wrote him? Did she somehow know that he hadn't thought about her in months? Was this her way of torturing him? Damn. *Damn!* He reread the short letter over and over. He imagined that he smelled cherry blossoms. He held the beautifully written thin paper up to his lips. He knew that she had kissed it when she sealed it. He cursed her and said, "God help me. I still love you, Vienna."

He hadn't even been married three months and he already knew that it was a farce. This was just the icing on the cake. He did what he always did: he phoned his cousin.

"Lara, I heard from her."

She didn't need to ask who "her" was. The only time Rainey phoned her was when it had something to do with Vienna. *Now what had that girl gone and done?* "She was in touch with you, Rainey?"

"She didn't call and I didn't see her. She sent me a letter of apology and wished me well. I take it that somehow, you told her that I had married."

"Her mom must have told her. They talk every so often." She was lying again.

Rainey read her the letter. His voice was hushed. "Does that sound like someone who has forgotten me, Lara? I can read between the lines. She still loves me."

"Oh, Rainey, I know what you want to hear but I am not the one to tell you. She is not coming back to you. I cannot make it any clearer. She has made a new life away from here. She's married and has two daughters. Now, you need to accept her letter as a good-bye and make your life work. Please, let her go."

He swallowed. "It's not working. Just when I think I'm done, she's back. I think that she really did put a spell on me and I can't break it."

"Now you are just being melodramatic! I am quite sure that this is the last time that you will hear from her."

"And how would you know that? Are you part of her conspiracy?"

"What conspiracy?"

"Yeah, her plot to drive me crazy."

"Don't say that, Rainey. You are scaring me."

"Don't be Lara. I have everything going for me—great job, staggering income, great health, and, oh yeah, did I mention a new wife that I am not in love with? See you soon, kid. Thanks for listening." He hung up and folded the letter. He went to his new library and stowed it away in a locked drawer, along with the one she had sent to Lara, the Saint Christopher, the bracelets, and the picture of them at New Year's. That was all he had left of Vienna. It was better being locked in a drawer than in his heart.

Louise was not having any luck at conceiving. He overheard her tell her mother that perhaps something was wrong with her. She so wanted to give her daddy a grandchild. When they got home that night in February, Rainey went into her medicine cabinet and presented her with her birth control pills.

"Perhaps if you quit taking these, you will get pregnant," Rainey said.

Louise was defensive. "You knew I was taking them? Why didn't you say something?"

"Hey, you're the one who wants to give 'Daddy' an heir. It really doesn't matter to me. A baby will just inconvenience you. How could you play tennis?" He walked away from her.

"Rainey, please, let's talk. I do want to have your baby. I'm scared. I don't know if I am mother material."

He knew that she wasn't. "Whatever, Louise. At the rate we have sex, it could take a very long time, so I wouldn't worry about it. Keep the pills. I don't care."

Within two months, Louise was pregnant and it was a nightmare for them both. She was sick from the moment of conception. She couldn't keep anything down and was so weak from being nauseated all the time that her doctor ordered complete bed rest. She had been in perfect health prior to the pregnancy. She was a fanatic about her physical fitness and diet, so this unexpected illness played havoc with her. Rainey was not exempt from her discomfort, as he was kept at her beck and call from the minute that he arrived home from work until he left the next morning. He was concerned for her and the baby's well-being, and truly felt sorry for the discomfort that she was in. Her mother spent most of the day with her and brought her cook with her to make sure that Rainey, at least, had proper meals. He hired a housekeeper to come in twice a week, though there was little to be done. He soon told Bernice to quit bringing her cook, as he could not do justice to her cuisine; perhaps when Louise regained her health, he would reconsider. He decided that it was high time he honed his own cooking skills. He had always managed to keep himself fed in his college years.

He was sitting at the kitchen table, rifling through some recipes that his mother had sent him, when he started to laugh at what he had been thinking. "Where are you when a guy really needs you, Vienna?" He had suddenly had a vision of her in the pantry at the Palace, baking up a storm for the fall fair. "Well, well, well, this is an improvement. I can actually see her and feel good with the memory. I'm not too sure that I should be thinking of her when my pregnant wife is upstairs suffering, but how does one stifle a remembrance?"

Rainey had been sleeping in the adjoining bedroom so as not to upset Louise. Early one Sunday morning in July, she called him into her room.

"Rainey," she said, "I have been up for hours and I am not sick. Could it be over?"

She slowly regained her strength, and within three weeks, she was back out on the golf course and chairing a charity ball. Tennis would have to wait. Life went back to normal. Rainey started spending more time at the plaza site, as it was in its first stage of completion. He was a hands-on guy and liked to be at the forefront of any crisis. The only problem he had was Louise's dad. Calvin was constantly in his face; his solution for any difficulties or setbacks was to fire the whole crew. According to him, no matter the tradesman, they were a dime a dozen. Rainey was proud to admit that he didn't roll that way and there was always a solution to any problem. He was highly respected by his workforce, associates, and staff. He knew it and wondered why he didn't have the same qualifications to have a successful personal life.

Morgan Paul Quinn arrived at 2 A.M. on January 13, 1966. He weighed in at 7 pounds 2 ounces. Louise was in labor for fourteen hours and she swore never again. Surprisingly, she fell in love with her newborn the second he was placed in her arms. Needless to say, Calvin was ecstatic and immediately had Morgan added to his will.

Rainey was pretty happy himself. The first thing he did was call his parents. He invited them to come down and meet their newest grandchild. They accepted the invitation and said they would await word for when Louise was up to house guests. Rainey knew the answer to that was "never," but it was his house and they were coming. Patsy and Paul arrived on a chilly February afternoon. They soon learned that the chill inside was greater than the one outside.

Rainey was not at all happy with Louise. They had a heated discussion after his parents' sudden departure. He told her that the next time they visited, she could go and stay at her parents' house, but that Morgan would be staying here. She could tell that he was serious and immediately phoned his parents and apologized for her behavior. She even cried. Rainey knew that they were just crocodile tears, but knew that he had made his point.

For weeks, she did everything she could think of to make Rainey happy. In late June, she found herself pregnant again. Rainey found her sobbing when he got home. She told him the news. He was shocked, as he knew that she was on the pill again.

"What are we going to do, Rainey? Morgan is only five months old! I can't go through that again. Please don't make me. I just can't."

"I'm not asking you to. What is it you want to do?"

"I can't say it, Rainey. Don't make me say it!"

"Louise, I do not believe in abortion, but it is your body and your decision. I will not stand in the way of whatever you decide. I had hoped that we would have a brother or sister for Morgan, though, one day."

"Easy for you to say; you are not the one whose body gets punished. I can't make the decision alone."

"Did you discuss it with Dr. Davidson?"

"Yes, she said that the pill is not 100%. Oh, really? Did I discuss terminating the pregnancy with her? Sort of. She said that I had lots of time and that I should take time to think it over. It's not just my decision. You're the father."

"Let's do that. How far along are you?"

"Approximately twenty-nine days."

"Is it the morning sickness that has you the most worried or do you not want to have another child?"

"Morning sickness…is that what you call it? Men, you have no idea!"

"I am sorry. I didn't mean to be insensitive. I know that you suffered, and believe me, I do not want to see you go through that again. Have you been ill yet?"

"No, but that doesn't mean that I won't be. I'm going to call my mother."

Bernice's advice was to give it a while, but she cautioned her against terminating the pregnancy because she would surely regret it. Apparently, she had an abortion before she was married, and after four miscarriages, she had finally carried Louise to term, but there was never to be another child. Louise had never heard the story before and it only made her decision harder.

Mason Dean Quinn was born on February 26, 1967 at 4 P.M. He weighed in at 7 pounds 12 ounces. He was as fair as Morgan. Neither had Rainey's blue eyes. Louise's pregnancy fared much better than the first and even the delivery was easier, but she made sure that she would never have another child.

Rainey wasn't sure when their marriage completely turned sour. Maybe he was too busy to notice. He blamed himself as much as he did Louise. He was disinterested and she was just cold. Morgan was six and Mason five when it all unraveled. It was Friday, July 14, his thirty-third birthday. He would not soon forget the day. The boys thought he should stay home, seeing it was his birthday. He promised them that he would be home early, as it was imperative that he keep his appointment with Mr. Chan.

His business luncheon went exceedingly well and it appeared that he was going to have another very long housing project. The Centennial Plaza had been completed nearly a year ago and he had only accepted small jobs since. He had moved his offices to a brand new building in an engineering, landscaping, and manufacturing area. He employed four architects and five office staff. Various tradesmen were always at his disposal.

He was whistling as he drove down Sutton Street and pulled into his parking spot. He briefly took notice of a black limousine parked in front of Avery's Landscaping. He was just about to enter his building when, for some reason, he turned and looked back across the road. What was it? He shrugged it off and went inside. Immediately, he knew something was different. He ran up the three flights of stairs and threw the door to his offices open. Sylvie smiled and wished him a happy birthday, and asked him how his luncheon went.

"Thank you. Very well," he answered. "What is that I smell? I know you don't wear perfume."

"I don't know, Sir. I have been trying to nail the scent down. Is it apple or lilac? Anyhow, it seemed to linger after that young lady left."

"What young lady? What did she want?" He had a gut feeling that something wasn't right.

"Well, she asked if you were in and I said that I was expecting you at any moment. I asked her if she would please take a seat and wait. She uttered something and bolted. That was only a few minutes ago. You must have just missed her on the stairs."

"Good God, it's cherry. It's cherry blossoms!" He was out the door and down the stairs, breathing hard. He flung open the door to see the limo pull away from the curb and disappear. He swore and thought, *Why didn't I get the license? How hard could it be to track down limousine companies in the area?* He ran back upstairs.

"Are you all right, Sir?" Sylvie asked.

"It might just be the best day of my life, or the worst. I need you to get me every company that rents out limos in the district, private or cab companies, okay? First, I need you to describe that young lady who was here. What do you remember about her?"

"Carla saw her first. Apparently, she was standing outside the door and was startled when Carla came up behind her. She appeared to be very unsure of herself. Oh, she was a lovely woman. She had the most unusual, dark eyes and gorgeous auburn, shoulder-length hair. She was very thin and fragile looking. Does that sound like someone you know?"

"I'm not sure, Sylvie. Will you see what you can find out for me please?"

Rainey paced back and forth, waiting for her. He played out a hundred scenarios as to why she didn't wait for him. If she came here to see him, why did she leave? Was it even her? He knew it was her. So what, she had lost weight and changed her hair color? That wasn't unfathomable. He phoned each and every company that Sylvie had tracked down. Nobody had a fare that came to Sutton. Every limo was accounted for except those that were rented for several days or weekly. He left messages for them all and assured the receptionists that there was a healthy reward waiting if anything turned up regarding rentals that brought a client to Sutton. He was to be reached at any time of day and he left them his home phone number. There was nothing to do now but wait and he wasn't a patient man, not when it came to Vienna.

The boys were waiting patiently for him. Morgan said, "Dad, you said you would be home early."

"Sorry. I got hung up. You all ready to go out to dinner?"

"Yup," Mason said. "Mom is waiting for you."

Of course she was. Calvin and Bernice were taking them all out for dinner to celebrate his birthday. He gave the boys a hug and asked if their mother was in a good mood. They shrugged their shoulders. He was already infuriated, so she better not tick him off. Right away, she sensed his mood.

"Who pissed in your oatmeal?" Louise asked.

"I'd rather not talk about it if you don't mind." He jumped into the shower and wondered how he was going to make it through the night. When he returned to the bedroom, he saw that Louise had laid out a light yellow shirt and tie for him. He said, "Really, Louise?"

"What? You know father always wants us to look well dressed. Would it kill you to wear a tie on your birthday?"

"You know what, Louise? I don't give a horse's ass what your father wants."

"Well, of all the ungrateful—"

"You don't think that I could have made it without his help, do you? Well, lady, I have news for you. By this time next month, I will have paid him back every red cent he lent me, and with interest, I might add. So put that in your soapbox and shut up."

He tried to make the best of the evening for the boys' sake, but even they knew that something was wrong.

Rainey called his realtor the next day and asked her to find him a suite downtown. Louise and he were barely on speaking terms, and that was why he was so flabbergasted when she said that she was going to accompany him and the boys to his parents' anniversary party in Hawthorne next month. He wasn't all that pleased because now he was going to have to pretend that his marriage wasn't in jeopardy.

She put on quite a show for his mom and dad and was even polite to all his friends. He was more than a little suspicious when he found her head to head with Jimmy's wife, Ruth. She waved to him, as if to signal that she was having a wonderful time. He thought nothing more about it until he received a phone call from Jimmy a week later.

"Buddy, I don't mean to be the bearer of bad tides, but I thought that I should warn you that Louise was asking a lot of questions at your parents' party."

"What kind of questions?"

"Well, she started out asking Ruth if she knew Vienna."

"What? She doesn't even know Vienna existed. I have never told her a thing."

"Yeah, that is what Ruth thought when she called her Vienna and not V. She played along with her, and when your little wife asked what happened between you and her, then she knew she was fishing for information."

"Good for Ruth. What did she tell her?"

"The truth. She said that V left you for no apparent reason. She then put a twist on it and told her that she was glad to see that you were finally over her."

"Christ, Jimmy, our marriage is all but over, but I think this just puts the final nail in the coffin. I can't, for the love of me, figure out how she found out about Vienna. But it's sure as hell clear now why she wanted to go to Hawthorne. She wanted answers to questions I didn't even know she had."

Rainey never brought up the subject of Vienna with Louise. He had no idea how she found out about her but didn't care enough to pursue the matter. He did check his locked drawer where he had stashed her memorabilia, but he found nothing amiss. He had chosen a suite at the Seven Bays and would move his personals there. He sprung the news to the boys and Louise at dinner one night. He informed them that due to his latest undertaking, he would be spending the odd night uptown, so he might as well be comfortable. Louise was not surprised, but the boys were not happy that their dad wasn't going to be home every night. In all fairness to Louise and her active social life, he suggested that they hire a full-time nanny slash housekeeper. She readily agreed, and within a week, they found a suitable middle-aged woman whom the boys liked. She was more than agreeable to spend occasional evenings when neither parent could be home.

Rainey was happy with the new arrangements, as it also meant that his parents and friends would have a place to stay when they visited…away from his shrew of a wife. His work kept him fully occupied. He had no time for anything else except Morgan and Mason. They were doing well in school and excelled in sports. Rainey took on the job as coach for their soccer league, which meant that he was tied up with that once a week and on weekends. He spent as much time with them as he could to make up for Louise's absence. He assumed they would divorce as soon as the boys were a little older. He was sure that he would never marry again.

The calendar read May 1974. He couldn't believe how the days had fled by. The boys were eight and seven. It was a rainy Thursday evening. Soccer practice had been cancelled due to the weather. He had spent an enjoyable day at home. Louise was away. He sent Janise, the nanny, home, and he and the boys made dinner and played board games. He was relaxing in his den, listening to the radio, and decided to go through his mail. He usually discarded all the junk mail, but he found one that had an offer for free tapes or records and decided to open it. His music collection had not been updated for years. He opened the advertisement.

> *Dear Mr. Quinn,*
>
> *You have been selected to receive a selection of classical music recordings absolutely free. The first of ten installments highlights the intoxicating melodies from the waltz king, Johann Strauss II, including The Blue Danube and other Viennese-inspired tunes from Beethoven, Mozart, and Hayden, just to name a few. If you have ever been in love or mourned for love lost, you deserve to hear these tender and enchanting pieces of music. There are tales of moonstruck lovers and serene beauty that haunt the soul. There are melodies of longing, melancholy, pain, and abandoned memories. There is music for sweethearts, especially in the operetta Morning, Noon and Night in Vienna…*

"Oh, for the love of Mary! Vienna, really?" He threw the pamphlet across the room just as "The First Time Ever I Saw Your Face" was playing on the radio. He hadn't heard a word about her for almost a year. She had not come to Lara's wedding last June. He hadn't expected her to. Lara had pleaded with her, but to no avail. She wasn't ready to face him yet. That had given him fleeting hope that someday, she was going to come back to him. Then he reminded himself that she was married and it wasn't going to happen…too many years had passed. And now, this reminder of her in an ad. Was he going to be haunted by her in one way or the other for the rest of his life?

Chapter Nineteen

Vienna, 1981

I cannot believe that twenty years had passed since I came to Scotland. Some days, it seemed like only yesterday that I arrived with a heavy heart and a little life growing inside of me. Other times, I had felt as though I lived three lifetimes. I was thirty-seven, and if it weren't for my beloved daughters, I would have withered up and died years ago. So much had happened since I last wrote about my life, so I guess I might as well start with the last time I saw Rainey.

I knew that it was his birthday that ill-fated day when I went to his office. I came back to the hotel room and curled up on the couch, hating myself for being so foolish. Suppose he had seen me? Well then, it would all be over now, wouldn't it? I even had the audacity to telephone his home address. I only wanted to hear his voice, and I did. It was a recording: *"You've reached the home of Louise and Rainey Quinn. We are sorry we missed your call. Please leave your name and number and we will get back to you as soon as possible."*

I sighed. Of course he was still married. I might have to do with that message for the rest of my life. When Jeremy came back, he asked me why I was so upset, and I told him what I had done. He told me that I should try and make contact with Rainey because, obviously, I wanted to. I told him that I couldn't do that, and he offered to do it for me. I made him promise never to do that and, furthermore, he had to make sure that Manuel would never reveal where he had taken me if anyone should ask. I was sure that we could count on his discretion, but just to be safe, I gave him $10,000. I did not consider it a bribe; he needed the money to bring his family to Canada.

Lara got married in 1973 to a man who had been a patient in Bridge Falls Hospital. He had been in a car accident and she helped him to recuperate by becoming his personal nurse once he was released. His name was Cooper

Stewart. I didn't go home for their wedding for one reason and only one reason: Rainey would be there.

In 1974, Addy became very ill. She had eloped with an older man when she was eighteen and he left her with a three-year-old daughter when she became ill. She had no choice but to move back home to live with our parents in Bridge. I went over as soon as I found out and did what I could to help out. It was then that I bought the little house on Cedar Avenue. It wasn't really small, but compared to Avanloch, it was insignificant.

I visited briefly with Jimmy and was pleased to find out that he and Ruth were trying to make their marriage work. Their daughter, Constance, was already ten years old. He said that there wasn't much hope for Yates's and June's woes, though. Marley and Zane were still happily wed but childless. It appeared that out of all of us, they were the only two to have a successful marriage. There was hope for Lara, though. He hadn't seen or talked to Rainey for almost two years.

Avanloch had undergone many changes through the years. As far as I was concerned, the updating was complete. We had brought the tower rooms into the twentieth century as much as possible. The biggest change was to the space in between them; we had turned it into a courtyard. It was complete with seating that mimicked an outdoor Parisian café. We had installed a fountain in the center and the entire area was landscaped with local trees and seasonal plantings. It was a most pleasant place to relax and view the valley.

The only room that I left untouched was the grand drawing room. I still found it grandiose. When we hosted large dinner parties, we did end the evening there, but I was never comfortable. I always had visions of Romans and their orgies that took place in just such settings. Ash and her friends made it their headquarters whenever they visited.

The room I loved the most was the informal drawing room. I had tried to follow the theme colors that had been prominent throughout Avanloch for a century—creamy and bold golds, deep reds, chocolate browns, and hints of black. The large, ornate fireplace was inlaid with figures of Greek gods and goddesses, and a bronze mirror hung above it. On the mantel was a selection of antique clocks. A copper chandelier hung from the plastered white ceiling. The walls were adorned with works of oil paintings, which dictated the romantic era. The floor was imported maple and vintage carpets of reds and golds enhanced the sitting arrangements. There were many comfortable armchairs and chesterfields that had been upholstered in rich brocades and crimson velvets. Oak side tables and floor lamps with frilly lace shades completed the room. In the center of two bookcases, which were filled with volumes of history, past and present, sat a seventeenth-century mahogany writing desk and a sunshine gold Queen Anne wing chair. As with all the other rooms, I gave it my signature—potted plants and fresh seasonal bouquets of delightful scents. I had oil created for me from an apothecary in Waverly that mimicked the scent of cherry blossoms, and I would infuse it into rose petals and nosegays. This and the conservatory were my favorite rooms in the whole house.

I was through decorating. Anything else would be up to the girls. Just in time, as in 1975, Jeremy became terribly ill. He had a cough accompanied by chills that could not be contained. He was diagnosed with tuberculosis. I never want to watch anyone die ever again. For a whole year, he suffered, and the whole household was lamenting. Rosy was seventeen and in her last year of school; Ava was fourteen. I had to force them to attend classes, as they wanted to be by their father's side continuously. They realized that he needed rest, so they reluctantly agreed. The day came when it was obvious to us all that he wouldn't make it through another night. Ash had arrived in the morning and we were all at his bedside when he exhaled his final earthly breath on January 26, 1976.

Mourners came from near and far for the funeral. We had to open up the entire house to accommodate the guests. The little chapel was no way large enough. Thank heavens for Reverend Peters and his wife, Betsy. They were the counsel who held the girls together. Jeremy was cremated and the urn that held his ashes was placed next to his beloved Maveryn. I composed the solemn words that hopefully would bring him peace.

> *On January 26, 1976, Jeremy Bruce McAllister passed from this world into God's holy realm. He will always be remembered by his daughters, Rosalyn and Ava, as a kind and devoted father, and a generous friend and husband to Vela. May he rest in peace and find comfort in the arms of his beloved Maveryn.*
>
> *Amen*

Shelley and Keats lived longer than any of us ever expected. We accredited the new dogs, who were named Barrett and Browning, with keeping them alive for so long. Shelley passed away first in the winter of '74 and Keats followed shortly after, probably of a broken heart.

Mollie Magan departed this life on October 31, 1976. She was very old but had remained in her own house until the very end. It was fitting that she passed on Halloween.

In the spring of 1977, I received some very sad news from Lara. Her Aunt Mavis and Uncle Saul were killed in an accident while they were visiting their children in Saskatchewan. I sent her a card of grievance. I wanted to send Rainey, Patsy, and Paul one also but thought better of it and didn't. In her next letter, she sent word that Marley Haggard had died of ovarian cancer. She passed away three months after her diagnosis. She said that Zane was inconsolable, and that he had left town immediately following her burial and hadn't been heard from since.

Too many deaths in such a short time. My sister Addy was not improving. She was yet to receive diagnosis of her condition. The expert opinion was that it was an autoimmune disease, lupus, rheumatoid arthritis, or a combination of many debilitating illnesses. They advised a warmer, dryer climate, and Mother and Father were taking her to live for the winter in Arizona. Mother was able to lease the restaurant out and Lara was going to take care of the house. I should be there.

In the fall of '77, I started putting my stories that I had been composing into print. I had made up tales of all the farm and wild animals for the girls when they were young. Ava was a gifted artist and she did all the drawings. Rosalyn handled the promotions and the marketing, and she and Ava also helped with the compositions. We published the books under the name Velavarose. They were well received and were distributed throughout Great Britain . We had no need for the income generated from the sales, so it was all donated to our charities, the main one being an orphanage in Scotland. By the end of the year, the books were being marketed in Canada. Over a period of three years, we composed fourteen books and I was working on the fairy tale Laddy and Emerald.

I had a rather disturbing visit from Roberge in the summer of 1980. I was in the stables, preparing for my daily ride on my new steed, Arabesque, when I was surprised by a man's voice. "Lady V."

Startled, I turned, half expecting to see Rainey. Who else would call me Lady V? "Monsieur Farradan, to what do I owe the pleasure?"

"You have not returned any of the many messages that I have left you. I thought that I should journey to see for myself that you are well."

"I am sorry that I didn't return any of your calls. I was assured by Ash and Amma that you were told that I was well. If you made the trip only to see me, then I am sorry to tell you that it is a waste of your time."

"Surely, you are not still in mourning for a man you didn't love?"

"That is hardly any of your affair."

"Is it not time you accept that I am going to continue to woo you until I win?"

"You are wasting your time, Sir . That is never going to happen. My heart belongs to another and soon I shall be joining him in Canada. I bid thee farewell." I was on Arabesque and out the gate before Roberge could utter a word. I hoped that I had seen the last of him and that he took me seriously when I had said that I was going to Canada to be with my love. I wish that it were true, but it was just a ruse.

The past few winters had not been easy for the girls and me. We were used to Jeremy taking us on winter vacations to foreign cities and countries. We had the pleasure of escaping to places like Bordeaux, France; Antwerp, Belgium; Athens, Greece; Barcelona, Spain; and Rome, Italy, to name a few. Jeremy was keenly aware that winter was the time of year my depression was at its worst, so we would have a quiet Christmas at Avanloch and then he would announce where our next exotic destination was to be. I think I liked Italy the best. I made a point that we visited all the landmarks that Rainey had told me about in his letters.

The weeks would pass quickly and then we would be back in wintry Scotland. Jeremy would be gone again, the girls would be back in school, and I would resume my sessions with Dr. Jai. I never did disclose the reason for my sadness to her. However, I did confide in Amma my feelings for Rainey after returning from my regrettable visit to his office in 1972.

She knew of my situation with Jeremy, as I was sure the whole household did. She was very saddened to hear that Rainey was the cause of my despondency. She was very perplexed as to why I chose to suffer instead of proclaiming my love to him. I told her that he had a family, just as I did, and I could not and would not do anything to jeopardize them. Perhaps someday, our time would come. I thought, *Lord, may I live long enough to undo all the harm that I had did to myself and others.*

I was forced to take stock of McAllister Holdings. It was such a vast empire that I had wanted no part of, but now, with Jeremy gone, I had to make decisions that I was not capable of. Thankfully, Uncle John was there to guide me through the legalities. We had numerous meetings with the board of directors. Rosalyn and Ava were old enough to take part in decisions, and Ash put her theatrical aspirations aside to take over as CEO (chief executive officer). Rosy was pursuing a career in business, so I was sure she would be her father's replacement before very long.

There was only one thing left that needed to be dealt with, and that was Jeremy's personal effects. With trepidation, we entered his private quarters. I didn't know what we were afraid of finding. John and Jannie accompanied the girls and myself one dark and dreary day months after he had passed away. All of his clothes and personal effects went to charities. The girls kept whatever mementos they wanted. It appeared that he had no secrets, and then we unlocked his safe. He had left farewell letters to us all. They were dated in 1974. Apparently, he knew two years before he passed that the illness was not to be conquered. Besides a copy of his last will and testament, and thousands of dollars, were three gold-bound journals. I knew before we opened them that they belonged to Maveryn. One she had started for Rosalyn the day that she was born. The second one was of her life at Avanloch. The third one was the one that interested me the most. It was addressed to "The next Lady of Avanloch." I suppose that meant me. I opened it to a random page and the words "Black Russian" jumped out at me.

I decided that I best read the journal in the privacy of my own sitting room. The first dozen or so pages were definitely not meant for the next Mrs. McAllister, but only for her own recall. She described day-to-day life at Avanloch and how happy she was. It wasn't until July 20, 1958 that I noticed a change in her writing of everyday events.

> *I have an eerie feeling that I am being watched. It is not like me to be so skittish. I enlisted Duffy to help me move my desk. I am now sitting facing the door and the hidden entrance to the stairway. It is giving me a sense of well-being.*

The next nine months of entries were only regarding her pregnancy and how happy she and Jeremy were. The evening before Rosalyn was born, she wrote:

>*I found my desk askew tonight. Something is afoot. No one in the house would do such a thing. The windows were closed, so it was not the wind. I have no time to devote to the mischief, as I am in the throes of labor. I must go and find Jer…*

I flipped through the dated pages until I found one that wasn't all about Rosalyn.

>*Rosalyn is three months old. What a delightful child! I never knew that motherhood could be so fulfilling. And yet, I am afraid for her. I am having disconcerting feelings of confusion. Is it only my imagination, or is there really someone or something watching me? I no longer just experience it in this room, but now, it has spread to the hallway and the main stairs. Am I being paranoid? Do other new mothers have these sensations?*

>*November 3, 1958*
>*Today, I got the shock of my life. I inquired of the staff if there were any stories of hauntings at Avanloch. Seeing it was a castle and built on very old grounds, I wouldn't be a bit surprised. Mrs. D had laughed and said she, too, wouldn't be surprised but that she had never witnessed any such thing. She only hoped Taty would never come back. It took some doing, but I finally managed for her to tell me who Taty was.*

That was how Maveryn discovered who Tatylyanna was. No one had a kind thing to say about her and were glad that she was gone, though sympathetic to the way in which she had died. Apparently, Mrs. Duffy omitted the part where Liz Beth had done the deed. There were many more notations of Taty in the journal but nothing that suggested she was a threat to Maveryn or Rosalyn, until late in 1959.

>*I have been troubled for some time now. I am experiencing sudden bouts of unexplained pain in my abdomen. Tomorrow, I have an appointment with a specialist in Waverly. Perhaps, I will even reveal to him that I have feelings of being spied on but that no one is there. I suppose I won't, as he is a man of science and what I am dealing with is not explainable.*

>*December 14*
>*My tests were inconclusive. To leave it for now, but if the pain persists, I am to be further evaluated. Now I am having frightening dreams of death.*

December 20
Jeremy rushed me to the hospital in the middle of the night a week ago.
I have a cancerous tumor that is already too far advanced for surgery.

February 2, 1960
We are finally home. Jeremy has had me to doctor after doctor on two
continents. He refuses to accept the bitter facts. I am not curable. I am too
weak to continue looking for a miracle. I just want to spend my remaining
days with him and Rosalyn. I have been moved to the first floor, as I am
bedridden. Even in this state, she taunts me. She will not win. I will not let
her have the last word. With my dying breath, I shall banish her to room
six and there she must stay. The Black Russian will be no more. I am not a
ranting lunatic. Do this please, darling Jeremy, I beg you.

Her final words to the journal were almost unintelligible, but I interpreted them as:

Thank you, Jeremy. I can rest in peace now. Tell Rosy I love her. If I were going
to Hell, I would see the Black Russian there, but I am off to Heaven. I will wait for
you to join me there, Jeremy, my love, my life.

Tears streamed down my face as I pictured the lovely Maveryn, and Shelley and Keats, frolicking in the meadows of wild flowers. Jeremy was with her now and I was quite sure that I had not seen the last of them. I was also sure that I would one day read the journals more thoroughly and discover some facts that I had missed the first time, just as there were still many places in the castle that I had yet to explore, such as the hidden stairwells and even parts of the cellar. I had been too occupied with the important aspects to go on any adventures, but the day would come, and now I had two grown daughters to explore with me.

I decided to spend January and February with my family in Arizona in the New Year. It was 1980. The girls were preoccupied with their studies in Edinburgh and only came home every other weekend, and I hated these early months. From the minute I landed in Tucson, I could understand why my parents wanted to remain here. Addy had been rejuvenated by the warm, dry weather. She and Mother had a small catering business that they ran from the house in Beth, which was southeast of Tucson. My mother was fifty-six and father was sixty. He was still remodeling houses. My niece was ten and the spitting image of her mother. I had a very enjoyable stay and was all too happy to help out in the kitchen, baking, as I did very little of it back in Scotland. Mother was so thrilled to learn that Jannie and John were coming to visit in March. A few days before I was to leave, Mother had a talk with me.

"When are you going to tell Ava that her father is still alive?" Mother said. "Don't look at me like that, child. Of course we know that Rainey is her father and the reason that you ran away. If I live to be a hundred, I will never understand why you did it. I promised you that I would keep your secret and it has been difficult to keep my mouth shut. Did you expect to keep that blue-eyed girl away from the world? Do you think that we are blind not to have seen the resemblance to Rainey? Don't you think Ava has the right to know? He is probably the most decent man that I have ever known besides your father, and you just cast him aside. Addy's husband was rotten to the bone and Sissy's isn't much better. I know you weren't in love with Jeremy, and now he has been gone for four years. Are you going to be a bitter woman the rest of your life? How pitiful it must be to be you."

I was in tears, knowing that she was right but couldn't respond.

"I am giving you until this time next year, Vienna Emerald, to tell Ava about her father and vice versa, or I will. Make no mistake about that, child. I will." Then she hugged me and told me that she loved me, but it was time for me to be happy, and I couldn't be when I was carrying such a burden.

I told her that I had every intention of revealing the truth to both of them when Ava was twenty-one, and she would only be nineteen next year. Mother didn't understand. How could she when I didn't myself?

The summer of 1980 was very busy as usual with the girls and all their friends. The house was always full. Ava had a boyfriend and they seemed to be serious. In December, they became engaged. I was not entirely thrilled. His name was Randy. He was from Canada and was enrolled in culinary school in Vancouver starting in January.

Chapter Twenty

Bringing Vienna Home

I didn't have a chance. The three of them ganged up on me. Ava wanted me to come to Vancouver with them. They were going to stop off in Bridge first and pick up the car that we kept there. Then she would go with Randy to the coast and she didn't want to drive back alone, so she asked if I would please go with them. Randy wanted me to meet his folks.

Rosalyn was the one who insisted the most. "Mama, I am going to be so busy with the company and finals, so I won't be home for months. I don't want to see you alone for that long and we all know how hard these winter months are for you. Aunt Jannie and Uncle John will be on their cruise and Amma and Johnny will be busy moving into Brackenshire. Mrs. D wants to spend time with her family. There will be no one here to keep you company. Besides, you could always take a trip to Arizona, and remember, Lily and Papa Joe are going to sell the house in Bridge. Don't you want to say good-bye?"

"I should be here to help with Amma's children while they are moving, don't you think? And I am so tired of flying."

"We are not going to take no for an answer," Ava said. "Let's talk to Dr. Jai and get her to prescribe something to help you relax on the plane. Please, pretty please, Mama? I really want you to come. You haven't seen Lara for a long time."

She was looking at me with those puppy dog eyes that she shared with her father, so I couldn't refuse any longer. Besides, they had knocked down every excuse that I had come up with.

We rented a car in Potsdam and arrived in Bridge Falls late in the evening. We had phoned ahead and asked Lara's husband, Cooper, if he could turn the heat up in the house for us. He was thrilled that we were here for a while and would let me surprise Lara myself. I climbed into a nice, warm bed and realized that I was very glad that I had come. I had the most peaceful sleep that I could remember.

Randy and Ava went out to a bar for dinner and dancing one evening while I was visiting with Lara and her family. I was proud of myself. I hadn't asked about Rainey. But I was wondering if I could trust myself when I went to Vancouver. The kids came home excited, as there was an amateur Iditarod taking place in the valley and it was winding up tomorrow in Hawthorne. I must go with them. Did I dare? There were bound to be people there besides Jimmy who would remember me. Suppose Rainey's parents were there? No, I had better not go.

Back in Vancouver, Rainey did a last-minute check in at the office to make sure nothing serious had arisen. He was assured by all that there was nothing that they couldn't handle.

"Are you getting an early start then, Mr. Q?" Sylvie asked.

"As soon as I drop the boys off at school tomorrow, I'll be leaving," Rainey replied. "What are you up to there, Sylvie?"

"Just reading my horoscope. Shall I give you yours for the weekend?"

He laughed. "You know that I don't believe in that nonsense."

"Then what can it hurt? Cancer, right? Well, this is interesting. It says here that this is the month when old lovers find each other. Hmmm, the same goes for the signs Aries and Pieces. Are you holding out on us?"

Rainey waved good-bye at the door. He smiled at the prediction as he drove home.

Hawthorne, January 1981

Ava thought that I was shivering from the cold. I could not tell her the truth, and that was I had just had an encounter with her father, the man I had been in love with for twenty years. What was wrong with me? I had been waiting for this day for so long and now I had acted as if it were nothing. Where was the spunky woman from Avanloch who wasn't fazed by ghosts or insurmountable tasks? Was I still afraid of Rainey's rejection? The answer was yes.

Ava ushered me to the back of the hotel bar to join up with the two teams that they had become friends with in Bridge. They were a lively bunch and welcomed me.

Rainey had joined his friends at the front of the room. Jimmy could tell the encounter with V hadn't gone well.

Yates said, "'Scuse me people, be right back."

Rainey watched as Yates walked over to Vienna's table and put his arm around her, giving her a big hug and planting a kiss on her cold cheek. Vienna looked up at him and patted his hand.

"Mama, who is this big cuddly bear?" Ava asked.

"Yates Fielding, meet my daughter Ava Lane McAllister."

"Ava Lane." Yates released his hold on V and said, "I am delighted to meet you. You do know that your existence is somewhat of a mystery around here, don't you?"

Ava was puzzled. "No. Whatever do you mean?"

"He is just kidding, dear," I said. "Yates is an old friend and is just wondering why I never brought you over to visit before. Isn't that right, Yates?"

He smiled at me. "Yes, why haven't you? No need, you're here now. You are going to stay for a while this time, aren't you? Usually, when we would find out that your mother was visiting, she was already gone. I can't believe that we never ran into each other all these years. How long ago was it that we saw each other at that funeral, V?"

"A few years back. How is everyone?"

"Come over for yourself and see. The whole gang is there and a few new faces. Just a word of caution…do you know about Marley?"

"Yes, I do. Oh, here is Ava's fiancé. Randy, this is Yates, an old friend of mine."

"Well, well, I must ask, are you part of V's mysterious past?" Randy asked, shaking Yates's hand.

Yates glanced over at his table and shook his head. "Well, I guess I fit into the 'past' category, but I am no mystery. No, that is not me." He glanced over at his table and winked at Vienna. Then he motioned the waitress to bring a round of drinks to the table. He took his leave before he opened up a can of worms. "Nice to have met you all. Don't be a stranger, V."

Rainey had been watching and wondering why he didn't have the nerve to just waltz over as Yates had. He wanted to put his arms around Vienna and kiss her so badly. By now, Zane's new wife, Frieda, and her friends, Nola and Amber, had joined the table.

"Who were you sitting with?" Frieda asked Yates.

"An old friend from a long time ago, V LaFontaine, and her daughter, Ava."

"V?" Frieda questioned, looking directly at Rainey. "Do you mean the mysterious V, Rainey's V? She actually exists?"

"I'm right here, Frieda. Yes, she really does exist." With that, Rainey summoned up his courage and made the long walk to her table.

Jimmy whispered, "Good luck, buddy."

I felt a hand on my shoulder and I knew it was him.

"Vienna," Rainey said almost pleadingly. "Can we have that drink now?"

Ava's eyes opened wide as she looked up at the stranger. No one called her mother Vienna, not even her family. In the few seconds that she had to study her mother's reaction to the man, she suddenly knew why no one called her Vienna. This was him. This was the one from a long, long time ago. There was something so familiar about him, but she couldn't figure out what it was.

Not wanting to make introductions, I told Ava that I would be right back. Rainey held the chair for me, then led me through the kitchen and into the restaurant through the swinging doors. None of the staff seemed to mind that we had entered this way. He suggested that we take a table at the back. I sat but couldn't look at him. My mind was racing to yesterdays. How could he still have the same effect on me after twenty years? I felt naked. I was very warm and I struggled to remove my coat. He jumped up to help and I felt his warm breath on the back of my neck. "It's Only Make-Believe" was playing on the jukebox. I sensed that he was just as nervous as I was.

"Do you still take your coffee black, Vienna?" Rainey asked.

I nodded. I wanted to tell him to call me V. Vienna was too afraid to be here. I felt his eyes on me, those deep, blue eyes that had the power to hypnotize me. Oh no, I was wearing green—his favorite color on me. Why had I chosen to wear my green angora sweater and jade earrings? I quickly felt my neck to make sure I didn't have the sea-green topaz teardrop that he had given me in another lifetime. Satisfied that I wasn't, I told myself that I was being silly. Men didn't remember colors, do they? Now what?

"Do you know how long it has been since we have seen each other, Vienna? I haven't had a word about you in years. No one knew what happened to you. It's like you disappeared off the face of the Earth."

Is he waiting for an explanation? "I've been living abroad."

"That's not much of an answer. I want to know why you ran away. Why you ran away from me."

I looked down, as I could not lie to him if I was staring into his dreamy eyes. "I don't think that I want to get into that right now, Rainey."

"If not now, when? Am I ever going to see you again?"

I got up and grabbed my coat. "I don't think so. You shouldn't call me Vienna." I almost collided with the waitress as I ran for the door. I heard him calling me but I didn't stop. His pleas echoed in my ears.

"Vienna, please." Rainey scrambled to pay the check. The door was closing but she was gone. Again. Defeated, he went back to the bar and slumped into a chair.

"So soon?" Jimmy asked.

He shrugged his shoulders and his face said it all. He had a couple more drinks and decided to call it a day.

"You can't go home yet, Rain!" Yates said. "Hell, it's only 7. The party is just getting started. Come on, what do you say, buddy?"

"Sorry, Yates, I'm bushed. That 300-mile drive is a killer in the winter. And hey, you know what they say? Tomorrow is another day. I want to spend some time with my parents . Walk me to my car, Jimmy. I think you and I have a little talking to do."

As soon as they were out the door, Jimmy questioned Rainey. "I take it that things didn't go very well. What the hell happened?"

"You want the whole five minutes in a nutshell? She told me that she's been living abroad…no kidding. We shouldn't see each other again and I shouldn't call her Vienna."

"I don't believe it."

"What don't you believe, Jimmy? What do you know that I don't?" Rainey unlocked the car doors and they got in. It was colder inside than it was outside. He started the engine. "Do you want to drive or just sit?"

"Here is fine. No matter where we are, you're going to want to kill me."

"Come on, Jimmy, nothing can be that bad."

Jimmy looked his friend in the eye. "I told you that I saw V once or twice in Bridge, right? The truth of the matter is that I have been in contact with her for years, probably ten. Whenever she comes into town, she calls me. I haven't seen the girls since that first time, though."

"Are you saying that you and Vienna met on the sly?"

"We weren't hiding anything because there was nothing to hide. Sometimes, we only talked on the phone. I didn't know she was here this time; she never phoned."

"So, for ten years, you have been in touch with her and you never once thought to mention it. You bastard! And you want me to believe that you don't have a relationship with her. Come on…how naïve do you think I am? You've always had a thing for her, haven't you?"

"Get your mind out of the gutter, Rain. What you are thinking is ludicrous. Our relationship is purely platonic."

"Why is it ludicrous?"

"Because, you stupid ass, she is still in love with you!"

Sarcastically, Rainey said, "Oh yeah, I could see that! She couldn't wait to get away from me! Don't take me for a fool, Jimmy. Believe me, there was no love."

"Did you give her a chance or did you bombard her with questions?"

"What are you getting at?"

"She's fragile, Rain. Give her a chance to adjust to seeing you."

"How am I going to do that? She's probably already left town."

"I don't think so. Yates said that they are here for a few days."

"You still haven't told me why you didn't tell me about seeing her. Who gave you the permission to play God?"

"What was I to do? She didn't want you to know, and if I wanted to keep tabs on her, I had to respect her wishes. Don't think it was easy for me, buddy."

"I'm not your buddy right now! Christ, I can't believe what I am hearing. Did you even once think of telling me?"

"Yeah. Remember when I told you that I had ran into an old girlfriend of yours and she asked about you? Can you recall what you said?"

"Not really. What does this have to do with Vienna?"

"Well, it was Vienna. But you said there was no one in your past that you cared a flying fig about, so whoever it was, I should keep it to myself. After you sobered up, you asked me who the girl was and I said Sally Baines. Remember now?"

"Yeah, I remember. So what stopped you from telling me that it was really Vienna?"

"You. The bitterness in your voice. I didn't think that you would ever forgive her for leaving and I couldn't take the chance that you would hurt her beyond repair. You had stored up too much resentment. If it had of been fifteen, sixteen years ago when you confessed to me that you still cared for her…well, it would have been a different story. You're hardened now, Rainey. Did I make a mistake in keeping this from you? Yeah, probably. We all know that I am just a big screw up. Just ask Ruth about that."

"We're all screw ups when it comes to matters of the heart. You're not the only one. I am still searching for answers as to why she left me in the first place. Do you have any insight into that?"

"She has never said, not to me and not to Lara, though sometimes I think Lara knows more than she can share."

"The essence of the whole thing is that you knew where she was and—"

"Got to stop you there. I never knew where she was! She would never say. Periodically, she would send us a postcard from some exotic place like Singapore or Bermuda. There was never a return address . There is something that she is not willing to share with her old friends, not even Lara. Its twenty years, Rain, what could it be?"

"I have no clue. You know that it is a mystery that still haunts me. In all fairness to you, I did know that she came back to the valley now and then. Maybe you mentioned it or Lara, or even my mom…it doesn't matter. You see, she always knew how to find me, but she never tried. Except that one time. I should have tried harder to find her."

"What one time? What more could you have done?"

"I'll tell you about it some time. I could have hired a private detective. Lord knows I have the money."

"Now you do, but you didn't always. I have to say one more thing, Rainey. V would do nothing to interfere with your marriage and that may be why she stayed away."

"Hell, Jimmy, you know that's been over for years. What stopped you from telling me when I told you I was going to get a divorce?"

"But you didn't, did you, Rain? You're still married. V has scruples, which I know is foreign to you, being in big business and all."

"Look who is calling the kettle black. I will probably never forgive you for keeping her from me. I guess there is nothing more to say."

"Yes, there is. It was all for V. I have one question for you: How did you feel when you saw her today?"

"Honestly, I felt like I was twenty-one again and this beautiful young girl had come into my life. I wanted to hold her and tell all the things that I should have back then."

"Then don't let her get away again, buddy. Go get her, and no matter what, forgive her. Whatever you have to promise her to get her back, do it. I can guarantee you that she wants you probably more than you do her."

"I doubt that. But this is by no means over between you and me."

"After you two are reunited, you can come at me with both barrels."

"From your lips to God's ears."

Jimmy got out of the car and walked around to the driver's side. Rainey opened the window.

Jimmy extended his hand. "I love you, man."

Rainey nodded. "Me, too."

As soon as Ava saw the stranger return, she got up and said good-bye to everyone. "Come on, Randy. We have to go."

Someone from the crowd asked if they were going to be back for the dance, and Randy said he didn't know. He followed Ava outside and asked her who the man who had whisked her mom away was. "He called her Vienna. Who do you know who calls her that?"

"Honestly, I don't have an inkling. He was with that bunch that Yates was sitting with. I guess they are all old friends of Mama's. I don't think that we should mention it."

They found V sitting in her car with the motor running.

"Mama, are you all right?" Ava couldn't help it and asked, "Who was that man you went with?"

"Oh, he is just someone I used to know. I haven't seen him for a very long time, so it was a little awkward. I am so very tired, cold, and wanted to go back to Bridge."

"We're coming with you, Mama."

"No! You are staying for the dance. I don't require babysitting."

"Please let us take you home. We can come back for the dance; it's such a short drive."

"Yes, V," Randy chimed in from the backseat. "We have lots of time before the dance."

"You two are driving me crazy." V said. "Okay, I give in. Why don't you drive, Randy?"

Ava said to herself, *I hope that guy is still there when we get back. I need some answers and I know Mama is not going to talk. She has always been so secretive about the days before she came to Scotland.* However, she did know that there was someone from her past and that his name was Rainey. She knew that because her mother called out his name countless times in her sleep. She had been eight the first time that she had been awakened by her mother calling out for him in her sleep. She had rushed into her mother's bedroom and found her sobbing and calling out, "Rainey, Rainey." That was the first of many times. She had been assured that it was only a bad dream. That was the answer she received every time. Was it a possibility that the man tonight was indeed Rainey? He called her Vienna, and Randy was right, no one called her that.

As she got older, she noticed the sadness in her mother's eyes. It was most prevalent at night, when they were sitting on the settee together. Her mother would be brushing her hair and, now and then, she would say, "You are so lovely, Ava. And your eyes are the color of an azure sea." Over and over through the years, Ava had heard those words. Before she had found out that Jeremy was not her biological father, she had asked where she got the color of her eyes from because both of her parents had brown eyes.

When Jeremy had become ill, Rosalyn had let it slip that he was not her father. She had said, "You can't possibly be as worried as I am about his health because he is not even your real father." Of course, Rosy regretted it the minute it was out of her mouth. Ava had only known one father and that was Lord Jeremy McAllister; she was even named after his castle, Avanloch. She had gone crying to her mother, who then told her it was true and that her true father had been killed in an accident in Italy. No one would tell her anything about him, not Lily or Papa Joe or Sissy or Addy—not even Lara or Jannie. They all said they didn't know him. She quit asking about him many years ago, as it upset her mother too much. She vowed that someday, she would discover who he really was.

The years had passed and she had learned nothing. In her heart, she felt that the answer lay in the little hamlet of Hawthorne, and if it did, she was determined to discover it tonight. At least she hoped that she would find out who this Rainey person was.

Randy and Ava left, promising V that they would be home early. Ava was ever so anxious to return to Hawthorne and find the man whom she was pretty sure was Rainey. They were too late, everyone had left the bar. She reassured herself that they would all be at the dance and received directions to the Grange. The party was well on its way and Ava wondered how hard it would be to track down Yates. As it was, it wasn't hard at all, because his daughter, Alexia Fielding, was sitting with their friends.

"I know that name," Ava said to her. "Are you Yates's daughter?"

"Yes, I am," Alexia said. "How do you know my dad?"

"Actually, I only met—excuse me, I should say, we all met—this afternoon after the races. Is he here and his friend, Rainey?"

Randy was looking at her oddly.

"Oh, you know my Uncle Rain, too?" Alexia said. "No, I don't think he's coming."

"Rainey is your uncle?" Ava quizzed her.

"Not really. I have always called him, Jimmy, and Zane uncle since I was young. The four of them have been friends since they were born. They are known as the Four Musketeers. Rainey has always been my favorite."

"Why is that, if you don't mind my asking?"

"No, not at all. He has these deep, piercing blue eyes…something like yours. But yours are full of life and Rainey's are always sad. I asked Dad once why he always looks so unhappy, and Dad said that something happened in his life a long time ago that he can't let go of. He is just the kindest person in the whole world, though."

"Do you know where your dad is now?"

"Sure, they are all at the back. They always sit there. I think they own those tables." She laughed and asked if she could show Ava the way.

Ava told her, "No, thanks."

Jerry said, "Alexia, are we going to dance or what?" And off they went.

Randy asked Ava if she knew what she was doing.

"I have to get some answers, Randy," she replied. "I just have to. Mama is never going to tell me anything. The answers have to be here with her old friends."

"Ava, I don't want to discourage you, but why don't you just ask Lara?"

"She's had almost twenty years to tell me things and she hasn't, so I have no reason to believe she will now. Wish me luck." She edged her way toward the back of the room, trying to avoid the dancers. It was easy to spot them. Lots of empty bottles and glasses on the tables and a good deal of laughter. *Good*, she thought. *Liquor encourages loose lips.*

Yates spotted her right away as she was trying to weave her way through the crowd. She arrived at his table almost breathless.

"Well hello, V's daughter. Are you lost?" To his friends, he said, "Meet Ava Lane."

"Where's your mother?" someone asked.

"She didn't come." She was surprised to hear them all say, "Too bad," or something along those lines. She tried to remember all the names. There was a Zane, Jamie, Frieda, and Nola. The one called Jimmy interested her most for some reason. "Nice to meet you all. Yates, do you think that I could have a word with you?"

"Sure. Care to trip the light fantastic?"

"Why not?" Ava joined him on the dance floor. Thankfully, it was a waltz, so they could talk, or at least try to. As a way of opening, she said, "I just met your daughter Alexia. She's a lovely girl. Do you have any more children?"

"Two boys. Frankie is fifteen and Evan is almost nineteen. How old are you, Ava?"

"I'm almost nineteen also. Did I meet your wife back at the table?"

He laughed heartily. "That ship sailed a long time ago."

"I'm sorry."

"Don't be, no one else is."

"I don't know quite how to ask you this, but your friend Rainey, was he someone special to my mother?"

"I would like to think that we were all special to V back in the day. But what you are asking me is not my story to tell. What does your mother say?"

"That's just it, she doesn't talk about her past. I know she is haunted by something and coming here today really stirred something up. Are you sure you have nothing that you want to get off your chest?"

He laughed again and said, "Sorry, luv." He dropped her off at her table, smelled his daughter's drink glass, and, satisfied, gave a quick salute and departed.

Damn it, Ava said to herself. *How am I ever going to find out anything about this Rainey and his relationship to Mama?* She was figuring out another way to approach the subject when Jimmy sat down beside her.

"Let me introduce myself," he said to everyone. "Jimmy Douglas, another old friend of V's. I have to admit that seeing someone who resembles her so much is quite a shock. Takes me back to another day and age. I have met you before, though, Ava."

It was not lost on Ava that no one else called her mother Vienna. It was only the man from earlier who did. "You mean before today? I'm sorry, I don't recall."

"No, I wouldn't expect that you would. I met you and I believe your older sister in Bridge many years ago. You must know how much you resemble your mother…" He stopped in mid-sentence, as if he was trying to remember something.

"Thank you, Jimmy. I never get tired of hearing that, but I am afraid that I can't hold a candle to my mother. She is a remarkable woman. I'm sorry for not remembering you. This is my fiancé, Randy. I take it that you knew my mother quite well. What can you tell me about her and Rainey?"

The question caught Jimmy off guard. He paused and then said, "They had a relationship. They were very important to each other. Anything more is not for me to comment on. You need to have this conversation with your mother."

"Why does everyone keeps saying that to me? Is there some deep, dark secret? Did he do something so unthinkable to her that no one wants to talk about it?"

Jimmy had to think quickly. Obviously, V had not told her daughter anything about Rainey, or that she had left abruptly twenty years ago and they still didn't know why. "Listen, Ava, Rainey is and always will be my best friend, and your mother holds a special place in my heart from days gone by. Some things are better left in the past. Be assured, though, that Rainey is no monster. He cares very deeply for your mother."

Ava caught that. Jimmy didn't say "cared"; he said "cares."

Jimmy thought, *Jesus H. Christ, why did I stop and talk to her? Curiosity, that's why. What is it about her that I can't place?* And then it hit him, like the proverbial ton of bricks. One had to be blind not to have made the connection. Surely, Yates noticed it, too. *Well, finally, some of the puzzle is starting to fit. The question is: how is this picture show going to end?* He couldn't help wondering what the consequences of this twenty-year-old mystery would be. Whatever was to transpire, he was going to be available to both his friends if they should need him. He had the feeling that Rainey and V were going to find their way back to each other tomorrow. They had better damn well make their feelings for each other known once and for all. He wasn't going to be silent any longer now that he had figured out the truth. He sat down with his friends and lifted a drink, feeling like he had just fought a battle with himself.

Earlier that evening, Rainey arrived at his parents. He said a quick hello to them and told them he had to make a phone call.

She answered the phone on the third ring.

"Lara?"

"Rainey, is that you? Where are you? You sound funny."

"Lara, she's gone." His voice was flat.

Lara panicked. "Who's gone, Aunt Patsy, Louise? Who, Rainey?"

"Vienna."

Lara took a deep breath. *My God*, she thought, *he's seen her.* "Where are you, Rainey?"

"I'm at the farm."

"Did you talk to her?"

"Briefly. She doesn't want to see me again. I need to see her, Lara. Help me please."

He's drunk, Lara thought. *I had forgotten that V was going to Hawthorne today, but why is Rainey there?*

"Are you still there, Lara? I'm coming down first thing in the morning. Is she back living in the old house?"

"No, she is not in the house that she went crazy in." The minute the words were out, she wanted to take them back.

"What…what did you say?"

"Nothing, honey. You better stop here first, okay? Now get some sleep. It's probably going to be a long day tomorrow."

"Okay." The line went dead.

Lara was banging her head on the telephone desk when her husband Cooper came in from the kitchen. "What have I done? What have I done?"

"Who was that on the…what are you doing?" He wanted to know.

"Oh, Coop," she moaned. "I finally did it. I let the fabled cat out of the secret bag."

Cooper pulled his wife into his arms. He knew what she was referring to: the burden that she had been carrying with her for so many years had come to light. It had to be something to do with V and Rainey. "Who was on the phone? Was it V or Rainey?"

"Rainey."

They usually only heard from Rainey when he wanted some news on V, but he had stopped asking years ago. So what was up with him now that had Lara so upset? He said, "I thought as much. What's up with him now? Did he ask about V? He doesn't know that she is here, does he?"

"He didn't have to ask. He had seen her. I don't know what happened, but she doesn't want to see him. He says that he is coming down here tomorrow. He sounded drunk or heartbroken…I don't know. Anyhow, I just blurted it out."

"What did you say exactly?"

"Oh, just that V went crazy. I took it back, but it may be too late."

"It's time that he finds out the truth, Lara. For one, I am glad it happened. This cover-up has gone on far too long; it's taken its toll on you. You want to protect V's secret, and then, on the other hand, you have had to lie to your cousin. It's not fair to you, hon."

"I am so worried about how it will all end. There is nothing stopping them from being together except V's guilt. Jeremy's is gone and Rain is finally going to divorce that ice princess. I wonder what he will do when he finds out that Jimmy and I have been keeping things from him. I don't know what to do."

"There isn't anything that we can do about the past or, for that matter, tomorrow. What is going to happen is going to. We can only hope for a reasonable outcome and be here if they need us."

Coop is so logical, she thought. "Should I phone V? Maybe she will call me?"

"Let's just see how it all plays out. They will either come to terms with each other or it will all be over once and for all."

"It can't be over, Coop. I wish that you could have seen them back in the day. Rainey was so happy. He has never been the same since he came home and found her gone. He's never been able to let her go and I know that she has never stopped loving him. I think that she is still afraid that he will reject her. Even though both Jimmy and I have tried to tell her how he feels, she won't interfere with his life. God, she should be up for sainthood!"

The phone rang. They both feared it was V.

Cooper answered it and handed it to Lara. "Speaking of the devil."

Lara grimaced. "Hello."

"Hi, Lara," said Jimmy. "Sorry to bother you, but I want to give you a heads up. Rainey is here and he has seen V. She was not very receptive to him. What is her problem? Does she want him or not? Anyhow, he is coming to Bridge to find her tomorrow. Just wanted to let you know."

"Thanks, Jimmy. I already know. Rain called me."

"What do you think will happen? He needs to know the truth, Lara. I confessed to him that I have been in touch with her for quite some time, and as expected, he was not thrilled with my disclosure. Ava is here at the dance. She wants answers also. I think that I have finally figured it out, Lara. Do you know? Of course you do. Ava is the reason V ran away. How blind and dumb was I?"

"Jimmy, if it is any consolation, I didn't know myself until I saw Ava. V never acknowledged it until Ava was fifteen. She is almost nineteen now."

"Well, it's over. He finds out the truth tomorrow or I tell him."

Chapter Twenty-One

Bridge Falls, 1981

It was barely above freezing yet Rainey's hands were clammy on the steering wheel. He had spent a sleepless night anticipating what today would bring. He arrived at the Stuart home a little before 9. Lara opened the door and ushered him in.

"Did you call her and warn her that I was coming?" Rainey began.

"Well hello to you, too, cous," Lara greeted.

"Sorry, I'm a little on edge." He hugged her and gave her a kiss on the cheek.

Cooper joined them at the kitchen table, and after a few polite niceties were exchanged, Rainey asked Lara what she had meant last night when she said that Vienna had gone crazy.

"Sorry, Rain, poor choice of words on my part," she replied. "I should have said that she had a mental breakdown. She was very depressed when she left here, which I didn't discover until many years later."

"Why would you keep that fact from me?"

"She didn't want you to know. After you went to Wales and failed to find her and took off for Italy, I truly believed that you would forget her."

"Well, we all know how that turned out. At no time did you ever mention that she wasn't well. In fact, just the opposite. You said she was married and had a daughter."

"Do you remember the letter that I passed on to you? She did say in there that she wasn't always happy. I guess that was her way of addressing her problems."

"Do I remember the letter? I still have it and can repeat it word for word."

"I should never have sent it on to you. I'm sorry. Anyhow, as time went on and we started corresponding, she began telling me about her despondency and that she was receiving help. She begged me not to reveal it to you."

"So all of this time, you have been in contact with her and you have known where she was? Is this what you are telling me, Lara?"

"No. That letter was the first time I heard from her and there was no return address. To this day, I still don't know where she lives. My letters are forwarded to her through a PO (post office) box. A few times, the girls have mentioned a place called Avanloch. I think that V has cautioned them about revealing where it is. I don't know how she explains things to them, but I don't want to rock the boat so I don't ask too many questions. You have every right to be pissed with me and I don't blame you. I kept her secrets and I betrayed you. What kind of a person makes that kind of decision?"

Rainey pulled Lara close to him. "Don't cry, hon. And don't blame yourself. I probably gave you the impression that I had put her out of my mind, but if you want to know the truth, I never have. Oh, I have tried, Lord how I have tried. Just when I think I am making headway, I hear a song on the radio that we used to listen to or something silly will happen and I'm right back under her spell again. Do you know that if I had a daughter, I contemplated naming her Vienna? How do you think that would have gone over? I guess I called out her name in my sleep once too many times because my 'almost' fiancé in Italy questioned me on it. I have no idea if I have done it with Louise, but of course, I don't care. The last words that Vienna said to me were that she loved me, and too late I realized that I was in love with her. Now, seeing her, I know I still am."

"You should be telling her this, Rainey, not me."

Vienna opened the door to Rainey. "Come in, Rainey. I have been expecting you."

She surprised the heck out of him by not slamming the door in his face. Her hair, now auburn, was still wet and the morning sun brought out the red highlights. She was dressed in a longish, light-blue dress. Without her winter clothes on, he realized she was very thin. A fleeting thought occurred to him: *Perhaps she is ill.* "Thank you," he finally stammered. The aroma of freshly brewed coffee greeted him and he could see plump muffins, still in their pan, resting on the open oven door. He breathed in the scent of a loving home.

She motioned him to a chair and, without asking, poured him a cup of coffee and placed a blueberry muffin in front of him. "I hope you still like these." She sat opposite him.

He didn't answer. He was too busy drinking in her essence.

"I'm sorry I handled things so childishly yesterday. I was so surprised to see you; I didn't have time to process the shock."

"What did I do to cause you to run away, Vienna? Please tell me how I hurt you. I have been in the dark for all these years."

"Oh, Rainey, it wasn't you. I can finally say that now. I was so young back then. I guess I thought that you cared for me the way I did for you. When you went away to Italy, I truly believed that it was your way of ending our relationship. No…please, let me finish. I felt that my life was over at seventeen and that I would never find love again. That's right, I loved you and you knew it, but you weren't in love with me and that was breaking my heart. Then, I received your long-awaited letter and it sounded like you wanted to pick up where we had left off when it was convenient for you. For months, I hadn't heard from you, and then all of a sudden, there was that letter saying you were coming home and you were bringing another girl with you. I know you said that you were coming to see me, but I couldn't handle seeing you, only to find out that you would be leaving me again. I made the decision not to be here when you returned. I am so sorry that I made my family lie for me. You see, they always knew where I was because they helped me get there. I went through hell until Rosalyn came into my life, and then I had Ava and I was content to live my life without you. I finally forgave myself. I hope I have answered your question."

"You've forgiven yourself? For what? I am the one who is at fault here. I took a young and impressionable girl's heart and her innocence. I can see how you thought that I treated you like some plaything. I knew from Lara and Jimmy that I had hurt you badly. So you see, Vienna, I haven't been able to forgive myself and I sure as hell never forgot you. You are wrong about one thing. I did love you then and, if you really want to know the truth, I still love you. Tell me it's not too late, Vienna."

Tears came to her eyes. How she had longed to hear those very words for some twenty odd years. Rainey reached for her hand and she let him take it.

"Please don't cry, Vienna."

She said through her sobs, "It is too late, Rainey. You are married and have a family, and I can't love you anymore. There is nothing left for us."

The basement door burst open and there was Ava. She looked at Rainey and then noticed her mother's wet eyes. "Are you all right, Mama?"

"Yes, dear. This is Rainey Quinn. Rainey, this is my daughter, Ava Lane McAllister."

"I know who he is, Mama." Who was this man to her mother and why did he look so familiar? The questions were racing through her mind as Rainey rose and took her hand.

"It's a pleasure to meet you, Ava. When I first saw you yesterday, I thought that I had lost my mind. You look so much like the way I remember your mother."

So this really was the man whose name her mother had called out in her dreams. She looked into his eyes. They were the color of an azure sea. She quickly let go of his hand. "Yes, I know exactly who you are."

Rainey was taken aback by the animosity in her voice. But something made him ask anyhow. "How old are you, Ava?"

She wanted to say "None of your business," but her mother answered for her.

"She will be nineteen in July."

Rainey seemed satisfied but Ava wasn't.

"Mother?" she questioned, as if expecting some sort of an explanation.

"Ava, honey, Rainey and I need to talk a little more." She got up and poured two cups of coffee, adding cream and sugar to one. She placed them on a tray and added two blueberry muffins, handing it all to Ava. "Take this for you and Randy." She opened the basement door for her daughter. "See you soon." She closed the door behind Ava and listened until she heard her go down the stairs. She took her seat again and took a sip of coffee, and then continued on as if they hadn't been interrupted. "Rainey, how can you say that you love me? You never told me twenty years ago that you loved me, so it doesn't make any sense hearing it now. Nothing has changed. I left because I wanted to. Please believe me when I say that my leaving had nothing to do with you. You had a bright and brilliant career ahead of you and I couldn't be a part of it. You need to go home to your family. Are you listening to me?"

He was, but he was doing the math; Ava couldn't be his daughter. Why did she have his eyes? Neither of his boys had his blue eyes. "Is Ava my daughter, Vienna? Is that why you left, because you were carrying my child?" He looked at her, pleading for an answer.

Vienna was trembling, but she had to keep playing the lying game. "What's got into you, Rainey Quinn? What kind of a question is that? The last time we saw each other was late August. Do you think that I was pregnant for eleven months? I should be in some record book!"

He thought she was protesting a little too much. "Who is her father, Vienna? It certainly isn't your late husband."

"No one you know and maybe I don't even know. You have no idea what I became after you left. Ava believes her father died before she was born, so let's just leave it at that. I think we are done here; you have the answers you wanted. You should leave now." She got up to show him to the door, but he wasn't moving.

"Suppose I am not ready to go? Suppose that I don't think we are anywhere finished? I have let you talk and now I would like to have my say. Can you at least pay me the courtesy of listening?"

Vienna sat back down, but he noticed that she was wringing her hands.

"I have just told you that I love you. I have never been able to tell any woman that and now I realize why. It's because I have always been in love with you. If you really want me to go, I will, but only for a few days. Believe me when I tell you that my marriage has been over for a very long time, and now I need to make it official. Please say that you will be here when I return. Don't make me come looking for you again because this time, I can assure you that I will find you. I have no intention of losing you again."

"What are you talking about...you came looking for me?"

"Nobody told you? I went to Wales, the Isle of Anglesey, to find you."

She had started to laugh in a loud and peculiar way. Rainey didn't like the change in her demeanor.

"Wales? I was never in Wales! What gave you that idea? I was in Scotland! My home is in Scotland. I live at Avanloch Castle. I'm going back because if I stay here, I will surely go crazy again. Don't make me go crazy again, Rainey."

She was sobbing hysterically. He got up to comfort her and tell her that he was never going to do anything to hurt her ever again when Ava and a young man burst into the room.

"Get away from her!" Ava shouted. "Don't touch her! Haven't you done enough to her already? Are you a masochist? Get out! Now!" She led her mother into another room.

Rainey had no idea what had just happened.

"I think it is best if you leave, Sir. I don't know what happened here, but it doesn't look good. It will take a little while for Ava to calm her mother down. You're Rainey, aren't you?"

"Yes, and you are Ava's boyfriend I gather."

"Name's Randy and we are actually engaged."

"You've seen this happen with Vienna before?"

"No, not really, but Ava has told me all about her mother's bouts of depression. This seems to be something else. You're the man from her past, aren't you? Whatever transpired today, I guess she couldn't handle it."

"You need to know this, Randy. I love Vienna and I wouldn't do anything to cause her harm. I don't know if it was something I said that set her off or what, but I am not giving up. I have waited twenty years to find her and I am not going to lose her again."

"I believe you, Sir."

They exchanged phone numbers and Rainey left with a heavy heart. He decided he had better fill Lara in on what had just transpired. She was sympathizing with him when the phone rang. He could hear Ava on the other end.

"Auntie Lara, I don't know what to do. I can't calm Mama down. She is crying and shaking. She keeps saying, 'What have I done? What have I done?' I don't know what to do. I am so afraid she is going to go back to the dark side again."

"Ava, darling, she needs Rainey. It's time."

"Time for what? I don't understand. He's the one who put her in this state. He is the one who hurt her all those years ago and why she left home, isn't he? Anyhow, we sent him away."

"Yes, I am afraid so. But it wasn't from anything Rainey did. We'll be right over."

"Is he still here? If you think that is best. Hurry, Lara, please hurry."

Rainey drove like a maniac. Thank God they only had six blocks to go.

Randy let them in, hugged Lara, and nodded politely to Rainey. "Right this way. Ava managed to get her mom to lie down."

"I think it's best if you go in first, Lara," Rainey suggested.

Ava motioned Lara to come in. Rainey backed away but stood at the bedroom door. Vienna had not seen him.

"How has she been?" Rainey asked Randy.

"About the same since you left half an hour ago. Ava says V usually just takes to her bed for days when she has her spells. Her depression, or melancholy, as V calls it, is most prevalent during the winter months. As I've told you before, I have not been witness to any of her attacks. Ava doesn't know if it is the mention of a name or a person or just a memory that brings it on. She has been diagnosed with depression and sees a psychotherapist back home. Of course, her doctor can't discuss her observations with the girls, so they have no idea if V confides in her or not. Personally, I think that V keeps everything to herself. Would you know anything about that?"

"I hate to admit it, but I may be the cause of her problems. I have not seen this side of Vienna before, but you have to realize that I have not seen her for a very long time. Needless to say, I am deeply disturbed by her sudden about-face. It doesn't change anything, though. I am sure that she still has feelings for me and I hope that I can convince her of how much I love her. Don't they say that love can conquer anything?"

"Yes. I have often wondered who the 'they' is in all these clichés. Shall we see what's happening?"

They moved within earshot and heard Lara say to Vienna, "I brought someone to see you, honey. Rainey is here."

"I think he was here, Lara. I don't know. Maybe I just made him up because I remember him saying that he loved me and I know that isn't so."

"Don't be too sure about that, honey. You didn't make him up. He's right here." She motioned for Rainey to come in.

Whimpering, Vienna managed to say, "Rainey, did you come back for me?"

He moved closer to her and then he reached down and took her in his arms. "I'm here, baby. Yes, I came back for you and I am not going anywhere without you."

Vienna wrapped her arms around him and cried, "Oh Rainey, my love."

He lay down beside her, kissed her tear-filled eyes, and twenty years faded away.

Ava closed the door silently. She was the one doing the crying now. "Is it this simple, Lara? Is he the answer to Mama's depression? What happens when he leaves her again?"

"He wasn't the one who left, Ava, and I can pretty much assure you that he is not going to leave her now."

"Why are you so sure? You know something that you are not telling me, don't you?"

"I am the one responsible for your mother and Rainey meeting. I was worried from the start that he might hurt her, but he fell in love with her, though he didn't know it at the time. V is the one who left him, although she loved him deeply. I have watched Rainey go through hell trying to come up with a reason as to why she has avoided him all these years. I finally figured the whole thing out when I first met you, but your mother still chose to keep her secret. He married and had a family, but never forgot her."

"What do you mean by when you met me?" Ava was asking a question that she was pretty sure she already knew the answer to.

Randy left to give them some privacy.

Lara led Ava over to the sofa and sat her down. She wasn't sure how to approach the subject or if she had any right to, but she didn't want Ava to be thunderstruck by the revelation that was surely coming today. "I have been harboring too many secrets, Ava, and it is time for them all to come out. To begin with, Rainey is my cousin. I have known him forever and he is the kindest man under the sun. He tried so hard to make a go of his marriage, but when there is no love, it just turns into bitterness. His boys are everything to him and thank God he has them, just as your mother has you and Rosy. Some people are meant to love only one person all of their lives and it is so for Rainey and your mom. I could have brought them together so many times and I will always regret that I didn't, but it was your mother's wish and I honored it. Does anything I am saying makes any sense to you?"

"I think that you are trying to tell me something without actually saying it. You want me to come to the realization that Rainey is my father, don't you?"

"I was hoping that you would make the connection when you met him, as I did when I first saw you. You were only seven, but you had his eyes, those beautiful, deep blues that I have never seen on anyone before, not even his sons. I never approached your mother about what I knew, nor did Joe and Lily. We all knew, but because of her fragile state, we didn't want to risk a recurrence of her depression. She would tell us in her own time. The years went by and none of us broke our oaths. We are all to blame, Ava. We kept you from knowing your father and him from knowing you. We all share the guilt."

Ava hugged Lara and said she didn't blame her for anything. "Please, don't you cry, too. I have so many questions. Do I have another set of grandparents? Rainey has children…I have siblings? Lara, you really are my aunt?"

Lara tried to laugh. "Yes, to all your questions. Rainey's mom and dad live in Hawthorne, you have two brothers, and I guess, technically, I am your second cousin. I am hoping that your mother is confessing all finally, but I have a hunch that it will be no surprise to Rainey. I am sure he knew the minute he saw you. Your mother's health is still the big issue here. I realize that you will need time to process all of this, but please, don't be angry with your mother. She was going to tell you the truth on your twenty-first birthday. I have no idea as to why she was waiting until then."

"Rainey asked me this morning how old I was. Mama told him I would be nineteen in July. Something is off there, isn't it? But, no, I could never be angry with Mama. I have had a good life. Jeremy was a pretty good father, although he was away most of the time. I have the best sister in the whole world. Lord, I don't know how she is going to react to the news. She is more protective of Mama than I am."

"V doesn't need any more protecting, Ava. Rainey is here now. I probably shouldn't have taken it upon myself to reveal as much as I have to you, but I didn't want you to be blindsided. I have kept my yap shut for too long."

"Do you think she is all right? I don't hear any crying."

"Oh, I think they are both all right. I told you that I was the one who introduced them. Well, from that very first night, Rainey called her his lady and she thought that he was her knight in shining armor. Their fairy tale is finally going to have a happy ending."

Rainey couldn't stop kissing Vienna. He kissed her forehead, her eyebrows, and her moist eyes, and then her cheeks, and finally, her lips. She wasn't sobbing anymore but was making little whimpering noises. She would reach up and run her hands around his face, and he would take her fingers and caress them with his own. She was trying very hard to keep her eyes open, but the episode had taken a toll on her. He rocked her and told her to go to sleep.

"I am too afraid to sleep, Rainey. If I should wake and find you gone, I would die a thousand deaths."

"You could sleep for a hundred years, my love, and when you awoke, I would still be here. You may as well get used to the fact that I am here to stay."

Through have closed eyelids, she whispered, "Promise me, Rainey."

"I promise." He kissed her lightly and waited until he could feel her body relax before he relinquished his firm hold on her. If anyone had told him that he would be lying in Vienna's arms today, he would have told them they were stark raving mad. He hated to admit it, but perhaps it was a good thing that she had her breakdown and he had been here to comfort her. Fate had finally intervened. When she reached out to him and called him her love, he knew that this was exactly where he was supposed to be. He was still drinking in the smell of her, the taste of her salty tears and the warmth of her hands on his face. She had hardly spoken, but her voice was music to his ears. He knew that he truly loved her. He knew that yesterday, when he had first seen her, but today it was a reality that she loved him, too. He had only been playing at life, but he had been given a second chance and there was nothing that could stop him from being with her.

He watched her sleep for a very long time before he felt himself drift off. He awoke with a start just as she was opening her eyes.

"I am sorry I left you for a while. This isn't a dream, is it, Rainey?"

"No, darling. Because if it is, I am having the same wonderful dream, and I don't care if I ever wake from it."

"I need to move, Rainey. Can we go and sit on the love chair?"

He smiled at her. "What a fitting name."

She smiled right back and told him that she had something to tell him and that he wasn't going to be very happy with her.

"You can tell me anything, love. I won't waste a second of lost time being angry with you. Are you going to tell me the reason why you left so many years ago?"

"Yes, it is a burden I can no longer carry. It is no excuse that I was very young, but I thought I was doing the right thing...the right thing for you. For you see, my love, I was carrying your child and I couldn't let that interfere with your career." She started crying again, but it was all right because this time, she was in Rainey's arms.

He held her tighter and soothed her with his tender kisses.

"I kept you from knowing your daughter and her from growing up without her real father. You should hate me and I won't blame you if you never forgive me."

"Wasn't that my line? Wasn't I always asking you to forgive me for some stupid thing that I had done?

"Nothing you did was ever this significant, though."

"I knew that she was mine the moment I saw her this morning, and I think she knows it, too. She has my eyes you know."

"What? She has your eyes?" Vienna was laughing…a wonderful, calm, happy laugh. "What do you think kept me connected to you for twenty years? Every day, I would look into those azure eyes and see you. I knew that if you ever saw her, you would know, too. Lara, Mother, and Father knew, but they had promised me they would keep my secret. Oh, how I wish they had not been so dedicated. But it is my fault and not theirs. I was too weak."

"Thank you for taking such good care of our daughter. I may have missed the first nineteen years of her life, but I can promise you that I will never miss another day if she will have me. I am a little perplexed, however. How could she have been born in July?"

"She was born on May 13 in Brackenshire Manor at Avanloch. Her birth date was another lie I fabricated. Poor Ava, she is two months older than she thinks. Do you want to know what time she was born, Rainey? It was 4:44 A.M. Does that mean anything to you?"

Rainey was so astonished that he was speechless for what seemed an eternity. He swallowed hard and finally spoke. "Of course it means something to me…my nightmares of losing you and the time portrayed on the clock was always 4:44. Is this what it was all leading up to? Could it just be a coincidence, Vienna?"

"Quit trying to reason with it, Rainey. It is what it is. Stranger things have happened, I am sure. Do you still have the dreams?"

"Oddly enough, they quit shortly after you left. Just a minute, the last time I had one was the night before Mother's Day. I remember because I had fallen asleep on the couch. The dream had unnerved me as usual. The next day, I phoned to wish my mom a happy Mother's Day. I asked about you. She said all was well and, no, she hadn't heard a thing about you. It was one of the last times I called your parents. They said that they had talked to you a few days ago and you were well."

"The day that Ava was born was Mother's Day in Canada."

"Geez, Vienna. There was a difference with that dream, though. The time I woke was not 4:44; it was something else. I can't remember."

"It was probably 8:44 P.M. the night before. That would make up for the time difference."

"Can you explain as to why you were always falling into oblivion in my nightmares? That's what they were…nightmares. I couldn't save you. Then they just stopped. Why do you think that happened?"

"Rainey, I live in a land where people believe in fairies, witches, leprechauns, and such. I have met real gypsies and seen things I cannot explain. No matter who I evoked, no one could take away my dreams of you. Only the angels know the answers. The stories I could tell you—"

"And you will. I have missed your storytelling to no end. If only the boys had a mother like you to make up tales for them at bedtime. You did that for your girls, didn't you?"

"Oh yes. Perhaps you will read them someday, especially the fairy tale of Emerald and Laddy."

"You wrote them down…one about us?"

"Yes, darling. Now I think it is time we went and talked to our daughter. Do you smell fried chicken? I am suddenly famished. I think that I had better wash my face and comb my hair. What a sight I must be."

"Yes, you are, Vienna. You're the sight I have been dreaming of for a very long time."

"I am curious to know how many women you have charmed with your romanticism."

He stood at the bathroom door and watched her brush her hair. "I am not aware that I charm anyone, and the only person I am interested in romancing is you, my dear. I have been meaning to ask you, when did you change the color of your hair?"

She turned and looked at him. "This is my natural color. When you met me, I had black hair…well, it was from a bottle. I had dyed it on a whim, and then I met you and you liked it, so I kept it. I have not been 'raven haired' for twenty years. Do you want me to dye it again?"

"I love the way it is right now. If I had of known it wasn't your true color…well, it was the only way I knew you back then. Ava's hair is darker."

"Actually, she has hair the color of yours; she is just experimenting right now."

"And Rosalyn?"

"She has the most magnificent red mane I have ever seen, except on her mother. She has blue-green eyes and a few freckles on her porcelain-like skin. She is very beautiful."

"I am sure she is. I am still trying to make the connection with her and Maveryn. It will come to me, I'm sure. One other thing, darling, you are very thin. I hope it isn't a health concern."

"I have been this way for twenty years, Rainey. I was almost anemic when I was carrying Ava. I lost 20 pounds initially and had to fight very hard to keep my weight loss from endangering Ava's development. I eat well, but I guess I am just too active. I seem to gain 6 pounds and then I lose 3, and then I gain 2 and lose 6…it's a constant struggle. But I am very healthy and you wouldn't want me to be heavy like I was before, would you?"

"I don't know. Perhaps you seem so fragile because you are so slender."

"I'm not fragile, Rainey. I won't break. I have been broken for a very long time, but that is all behind me now. I am strong, and with you, I will be stronger."

"I think I am the cause of all your problems, but I am going to spend the rest of my life repairing the damage I have done." He had come up behind her, parted her hair, and kissed her on the back of her neck.

She turned and gave him a crooked little smile. "I might just take you up on that. I think we had better get out of here before I lose all my willpower."

They emerged arm and arm. They never took their eyes off one another.

Ava spoke first. "Are you all right, Mama?"

"I am wonderful, darling. Rainey talked me into having a little sleep, which I believed turned into a long one. I am refreshed and calm, and I am sorry, everyone, for having a meltdown. Lara, thank you. I love you."

"I love you, too, both of you. Randy has made you a delicious dinner. Coop is picking me up so I will see you all tomorrow."

They had a big family hug. Vienna never let go of Rainey for more than a second.

As Lara was going out the door, Rainey said, "Thanks, Lara, for everything. Will you phone Jimmy for me?"

"You read my mind, cous." She blew them a kiss.

"Randy, ole boy, excellent meal," Rainey said. "Are you sure you need to go to culinary school?"

"Yes, Sir. This is only plain, ordinary cooking, right, V? I need to refine my skills if I want to become a world-class chef. My ultimate goal is to attend schools in Provence, Bordeaux, and Nice, to name a few."

"What are your plans, Ava?" Rainey had been admiring his newly found daughter throughout the whole meal.

She had been trying not to be obvious, but her curiosity won over. *I can see why Mama is so infatuated with him. He is one attractive man, but it is not only that. He is a gentleman and obviously experiencing rekindled feelings for my mother. Rosalyn would call him Princely.* She stifled a laugh. *Is he the object of Mama's fairy tales? Could this be the Laddy to her Emerald?*

Finally, dinner was over. Randy motioned everyone to stay sitting as he would do the clean-up. But first, they must have a piece of Ava's coconut cream pie.

Rainey's mouth watered. "If it is anything like her mother's, then bring it on. So you have your mother's talents in the kitchen, Ava?"

"We have to sneak into Mrs. D's kitchen back home. She doesn't think that us so-called ladies should be doing menial tasks. When she comes home and sees all the goodies that we have cooked up, she just shakes her head. She is a good sport, though. She does let us help on the holidays without too much fuss, right, Mama?"

"Yes, and I am pleased to say that she has finally adopted our Canadian fare, but all too soon, she will be retiring and we will have to train a new cook to our ways." They all laughed. Vienna took Rainey's hand and reached across the table to take Ava's hand. Then she said to Ava, "Darling, we have something we want to tell you. Actually, it is me. Poor Rainey only found out a little while ago."

Ava squeezed her mother's hand, and to her own surprise, she reached out for Rainey's other hand. He gave it willingly and his smile said it all. "Would it make it any easier for you, Mama, if I told you that I already know?"

Vienna tried to hold back her tears, but it was a failed effort. Rainey got up and took her in his arms again and motioned for Ava to come over and join them. He kissed the tops of both of their heads. "Where have you two been all my life?" He was near to tears himself.

Randy came up from the basement with the pie and said, "What did I miss?"

"Ava will explain it to you, Randy," said Rainey. "Right now, Vienna and I have to go and phone my parents, and tell them that I have my life back and that they have a brand new granddaughter."

Vienna mouthed to Ava, "Thank you, darling."

Randy stammered, "What?"

The newly found lovebirds went into the living room and sat on the sofa.

"How do you think Paul and Patsy are going to react to the news?" Vienna asked.

"They better bloody well be happy for us, but it doesn't matter because we are all that matters and we will fit them and everyone else into our lives one way or the other. How will your parents take it?"

"Are you kidding? They will be overjoyed. My mother gave me an ultimatum last year...either I tell you the truth or she was going to. Thank God, we beat her to it."

"Mom."

"Rainey, where are you?" Patsy asked.

"Put Dad on the other phone please."

"Okay dear. Paul, pick up the other phone, it's Rainey."

"I'm still in Bridge," Rainey said. "I'm with Vienna."

There was a slight pause. Then Patsy said, "Vienna?"

"Yes Mom, Dad. I finally found her. We are together. She is right here beside me."

"Found her? You make it sound as if she was lost. You knew that she was living abroad and had married," Patsy said matter-of-factly.

"Did you know where she was, Mom?"

"Just what Lara and her mom told me. There was no specific residence . Where has she been for the last twenty years?"

"That doesn't matter. She is here now and I am never letting her go again."

"Rainey, what about the boys? Have you forgotten that you are still married?"

"Not for long. You know very well that my marriage has been over for a very long time. Don't worry about the boys; they will be fine."

His father spoke for the first time. "How is V, Son?"

"You can see for yourself in a day or two," Rainey said. Vienna leaned over and kissed him.

"Are you staying? I thought you told us that you had some pending business to attend to tomorrow and had to go back today."

Rainey laughed. "Screw that. There is nothing that can't be taken care of with one phone call; I am the boss after all." He winked at Vienna. "Dad, I have finally been reunited with the woman of my dreams; we need time together. You can't imagine my elation. Do you want to hear another miracle? Vienna has a daughter—no, *we* have a daughter. Mom, Dad, you have the granddaughter that you always wanted. I have my life back; I hope you will be happy for us."

His mom was crying. "Oh, Rainey, we are so happy for you. We love you and can't wait to see V and her daughter."

Rainey hung up and thought, *I don't think she believes me when I said "our" daughter. Oh well, she will know when she sees her.*

On the other end, Paul hung up the phone and joined his wife in the kitchen. She was sitting at the table with her head in her hands. Neither of them spoke for a few minutes. Finally, Paul broke the silence. "We have a granddaughter."

"If this is so, Paul, and I am not sure that she is indeed his child, how could she keep her from us all? Anne told me that Lara told her that V was emotionally unstable. I am so worried that if this is true, how it will affect Rainey. I mean, do her actions of the past sound rational? She broke his heart you know, and what if she does again? I don't think he could handle it."

"I think you are jumping the gun. We have no idea why she left. Could it be because she was pregnant and Rainey was in Italy, and she was afraid to tell him? Whatever. It happened, and I for one want to see my son happy again. Do you remember the way it was when she was here? The laughter that filled this house has never been duplicated. I never could understand why he married Louise. The only thing he got out of that union is the boys. Now, he deserves to live in peace with his beloved Vienna, don't you think?"

Ava watched her mother and Rainey. She couldn't call him father yet. They were sitting on the sofa in the living room. He had his arm around her and they were holding hands; they hadn't taken their eyes off each other since emerging from the bedroom. Ava sat in a chair beside them. "Can I ask you a question, Rainey?"

"Certainly, Ava. Anything."

"I am curious about your name. How did your parents come up with it?"

"I will let your mother answer that one; she is a much better storyteller than I am."

"Are you sure, Rainey?" V said. "I hope I remember correctly."

"You will, sweetheart. You still have your photographic memory, don't you?"

"That is just a little joke between us, honey. As you know perfectly well, I don't always remember things so well. Here goes. Patsy, your grandmother, was expecting her first child, and if it was a boy, she was going to name him after her favorite movie stars, who were Claude Rains and Claudette Colbert; I am not sure of her last name. Anyhow, the child was a girl, so she named her Claudia Alana. The Alana was for her grandmother. Then when Rainey was born, she didn't want to name him Claude, as it was too close to Claudia, so she came up with Rainey. Laddy was one of her favorite books as a child, and so Ladd became his middle name. That's all there is to that. I must say, I am glad she didn't call you Claude... Rainey is so much smoother and romantic, and suits you to a T."

Ava smiled. "I agree. Lara tells me that you have two sons?"

"Morgan will be sixteen this week and Mason is almost fifteen. They are good boys, very athletic and conscientious. I have only stayed married because of them, but I am beginning to think that the constant bickering has been more harmful to them than I had anticipated. I am only home when their mother is off on one of her never-ending crusades. They probably already think that I have a mistress, which, I can assure you, is not true. Well, let's say it wasn't." He stopped and looked at Vienna to see her reaction, and she was smiling mischievously. He went on. "I guess I have always been unfaithful to Louise because this lady here left her lasting impression on me, and I could never get her out of my mind no matter how hard I tried. I would have gone to my grave loving her."

That was a little more than Ava had expected for an answer. She had no idea that a man could be so idealistic when it came to love. She wasn't the writer in the family, but their story definitely needed telling. She knew there was a lot more to learn about her mother and father and was looking forward to hearing their whole saga. Through misty eyes, she said, "I don't know much about boys, having grown up in a household of women, so I have no idea how they will perceive me, but I am surely looking forward to meeting them. Now, if you two will excuse us, Randy and I are going to meet some of the sled teams at the bar before they leave tomorrow. I am very glad today happened."

Vienna and Rainey both got up and embraced their daughter. "Thank you, darling. Have a nice time."

Rainey was very emotional. "I am the luckiest man in the world tonight. I have two beautiful women in my arms."

Ava collected Randy and he asked her if she was sure she wanted to go out and leave her mom.

"Get me out of here before I turn into a blithering idiot," she answered.

As soon as the door closed behind Ava and Randy, Rainey pulled Vienna onto his lap.

"And what do you want to do now, Missy?"

She gazed into his dreamy eyes and said, "I want you to take me to the Palace."

"Honey, do you think that is a good idea?"

"Why do you say that?"

"Lara told me that was where you had your first episode of despair."

"It had nothing to do with the house, Rainey. Actually, the house was my refuge. I spent countless days contemplating my hopeless situation, but on the other hand, I had nothing but wonderful memories of the times you and I had spent there together."

"I remember, too. Put something warm on and I'll start the car. What about Ava?"

"I'll leave her a note."

He opened the car door for her. "Isn't it going to be cold in the house?"

She climbed in and said, "Oh no, I prepared it for us last night."

"What do you mean?"

"You'll see when we get there. I really don't care for these new cars. This one can't hold a candle to Gypsy Lady. Look how far away I am from you."

Rainey laughed. "You're right. I don't like you that far away from me. I guess I will just have to bring the Lady out of storage then."

Vienna was delightfully surprised. "You still have her?"

"You bet. I could never get rid of her even though I thought that I should. That car is part of us, Vienna. She has been in the old garage at the farm since 1963. Do you remember the day I tried to teach you how to drive?"

"Yes, I thought I was going to kill the car. Did you think of me often, Rainey?"

"What do you think?"

"I think perhaps that you did for a while. I am glad you went on and finished your schooling and life."

"What choice did I have? You left me no clue as to your whereabouts. I have to be honest. Sometimes, I came close to hating you. It was better than the alternative."

"What was that?"

"Loving you."

"Oh, Rainey." She reached for him, cursing the bucket seats. They had arrived at the Palace. "I shall work very hard to earn your forgiveness."

"I've already forgiven you. Tonight is not the time for any regrets. Wait here until I get out to help you. I don't want you falling."

"Do you not think we have winters in Scotland? I am as sure footed as ole slew foot Sue."

"I hate even to suggest that I have no idea of who that is. A friend of yours?"

She passed him the key. "Rainey, you are so funny."

"Me? It's not me who has friends with odd names!"

The door swung open to the warm, familiar entrance.

"Ahhh, home," Vienna sighed, and she threw her boots into the corner and placed her coat on the banister. She waited for Rainey to do the same and then pulled him along down the hallway. She opened the door to the library and he felt a twinge of nostalgia. He did love this room, this house, this woman. Yes, he had come home. Home was wherever Vienna was.

"Throw a match to the logs, sweetheart," she said. "I'll be right back."

By the time the fire was sizzling, she had returned with a tray filled with an assortment of cheeses, deli meats and crackers, and a bottle of red wine. Rainey didn't take his eyes off her as she flitted about the room, collecting glasses from the cabinet and turning the stereo on. He thought that he recognized the aria but could not place it.

"What is the name of this haunting melody?" he asked.

"This is a collection of tranquil and peaceful works...this is one of Beethoven's pieces called Romance. Do you know it?"

"As a matter of fact, I do. Your taste in music has changed."

"Umm, a little." She poured him a glass of wine and sat down on the floor at his feet.

He caressed her as she lay her head upon him. "Curious, my dear, but how did you know I was going to be here tonight? After the way you left me yesterday, how did you know that I would come looking for you?"

"Simple, I wished you here."

"Oh, you did now, did you? Do you have your own personal genie?"

"You might say that. One year at Halloween, Rosalyn was dressed as the fairy godmother and she granted me three wishes, and I could use them whenever I so desired. I used one right away. I wished that she and Ava would always love me. She told me that was a complete waste of a wish because, of course, they would always love me. The second wish I used when Addy became ill, and the third I used last night. I wished that you would come for me and that you would love me the way that I still loved you."

"I am so pleased to say that your wish has come true. That has to be the most enchanting story that you have ever told me. I am almost inclined to believe that it is true; your wish is my desire."

"When you meet my Rosy, you can ask her, but I assure you it is a true story. Will you dance with me, Rainey?"

"It will be my greatest pleasure, Lady V."

Their bodies swayed with the music and she whispered in his ear. "I really am a lady now you know, and as a lady, I always get my way. My desire right now is you, my love. I have stayed true to you for twenty years, but now has come the time for me to be yours again. Do you want me, Rainey?"

"Do I want you? You are flirting with a man who has envisioned this moment a million times over. But what are you trying to tell me?"

"Believe me, Sir, I am not flirting. I am perfectly serious, and what I am telling you is that I have never been with another man."

"Vienna?"

"Yes, I do mean Jeremy and I were never man and wife. He still loved Maveryn and I you." She put her fingers to his lips. "Shush…now, will you come and live with me and be my love?"

His answer was in the form of a passionate kiss. "Don't wake me if I am dreaming."

And they rekindled their love that had been denied for so many years.

They lay in each other's arms for a very long time, not saying anything. Suddenly, Vienna sat up and said, "I'm famished!"

Rainey laughed. "That's my girl." He got up and handed her the snacks and poured her a glass of wine.

She declined. "I'll just have a sip of yours, Rainey…the medication you know."

He sat down beside her. "We have a lot to talk about, don't we?"

"Yes, I suppose. Not tonight, though. Let's not spoil the magic."

"I have no intention of doing that. Come here, you little imp."

"You still think I have mystic powers?"

"I know you do. Look what you have done to me."

"I see a man who has just fulfilled a damsel's fancy. Now, I am going to go upstairs and take a long bath. Will you be all right without me?"

"It's not going to be easy, but I will try. I'll clean up."

"Thank you darling."

How had he lived without her? He prayed he'd never have to find out.

She was in the tub with only her head slightly above the bubbles. He hadn't knocked and she hadn't heard him come in, but she knew he was there.

"Hello, gorgeous," Rainey said.

"Hello, darling," Vienna replied. "Did you come to join me?"

"I came to wash your back and shampoo your golden copper locks, if you will indulge me the pleasure."

"Indulge you? Are you serious? I am yearning for you to do so again. Do you remember the first time that you washed my hair?"

He sat down on the bench behind the claw-footed tub. "I think I do. It's not like I have done it for anyone else, dear lady. We were at my house and it was the last night that we were together. I'm not likely to have forgotten that."

"It's the night that Ava was conceived."

"You know that for a fact?"

"Mmm, I do."

Rainey was massaging the shampoo into her scalp. She bent her head back and looked at him like she was in another world. She closed her eyes and he kissed her tenderly.

"Where are you right now, Vienna?"

"In Heaven. I'm in a meadow and I am on my beloved Atlántia. There is a mist rising on the horizon, and I ride into it and the spray engulfs me luxuriously. I see you riding over the ridge toward me. You are on the majestic Arabesque. We are coming closer and closer to each other…"

"Keep talking. Who is Arabesque?"

"He is the magnificent steed I bought a few years ago with plans to present him to you someday. He is the color of your old horse, Rusty."

"You bought me a horse? Vienna, this is a new sensation for me. I feel like I am there with you. I can see what you are seeing. I have never felt more sensual."

"Darling, I think that you had better get in this tub with me right now."

"Again, your wish is my command."

Of course, I couldn't sleep. My head was like a faucet that wouldn't shut off. What-ifs and doubts of uncertainty were running rampart through the cobwebs of my mind. I wondered if I had been stressing out loud as Rainey woke up and asked me what I was doing.

I said, "Watching you sleep."

"No, you're not. You're worrying about something. What is it?"

"Rainey, what is going to become of us? You'll go back to your practice and your family, and I'll go back to Scotland and my life there. Is tonight all that we will ever have?"

"Oh, you crazy little imp! Haven't I made it perfectly clear that I am never letting you out of my sight again?"

"That's me, Rainey, crazy as a loon."

"You know that I didn't mean it that way. Sorry, poor choice of words."

"I know you didn't mean it that way. I am usually in complete control of myself. No one gets the upper hand on me, not even those girls. I have been the so-called 'boss' for many years, but apparently not with my feelings. Now I am a quivering mass of nerves. I feel as though I could break into a thousand pieces. You've reduced me to an unsure teenage girl again."

"You were never unsure of yourself. You always knew what to say and how to say it. I loved you as a beautiful teenage girl, but I love you more now for the stunning woman you have become. What can I say to assure you that this, what we have tonight, is for keeps? It is I who should be scared to death that you won't want me to share your life. Remember, sweetheart, it was you who left, not me. I know I left you in a way, but not for twenty years."

"Rainey, if you could only read all the letters that I've written to you throughout the years, you'd know that all I have ever wanted was to be in your life."

"You wrote me letters?"

"Every Christmas, on your birthday, on Ava's birthday, whenever I didn't think that I could go on without you anymore."

"You're coming very close to making me cry."

"I'm sorry."

"Don't be. I've been a hard ass for too long. You're the only one who can bring me to my knees. I want to marry you, Vienna LaFontaine."

"That doesn't matter to me, Rainey. A piece of paper isn't going to change how I feel about you. I just want to be with you."

"It matters to me and it will be, two minutes after the divorce is final. Will you be mine, Vienna?"

"I will, but why two minutes, why not one?"

"You got me there, didn't you?"

I laughed with him and told him that I was going to get up for a little while.

"What do you mean you're getting up? It's 12:30 in the morning."

"It's what I do, Rainey. I'll take one of my little pills and wander the house until I feel sleepy. Now, go back to sleep."

"What do you mean roam the house?"

"That s how I met all the ghosts of Avanloch, roaming the halls on sleepless nights."

"Ghosts?"

"I'll tell you all about them someday."

"I'm not sure I want to know, do I?"

I told him that they made for good storytelling.

"Well, we know how I love your stories. Promise me you will come back as soon as you feel sleepy. You're going to be very busy tomorrow."

"Busy? How?"

"We are going to the coast, remember?"

"I'm going with you?"

"Well, I am not going without you."

I kissed him and told him that I loved him. "Sweet dreams."

"I love you, Vienna. I don't have to dream anymore because my dream is right here and she is real."

I awoke to the sweet, pungent aroma of coffee. I opened my eyes and found Rainey sitting in Joe's old ratty chair beside me. "What are you doing?" I asked.

"Watching you sleep. I woke up and you weren't beside me. I panicked for a moment until I remembered where I was."

"I'm sorry, love. I guess I fell asleep before I made it back upstairs. Do I smell coffee?"

"Yes, I will get you a cup."

"No, I'm up. I'll join you in the kitchen as soon as I wash my face."

We sat at the table. I leaned my head on his shoulder and said, "I think we have been here before."

"I know, a very, very long time ago. Do you remember Addy asking me if you were bossy to me like you were to her?"

"Oh yes." I giggled. "How is it that we have been apart for so long and yet it seems as if we have been together all our lives? Your thoughts are mine and mine yours."

He kissed my forehead. "It just is, but we have a lot to discover about each other and I am looking forward to every new day."

"Do you remember what you promised me last night?"

"Was that about midnight?"

"Umm, you said we were going to be together and you asked me to marry you."

"How can I make it anymore clearer? The only question is to where we will live."

"I've been thinking about that precisely. You know that Lily and Joe are finally going to sell this place? What would you think if I bought it?"

"I love this house, and what would you say if I said let's buy it together?"

I gave him a big yes and he said, "Good, then that is settled. I think that I want to stay here another day. Is that all right with you? Randy and Ava aren't leaving until tomorrow, right?"

I agreed, and he swooped me up into his arms and carried me down the hall. We started up the stairs and I said, "You know, if I were still a chubby teenager, you wouldn't be able to carry me."

He lost his footing and down we went, laughing until we cried.

When we finally gained control of ourselves, I told Rainey that seeing we were staying for another day, we should have a dinner party. I told him I would like to invite Lara and Coop, Jimmy, Yates, and Zane, and Ava and Randy of course.

"Are you sure, Vienna?"

"Yes, I want to share our joy with everyone and I feel like cooking, and Randy and Ava will help. What do you say?"

"You know that I am not pleased with Jimmy keeping your visits a secret from me?"

"Are you upset with Lara, too? You know they did it because I begged them to. Now, I wish someone would have broken their promise and spilled the beans. It was bad enough I had them betray you—"

"Vienna, I thought we weren't going to go there today?"

"It's on my mind constantly. I try to reason with myself that this was the way the story had to play out. Perhaps ten, fifteen, or even five years ago, you wouldn't have been able to forgive me, but when I see how you love me now, all my reasoning goes down the drain. Suppose you had fallen head-over-heels in love with someone? I would have never gotten you back. It plays heavily on my mind. Lara and Jimmy both warned me that I was waiting too long. Rainey, I thought that I had forgiven myself, but I don't think I have."

"You must stop this and stop it now. I have forgiven you and I couldn't possibly have fallen seriously for anyone else when I was still fatally lovesick over you. Are we good? I say yes, let's have a celebration. You phone Lara and Ava and I will call the boys."

He shook me gently and coaxed a sullen, tearful smile from me.

We made up a huge batch of meatballs to serve with spaghetti and garlic bread. Lara insisted on bringing salad and Ava and Randy were doing dessert and hors d'oeuvres. Rainey went shopping while I tidied up a bit. I had never liked housework. He knew it and offered to help, but I shooed him out. No one was living in the house so there wasn't much to do, and it beat choosing wines.

The doorbell rang. I answered the door. It had started to snow again and Jimmy and Yates looked as if they had been dusted with icing sugar. Jimmy had me in his arms and was looking over his shoulder at Rainey standing behind me.

"Can I hug your girl, Rainey?" Jimmy said.

I glanced back at Rainey and he had a hint of a smile forming. "Have you ever asked for my permission before?"

Yates put me in one of his bear hugs. "I don't intend to ask the ole boy for the pleasure of embracing an old friend."

I was laughing and told them I was sorry that Zane couldn't make it, but there would be other times. We joined the others in the living room, where more hugs and handshakes were exchanged. Rainey dispensed some of his famous eggnog out to everyone and handed me a cup of plain nog.

Jimmy rose to propose a toast. "To V and Rainey. Please, Lord, don't ever let them become separated again."

A loud "Amen" echoed through the room.

Rainey answered, "It will never come to pass if I have anything to say about it. We have a lot to make up for and so do a couple of you." He raised his glass toward Lara and Jimmy. "But tonight is for celebration, so because I love you, you're forgiven for keeping Vienna's confidence."

Rainey took my hand and continued. "If I had to choose Vienna over me, this fair lady would win every time. I am trying to understand you guys' dilemma, but damn it, I wish you hadn't been so noble. Enough said."

I wanted to say something but nothing would come out. Lara and Ava were both close to tears and I wasn't very far behind. Good old Yates lightened the mood.

"Okay, so is everyone happy? Good. Now I get to ask the question. Where in God's creation have you been, V? Have you really been living all over the world?"

"Not really. I've been living in Scotland. I went there because that is where my Aunt Jannie lives."

"You mean like Edinburgh, Scotland, or I guess I can't think of any other cities over there in the land of bagpipes," Yates confessed.

"No, we don't live in the city, although the girls go to school in Edinburgh. Our home is at Avanloch."

"Where is Avon…what?" Jimmy asked.

"It's not so much where as what. It is a huge estate covering many acres. We raise livestock of all kinds and employ about 150 people, what with the farm, gardens, and the dairy and mill in the village. There are several manor houses on the property, which the staff of Avanloch reside in."

Jimmy whistled. "Manor houses V? I knew you had married well…but a mansion?"

"Actually, it's not really a mansion, but a castle," Ava said matter-of-factly.

"Now, I think we should go into dinner."

"You're shitting me. Sorry, ladies. Really, a castle? You know all about this, Rain?" Jimmy was bowled over.

"Well, Jimmy, I am learning more and more by the minute. We haven't had time to discuss a lot yet. Shall we follow Ava into the dining room?"

As soon as the food was on the table and we were all seated, Rainey said, "Oh, by the way, in case you haven't figured it out, Ava is my daughter."

"Yeah, Rain," Yates said. "We both came to the conclusion after seeing and talking with Ava at the dance. I think the eyes were the giveaway. Did you know, Lara?"

She squirmed in her chair and looked at her cousin. "Guilty as charged."

Rainey smiled at Lara. "It's okay, hon. I know why you kept it from me."

"Ava, you never told me that you had talked to Yates and Jimmy?"

Ava answered, hoping her mother wouldn't be angry with her. "I had to, Mama. I had to find out who Rainey was to you."

"It's all right, darling. I should have told you long ago."

Her father said to her, "And I should have figured it out myself. Hell, all those years of schooling and never once did I think that your mother left because she was carrying you. I always thought that it was something I did."

"Well, in a very special way, it was something you did, wasn't it, Rainey?"

He blushed and we laughed with him.

"You have a stepdaughter, don't you, V?" Jimmy asked.

"Rosalyn is my daughter. Actually, she was the one who adopted me. She took me to be her new mama even before Ava was born. I legally adopted her when I married her father, as he did Ava. The girls are the only reason we married." I smiled up at Rainey. "Jeremy was still in love with his deceased wife, Maveryn, and my heart was and always will be with this man here."

"What happened to Maveryn?" Jimmy asked.

"Rosalyn's mother, Maveryn, had the same dreadful cancer that Marley died from; she just hung on a little longer. Jeremy had her to doctors in three continents until she begged him to take her home and let her die in peace at Avanloch."

"So you never knew her? Did she have family in Scotland?" Yates questioned.

"Yes, I had met Maveryn on a previous visit. She was most gracious and beautiful. I always wished that I could be like her one day."

Ava slid her arm through mine. "You are, Mama. To answer your question, Yates, her family is from Wales."

Jimmy said to Rainey, "Does V know that you went to Wales to look for her?"

I saw a light go on in Rainey's eyes just as he was about to answer Jimmy. He looked directly at me and I sensed panic in his voice. "What was her maiden name?"

"Maveryn? Why?"

"Just answer me, Vienna. What was her maiden name?"

Ava also noticed the change in his demeanor and answered, "De La Mare."

Rainey stood up and stared down at me. I was sure everyone felt the tension building in him. "I suppose you're going to tell me that her father's name was Louis, that she had two sisters, and that they live in the south of Wales?"

I suddenly became very cold. "How would you know that, Rainey?"

He interrupted me. "Because I was there at Louis De La Mare's house. I told you that I knew those names, Rosalyn and Maveryn together, didn't I?"

Everyone was speechless and staring at Rainey, except me. I got up and put my arms around him, but he was unresponsive.

He looked into my teary eyes. "I was that close to you, Vienna." He made a minute measurement with his fingers. "That close. Well, isn't this just a kick in the ole reality psyche?" He walked out of the room without another word.

"He will be all right. Excuse me, I must go to him." I pleaded with our guests to continue with their dinner even though I felt it was hopeless. I heard Randy asking if anyone would like more wine and I was sure they all said yes.

I found Rainey in the conservatory, staring into the fountain. "I'm so sorry, darling."

His laugh was almost maniacal. "Look at me, I am shaking. This happened twenty years ago and I feel like it was yesterday. I will never forgive myself for not finding you." He was openly crying. "I should have found you…I didn't look hard enough."

All I could do was hold him as he had me.

Finally, the trembling subsided and he said in a broken voice, "If I should ever lose you again, I will surely die."

"Well, that is never going to happen, is it? Things were so different back in the early '60s, Rainey. The world was not as assessable as it is now. But now, you must listen to me. It wasn't the right time…Morgan and Mason weren't born yet. You have to believe that it was not our time. I love you so much. I can't stand to see you do this to yourself. I told you that I had a good life. I wanted for nothing except you. No one was holding me against my will. You didn't have to save me. I had to do that myself. Now we are together and we are going to be one big happy family. Do you believe that?"

"Yes," he answered me, but I was not convinced. "I can't go back in there, Vienna."

"Oh yes, you can! They are our friends and our daughter is out there. They all love you and understand that we are still going through some trying times. Come on, stiff upper lip."

"For you, my lady. Perhaps a kiss for the wounded ego?"

I was happy to oblige.

Rainey apologized, but of course, there was no need to. Ava poured us a cup of coffee and cut a piece of her banana cream pie for us all. Yates said he hadn't been treated to such tasty fare since my mother's last meal at the diner. It was indeed a compliment.

Ava said that everyone was eager to know more about our life at Avanloch and that she and Randy would do the clean up while I narrated. We benched that immediately and all proceeded to clear the table. Once the dishwasher was started, we adjourned into the living room. Jimmy and Yates were like two kids with their questions. Lara was still amazed that Addy and Sissy had not let it slip as to where I was.

"Me, too, Lara. I wished they hadn't been so loyal," Rainey lamented.

The questions were coming fast and furious. How big was the castle? How many rooms? Was there a moat and a drawbridge? How many servants did we have? Were there towers and turrets?

"Hey, kids, one at a time," Rainey pleaded.

"Well, I have never measured it, but if I were to walk through the whole house, and, yes, we do refer to it as a house, it would probably take me half an hour. What do you think, Ava, is that about right?"

"I think longer, Mama, if you were to count the tower rooms, the courtyard, and depending whether you took the elevator or the stairs."

"It's freaking *big*," Randy chimed in.

Ava continued. "It is possibly as tall as a six- or eight-storey high rise, though there are only three floors, not counting the cellar. How many rooms is there, Randy? You counted them."

"Let's see if my memory suits me correctly. There are twelve bedrooms and three of those have suites, sitting rooms, whatever. The two towers each have three rooms, the Duffys have three, and the almost never used maid's room, about twelve more, and that is not including the grand foyer or Eden. Did anyone keep track? More like forty, right? Anyhow, as I said before, it is *big*. Ava never led on where she lived, so it was a complete surprise to me when I first came upon it."

Rainey looked at Ava and then me. "Eden?"

"You, being the architect, will be amazed at what Mama had built," Ava said. "It's a grander version of the Palace's conservatory. She made her own blueprints. You'll be very impressed with her, Rainey."

"Oh, I am already impressed."

"Ava will dig out Lily's photos of Avanloch and then you will all have a better understanding of it and the lands. First, I have an announcement to make. Last night, I received a proposal. Rainey said that two minutes after his divorce is final, he is going to marry me. What do you all say?"

"Well, I say, two minutes? Why not one minute?"

"My sentiments exactly, Jimmy!" I teased.

"I guess I will never hear the end of that, will I? Ava, what do you think?"

"As Mrs. Sharpe would say, 'Mary Queen of Scots, 'tis a bonnie idea. Lang may yer playing,' which means what a beautiful idea and live long and well. I am so happy for you and Mama, and Rosy will be, too."

"Thank you, Ava. Does everyone at Avanloch speak with the brogue? I notice more of an accent in you than your mother, and how in the world do you understand everyone?"

"Because I was born there, I have no problem with the language, and neither does Rosalyn. Mostly, everyone speaks the Queen's English at the castle and even in the village. The older folks like Mrs. Sharpe, who is the cook at Brackenshire, and our own Mrs. McDuff and her husband, speak more of the old dialect. Mama had a little problem at first, didn't you, Mama?"

"You either adapt or play dumb. I learned to do both. I had a great teacher in my Aunt Jannie. You will all see, as I want you to be our guests at our wedding; that is, if Rainey still wants to marry me when his divorce is final…"

I think I wounded Rainey as he said in a downtrodden voice, "Nothing will keep me from wanting to marry you, my lady, but perhaps it is you who will change *her* mind."

"No, that is not going to happen. I am sorry. I didn't mean it that way. Please forgive us, we are still finding our way with each other and I am sure that we are going to step on a lot of toes, but mostly our own. What I started to say was that I would like us to be married in the chapel in the village at Avanloch, and we would want you all to come as our guests."

Rainey agreed. "I shall marry you anywhere, but if that is your desire, it shall be so. I cannot think of a celebration without all of you."

"Guess we better start saving our pennies, eh, Yates? Because I for one would not miss it for the world," Jimmy declared.

"Oh no, you misunderstood me. You will be our guests. I have a fair bit of money, and from what I gather, Rainey is not exactly derelict, so there will be no expense on your part. Heavens, we would not expect for you to come all that way on your own."

Ava had her hand over her mouth to stifle her giggles. I asked her what little joke she was concealing.

She managed to get a few words out. "Did my mother say that she had a little money? What with the incomes from Avanloch Ventures and McAllister Shipping Enterprises, she has more money than the Queen of England!"

Even Rainey looked startled. "Is she right, Vienna? I understood that you were well off, but wealthy beyond means? I had no idea."

I could only smile. "It is none of my own making. I married into it. I never consider myself rich. The girls and the people around me are who have enhanced my life, so in that aspect, yes, I am rich, and even more so now that I have Rainey."

"You all know that I started out with nothing, so I made a go of it with my architectural business, but what does it matter if you are unhappy? I will never be that way again as long as I have this lady with me, so it matters not to me if I lose all that I have built. But," Rainey smiled broadly at me, "apparently, it doesn't matter because I am going to be taken care of."

Everyone laughed at that and Ava rambled on some more. "Mama is the most generous person ever. She doesn't just sit on her investments; she makes them work. She finances an orphanage and finds homes for hundreds every year. She puts many through college. She volunteers at the hospital in Waverly and funds the local libraries, and all the proceeds from her book sales go to charity—"

"Enough, Ava. You make me sound like a saint, which I surely am not."

"I can attest to that," Rainey said.

"Really, Rainey?" Ava quipped.

We both broke out into laughter.

Lara shook her head. "Another private joke between them, Ava. It seems as if twenty years apart did not impede their memories. But books, V, you write books?"

"Ava makes it sound as if it is all me. It isn't. I write the stories—they are children's books—with help from both girls. Ava is a very talented artist, so she does all the illustrations, and Rosy does the marketing. It is just an enjoyable collection of stories I made up and told the girls as they were growing up. We certainly do not need the money, so it is distributed to charities that need funding. Enough about that. I only have a few more things to say and that is regarding Avanloch. I know that Randy has told you that it is large, but as far as castles go, it isn't. It would fit three or four times easily into the likes of Dome or Bellmore Castles. It is what is known as a lesser castle. It was resurrected on the site of a formal fortress by the McAllister family after the Scottish wars. It was not built as a military stronghold and has undergone many changes in the last fifty years. From the outside, it looks like a castle, all grey stone and rock walls, and the turrets and towers. There are hundreds of windows of every size, many are stained glass. There are beautiful mosaics set into the walls, so it does not look too foreboding. The inside is very modern and most rooms have had their ceilings lowered. I feel very fortunate to have had the opportunity to make my home in such a delightful setting. I cannot wait for you all to visit. We do not employ servants; they are all friends and we consider them family."

"Crazy question, V. Do you have any ghosts?" Jimmy asked.

Ava answered him. "Of course, Jimmy; it is a castle after all."

Randy said, "I myself have not seen any. Apparently, they only come out on special occasions and I have not missed meeting any, especially the one they keep locked up."

They all looked at me and Ava said, "You tell them about Tatylyanna, Mama."

"The Black Russian, as Maveryn named her. Ummm, she and I have an understanding. A story for another time."

"We are all intrigued, V. You have made no mention of your encounters with the spirits in your letters. How come?" Lara asked of me.

"I don't know. Maybe it's just part of living in a castle. Anyhow, they are all friendly, with the exception of Taty, but she is under lock and key."

Lara wondered how we could keep a ghost from escaping.

I smiled and shrugged my shoulders. "I have no idea."

"Rainey, do you know what you are getting yourself into, buddy?" Jimmy asked.

"To be sure, no. But I am sure that it will be a very intriguing life with these girls."

Lara said it was time to go, as we had to get up early tomorrow. They thanked us for the dinner and evening. We all hugged with promises to get together again as soon as we got back into town. Jimmy said that I was not off the hook regarding ghost stories, and I assured him that there were plenty, just waiting to be told.

Chapter Twenty-Two

Vienna and Rainey

Rainey closed the door behind them and leaned against it, pulling me into his arms. "I was beginning to believe that they would never leave." I scolded him and he answered that he still wasn't up to sharing me.

The next morning, while we were having a quick cup of coffee, I phoned my parents and told them that I was with Rainey. Mother let out a huge sigh of relief, and when I told her that we wanted to buy the house, she was too elated to speak. I told her that we were going to the coast so that Rainey could deal with his wife and business, and then we would make the final arrangements for the sale of the house when we returned to Bridge. Perhaps somewhere along the way, we may fit in a visit with them. I passed the phone to Rainey and left the room, as I could hear my mother crying and apologizing to him. I didn't want to deal with anyone's guilt but my own, and there was plenty of that to go around. I was dreading facing Patsy and Paul, and if it were my choice, I think I would have preferred to run away with Rainey and forget everyone else. But he had two sons and I already did that "running away" thing that had cost us all twenty years of sadness.

Ava and Randy arrived and we left in separate cars. Ava made a funny little face as she was closing her door and said, "And we are off through the woods to Grandma's house. Did you pack a picnic basket, Mama?"

Rainey shook his head and said we had nothing to worry about.

Easy for him to say.

He asked me how I was feeling today and I said that I was as happy as a lark and to ask me again after I had met with his parents.

"No, I mean, how are you? Do you have any feelings of repentance? Are we going to be able to talk about twenty years ago or am I going to cause you to have another episode?"

"If you mean, am I going to breakdown and go to my dark place again? I can never be sure, but I hope that is all over and done with now. If you are worried that every time you bring the past up I am going to retreat into another world, don't be. I've been there and I never want to return."

"Just checking. I want to be sure that I am not going to upset you. I told you that I have forgiven you, Vienna, and I have to go with the premise that all those years we were apart was for a reason. However, I have a thousand and one questions that I seem to require answers to, and we have a six-hour trip to satisfy my curiosity."

"Really, Rainey? You're going to put me through the third degree?"

"Really, Vienna. Will you have answers for me?"

"Perhaps."

He squeezed my hand and no more was said until we drove into the Quinn ranch. I was shaking ever so slightly as Rainey opened the car door for me.

"Relax, sweetheart," he whispered.

"Oh, V, is it really you?" Patsy put me at ease immediately with a warm hug.

Paul did the same and said, "Welcome home, young lady. We have missed you."

They were gazing toward the other car. Rainey helped Ava out and proudly introduced her to her new grandparents. Patsy covered her mouth with her hand as she gasped, "Ava! Oh my God, Rainey, she has your eyes! Welcome, my dear. We are so delighted to meet you."

I knew she could no longer doubt that Ava was truly a Quinn.

Rainey laughed. "I'm pretty sure that Ava has her own eyes, Mom." He introduced them to Randy and asked his dad if he had located the walkie-talkies.

The men went off to retrieve the radio phones and Patsy led Ava and me into the house. I excused myself and snuck upstairs to the room in which I had spent so many nights long ago. Rainey found me in his old bedroom, where I was remembering the night that I had come into his room to watch him as he slept. Where had that young, naïve girl gone?

"What are you doing?" He went to his closet and took out a clean white shirt and khaki pants and proceeded to change. "Next time you kidnap me, will you please bring me a change of clothes?"

"Yes, dear. I am just reminiscing."

"Correct me if I am wrong, but we never spent a night here together, did we?"

"Of course not."

He came up behind me, and started kissing my neck and caressing me. I broke free and ran down the hall. He caught up to me and I pretended to fight him off, giggling like a schoolgirl.

"You're not getting away from me that easy, young lady."

We spotted Patsy at the foot of the stairs, staring up at us.

Rainey cleared his throat. "Sorry, Mom."

"Sorry, for what? This house hasn't echoed with laughter for so long. It's like a sweet melody to hear you two. Now come on down here, breakfast is ready."

We descended the stairs and both hugged her, and she said, "Thank you for coming home to my Rainey, V, and for bringing us a beautiful grand-daughter."

That was all that was said about my being gone for so many years. We gathered the rest from the living room, where Paul had been showing off family pictures. Ava touched Rainey's boys' photos gently, and she and Rainey shared a special smile. I wondered again why Rainey and I had never taken pictures of ourselves together. Actually, except for pictures of me and Lara, I had no photographic memories at all from my time here or in Bridge. It was almost as if I had never existed. I suddenly felt very sad.

We had a lovely family breakfast. Patsy wanted to know everything about our life in Scotland and we filled her in as much as we had time for. We were all a little teary eyed as we said our farewells. Rainey promised that he would bring us back soon.

The sun came out from its hiding place among the clouds as we were leaving. I took that to be a good omen. The roads had been plowed and sanded, and Rainey said that we should arrive at our destination in late af-ternoon. The guys synchronized their radio phones and we were off.

"I think that we are going to have to start acting like adults in light of what happened back at the ranch," I said to Rainey.

"Why? I don't feel like an adult. In fact, I feel like a boy who has just dis-covered how to open the cookie jar with all its earthly delights. But I cannot keep dwelling into the future until I have some answers about the broken pieces of yesterday. Do you understand what I need, Vienna?"

I put my seat into the reclining position and closed my eyes. This was going to be a very long trip. I sighed. "What's question number one?"

"This is not going to be like the Spanish Inquisition, my love."

"Good to know."

I understood that Rainey had been patient with me and that he was afraid of upsetting me, but I had nothing to hide and hoped that my answers would be sufficient for him.

"First off, I want you to know how much I am in love with you. When you are gone from my sight for even a minute, I lose track of time and I feel disoriented until I see you again. I get weak in the knees and feel a bolt of electricity pass through my body as soon as you touch me. I was happy with our relationship before, but this is different. You take my breath away when I am with you, and when I'm not near you, I can't breathe. Is this what twenty years of longing for you has done to me, Vienna?"

"I don't know what to say, Rainey. You see, I have been in love with you from the minute I met you and it has never faded, not even when I thought we were through. When I went away, I thought that I could forget you, but obviously, that didn't happen. So, I have had those feelings you describe for a lot longer than you, and for me, the tingle has not gone away."

"If you had these feelings for me all this time, why did you stay away so long? I understand that you felt that you would be jeopardizing my career by revealing that you were carrying my child, but, Vienna, did you have such little faith in me that you thought that I couldn't handle both?"

"Oh, I had all the faith in the world in you. I knew exactly what you would do. You were and still are this sweet and tender gentleman, and you would make things right because that would have been the thing to do. I didn't want you that way. You didn't love me then…okay, okay, you say you did love me, but you didn't know that until I was gone. You must remember that I was only seventeen and things were very different back then. I did what I thought was best, not only for you, but for me. I was not ashamed of our love child, but I couldn't handle what I may have cost you."

"Did you get pregnant without me? Didn't some of the burden rest with me?"

"I never blamed you. I was under the mistaken premise that it couldn't happen to me. I was in denial for months, even through the sickness. Lara was gone and I felt so alone. If you had come home earlier and surprised me, I would have fallen into your arms and confessed all, but that didn't happen and there is no sense in conjecture. We can't go back and I try not to dwell on what-ifs. It doesn't solve anything, Rainey."

"Do you know how much I hate myself, Vienna? I should have tried harder to find you. I should have hired a private detective. I should have badgered your little sisters until they gave you up. Why didn't I? Maybe because I believed that you had run off with another man. I was sick over that thought. Even after Lara told me that it wasn't so, I did nothing. Nothing. I couldn't handle the fact that you had left me for whatever reason."

"How many times do I have to tell you that it was not your fault? It was mine. And even though I wanted to find you when I finally started to return to Bridge, you were married and had the boys, so I had to let it be. You had them and I had the girls. I would never have become Rosalyn's mother if I hadn't have gone to Scotland. I have tried to find solace in that, not that it did me much good. I still ended up in therapy, and my poor Dr. Jai has no idea of what my real problem was. She could not drag it out of me. It was my burden and mine alone."

"Nothing you are saying makes me feel any better. I tried to accept the fact that you were not coming back. Your family gave me no hope. I cursed you and let your memory play games with me. I thought that I had found solitude in the bottle, but my father set me straight about that. After my ill-fated trip to Wales, I knew I had to get away. I could no longer stay in the house or sleep in the bed that we had been lovers in. And just in case you are wondering, I have never been back to the line shack in Hawthorne. So I went to Italy again because there were no reminders of you there."

"I am so sorry, Rainey." I adjusted my seat so that I was erect again, and I reached out to touch him, wishing that I could hold him in my arms. "One of us is always comforting the other. This has to stop soon, Rainey."

He sniveled a little and said, "It will. After several months in Milan, I finally realized that I may never see you again. I could only hope that you were happy and try to go on with my life."

"Tell me about your job in Milan. Did you find someone to console you?"

He looked at me and there was something dubious in his voice and eyes that I wasn't used to seeing. "You don't want to know that, Vienna."

"Why not? I certainly didn't expect you to be faithful to me. Tell me about her or them; I am not going to get upset."

"There was only one. We shared a residence mostly for financial reasons. She was hardly ever there, as she traveled a lot with her job. I did not love her and I was never more aware of that than the day I got your letter."

I was confused. "I never wrote you any letter."

"It wasn't to me; it was the first one that you sent to Lara. She forwarded it to me."

"Oh, she shouldn't have. I never meant for her to."

"It just so happens that the night Zeta told me there was a parcel from my mom, we were going to some benefit gala. I didn't get a chance to read the letter until I got home, but not before I recognized your handwriting. That threw me for a loop. Just when I thought that I was making progress with putting your memory away, there you were right back again." His laugh was scary. "I wouldn't dance with Zeta or any of her model cohorts. One of them, and believe it or not, was from Borneo. I don't remember her name or if I ever knew it. You remember Borneo, don't you?"

I shook my head no.

"Sure you do. You once said you must look like the wild woman from Borneo and I had no idea who that was. Anyhow, she came up to me and said, 'Dance with me, Rainey Quinn.' I looked at her and it was you. No one ever called me that except you. I thought that I had finally gone bonkers. I refused her of course and had another drink. Yup, I was drinking again."

I didn't know how to respond to that, so I said something utterly stupid. "Zeta, that is a very unusual name. Is she Italian?"

"Is that all you can say? I am pouring my heart out to you and you ask what her nationality is? Well, she is Portuguese. Are you satisfied?"

"I am tired of saying that I am sorry, but I am. I just don't know how to respond to you." I didn't realize that I was biting my nails, something that I never did, until Rainey lightly slapped my hand and told me to stop it. I realized what I was doing and stopped, not sure where this conversation was going. I said, "Do you want to tell me anything else? I promise not to ask any more silly questions."

"I'm sure that I am going to have a lot for you. I don't even know how this became about me…I thought I was the one seeking answers."

"Please go on with your time in Italy."

"There is not much more to say. I had a good job and was very busy. Zeta and I had an understanding. Neither of us wanted a commitment. That all changed the day she asked me to marry her."

I was a little astounded. "*She* asked you to marry *her*? What did you say?"

"Well, *no*, of course! I told her I was not in love with her and she asked me about you. I had no idea how she even knew your name and I wondered if she had read the letter. Apparently, I used to call your name out in my sleep. She asked me if I still loved you and I said, 'Probably.' That was pretty much the end of that, for me anyhow. Then Dad had the heart attack and I came home. She wanted to come with me but I vetoed that. Does that satisfy you?"

"Don't be snooty! I only want to know about your life before you met Louise. I guess you spent Christmas by yourselves in Italy, or did you go to her family in Portugal?"

"As a matter of fact, I went to London to spend the holiday with my friend, Stu."

"I didn't know you knew people in England."

"Just Stu. He is the one who took me to Wales, where we hooked up with his Aunt Maddie to look for you. That was the biggest misadventure of my life."

I tried to hide my dismay by saying, "I know a Stu from London also."

He looked at me quizzically. "Well, I hardly doubt that it is my Stu."

"Why?"

"Come on, Vienna, seriously? How much of a coincidence would that be? Astronomical! Besides, Stu knew what you looked like and he would have made the connection immediately despite the hair color."

"Well, I never actually met Stu. Ash brought me books from his sizeable collection. I was supposed to meet him… What's wrong, Rainey?" I thought that he had stopped breathing; he was so white.

Barely whispering, he instructed me to call Ava and tell her we were pulling over.

He scared me. "Rainey?" I cried.

The car had come to a complete stop on the side of the road. Ava and Randy pulled in behind us. They came over to us to ask why we had stopped. Rainey told them that we needed a break. He was back to normal.

"Don't do that to me again!" I said as soon as the kids were out of earshot. "Lord, I thought you were having a heart attack! Are you all right?"

He nodded.

I suggested we get out to stretch, but he put his hand on me to stop me. He had the peculiar look on his face again.

"Is your Stu married?" he asked.

"What a strange question. Yes, his wife's name is Daisy."

"The coincidence just became fact. Your Stu is my Stu."

"How can you be sure?"

"Two people in London named Stu who have enormous book collections and are both married to someone named Daisy? I hardly doubt that they are not the same person. You said you never met him. How come?"

"Well, the obvious. He lived in London and I lived in a remote part of Scotland. Twice, when I visited Ash, she had made plans for me to meet him, but it never panned out. He was either away or giving a lecture. Is your Stu a highly educated man?"

"Yes. Tell me who Ash is again."

"She is Jeremy's sister."

"What does she do?"

Again, I found his question very odd. "She works for McAllister Shipping. Before Jeremy passed away, she wrote and produced plays."

"I think I met her at Stu's wedding. Is she rather manly in her ways?"

"Yes, she is. You were at Stu's wedding? That was in the spring of '63? I was in London also."

"This just keeps on getting stranger. Why were you there?"

"It was the winter after my discontent, so to speak. Ash's play was premiering and Jeremy wanted to get me out of my doldrums for a few days. It was the first time I was away from my girls, so I had a dreadful time. Ava wasn't even a year old yet. Do you realize that we could have run into each other?"

"I met Ash at the wedding. She had to leave prematurely because of her play. If she had stayed around for the reception, perhaps we would have talked more."

Ava had come back to the car. "What are you two doing? I thought the purpose of this stop was to get out for a short walk."

Rainey opened the door and said, "We were just finishing up a conversation."

"Is everything all right with you two?"

"Yes, darling. I think it would be a good idea if you rode with Rainey for a while so that you can get to know each other better. What do you say?"

Rainey took hold of me and said, "Not so fast, my lady, we are not through with our discussion yet. Can we do that later, Ava? I am looking forward to getting to know you better."

"Damn it! I thought I could get off the hook for a little while," I joked.

Rainey smiled. "Such language and from a lady!"

Ava agreed. "Mother never swears."

"And you only call me mother when you are annoyed with me."

"I am never annoyed with you, Mama."

"Ha!" was my reply. "Let's go, it's cold out here."

Rainey kissed me and we resumed our journey. We talked more about the ifs and why hadn't our paths crossed in England. It was all so non-sensible. He told me more about his quest in Wales and pressed me for information about my life at Avanloch.

"You've told me that you weren't in love with Jeremy, but it is hard for me to believe that there was no one else who took a fancy to you or you to him."

"Is that a question or a statement? Was I tempted, is that what you are asking me?" I was not going to burst the bubble and tell him about my unresolved affections for Jack or Roberge. "There was no one to speak of." It would not have been fair to anyone to pretend that I had feelings for them when I was still in love with you."

"My dear, I am not talking about love—"

"I know what you mean and the answer is still 'no.' I told you at the Palace that I had been true to you. Did you not believe me?"

"Yes, I know. It is just that you have so much love to give; the happiest day of my life was Sunday, when you invited me into your house. Even when you asked me to leave, I had hope. Then you took me back. Darling, I was on an emotional roller coaster. Even after you told me you still loved me, I wasn't sure that I would be able to convince you of my feelings for you. But at the Palace, that all changed." He reached over and squeezed my hand. "You truly have lit up my life. Every time I look into your eyes I see happiness. You make every kiss seem like the first and I never want them to end. I can't wait to hold you in my arms. How do you do that Vienna?"

"It isn't any different for me, Rain. I have to tell you something and I don't think that you are going to be happy with me."

He looked at me questioningly.

I continued with my confession. "I came to see you once about ten years ago."

"What do you mean?"

"Jeremy had to come to Vancouver and Seattle and invited me along. I didn't want to come but everyone convinced me to. The girls were going to summer camp. Yes, it was ten years ago because Ava was ten. I knew exactly what I would do if I came, and I did. I found your business address in the yellow pages and I had the limousine driver take me there."

Rainey's voice was trembling as he instructed me to call Ava again and tell her we were stopping. By the time I had picked up the phone, he had already abruptly braked and we were on the side of the road in a foot of snow.

Ava and Randy pulled up behind them.

"What the hell is going on with those two? He better not be saying things to upset Mama." Ava had her hand on the doorknob when Randy grabbed her arm.

"Don't go storming up there. Let's just see why they stopped. I don't think you have to worry about Rainey saying or doing anything to upset your mother. He loves her more than life itself."

She ignored him. Her mother already had the window open, anticipating her daughter's reaction. "Hello, dear. Again. Your father is a little annoyed with me and thought that he shouldn't be driving right now until we have the newest revelation talked through."

"You don't have to worry, Ava," Rainey said. "I am not going to scold your mother too much. I have just found out that she came to see me ten years ago but never let me see her. I am a little shook up."

"Is that right, Mother?"

"Another of my blunders, yes."

Ava sighed. "All righty then, I'll leave you be."

She trudged back to the car and slammed the door.

"Well?" Randy questioned.

"It appears as though my mother went to see Rainey ten years ago but never actually made contact. That's all I know. It's safer to be stopped right now while he vents."

Rainey was staring straight ahead as if he couldn't bear to look at me. "Exactly when was this, Vienna?"

I tried to keep my composure. "As it so happened, it was on your birthday, July 14."

"My thirty-third to be exact. That would have been the best present that I had ever received if you had of waited for me. Instead, you came into my office, talked to my receptionist and secretary, and left without as much as a, 'How do you do?'"

"You knew I was there?"

"You left your fragrance behind. The minute I entered the stairwell, I noticed the delicate scent but could not place it. After all, it had been many years since I smelled cherry blossoms. I asked Sylvie what it was because she is allergic to perfume and no one in the offices wears any. It took a second or so for me to make the connection, and when I did, I ran down to see a black limo pulling away. That was you, wasn't it?"

"Yes."

"Why did you even bother tracking me down if you had no intentions of actually making contact, pray tell?"

"Here we go again. *If* you had been there at that moment, who knows what I would have done? But you weren't, so I left. We probably missed passing on the stairs by mere seconds. I watched you from the car. You glanced my way and I thought that you looked happy. I couldn't interfere with your new life. It was another huge mistake. Can you look at me, Rainey?"

He turned toward me. "I searched for that limousine for weeks. No one would admit to bringing a fare to Sutton Street. How did you manage that?"

"I paid Manuel, the driver, to keep my confidence."

"I offered a reward, but still no one would come forward."

"Manuel would not have given me up. We became friends. He tried to convince me to seek you out again. I told him that I would soon, but the timing was not right that day. He had come from a small town in Mexico to make enough money to send for his family. I helped him out with that."

"So you bribed him. How much?"

"I didn't consider it a bribe. Is the amount important? Okay, I gave him $10,000."

"Wow, I guess you really didn't want me to find you!"

"It wasn't like that, Rainey. I just needed to see you and hear your voice, that's all."

"Hear my voice? Well, you didn't, did you?"

"Yes, I did. I phoned your home phone and listened to your answering machine, not once but twice. When the message said, 'Louise and Rainey Quinn,' I knew that I had done the right thing."

"Geez, Vienna, it wasn't right!"

"Do you hate me, Rainey?"

He didn't answer me but opened his door, and I watched him walk around the front of the car, not knowing what to expect. He opened my door and pulled me out.

"Should I start walking back to Bridge?" I asked.

He opened his coat open and folded my trembling body into his. "You silly little minx. Thank you for telling me." He kissed my forehead.

"But you already knew. Would you have mentioned the occurrence ever?"

"We'll never know, will we? Chin up. I think I deserve a kiss."

"Oh, Rainey, I love you."

Ava had joined us. She said to Rainey, "Mama isn't crying and you aren't steaming, so are we all right?"

"I'm dealing, Ava. Your mother is a lot more in control than I am."

"You have not been the one keeping secrets, Rainey," I responded.

"Will we be stopping anymore?" Ava asked.

"About 20 miles down the road is a wayside diner I always have a coffee break at. How does that sound?" Rainey answered.

"That's not exactly what I meant. Mama, are you harboring any other surprises?"

Ava was definitely on her father's side with regard to his reaction at my latest revelation. "No, I have nothing else to confess. From now on, we shall only speak of cabbages and kings and castles."

"Sounds good to me. You can rest easy, Ava. There is nothing that your mother could tell me that would make me turn away from her." Rainey hugged our daughter and helped me back into the car. "See you at the rest stop."

"You're too forgiving of my mistakes, Rainey. It's more than I deserve," I said to him when we were on our way again.

"Who's the judge of what you deserve? I think that you have been punishing yourself for far too long. Everything outweighs the fact that we are together again, don't you agree?"

"Yes. Right now, I wish that we were in Scotland at Avanloch. I so wish to take you walking on the glen where the mist rises above the heathers and watch the sun rise over the meadows. I want to go riding with you over the moors and make love on the cool, lush mosses. I want you to witness the storms that take over the senses and make one oblivious to anything else, and

I can't wait for us to roam the halls at midnight, seeking out the spirits that rendezvous in the wee hours of the morning."

"You have painted me into your paradise and I assure you that I am looking forward to exploring with you just as much. I don't know if I will be able to share your enthusiasm with the ghosts, though. I don't think that I believe they exist."

"Oh, you will! That will be the fun of it…watching your reaction the first time you come to grips with the fact that visits from the other side are truly possible. I hope the first apparition you encounter will be Maveryn. Sometimes, we don't see her for months and we worry that she will not be returning. Can I recite for you a little poem?"

"Please do."

I said,

"Maveryn came again to Avanloch last night
She came with the breeze in the pale moonlight
She walked the halls in her long white gown
She filled our hearts with love and joyous song
She passed through us like a wisp of air
Then gone again was our Maveryn fair."

"There is no doubt in my mind that you composed that," said Rainey. "You almost have me believing in her existence. Imagine that, me, a man of tangible facts, contemplating such a frivolity."

I laughed with him. "Not only do we have Lady Maveryn, we have phantoms in the mist and fairies in the gardens."

"The boys are going to be so enchanted with you and your stories."

"You think? I don't know how teenage boys are. I am sure that they are only interested in sports and girls."

"They are definitely into sports; girls, I can't say."

"I think I will close my eyes for a few minutes, Rainey, unless you want me to drive for a while?"

"Do you still close your eyes when you cross over bridges?"

"I have no idea, but I have never had an accident and I have been driving for a long time. What kind of music do you listen to now?"

He reached in the back and passed me a blanket to wrap up in and replied, "I quit playing all those sad country songs soon after you left. Now and then, I catch one of your favorites on the radio and it immediately takes me back. I learned to appreciate operettas when I was in Italy and I discovered this French songstress whose love songs are quite haunting, not that I bother to take the time to translate. I just enjoy listening to her. There is one song she recorded a few years back that reminds me of you. She recorded it in both English and French. Her name is Gizelle Marchant. Have you heard of her?"

"Indeed I have. Does the song you are talking about go like this?"
"Mademoiselle, will you come walk with me?
Take my hand and I will lead you to our destiny

I told him no, no, no, a thousand times
For I was yours and you were forever mine
Mademoiselle, will you please come dance with me
Paradise is in my arms, you will surely see
I told him no, no, no, no, farewell, adieu
My dances were all reserved for you
Mademoiselle, let me take you from this life
Come with me to Vienne and be my wife
No, No, No, No, No, a thousand nos I cried
Let me go, leave me be, I am betrothed I lied
I left him there alone, so forlorn and wondering
I hadn't meant to be unkind but you were calling me
Tomorrow at the dawn I must cross the seventh sea
Mademoiselle is coming home to you at Avonlea"

"I can't believe it, Vienna. You still memorize all the lyrics to the songs you like."

I laughed. "Of course I know all the words, for they are mine. And they remind you of me, for I wrote it with you in mind."

"Excuse me, dear, did you just say that you wrote that song?"

"Don't look so flabbergasted, Rainey. Yes, they are my lyrics."

"And Gizelle recorded them...so you know her. I'm sorry, I'm a little miffed. Hell, I'm a lot miffed! How did this come to be?"

"Simple. I had written the poem/song a while back, and when I discovered Gizelle, I thought, what the heck? I sent them off to her. Actually, the girls came up with the music and sang the tune to their piano and harp rendition. We made a cheap tape for her, and lo and behold, she contacted me immediately and asked me if I would sell her the rights to record the song. I knew nothing about the ins and outs of the music business, but Uncle John handled all the legal aspects. To your other question, no, I have never met Gizelle, but we have talked numerous times on the telephone. She is patiently waiting for me to write another song for her. I told her that I was much too busy, but if something came to me again, she would be the first to know. Whoever thought it would be such a hit not only in France but elsewhere? Obviously, you never read the cover story on the album or you would have known it was me and that my royalties all went to charity."

"Is that right, Vienna? And what was your nom de plume, Vienna LaFontaine?"

I realized at once my mistake. "Oops, you're right. I guess you didn't know I was Vela McAllister, did you?"

"No, my dear, I didn't. Where did the Vela come from?"

"Maveryn gave me the name when I was twelve. She knew that I didn't like to be called Vienna and she didn't care for V, so she used 'Ve' with 'La' from LaFontaine and I became Vela. When I returned, Jeremy asked if he could call me that, so it stuck."

"Thank you for clearing that up. I am still in shock to know that my favorite songstress has recorded a song that the woman I love wrote. Don't you think that is uncanny? I am glad she kept the harp as an instrument. Along with the violins, it solidifies the mood, which I find romantically haunting. Lord, Vienna, what other things have you done? Will you ever quit astonishing me?"

"I hope not, darling. I think I like her version in French much better. English is just English, but French is one of the romance languages. Now, please put on the tape and I will dream about us in wonderland."

"Sounds like a title for a new song to me."

"Please don't put words in my mouth. I have enough to contend with right now."

I guess I slept, for when I opened my eyes, we were only 30 miles outside of Vancouver. "You must be exhausted, Rainey. I'm sorry that I slept so long."

"Not to be. I've been listening to Gizelle and planning our future together, so the time has gone by quickly. I have made this trip so many times its like clockwork to me."

"Still, I should have been keeping you company. By the way, does Gizelle know that you are planning a future with her?"

"Very funny, my dear."

His grin set my heart afire.

It wasn't very long until he pulled into the parking lot at the Seven Bays. He let me into his suite and walked Ava and Randy to the room he had booked for them. I anxiously awaited his return.

Rainey almost tripped over Vienna's boots as he entered his apartment. He picked them up along with her coat, which she had flung in the corner. He gathered them up and placed them with his in their respective places. On the way to the bedroom, he retrieved her sweater and then her blouse and her socks. He found her beside the bed, attempting to wiggle out of her jeans. He leaned up against the door with an amused smile on his face.

"What are you doing?" she asked.

"Just picking up after you; not all of us have the luxury of a maid."

"I'll have you know, Rainey Quinn, that no maid picks up after me. I make my own bed and help with the housework, and I still saddle my own horse, so there! Now quit standing there with that silly grin on your face. I don't like you seeing me in my old granny underwear. Tomorrow, I'm going to go shopping for some sexy red lingerie."

"Makes no difference to me, my love."

"Before I climb into this bed, I have a question for you. Think before you answer for I will know if you are lying."

"Why would I lie? Fire away."

"How many women have shared this bed with you?"

"That's easy, none."

"No woman has slept in this bed?"

"I didn't say that. You asked who had shared it with me and the answer is still no one. But there have been women in this bed." He was still smiling sheepishly.

"Ha! I knew it."

"Does my mother or sister count?"

"Don't be silly. Of course not. Why would they sleep here and not at your house?"

"Louise."

She slipped out of her bra and panties and said, "Well, what are you waiting for? Do you need a written invitation?"

"No, Ma'am. Coming right now, Ma'am." He dropped her clothes in a heap on the floor and sat down on the bed beside her.

"Have I not threatened you with the consequences of calling me Ma'am?"

"No, but I think I'm willing to find out."

"I have never actually harmed anyone, but there is always a first time." She started to unbutton his shirt.

"You know, Vienna, sometimes I think you are two very different people. One is this tender, demure young girl, and then, you are this brash, authoritative woman. Are you harboring two personalities?"

She wrapped her arms around his neck and whispered, "Which one do you like best?"

He untangled her and held her away from him. "Mademoiselle, it is my turn to ask the questions now."

"Really, again?"

"Yes. Who is the 'he' in your song?"

"Who says there is a specific 'he'? It's just a song."

"Vienna, who was the man—or who *is*—the man pursuing you?"

"That's a story for another time. The only thing important now is us."

Rainey had ordered room service and Ava and Randy joined them for a late supper. He commented on Vienna's appetite. "My mother voiced concerns over your slim frame the same as I have, Vienna, but there is certainly nothing wrong with your appetite, is there?"

Ava answered for her mother. "You shouldn't worry, Rainey. Mama is very healthy. I have never known her any other way."

"Yes, I am sure she is, but I would still like to see her a little rounder."

"You mean like me?" Ava queried.

"Hello. I am right here, you two. You will have to excuse Rainey, honey. It appears he likes his girls plump. He remembers me from when I was a teenager, always fighting with keeping my weight down. Now I struggle to put weight on. Yes, I would like to find a happy medium and maybe I will. I already have trouble buttoning up my jeans. For almost a week, I have been idle and you just may get your wish, Rainey Quinn."

He smiled at her and said that he would love her no matter what. They moved to the sofas in the living room area and Rainey advised them of his plans for tomorrow. He had his arm around Vienna and said that as much as he hated to leave her, he had some business to take care of at his office. He said again to Ava, "I can trust you to look after your mother. She has said that she would like to do a little shopping. I am going to make my driver available to you. I don't want the two of you to be wandering the streets alone. Henry has been an employee for a number of years and will take good care of you. Unfortunately, he will be retiring this year and I will have to replace him."

Vienna thanked him and turned to her daughter. "You will have to be patient with your father, Ava. He seems to think that I need protecting, though from what? I am not sure. He thinks the earth is going to swallow me up if I am out of his sight."

"It's more than that, Ava. You tell me, is your mother not adventuresome? Does she not go off riding all alone at Avanloch, and does she not consort with ghosts in the middle of the night or close her eyes when she is driving over bridges?"

Vienna struck him ever so lightly. "Rainey Quinn!"

They all laughed and Ava said, "Well, to be perfectly honest, we do worry about some of her escapades, but as you will soon learn, she *is* the boss."

"Just as I feared. Vienna, I have a question for you."

She hung her head. "Oh no, not another?"

"This one won't hurt a bit. Where were you the day that JFK was assassinated?"

"Oh, surely you don't think that you are going to catch me with that one, do you? Can't you come up with something a little less known? Like perhaps when did Marilyn Monroe die?"

"What are you two talking about?" Ava wanted to know.

Rainey enlightened her. "Your mother used to play this little game with me like asking me strange facts about celebrities…some of them, I can assure you, I never even heard of. So, I just thought I would see if I could catch her off guard."

"You have heard of John Fitzgerald Kennedy, I know. To answer Rainey, he died November 22, 1963 in Dallas, Texas. I was at Avanloch and we watched it all on T.V. In case anyone is interested, Marilyn was found dead at her home in California on August 5, 1962, just a month after I was married to Jeremy. She was only thirty-six years old."

Rainey chuckled. "Just as I thought. I should know better than try and catch you at your own game. Perhaps I should have found a more obscure fact to test you with…like something about Attila the Hun?"

"I wouldn't even go *there* if I were you, Rainey," Ava warned him.

"Right. Are you still fascinated with Hollywood, Vienna? Did you name Ava after one of your favorites, Ava Gardner?"

Before Vienna could answer, Ava did. "I know the answer to that one. She named me for Avanloch, didn't you, Mama?"

"You are both wrong. I named you for Avastavalley. You do remember that, don't you, Rainey?"

"It's not likely that I would forget. I had no idea. I never put the two names together. I should have known you would have romance associated with our daughter's name." He kissed her on her forehead and squeezed her hand.

"Well, I am really in the dark," Ava stated. "All of this time, I thought that you named me after Avanloch. What is Avastavalley?"

"It's a quaint little place in the interior. Your father took me there one weekend in 1961...do I need to say more? And it is pronounced Ava, not Avan like the castle."

"Mother, you are full of surprises."

"A woman has to have some secrets. I couldn't reveal that to you without telling you the whole story, but I vowed you would know someday, and now you do."

"I suppose we should call it a night. What time do you want to leave in the morning, Mama? Randy has to be at the school by 10."

"I have plans for your mother first thing, but we will be back by then I am sure," Rainey said. "After my meeting, I am picking the boys up at school and having the little powwow with them. We should be back here by 4 so that you can get acquainted with them, and then dinner. How does that sound? Is that enough time for shopping?"

"It sounds fine, Rainey. What are we doing so early in the morning?"

"And that is *my* little secret, my love." Rainey winked at Ava and Randy but they had no clue as to what he was planning.

As they got up to leave, Rainey said, "What would you all say if I told you that this past weekend was predestined?"

Vienna stood up with him and put her arms around him. "Since when have you believed in fate, sweetheart?"

"Since you. I just don't know why it took so long in coming. Before I went to Hawthorne, and I almost didn't you know, Sylvie, my receptionist, read my horoscope for me. Really, as if I believe in such things. Anyhow, it said that I was going to be reunited with a past love. Can you imagine what I said to that?"

"Yes, I think we can, Rainey, and I don't think that it is fit for our ladylike ears," Vienna teased.

"That's not all. The same was for the sign Aries, and you're an Aries, aren't you, love?"

"Yes, I am. I'm impressed. You remember my birthday."

"Don't give me too much credit. I'm still not sure of the date. Something to do with the day Liz Taylor's husband died."

"Oh now I am really impressed! You actually remember me telling you that?"

"Yes. It is odd that I can have a total recall of conversations with you from so long ago and yet if you ask me who I had a business meeting with last week, I wouldn't be able to recollect what transpired."

"It is a mystery how the mind works. I am just so happy that you kept me in your thoughts or this reunion may not be taking place." Vienna smiled up at Rainey as they said good night to their daughter.

Rainey ruffled Ava's hair and said, "I remember when your mother's hair was this black. When I first seen you at Hawthorne, I thought that I was hallucinating." He kissed the top of her head.

Ava answered with, "I think that I had better take my natural shade back so I don't cause you anymore grief."

"I didn't mean that you should change, Ava."

"I know you didn't."

As the door closed, Vienna asked Rainey again if he would like her to dye her hair dark again.

"Never," he replied. "I love your caramel locks. They do look better this way, though." He undid the pins in her hair so that it cascaded to her shoulders. "There, that's better."

As they proceeded to the bedroom, Vienna commented on how quiet Randy was at dinner. Rainey said that he noticed it to too. "Do you think that they have had a spat?"

"I'm sure that we will find out tomorrow."

Vienna awoke to the aroma of freshly brewed coffee. Rainey had been holding a cup under her nose, and as soon as her eyes opened, he pulled it away. "Well, that certainly isn't your best move to awaken a girl with. What time is it anyhow?"

"Time? It's time to get a move on. You have overslept, my beauty."

"Oh yes, you have some mysterious plan for me this morning."

"It won't be for long. Now drink up and get a move on!"

"Now who's the bossy one?"

Half an hour later, they were out on the street. They walked for several blocks until they reached Centennial Square. Rainey told her that this was his first big project and that its success propelled him into the higher brackets of the architecture trade. Vienna thanked him for bringing her and asked why he hadn't taken an apartment here.

"I make damn good money, honey, but I am not frivolous. For the amount of time I spend at my suite, here would be a complete waste of funds. The rent would easily be five times what I pay at the Seven Bays. This is not why I brought you here, though."

He steered her into a revolving door that led into the mall. Hand and hand, they walked until he came to a stop in front of Miller's Fine Diamonds.

The clerk, a man in his late fifties, approached them and asked if he could be of some assistance. Rainey asked that they be shown his best engagement rings.

"Yes, Sir!" the man replied and asked them to follow him.

With a quivering voice, Vienna said. "Rainey, this isn't necessary...just because we talked about it with our friends doesn't mean—"

"You do want to marry me, don't you, Vienna? Is there some reason…perhaps someone who is standing in your way?" He thought of the man in her song and felt ill.

"Oh no, Rainey! I have wanted to be your wife all my life. It has been my fantasy."

He had thought that his heart was going to stop for a minute but her response reassured him. "And I want to marry you more than anything in my life. It is just a matter of time. But for now, I want everyone to know that you are mine and I think that a large rock will do the trick."

"I hope you won't regret this, Rain. You've only known me a few days. I am not seventeen anymore. I am very headstrong and used to doing things my way. I have tried to be on my best behavior for you, but I can be very moody and withdrawn. I don't want to delude you into thinking that I am always going to be this lovable and consistent lady."

"I look forward to all of your faces and moods, and I can assure you that you, too, will have to deal with my alter egos. Now, do you want a ring or not?"

"Yes, very much so."

It was not the ring that he would have chosen for her. She did not want a huge stone and had picked out a solitaire diamond surrounded by tinier ones in a gold setting. She was worried about the price, but Rainey assured her it was not a problem and wondered if it was even enough for the mistress of Avanloch. As they walked back to the apartment, she told him that it was beautiful and that she would wear it always with pride.

"I am having a hard time grasping the fact that we are really together and that you have forgiven me. A lesser man wouldn't have you know."

"I consider myself the luckiest man in the world. All these years that I was without you and managed to get by is a mystery to me. I knew that you were alive by words dropped here and there by 'certain people.'" He chuckled. "No one ever said that your marriage was not one of love; I just assumed that it was and tried to go on with a life that I now know was a farce."

"Please don't say that, honey. Just think of all that you have accomplished; the magnificent structures that you have built, and the rearing of your sons."

"Yes, of course, but I was always lonely, Vienna. I never found comfort in any woman's arms like I do in yours."

"Nor have I. We will never be lonely again, Rainey, never."

Ava was waiting for them and was not at all surprised when her mother showed her the ring. She smiled at her father and knew that she had made the right decision regarding her engagement to Randy. They went off on their shopping escapade and Rainey left for his appointments, instructing Vienna to keep in contact with him through the car phone.

"Quit worrying will you? I have been in the city before you know. I'll either be in a store or the car. You're not expecting an earthquake, are you?" she teased.

"Don't even suggest such a thing!" Rainey gave her a quick pat on the behind.

Everyone at the office was delighted to see him but quite astonished to hear about his future plans. Briefly, he told them about Vienna and winked at Sylvie.

"I know it comes as no shock to any of you that my marriage is over. I've been dragging my feet far too long, but now, with Vienna back in my life, I hope to make it official before the month is out. I want to take a backseat in the company, as I have no idea where my life with her is going to take me. I won't dissolve the company, but I don't plan on being actively involved for a while, and maybe never. The three of you, Clive, Stan, and Gregg, if you can agree, and I think you can, will become equal partners."

"You're serious, Rainey? You want us to take over the company? What about all the projects that you have in the fire?" Stan inquired.

"I'm dead serious. You all have your own dealings so you will just have to add mine to them. Anyone of you can run the business. I'll leave you to mull it over, but I shouldn't have to tell you what the alternative is… I'd have to sell off, and make no mistake about it, I am ready to do whatever it takes for me to be with the woman I love. She will have no desire to live here. We are buying her old family home back in Bridge Falls and she owns a huge estate in Scotland… Hell, it's not an estate, it's a castle!"

"What? Did we hear you right, Sir? Did you say castle?" Sylvie exclaimed.

Rainey put his arm around her as they, along with the other secretaries, left the guys to consider his proposal. "You have me believing in the occult, Sylvie. The horoscope prediction was bang on. There must be a lot of happy people out there who share the same fortune."

"I don't think it works for everyone in the same way, but I am so glad it has come true for you. I have never seen you so elated. How are the boys taking it?"

"That's my next task as soon as I am finished up here."

The doors to the boardroom opened on three men with huge smiles on their faces. They came over and one by one shook Rainey's hand, who said, "Get Stanton up here, will you, Sylvie? He is expecting the call."

Two hours later, all the legalities were taken care of and Rainey left to pick up Morgan and Mason. He had planned what he would say, but in the end knew that he would just wing it, depending on their reactions. He arrived before the final bell sounded. They came out together, which Rainey was sure was a first. They got along as far as brothers go, but they had separate lives outside of home. Not even a week had passed since he had last seen them, and yet it felt as though an eon had passed. Morgan jumped into the front seat, leaving Mason to take up his usual position in the back. They exchanged the usual "how are you and glad to see you."

"You're sure that your mother isn't home?" Rainey asked.

"No, she won't be home until tomorrow night. You really don't want to see her, do you, Dad?" Morgan asked.

"Not until I have a chance to talk to you boys. Do you need to stop anywhere before we go home? Snacks?"

"We have lots at home. You seem different, Dad. Is something wrong?"

Rainey swung the car around and headed for the house six blocks away. "On the contrary, Son, all is finally all right with my world."

"I didn't know anything was wrong except between you and Mom. You're going to ask her for a divorce, aren't you, Dad?" Morgan was too perceptive.

"I want to tell you the story from the beginning. Can you wait another few minutes until we are home?"

They both echoed, "Sure." Morgan shrugged his shoulders as if in a question as he looked at his brother in the backseat.

Once seated in the comfort of his den, with the boys sitting opposite him, Rainey started his saga. "I need you to go back with me to the summer of 1960. I was turning twenty-one and I met this young girl whom I fell head over heels for. Her name was Vienna LaFontaine.

"She was only sixteen. We spent two summers together plus more when I could get home. I was still enrolled in university down here and she lived in Bridge Falls. I had met her through your Aunt Lara; they were best friends. Anyhow, I thought that I would someday have a future with her when I was done with school and had secured a future in architecture. Unfortunately, I forgot to tell her that. Hell, I was too cocky. I always thought that she would be waiting for me no matter what. I don't know who I thought I was, but I had not considered her feelings. When I went off to Italy for those four months, our communications broke down and she thought that I had found someone new. Most of my letters to her were lost. When I came home at Christmas, she was gone." His voice had suddenly gone flat.

Morgan picked up on it. "Do you mean…had she died?"

Rainey regained his composure. "Sorry, I still feel the hurt. No, thank God, she hadn't died. She was just gone. She had run away. Her family didn't even know where she had gone, or so we all thought. There was even talk that she had left with some guy named Jack, which turned out to be false. Anyhow, I tried to find her, realizing that I was in love with her. Only, it was too late. I never really got over my love for her even though I tried with your mother. Anyhow, as you may be guessing…I found her last Saturday in Hawthorne." He quit talking to see how they would react to that revelation.

Mason was the most curious. "Did you recognize each other right off, Dad? Was she happy to see you? Did you find out why she had left?"

Rainey smiled. "Well, she had changed a little, but there was no mistaking that it was her. And, no, she did not appear to be happy to see me at first. I'm afraid I bombarded her with too many questions and she couldn't handle it, so she left me with no answers. I had been heartbroken when she had left twenty years ago and I was not about to let her go again. I went to Bridge the next morning to try and talk to her."

"She lives in Bridge Falls and you never knew? Lara didn't tell you?" Morgan asked.

"No, she only visits. Although her family still has a house there… I've shown it to you guys, the Palace, as it is known on the river. She bought her own house there for some reason.

"Where does she live usually, Dad?" Mason asked.

"Scotland."

"Scotland? You mean like in Britain?"

"Yes, Mason, that Scotland. She had an aunt there and that is where she escaped to. The reason she left all those years ago was because she was going to have a baby. She didn't want me to know because she thought that it would jeopardize my career. The baby was mine. I had no idea; the thought never even entered my head. That is how stupid I was. She did what she thought was right and her family kept us all in the dark. Lara didn't even know that she had my child until I was married and had started my own family. Vienna did marry, but that is another story for another time. The important thing is that Vienna and I have found each other again, and more than that, I have a daughter. Her name is Ava and she is just as beautiful as her mother."

The boys were speechless for a minute, and then Morgan said, "Does that mean that we have a sister? And how do you know for sure that she is yours? Sorry, Dad."

"Yes, it does, Son, and when you see her, you will know that she is mine."

"Is she here? Are they here? Is that why you didn't come home last night?" Morgan appeared to be wounded.

"I know it will be hard for you to comprehend that I have a daughter and that I am leaving your mother. But the truth is that we have been estranged for a very long time. I only stayed married to her because of you two…perhaps that was wrong. We do not love one another and perhaps we never did. I am forty-two and I think I have earned the right to be with the woman whom I truly love."

"It's not like we haven't been expecting this, Dad," Morgan said. "In fact, we have wondered what took you so long. I think that we have both suspected that you already had a girlfriend."

"I didn't. I have pretty much been married to my job and keeping you boys on the straight and narrow. I had always hoped that Vienna would come back to me and I would have taken her back no matter what. But I pretty much gave up on that idea a long time ago, and then Jimmy invited me to come to Hawthorne and, as they say, 'the rest is history.' If this is all too much for you guys, I understand. They are waiting back at my apartment to meet you, but we can put it off for another day if you prefer. Up to you."

"I want to meet them, Dad." Of course Mason would.

Morgan seemed to be mulling something over in his mind.

"What is it, Son?" Rainey asked him.

"Does Mom know?"

"I haven't spoken to her yet…you mean about the divorce?"

"No, I mean, does she know about Vienna?"

"No, how would she? I have never spoken about her."

"Oh, I think she knows, Dad."

"Why would you say that, Morg?"

"I've heard her mention that name. It's not such a common name that you would forget. It was a long time ago, but I heard it and I have proof."

Rainey leaned forward, not quite comprehending what his son was saying. "Proof? Proof of what, Son?"

Morgan got up and said he'd be right back. Mason shook his head. No, he had no idea what his brother was talking about. Morgan returned and laid a crumpled piece of paper in front of his dad. Rainey straightened the single note paper out and read the bold letters—Vienna LaFontaine. He was stunned. It wasn't his handwriting.

"Where did you get this?" He hoped he didn't sound annoyed.

"I've been mulling it over ever since you told us the name of your old girlfriend…something was tickling my memory, but it just came to me now. Mother wrote it. I remember because she was thoroughly ticked off at me. I had come barging in to the living room, as she so put it, and interrupted her phone conversation. She called me a rude brat and ordered me out of the room. I left, but I didn't completely close the door, as I was curious about who was on the other end of the line and I was mad at her also. She was talking to that detective friend of Grandpa's. She said his name, Mr. Reeves. She thanked him for the long-overdue information and there would be no need for you to ever know. She mumbled something…I think it may have been Vienna. Dad, it was a long time ago, but that is what I remember."

"Think, Morgan. When was this? Can you remember approximately?"

"Yeah, it was right after we got home from Hawthorne and the party."

"Son, we have been to a lot of parties in Hawthorne. Can you narrow it down a little more? And I still don't know where you got this piece of paper with Vienna's name."

"After Mother hung up the phone, she got up, got a drink of something, went back to the telephone table, and wrote something down. She looked toward the door and I thought that I had been caught, so I hightailed it out of there. I went back later and did that trick you showed me of how to scribble over the paper and draw up the message from the previous page. That's what you have in front of you. I have kept it hidden and I guess I forgot about it until today. I don't know why I kept it, honestly, Dad."

"That's all right, Son. I don't know what it means." To himself, he thought, *But I am damn well going to find out!*

"How many times has Mom come to Hawthorne, Dad? The last time was at your dad's birthday party. Remember how she decided to come at the last minute? I think I was nine."

"You've got a good memory, Son. That would have been 1975. I can't think of anything significant that happened then. Let's just leave it for now. Though I must admit I am a little curious as to what your mother was up to. What is the word on tonight? I thought that we could all go out to your favorite restaurant. What do you say? Oh, one other thing that I might temp you with… I told you that Vienna and Ava live in Scotland, right? Well, not just anywhere but at Avanloch, which just happens to be a castle!"

The boys were dumbstruck.

Got ya, Rainey said to himself.

"Really, Dad? A castle? People don't live in castles anymore." Mason denied it but was so hoping it was true. He had a sister who lived in a castle?

"How about we let them tell you? If you're coming, go get tidied up."

The boys left the room, but not before they heard their dad dial a number and say in a soft voice, "Sweetheart…"

Morgan followed Mason into the shared bathroom where they both sat on the tub. Morgan told his brother that he could shower first, as he needed to get some of the peach fuzz off his face.

Morgan yelled over the running water, "What do you think? Is he off his rocker?"

Mason replied, "Well, you sure as hell didn't help any when you told him that cock and baloney story about Mother."

"It's true and I don't know why I brought it up, either. I feel sorry for him. He has been miserable and now suddenly he is happy. Suppose if something goes wrong? I mean, she left him before."

"Why are you so negative? I want it all to be true—the sister, the castle, Vienna."

"What fairy tale world are you living in, little brother? What the hell would we do with a sister? Anyhow, Dad is probably going to move to Scotland with them and we'll never see him again."

"Fatalist! If I have to choose between parents, I'm taking Dad."

"Where did you learn such fancy language? Do you really think that Dad would want you?"

Mason came out of the shower. "He would never leave us. You maybe, but not me."

Morgan gave Mason's head a tussle and said as he climbed into the shower, "I guess time will tell, won't it, little brother?"

Rainey turned the key in the lock and saw Vienna and Ava standing near the door, waiting for them. He started to close the door and pretended to be backing out.

"Sorry guys, wrong apartment."

Vienna grabbed him by his coattail and said, "Get back here, Rainey Quinn!"

The boys were confused.

Rainey laughed. "When I left this morning, these two were in their farm clothes—jeans and knee boots—and now they have transformed themselves into the true ladies of Avanloch. Boys, may I present your sister, Ava, and the love of my life, Vienna."

Their dad had put his arm around the woman he called Vienna; she smiled and nudged him, and said, "Very funny."

Ava stepped forward and said, "Don't mind those two. They are always fooling around." She extended both her hands to them and then said, "Heck, you're not too old for hugs, are you?"

Mason assured he wasn't by saying, "No, Ma'am."

They hugged and she laughed. "A gentleman just like your dad I see. Morgan?"

He was a little hesitant. He had taken in the whole picture in less than a minute. He was seeing a whole new side of his father—jovial and beaming with happiness. He had an eye for a pretty girl, but Ava and Vienna were exceptionally beautiful. They could be movie stars. It had only taken one look to see his dad in Ava. Her facial expressions were a female version of him; her hair was a darker shade of sand, just like the three of them. Her eyes were the same distinctive deep blue as his father's. He was tense, but he let his newly found sister hug him. She was so warm and free with her affections.

Vienna reached out and said she was delighted to meet them, and motioned for them to join them in the living room. They followed her lead. She and their father sat on one of the sofas and Ava sat between them on the opposite one. There was no awkward silence, as Rainey and Ava kept the conversation rolling, encouraging the boys to speak about their interests, which were mainly sports.

Vienna had already laid out snacks and drinks for them all. "I don't want to spoil your appetites as your dad says we are going to the Spaghetti Factory for dinner. Can someone please tell me why we are going to be eating spaghetti in a factory?"

Mason was only too eager to explain to her the concept of the restaurant. It didn't take him long to fit in that it even had a caboose, which, if one was fortunate enough, one could have her dinner in. The whole place was filled with old things that they would surely find interesting, seeing that they lived in a castle.

The reference wasn't lost on Ava. "So Rainey told you?"

"Yes, Ma'am."

"What's with this ma'am bit, Mason? I dare you to call Mama that."

Mason wondered what she meant. He looked at his dad and Vienna.

"Son, I forgot to mention to you that these two ladies are really ladies. The title comes from the McAllister name, you know, dukes and duchesses, and lords and ladies, and such. Vienna states that she is just an ordinary person despite the title and hates to be called ma'am, which, I am assuming, the girls don't like, either."

"Girls?" Morgan asked. "Are there more?"

"Just one, my sister Rosalyn. We are not related by blood, but that doesn't matter as we are sisters in our hearts. Her dad was Lord McAllister, so she is the true heir. Mama married him to give us parents, so became Lady McAllister. Rosalyn's mother had died before she was even two and she claimed Mama to be her new mother before I was even born. Her dad never got over her mother, Maveryn, and though we didn't know it until just a few days ago, Mama also had a love that she was holding on to, my father and yours. Anyhow, though there was no real marriage, they kept up appearances and each respectively adopted us girls. Jeremy was hardly ever home. Mama is the one who kept it all together, the running of the castle, the farm, and local businesses. She turned Avanloch into a home."

"You give me too much credit, darling. I am sure the boys would rather hear about other things," Vienna stated.

"I think you are too modest, my dear. I'm sure that every word Ava says is true. Can you believe it that these brave souls live among ghosts?" Rainey asked his boys.

Mason was first to respond. "Ghosts? Not really, right, Ava?"

She laughed. "Why, of course. It is a castle after all."

Vienna enlightened them, seeing that their interest had gone up a degree or two. "To be sure, we do have spirits. They are all friendly, though, except for one and we keep her locked up. Our favorite is Maveryn, Rosy's mother. She visits us often and looks after us."

"I don't understand. How can you keep a ghost locked up? Can't they go through walls and doors?" Mason questioned.

Morgan was less inclined to be convinced. "Mase, I think that they are just pulling your leg. Ghosts don't really exist."

"That is just what I thought at first, Morg, but the more I hear, the more I am convinced. The true test will be to encounter one for myself." Rainey smiled.

"It doesn't matter to us whether anyone believes us because we know they are there. To answer your question, though, Mason, I have no idea how we keep the Black Russian from escaping…perhaps she doesn't want to."

Both the boys leaned forward. "The Black Russian?" Mason asked. He was definitely mesmerized.

"I myself have not met her. Mama has had some contact with her. Some of the other household staff swear they have felt her presence. As a matter of record, she was once engaged to Jeremy but was deceiving him, and was pushed to her death by his dead sister. That was witnessed by four people." Ava's account was received with curious stares.

"Ava, quit teasing," her mother said. "You can't just tell them little bits and pieces of the whole sordid story."

Ava's eyes were twinkling. "Why not? I want to keep them interested but not too surprised when they come to visit. You will be coming to visit us, won't you?"

Mason lit up. "Will we, Dad?"

"Of course. Myself, I can hardly wait." Rainey winked at Vienna.

"Good." Ava piqued their curiosity a little more. "We need to have some help in discovering the hidden rooms and finding Liz Beth, the lost soul."

Rainey said a silent thank you to Vienna and Ava for captivating the boys.

"Excuse me, Ava, but did you say there are rooms that you don't know about at Avanloch? How can that be?" Rainey looked at Vienna for confirmation.

"Oh, we know about them, we just can't find them," Ava stated.

"That doesn't sound plausible. How do you know they exist then?"

"Jeremy told us. One cold, snowy evening in December, when I was about ten—that would have made Rosalyn thirteen—he told us about them. Apparently, there are three such rooms. He laughed when he told us about them and said it would give us something fun to do, trying to discover their whereabouts. He said that the third concealed room we would never find and so just to concentrate on the other two. We figured that one room was in his tower quarters, which we were never invited to visit." She looked at the boys and asked them if they had read *Wuthering Heights* or *Jane Eyre*, works by Emily Bronte and Charlotte Bronte, respectively. She answered her own question. "Of course you haven't. I doubt that they are standard reading here in Canada, and they are girls' books."

"Do I count, Ava? I have read them both," Rainey confessed.

"Well, then you know about the brooding Heathcliff and Mr. Rochester…well, Father was of the same breed. He was hardly ever home, and when he was, we saw very little of him. Oh, he was kind to us, but I dare say, he had not a clue as how to care for us or ever considered our feelings."

"Ava," Vienna scolded. "Why are you so down on Jeremy?"

"I'm just explaining things the way they were, Mama. You know perfectly well that we were all a lot happier when he wasn't home!"

"I don't think that this is the right time to be discussing his character, dear."

"You're right, Mama. Sorry. Anyhow, back to the mystery of the unknown rooms. We were given no further information except that they were on the main floor. Rosy and I were quite intrigued at first but lost interest soon after. Every year, about the same time, though, we would take up the quest again for a few days and then give up. We enlisted Amma and Shalla to assist us. They are our dear friends from Avanloch. We would make a game of it, but alas, to no end. I'm sure that we looked behind every book, mirror, or painting in the whole castle and never once found any clue. We would knock on walls and push or pull anything we thought might pop open a door. Nothing. Mama brought us all her old books of the Hardy Boys, Nancy Drew, and Ginny Gordon from Bridge Falls that she had read as a young girl. She said that those young sleuths were always discovering secret passages and rooms, and perhaps, one of their episodes would prove useful to us. I can't tell you how many nights we would read a chapter that described some clandestine space and we would run downstairs, thinking, at long last, that we had solved our dilemma. Of course, we always came up empty. Perhaps you boys will have more luck than we girls did."

"Dad, you should be able to detect a hidden room, shouldn't you? With all of your knowledge of architecture, you could, couldn't you?" Mason asked of his dad.

"To be honest, Son, I have no idea. These fortresses were constructed a long time ago and, I am sure, very discretely. They were meant to be secretive and would not be easy to detect, but it may be a hell of a lot of fun trying to. What do you say to this, Vienna? You have been relatively silent. Perhaps they don't even exist. Is that a possibility?"

Ava answered, "They exist all right. Father gave us another clue on his deathbed."

"Ava, you are just full of interesting little tidbits, aren't you? Are you going to leave us hanging or what?" Rainey asked.

"You tell them, Mama. Tell them the last thing that Jeremy said."

Rainey felt that it was a painful time for Vienna and squeezed her hand, letting her know that he understood.

"It was nothing really. We were all holding hands, as we knew the end was near, when he spoke his last words. They were, 'The plans…girls, find the plans.' Then he whispered something unintelligible, but it sounded like 'Liz Beth.' I'm afraid that is it. Not really any big revelation. No one thought much of it at the time, but weeks after his funeral, the girls started to put two and two together and figured that he had given them one last clue as to the whereabouts of the two secret rooms. But, in reality, he could have meant anything. His sister has no knowledge of any such mysterious hidden spaces and she has no idea where the blueprints to the house are."

Morgan, who had been quiet, spoke up. "Perhaps they are in his secret tower."

"Perhaps. We have searched his rooms but so far have only found several diaries, three are Maveryn's and one is his life and the history of Avanloch. I have not read it, but Rosalyn has and says that unless he wrote in code, she cannot find anything that solves the mystery. I must admit, though, that sometimes, late at night, when I can't sleep, I have had visions of walls opening at a simple touch or even a command. If we are to take him at his word and they do exist, what would it accomplish if we were to discover them?"

"I, for one, Mother, would have my curiosity satisfied. And, who knows? Maybe one room is filled with gold!"

They all laughed with her, then Vienna said, "Yes, and perhaps that gold will come from a little withered man sitting at a spinning wheel. We all remember our fairy tales, right? Do you think that we should get ready to go to dinner before they close that factory down?"

Ava and Vienna got up to go to the bedroom just as the telephone was ringing.

"Get ready, girls. I'll see who is on the phone." Rainey picked up the receiver. "Hello. Nice to talk to you, too, Louise. They are right here. Why are you suddenly concerned for their whereabouts?" He motioned to the boys that their mother was annoyed. "What do you mean you are home? It was all of our understanding that you wouldn't be back until tomorrow night. Hold on, nothing is going on…what are you insinuating?"

The boys looked at one another and then their dad, indicating that she wasn't supposed to be home until tomorrow.

"We are going out to dinner. What do you mean with whom? I don't think I like your attitude. They will be home after. Yes, I am fully aware that it is a school night! Good-bye, Louise." He handed the phone to Morgan and left the room with a disgusted look.

Rainey met Ava at the door and lightly touched her hair. "I like the new color. You didn't do it for me, did you?"

She smiled. "So what if I did?"

Vienna asked who was on the phone and he replied, "The wicked witch."

Jokingly, she said, "Priscilla?"

He picked her up and twirled her around. "No, her sister!"

"Oh my word, there are two of them!"

"Yes, and I hate to say but this one could be more evil. Enough. I haven't had the chance to tell you how gorgeous you look tonight. I love your hair curly and flowing around your angelic face. I have a weakness for you in dresses and this one is exceptionally lovely."

"Thank you, and thank yourself, for you bought it for me."

"I did? I don't recall."

"I see you still have that razor sharp memory! You gave me $200, darling. But if it wasn't you, then I wonder who I bought the lingerie for."

"It better have been for me," he said, kissing her.

"Quit fooling around, Rainey. Help me with my coat."

"Yes, my lady."

After being seated in the restaurant, Ava and Vienna commented on the décor.

"Perhaps we should open up one of these in Waverly, Mama. There certainly are a lot of old and rundown brick buildings in the warehouse district."

"Oh yes, dear, as if we need something else to do."

"Well, it's a thought. We could open up a whole new employment opportunity."

"Pay no intention to her; her mind starts to wander," Vienna teased.

Morgan announced that his mother was home a day early and that had spoiled his and Mason's plans.

Rainey put his drink down and said inquisitively, "And, pray tell, what sort of plans were those?"

Mason answered, "We were going to invite Ava to spend the night at the house so that we could get better acquainted, but that is out the window now."

Rainey had not expected that reaction, especially from Morgan. "That was very thoughtful of you guys. I can guarantee you that there will be many opportunities for you all to get to know each other better."

Ava patted both their hands and said, "Thanks. It would have been fun."

Mason pointed to her ring finger. "I've been meaning to ask you, are you engaged?"

Vienna quickly covered up her left hand with her right. Rainey realized what she did and placed his hand on top of hers.

Ava nonchalantly spoke, as if it meant nothing to her. "Oh that. I was engaged, but I am not anymore. I should have taken it off." And she proceeded to do just that.

Vienna was shocked. "What do you mean, honey? What's happened?"

Ava glanced at her father. "Rainey."

"Did I give you the impression that I didn't like, Randy?" Rainey asked. "It was really none of my business. I don't understand, Ava. What did I have to do with you breaking off your engagement?"

"Everything, Randy has never once looked at me the way you look at Mama. Love shines from your eyes. When she leaves a room, I swear you become anxious, and when she returns, your whole presence lights up. You're always holding hands or touching. Your memories of twenty years ago are so profound. You always give her the benefit of a doubt and are so eager to forgive. I can't settle for anything less than what the two of you have. I realize that your story is somewhat of a fairy tale come true, but I want it for myself. It wasn't going to happen with Randy and that's that. Please don't cry, Mama."

Rainey put his arm around Vienna. "It's all right, babe." To Ava, he said, "Those are, without doubt, the kindest words anyone has ever said about me. Thank you, but I cannot take credit…your mother brings out the best in me."

Ava noticed that the boys were a little uncomfortable with her talking about their father and his love for her mother. "Excuse us. Come on, Mama, let's go powder our noses."

Rainey helped Vienna out of the booth. He gave her a quick peck on the lips. "Don't be too long, girls." He winked at Ava, who smiled and shook her head, eyes reaching for the ceiling.

Once they were gone, Morgan said, "You're not fooling us you know, Dad."

"I beg your pardon?"

"Vienna is wearing a ring also. Did you ask her to marry you?"

Rainey smiled.

"Isn't there a law or rule or something against being married to one woman and engaged to another?" Mason asked.

Rainey burst into laughter. "You have to be kidding. Do you think I care? I would break every rule in the book to be with Vienna. You boys are a little too young to understand what love can do to a man, but I have every hope for you that you will someday. I just pray that you don't have to wait twenty years like I had to."

"Dad, do you think that you should be giving Mom reasons for a fight?"

"Do you think that she is going to sue me, Morg? What for? Alienation of affections? Adultery? What would she have to gain? She can have the house and she already has a large share in the business. Believe me, this won't even see the inside of a courtroom."

"How can you be so sure?"

"I am very sure. You boys don't need to know the hows and whys."

"Have you figured out what happened in 1975, Dad?"

"Yes, it is all starting to make sense to me now. You've given me a heads up, Morg. That bit of info might just come in handy."

Mason said that he knew that a divorce was inevitable but that he didn't want to have to choose sides.

"I would never ask you boys to do that," Rainey replied.

"Mason is just worried who he is going to have to live with, you or Mom."

"No, I'm not! I'm going with you, aren't I, Dad?"

"It's too early to be talking about that boys. Here come the girls. Let's enjoy the rest of the evening. By the way, I am proud of you for the way that you have accepted Ava. It means a lot to me."

"She's really nice, Dad, and Vienna, too. They're not girls."

Rainey laughed as he knew exactly what Mason had meant.

Their dinners arrived and the conversation became light again.

Rainey said to Vienna, "The jig is up, honey. The boys know we are engaged. They were just concerned that maybe we were breaking some rule."

She blushed but said, "Rules? I guess I should tell you all that though I don't knowingly break the law, rules are meant to be broken, and I am sure that I have done my share of that, so one more won't hurt."

Rainey changed the subject. "Ava, finish the story about the lost spirit of Avanloch."

"Oh, that is Mama's story, not mine."

Vienna made a funny face but did not respond.

"Apparently, she is leaving it up to me," Ava said. "One stormy night…funny how it is always storming when something eerie transpires. Keep in mind, I was just a baby so I have no recall of any of this. Anyhow, Mama and her friends were stuck at the castle alone. All the men were at a stag party in the village. They decided to play a game and that game turned out to be with the Ouija board." She asked the boys if they knew what that was and they nodded that they did. "This game was frowned upon by Mrs. D, our cook and eldest member of the household. She called it a witch board and had hidden it high in the back of a shelf in the games room. Anyhow, Amma found it. They had fun with it for a while and then out of the blue, the pointer took control and spelled out 'Liz Beth.' When they got over the shock, they asked her if she was going to talk to them, and she said, 'Yes, help me!' They were interrupted by Mrs. D, who unexpectedly had come home. She did not approve of the use of the Ouija board and was upset with them all. Liz Beth was never heard from again, even during the séances; at least, we think not."

"Vienna, you held séances?" Rainey asked somewhat surprised. "And what do you mean 'you think not,' Ava?"

"We did not make contact with Liz Beth. But we all felt that Maveryn was with us, and soon after, she started making her presence known. End of story."

"Who is Liz Beth?" Mason asked.

Rainey rescued her. "Let's leave that for another day. With all this talk of ghosts and the like, you'll probably have a hard time sleeping."

"Come on, Dad, we're not children!" Morgan emphatically stated.

"Oh really? Ava, I think you have inherited the art of storytelling from your mother. I cannot wait to hear more from both of you. I dare say you have a 1,000 and 1 tales."

"Why do you people over here say 1,000 and 1, why not just 1,000? Is it like 'more than you can shake a stick at'? Why would you be shaking a stick at anything for anyhow, unless it was a dog? You Canadians! Do you know, boys?"

They shook their heads. Rainey and Vienna were amused by her questions, especially Rainey. "Oh, you're one to talk. The Scottish have their own language…like daft and ken and *dinnae* and *bairn*."

"But, Rainey, those are just words in their language. It's much older than yours. The Scottish dialect goes back thousands of years and yours is an adaptation of all the countries that settled in Canada. I guess we all have funny sayings, but sometimes I think that Mama makes up her own."

"I agree with you on that, Ava," Rainey said, and Vienna poked him.

"Do you all drink tea instead of coffee?" Morgan asked.

"Most prefer tea, but coffee is becoming more and more popular among the young. Do you know that high teas are held at Avanloch once a week from spring to autumn?"

Rainey asked who presided at these teas.

"Why, we all do. Whoever is home is the host. Most of the ladies want to see Mama, but she does not always attend." Then Ava continued in her best British accent. "Hallo, this is the Duke of So-so, my wife and I will be in your area. It would delightful if we could take tea with you, Lady McAllister…"

They all enjoyed Ava's accounts of teatime at the castle. Some of the stories, Vienna herself hadn't heard. The boys expressed their dismay that they had to go home, but Rainey didn't want to rile their mother anymore, considering that he was going to ask her to divorce him the next day. Vienna was looking very tired. He offered to take her back to the hotel while he drove the boys home, but she wanted to go with him.

Rainey parked in the sheltered driveway and escorted the boys in. He waited for them to find their mother.

Morgan yelled, "Mom, we're home! Dad wants to talk to you."

He waited patiently for her in the living room.

She entered in her usual hullabaloo. "What is it, Rainey? I was just about to make an overseas call."

As if he cared if he had interrupted her. "This won't take long. I want you here tomorrow. We need to talk. Will 10 A.M. be all right…won't interfere with a golf date or tennis game?"

"You don't have to be so sarcastic. I will try and be up by then."

"Don't you have to get the boys off to school?" Why was he badgering her?

"You know perfectly well that the boys can look after themselves. What's this all about anyhow?"

"It's long overdue." He yelled good-bye to the boys.

Mason came out with him and hugged him. "I had a blast, Dad. Can't wait until tomorrow." Rainey cautioned him with his fingers to his lips. "Don't worry, Dad. You can count on me."

Vienna asked if it went all right with Louise, and he told her that she said she would be home but sounded a tad suspicious. They said good night to Ava at her door and she assured them for the tenth time that she was fine being by herself.

Rainey tucked Vienna into bed. He pushed her hair away from her face and kissed her forehead. "Get some sleep, baby. I love you."

"I don't know why I am so tired, Rainey. I'm sorry."

"For what, you silly goose?"

She smiled and mouthed "I love you" as her eyes closed.

He kissed her fingertips and turned the lamp off. At the bedroom door, he stopped and smiled as he looked at her in his bed, wondering how he had been so lucky as to have her back in his life. He went into the kitchenette and retrieved a key from the back of one of the cupboards. He sat down at his desk and opened a drawer, which housed a hidden compartment. He unlocked it and stared at the contents: a cassette tape and an oversized envelope.

That's what it was all about. He was sure that this information was why Louise had tracked down Vienna's whereabouts. She had needed a bargaining tool so that he wouldn't take the damaging evidence that he had on her father to the authorities. He had never discovered who the traitor was who sent him the incriminating information on his father-in-law. He had known for a long time that Calvin Morgan was a liar and a swindler, but he had never suspected him of bribing elected officials or insider trading. Hell, it appeared that he even had ties to organized crime. Rainey had confronted Louise with the allegations and she denied any knowledge of the accusations, stating that they must have been trumped up. He hadn't believed her for one minute. He made copies of everything in triplicate and stashed them at three different locations, one being right here.

Calvin was not the least bit intimidated to learn that Rainey had somehow uncovered the damaging information. He denied nothing. He hadn't even been curious as to how his son-in-law had come upon the material. According to him, that was the way business was run. How the hell did Rainey think that he got the contract for Centennial Plaza? Did he think that it was simply handed to him, a rookie architect? Calvin had laughed a deep, obnoxious laugh. He had to grease a lot of hands to land that deal for his daughter's husband. Rainey suddenly realized that he had been an unwilling partner in laundering dirty money for the old man. He himself had made some shrewd business deals, but they were never illegal. He threw the incriminating documents at Calvin's feet and never had another thing to do with the man. His loan had been repaid years ago. He only went to the funeral for the boys' sake. They needn't know the ugly facts.

Louise had used her father's private detective to locate Vienna; he was sure of it. She hadn't trusted him to keep her father's illicit dealings to himself. If any of it was ever leaked, the Morgan empire would come crashing down. She had discovered Vienna's existence. She must have found the key to his locked drawer where he kept his few mementos of her. Then she had it affirmed when she had the discussions with Ruth in Hawthorne. He didn't think that she did anything about it at first, but once the allegations about her father were made known to him, she set her plan in motion. That was the sudden reversal of her attending his father's party in 1975; she needed more info. Hell, now that he thought about it, she had even gone to Bridge. He wondered what she had unearthed there. How come she was able to find Vienna when he wasn't?

Obviously, he hadn't tried hard enough. His wife had an agenda and her father's reputation was at stake. She must have figured that he would have done anything to find his old flame, and she was right, he would have. But now, the ball was in his field. Thank you, Morgan.

He glanced toward the bedroom again. He knew he didn't deserve her. How many times had she forgiven him and taken him back after his indiscretions? She knew that he had seen other women after she had told him that she loved him; she just didn't know how many. She took him back. Then there was that ridiculous affair with Priscilla. She forgave him again. He had told her about Zeta and she took that in her stride because, as far as he knew, she had left and was never coming back to him. His marriage was just a natural progression. Thank God he hadn't lied to her when he told her that no woman had ever shared his bed with him here...not even Jorja.

He put his head in his hands and tried to shut her out of his sight. He had told Vienna everything, why didn't he tell her about Jorja? He couldn't because he had said that he had never loved anyone else but her for all of those twenty years. To this day, he still wasn't sure if it had been love or just depraved lust. He was ashamed of what had transpired between them. He had almost lost everything because of her—his family, his business, but most of all, his self-respect and dignity. He shuddered when he thought of the night he had wanted to kill her. So much for self-hypnosis to forget those perverted months of his life. No, that sweet woman sleeping in the other room would never know about Jorja. He would take her name to the grave with him because that was where she belonged...in the ground. Oh, Vienna, if you had only waited for me in 1972, that sordid time would never have taken place. "Oh, dear God, it sounds like I am blaming her!"

Nothing could be further from the truth; he didn't blame her for anything. An ugly thought just came to him: did Louise know about Jorja? It wouldn't surprise him if she did and that she might use it against him someday to destroy his relationship with Vienna. There would be no coming back from that. He would have to see if she would show her hand tomorrow. He needed a positive distraction and went to sit at Vienna's bedside. Sleep was out of the question. Her hands rested on his pillow; her eyes were fluttering. He hoped she was having sweet dreams about him. On one hand was the ring he had given her. Her wrists were so delicate and small. Would the bracelets slide right off? What?

In a flash, he was gone, throwing a shirt on and buttoning it as he ran down three flights of stairs. In his haste, he lost a shoe and had to retrieve it from two steps up. He was pleased to see that Manuel was at the night desk.

"Mr. Quinn, you're up late. Is something wrong, Sir?"

"On the contrary, Manuel. Do you think that I might have access to one of my safety deposit boxes? I know it is late, but I would take it as a personal favor if—"

"Certainly, Sir. No problem."

Rainey followed him into the back room and produced his key to box 1962. He signed the ledger and waited for Manuel to produce the duplicate, and together, they turned their keys. Manuel backed away as Rainey opened the metal receptacle. He pulled out a cardboard package, and from it, he retracted a small rosewood box. He peeked inside and, satisfied, called Manuel back and handed him the second key. At the desk, he slipped a $50 bill toward Manuel.

"What is this for, Sir?"

"For your help, my good man."

"I did nothing but my job, Sir. I cannot accept this."

"Yes, you can. I'm sure you have been tipped many times, especially when you were a limo driver. Here." Rainey fished out another fifty from his wallet. "Take that precious family of yours out to dinner. Will you not share in my good fortune? Upstairs, waiting for me is the girl of my dreams. In this tiny box is a gift I bought for her twenty years ago. She has been lost to me for that long. I was so close to finding her, but it was not to be. She even came to see me here one year but changed her mind. Fate has finally intervened and we are together again. When my Scottish lass sees these, she is going to know that I never forgot her. Will you be part of my happiness, Manuel?"

"Did you say Scotland, Sir? Your lady was from there?" Manuel had formed the words slowly one at a time.

"Yes. Is something wrong?"

"Sure that you are not that Mr. Quinn! No, that would be crazy."

"You know me, Manuel. What do you mean *that* Mr. Quinn?"

"Sir, I think I have done you a great injustice. I think I have, without knowing, kept you from her. Once, many years ago, I drove a beautiful young woman to meet with an old love, but she could not go through with it. Tell me that was not you, Sir, and that you did not try to find the driver who took her there."

Despite Manuel's obvious discomfort, Rainey started to laugh. Finally, he regained his composure. "Well, it has come full circle, hasn't it? You're the Manuel who Vienna told me about. Is she the one who helped you bring your family here from Mexico?"

"Yes, Sir, the lady did, but her name was not Vienna. Perhaps she is not the one."

"Oh, she is the one all right. Her name was Vela McAllister, am I right? And did she give you $10,000 to keep her a secret?"

Manuel hung his head. "I was desperate to bring my family here. I should not have taken her money. It was wrong and I have tried and tried to pay her back, but she keeps sending me more. It goes straight to my bank and they will not reveal to me where it comes from. I know it is somewhere in Scotland because every Christmas, she sends a card, and soon after, another $10,000 shows up in my account. I have not spent another dime, only to use it as collateral for a loan for the house. You will help me to return it to her, Mr. Quinn?"

Rainey was still smiling. "I am guessing that with interest, there is well over $100,000 in your account. It is your money, Manuel. It is what Vienna does. Never in a million years would she take it back." He patted Manuel on the back. "I say it was your lucky day that you drew her from the limo pool, just as it was mine the day I met her. We are two lucky devils! She is going to blow a gasket when she sees you." Still chuckling, he left Manuel with a puzzled look on his face and $100 on the desk in front of him. He took the elevator and let himself into his suite.

"Rainey, is that you?" Vienna asked.

"Yes, darling. I'll be right there." He sauntered into the bedroom, still sporting the same grin. He'd tell her about Manuel later; one thing at a time.

"Where in the world have you been? Rainey Quinn, if you have another damsel in this hotel…if you do, you are in big trouble, Mister."

He sat down on the bed beside her. "You're so funny, my love. I had to retrieve this for you." He passed her the little floral box. She pulled herself up. He placed a pillow behind her and switched on the lamp.

"What's this? And where did you get it at this time of night? It is exquisite. Is it rosewood? Are those iris and forget-me-nots inlaid in the wood?"

"I think so. Open it."

"There's more?" Gently, she undid the delicate clasp to the receptacle that had safeguarded the bracelets for two decades. "Oh my," was all she could say. She slipped them out of their satin protective bed. One by one, she admired them. "Rainey, I don't understand. Where did you get these?"

"I bought them for you twenty years ago. They came from Italy. They were my Christmas present to you. I kept them, hoping that I could give them to you someday. I had almost forgotten about them until tonight."

"Oh, Rainey, you're going to make me cry."

He handed her a tissue. "That wouldn't be anything new now, would it?"

She was running her fingers around the outside and insides of the baubles. "They came from Vienna. I couldn't refuse them. Do you like them?"

"I love them because you bought them. This light is so poor. Do you have a magnifying glass? Does one say yesterday, today, and tomorrow in Spanish?"

Rainey helped her on with her housecoat and she followed him into the living room. He sat her down at his desk and found a magnifying glass for her. She started to examine the first bracelet. "Yes, see? Among the lilies and lotus vines are the words *ayer*, *hoy*, and *manana*. Rainey, do you have something silk?"

"Silk? No, I don't think so. Why?"

"I need something to polish these with. Do you think that you could bring me one of my new silk nighties?"

Rainey returned and asked if the white one would suffice.

"Thank you, darling."

"What are you looking for?"

"I will tell you in a minute. Tell me more about the shop where you purchased these."

"I was leaving for home and I had found gifts for everyone except you, so I made a last-ditch effort into Rome to find the perfect present for you. I had just about given up, as nothing was appealing to me. I decided to take a different route back and, as luck would have it, I became lost. I inquired into several shops for directions, only to find that no one spoke English. Eventually, I found a shopkeeper who understood me. I had been reluctant to enter the shop, as the windows were filthy and the whole building was in disrepair. We started up a conversation, and although he spoke in broken English, I was able to ascertain directions from him. The interior was in much better shape. His name was Xavier but everyone called him Ax. This had been his father's store, but, due to his ill health, could no longer run it, so Ax had left his repair business to take it over. He was in the process of rearranging and cleaning but was open to business, and I was welcome to look around. It didn't take me long to spot the bracelets under a glass in a cabinet. I asked to see them. Ax said that he had found them in storage and hadn't the chance to clean them up, but he took them out for my inspection. I knew at once that I had to have them. They were from Vienna and were made from Austrian silver…was there anything more fitting? I didn't pay much attention as to what else was written on them. I did notice the flowers and doves, however. I bargained with him and he finally let me have them for $700 in American. He let me have the little box for nothing. I think I made a very good deal. What do you think?"

"Rainey, that was a lot of money for a student. How did you manage it?"

"So what if I had to steal, beg, or borrow? I had to have those bracelets for you."

"Thank you. They are very precious, as you bought them for me. I am only sorry that I wasn't home to receive them. Now, I am going to tell you just how precious they are. You will have to use the magnifying glass. I have cleaned them as best as I can. They definitely require professional care." She showed the inside inscription to him on the one that had *aye, hoy*, and *manana* etched on the exterior. It said *Amado*. The second bracelet was imprinted with violets in a faded shade of blue and lavender roses, all cascading out of honeysuckle vines. On the interior, it had the word *Querido*. Doves sitting on olive branches and lily-of-the-valley decorated the last bracelet that she showed him. The inscription read: *Mi muier Kat…Para siempre Anton…Infinidad.*

"What does this all mean, Vienna? Did these belong to someone named Kat?"

"I believe they did and I am sure that they are the real thing. Rainey, you have stumbled upon the Infinity Bracelets that have been lost for over 100 years!"

"I am sure that I have no idea what you are talking about. Please enlighten me."

"While searching for some history on Avanloch in the vast libraries in the castle, I came upon a volume titled *Unsolved Romantic Mysteries through the Ages*. I was somewhat intrigued and started to read some of the stories. The one titled "The Infinity Bracelets" captivated me. It was a very short story and I will make it even shorter. Spain was at war with France again some time in the 1850s and the heir to the Spanish throne had been abducted or killed, no one knew which. In truth, his father had sent him to a monastery in Andorra, in the Pyrenees Mountains. He had been wounded and required rehabilitation. One day while walking along the river, he became faint and collapsed. His name was Anton Christoval; he was twenty-three. Luckily for him, he was discovered by a maiden from the village. Her name was Katarina. I don't remember if her last name was mentioned. She managed to get him to her home, where she cared for him, and they became lovers. She was only sixteen. Before he returned to Spain, they were married. He promised that he would return, but two years came and went and he did not. He had the bracelets made for her and had them delivered by courier so she still knew that he loved her. Correspondence was scarce. He had been betrothed to another when he was just a child. The wedding was to take place in October, and in September, he returned to Andorra only to find that Katarina had been killed two days before. Her body was still lying in her coffin in the church. Her bracelets had been ripped from her arm, the chains leaving their mark on her pale skin. The priest took him aside and said that the child had been spared, but that she had been whisked away by the same soldiers who had slain her mother. Anton vowed to find the child, whom he had not known existed, and to avenge his lover's killers. He did return to marry Castilla, as she was heir to an empire greater than his and he would have unlimited resources to search for his daughter. He had no children with Castilla. Wars broke out again in Europe and all the monarchies were in danger of falling. It was extremely important that he find his daughter, Catalina."

"Why are you stopping? Did he find her?"

"Honey, I don't know. That is how it ended…with him searching for her. I have not had the time to do anymore research, and to tell you the truth, I almost forgot about the tale, and then you give me these marvelous bracelets."

"Well that's a bust! Tell me, how can you be sure they are the real deal?"

"Well, they will have to be authenticated by an expert, but if someone wanted to duplicate them, would he have used this quality of silver? And I am sure that there is some little detail that we have missed that will prove they are the true Infinity Bracelets. As for the Spanish, I know the days mentioned are yesterday, today, and tomorrow. I do not know for sure what the rest of the words mean and I think the flowers are also significant. Ava knows Spanish and she can translate for us tomorrow. Rainey, you have made this one interesting evening. Tomorrow is a big day for you; I hope that you will be able to get some sleep. Can you come to bed now?"

Arm in arm, they went into the bedroom. Vienna folded the blankets back and slid in beside Rainey, who cradled her in his arms.

"You know something, hon," he said. "They remind me of you and me. Star-crossed lovers."

"There is one big difference, Rain. I am still alive and Ava is right down the hall."

"I like to think that Kat didn't die, that it was all a ruse and they lived happily ever after."

"I see you are still the romantic."

"Me? I am not the one who writes poems and songs, and I bet that back in that castle of yours, you own a wardrobe right out of the Victorian age."

"You're right about that, but if I don't start exercising, I won't be able to fit into anything soon. Speaking about gaining weight, would you like to have a baby with me, Rainey?"

He sat straight up. "What…what did you say?"

"You heard me. Don't tell me that you have done something to prevent you from fathering a child."

"The answer is no, but tell me you are not serious."

"Well, apparently, we are not doing anything about not getting pregnant, so I guess we will just have to wait and see."

"Vienna, don't you think we are a little old? We should be thinking about grandchildren, not a baby of our own."

"How old do you think I am anyhow?"

"I know exactly how old you are. I would be worried about you constantly. Didn't you tell me that you had a difficult time with sickness when you were expecting, Ava? And weren't you depressed?"

"That is because you weren't with me…it would be different this time. It could be a magical time for us, Rainey."

He slipped back down beside her. "It is already magical, sweetheart. I might sound selfish, but I don't want to share you more than I have to."

"Umm, we'll talk more another day. Good night, my love."

He mussed up her hair. "Good night, my sweet lady."

Ava arrived in time to have coffee before Rainey left for his confrontation with Louise. Vienna immediately asked her to translate the inscriptions on the bracelets.

"Where in the world did these come from?" She looked inquisitively at her father, who left it up to Vienna to tell the tale, which she did. "You're just full of surprises, aren't you? What else do you have up your sleeve?"

He laughed. "Just tell us what they say; we have been curious all night. Your mother has a faint idea but wanted to wait for you to tell us for sure."

"Okay, this one says yesterday, today, and tomorrow…you knew that right, mama?" Vienna nodded. "*Amado* means beloved. This one with the roses says *Mi Querido*…it translate to sweetheart or darling."

"Oh, I missed the *mi*."

"It is barely visible." Ava read the inscription on the last bracelet. "My love, Kat…Forever, Anton…*Infinidad*, which means infinity or eternal. Who are Kat and Anton, do you know? I think these are very, very old. We should get these chains repaired, Mama, before the bracelets become separated."

"Yes, we will today. I need to try and have them authenticated. I'll tell you the whole story on the way to the jewelers. Are you ready to leave, Rain?"

"Yes. Will you please walk with me to the front door?"

"I'll get dressed while you are gone, Mama."

"I thought you were a big boy," Vienna said. "Do you really need me to walk you to the door?"

"Very funny. I want to show you something—no, I mean someone." Rainey walked Vienna up to the front desk.

"What's going on here, Rain?"

Manuel turned from sorting messages and stared at the woman facing him. It was obvious that she did not recognize him. He wondered if he would have known who she was had Mr. Quinn not told him about her last night. He didn't know what to say.

"Vienna, I would like you to reacquaint yourself with Mr. Demarco. I think you know him better as Manuel." Rainey watched her eyes light up.

"Manuel, is it really you? This is too much! Rainey, where did you find him?"

He laughed. "He has been here under my nose for what, Manuel, three years now?"

"Yes, Sir. Miss Vela, it is so nice to see you. I did not make the connection to the name Quinn until last night. You have been well?"

"Yes, very well. Thank you. And you?" She smiled at Rainey. "This is incredible, another coincidence. What are the odds? Manuel, when does your shift end?"

"In fifteen minutes, Ma'am."

"Please call me, Vienna. Would you join me and my daughter for breakfast? Perhaps your wife would like to come? Rainey has a previous appointment. I would so like to catch up with your life even if we only knew each other for two days. I have thought of you and your kindness to me."

"Miss Vienna, you must to stop sending me money. Today is my wife's day for the library at the school, but I would be honored to meet your daughter."

Rainey said, "Good luck, Manuel. I best be getting a move on." He kissed Vienna and reluctantly left for his overdue meeting with Louise.

Rainey found Louise at the kitchen table, coffee in her hand. She motioned for him to get his own. She was still in her night clothes. She wore flannel pajamas…Vienna wore silk and satin gowns. He sat down opposite her.

"There is no longer postponing the inevitable, Louise. We need to get a divorce."

"And hello to you, too. Now don't beat around the bush, come on, what is it you really want? It can't be as simple as a little divorce?"

"That's it, I want a divorce. It can be amiable or we can do it the hard way, entirely up to you. You already have half the business and you can have the house. Anything else, we can bargain for."

"What else is there? The boys? You've been content to leave things the way they are, why all of a sudden do you want a divorce? Another woman, I suppose."

Rainey said in a snide tone, "Oh, I have been anything but content. The boys are not a bargaining chip. I will do nothing to harm them. I think they are old enough to make their own choices. And, yes, there is another woman. I don't know why we say 'other,' because you haven't been the woman in my life for fifteen years."

"So, who is she? Is she someone I know or one of your little tramps?"

Here it comes. But he refused to take the bait. Instead, he hit her with the truth. "I don't know. Do you know her, Louise? Her name is Vienna LaFontaine."

She turned white but quickly recovered. "I know no one by that name."

"There is no use denying it, Louise. You have known all about her for a very long time. How long did it take you and that shyster detective to find her? And just what were you going to do with the information? Were you thinking of blackmail? Well, the jig is up. I have finally been united with the love of my life and you *will* not stand in my way!"

"You son of a bitch, Rainey Quinn!"

"Don't call me that."

"I'll call you a son of a bitch as much as I want because that is what you are!"

"That's not what I meant."

"What?"

"Never mind. Look, Louise, you don't want me and you surely don't love me, and I don't love you. We haven't had a marriage for a very long time. Why are we prolonging the agony?"

"Why did you marry me? You never loved me, did you? You could never even say you loved me, not even when we were in bed. Do you tell your little trollop that you love her? Well, do you?"

Rainey let the name-calling go unnoticed. "Can we keep this between you and me? Look, we gave it a try and it didn't work, but we did get two great kids out of it. Do you want to do this peacefully or not?" He got up to leave.

"I'll give you a f...in divorce because I don't want to deal with your insults anymore. I don't want you coming around here anymore. You can see the boys same as before, but no more. Is that clear?"

"When have I ever insulted you?"

"Every time you called *her* name in your sleep, every time you told me that I was made out of stone and that I had no idea how a real woman knew how to keep her man satisfied, and every time you accused my father of unspeakable things, and when you walked out on me and the kids. Oh, how I loved explaining that to the neighbors!"

"You never cared what the neighbors thought, but for the rest, I am sorry. I never set out to hurt you. I wondered how you found out about Vienna. Is that when you decided to quiz Ruth about my involvement with her? I could have saved you the trouble if you had discussed it with me."

"Oh sure, easy for you to say now. If you were so enamored with her, why didn't you look for her yourself?"

"I did, before I even met you. I just didn't try as hard as you did, obviously. Whether you believe me or not, my intentions toward you were honorable. I have no excuse for my subconscious, but again, I am sorry. Just a matter of curiosity, how long did it take you and Reeves to find her?"

"A while."

"It was about the time that the info on your father came into my possession, wasn't it, around 1974, '75? Did you need a bargaining chip? You thought that if I went through with the threat to expose your dad, you'd blackmail me with what you knew about Vienna's whereabouts. Is that it? Well, you were right. I would have backed down. But it never came to that because of what it would have done to you and your mother, not to mention the boys. Yet, you chose to keep your information from me. And what about my daughter? You discovered that Morgan and Mason had a sister, but it meant nothing to you. You were just putting another nail in my coffin. You had no intentions of ever telling me anything, did you, Louise?"

"What...what daughter?"

"Don't play innocent with me! Were you ever going to tell me or the boys about Ava?"

"I didn't know for sure. Logan only thought that she might be yours when he saw her. I never knew her name."

"Are you telling me that sleaze ball saw her? When?"

"When he found *your* Vienna in her castle in Scotland. Vienna...where did she get a name like that?" Louise laughed a hard, malicious laugh. "I couldn't even pay her to stay away from you now, could I? She sure as hell didn't need the money! Is that why you are with her now—the same reason you married me—for the money?"

"Yeah sure, Louise, I need the money. Think what you may, but I did not marry you for the money, thank God, as it was all tainted. Look, we are not accomplishing anything here. I have to let it go; you found Vienna and kept it from me. Did you ever have trouble sleeping at nights?"

She didn't answer him.

This time, he was really leaving. "I'll be here with a moving van on Monday to pick up the rest of my stuff. If you want to make sure that I don't take anything that doesn't belong to me, then you had better be here."

"Where are you taking it all to?"

"Bridge Falls."

Her expression was one of spitefulness. "You're moving there? What about the business and the boys? I'll tell you one thing: they are not going with you!"

"I don't intend for them to live with me. The company has already been dealt with."

"Of course not! They would just interfere with your new life!"

"Make up your mind, Louise. Do you want me to take the boys or not? Because I will in a flash. Vienna will be a wonderful mother to them."

"There is no way in hell that that woman will ever be a mother to my children, so just get that out of your head, Mister! You've been blaming me for keeping her a secret…how did she explain her disappearance to you? Aren't you the least bit worried that she will leave you again when something better comes along? She isn't the saint that everyone makes her out to be, is she, sonny boy?"

"Think whatever you need to. If making her the villain eases your conscience, so be it. Now, are you going to call our…your lawyer? Oh, I almost forgot. I need to pick up the bags the boys left for me." Rainey smiled at her and walked toward Mason's and Morgan's rooms.

"You're not taking them to your den of debauchery!"

He shook his head, mocking her, as he returned with the backpacks. "Too late, Louise. They have already been there and they so enjoyed the belly dancers! But for your information, they will be staying with their sister in a separate suite."

"I can't believe that you have exposed them to your lover. Do you not have any self-respect left? It's Morgan's birthday, or have you forgotten?"

"Nope, you pretty much took that away from me. Look, I am sorry that I was such a rotten husband, but you can't deny that I was and am a damn good father. Don't make them choose. You wouldn't like their choice. Yes, I know it is Morgan's birthday."

"You really are the bastard of the century, aren't you? I won't fight you on the divorce, but only on these conditions. You will not sue for custody of the boys and you will destroy all the evidence you have on Daddy."

"Good as done. I'll have the boys back on Sunday. Have a good day."

He heard a coffee cup hit the door as he closed it. He went straight to his office to talk to the company lawyer about representing him in the divorce. Doug Stanton had been a divorce attorney before changing to corporate law. He said nothing could be more malicious than divorce proceedings. Rainey hoped that he would take his case as a favor, and he wasn't wrong. Doug said that he would represent him if it was to be as cut and dried as Rainey promised him that it would be. He made the trip back to his apartment and found Vienna curled up on the sofa. He settled in beside her, reaching for her hand.

"You're just what I need right now. A soft place to lay my head."

She pulled him down to rest alongside of her. "Was it that bad, Rainey?"

"No, not really. We traded insults, but hopefully, the divorce will go through without a hitch. I'm a realist, though, so I trust no one, especially her, and I expect the worst."

"Stop being such a pessimist. You have to believe that there is a rainbow at the end of the tunnel. We deserve it, and if there are complications, then we will deal with them. I told you that I will live with you in sin if I have to…oh, I think I am already doing that. I don't know what Reverend Peters will think of me, but I am willing to take the chance."

"It can't be sin when two people love each other as much as we do, can it? Now, tell me about your day. What did you and Ava find out about the bracelets and how was your reunion with Manuel? Did I tell you that I am going to offer him the job as company chauffer? He will make twice as much money as he does here at the hotel."

"Which question do you want me to answer first?"

He pulled her down and kissed her. "All of them. We don't have much time. I have to pick the boys up soon. Where is Ava?"

"She is resting. What do you have in mind, Sir?"

"I missed you last night."

"I'm sorry. I was so tired and then you surprised me with the bracelets, and then—"

"Shhh."

Two hours later, Rainey had Morgan, Mason, and Ava settled in the suite across the hall. "Shall we order room service or do you want to go out for a quick burger? I am hoping you will be able to amuse yourselves tonight while I take Vienna to a concert."

"I've found a movie theater a few blocks away, and if the boys agree, we can take in a couple of shows." Ava looked at them for conformation and they both nodded.

Morgan said, "Dad, why don't you take Vienna out for dinner before the concert?"

"Are you sure, Son? This is supposed to be your big birthday celebration."

"It is. It's my first birthday with my sister. Tomorrow, we can do something."

The girls were both misty eyed. "Okay you guys, what concert?" Vienna pleaded.

"It's not really a concert, but there will be music. That's all I'm telling you for now. Shall we get dressed?" Rainey winked at Morgan and mouthed, "Thanks, Son."

"How do I know what to wear if I don't know where I am going?" Vienna asked.

"Come on. Let me pick something out for you."

They went into the bedroom, where Rainey pulled a box out from under the bed. He laid it on the table and told her to open it.

"How did you sneak this in here, Mister? What are you up to?" She untied the ribbon and found a silk, coffee-colored blouse and a chocolate-corduroy long skirt. "Rainey?"

"Do you like the outfit?"

"I love it. How did you know my size?"

"Believe me, I know every inch of you. I thought that they would go nicely with the boots that you just bought, and these." He opened the nightstand drawer and produced a string of pearls and earrings.

"Oh, Rainey." She turned so that he could fasten the clasp.

He held his hands up to her neck and a tear slid down her cheek. He felt her body trembling and turned her to face him. He wiped the tears away. "Hey, no crying. Whatever am I going to do with you?"

"Why are you showering me with gifts?"

"I know that anything that I give you can't compare with what you already have, but I want to make up for every birthday and Christmas that I missed with you. Will you let me do that?"

"Yes, but only if you know it is not necessary. I have nothing for you except this." She went over to the dresser and retrieved a little package. She opened it and handed him the Saint Christopher amulet that she had bought him so many years ago.

"Vienna, you had the chain repaired. It has been broken for a very long time, just as I was.

Thank you, darling. And when you say you have nothing for me, that is not true. Didn't you tell me that you wrote me letters? I can hardly wait to read them, but most of all, you have given me my life back by loving me."

She had a very difficult time getting dressed as her tears kept falling and she couldn't put the silk blouse on until they subsided. He told her he wouldn't talk anymore if that would help. She nodded that it would.

Finally, they were ready to take their leave. Ava asked when Rainey was going to have her mother home. He laughed and said, "By midnight."

At dinner, Rainey asked Vienna if she still had the blue turquoise teardrop.

"I always carry it with me and wear it whenever I am feeling blue. It was the only tangible part I had of you. I don't know why I left it home this time. Rosalyn and Ava have been most curious about its origin and I always promised them I would tell them someday. Well, they grew up and quit pestering me, but now, I will have another romantic story to tell them about you and me."

"And the cherry blossom fragrance you wore when you came to my office, you don't wear it anymore?"

"That was the last time. I wasn't even aware that I was wearing it as I always did, but when I got back home to Avanloch, I rid myself of all my cherry essences and have not used them since. I guess I thought that in a way, I was putting you away, too. I can always make more, though, if you like."

"You make your own?"

"It took me a long time to find just the right proportions, but after many unsuccessful tries, I finally came up with a fragrance that was acceptable, but it was nothing like what I experienced the first time we kissed. I have never found an explanation for that."

"Me neither, but there was no mistaking that scent that penetrated the stairwell that day. Do you still believe that we weren't meant to be together then?"

"Yes. If it had been our time, then we would have met on the stairs. All good things come to those who wait, and now our waiting is over."

"Do you ever wonder what the consequences would have been if one of us had died? Some nights, I am haunted by that thought."

"Don't be, Rainey. It didn't happen, so why should we dwell upon despondency?"

They walked the short distance to the nightclub, where Vienna discovered where they were going. The billboard read:

The Paradise Club Presents
Tribute To
Elvis, Buddy Holly, Patsy Cline
and
Marilyn Monroe

"Oh, Rainey, how perfect! This is the best present ever!"

When they returned to the Seven Bays, Vienna insisted on knocking on the kids' door and waking them up. They were not asleep but watching a horror movie, which Ava was only too glad to shut off to hear how her parents evening had gone. How strange to say the word "parents." She wondered if she would ever be able to call Rainey "Father." Not important, as she already had a special place in her heart for him, and listening to her mother describe her amazing surprise only endeared him to her more.

When Vienna and Rainey were settled into bed, she said to him, "Darling, I think it is time that I went home. I have just about had it with the city. First, we have to go to Bridge and finalize the purchase of the Palace. I suppose we will have to make a quick trip to Arizona, but then, I want to take you home. Yes, I need to get home to my family in Scotland and the ghosts of Avanloch.

Will you be able to come with me? After all is taken care of, what would you say about going on an adventure with me?"

"I am free to be with you wherever. I am so looking forward to going to your Avanloch. Every day is an adventure with you, my dear, but what do you have in mind?"

"I never did finish telling you about the bracelets. We went to three different jewelers and one pawnshop. No one knew anything of the Infinity title, but they all confirmed that they are genuine Austrian silver and that they are old. Apparently, there is a date on each of them, which is not visible to the naked eye. It is 1852. That seems to fit in with the story I read. I need to satisfy my curiosity and I fear that the only way I can do that is to travel to the land where Kat's child disappeared. First, I have to do a lot more research and will do that when we are in Scotland. I think I know just the person who may be able to give me some insight into whether the account of the bracelets is true."

"And just who is that, my love?"

"His name is Roberge Farradan. He is the Duke of Hennessey and his ancestry is Spanish."

"And just how do you know this Roberge fellow?"

"He is an acquaintance of Jeremy's, but one thing is for sure, Rainey, you are not going to like him. No, you are not going to like him one single bit."

"Oh really, Vienna?"

"Really, Rainey."

It was Monday. Rainey and Vienna had been together for a week now. They were still discovering and exploring new aspects of their love for one another.

"Are you awake, Vienna?"

"I am now." She opened one eye.

"Are you still tired from Morgan's birthday celebrations? Do you want to go back to sleep? I shouldn't have awakened you."

"No, I don't want to go back to sleep. What's bothering you, Rain?"

"Nothing really. I've been thinking about what you said and I agree. It's time to leave the city and get on with our lives. Let's go tomorrow. I have the lawyer thing today and, hopefully, that will be the end of my so-called marriage. I know there will be a mandatory three- or four-month wait for it to become final, but in all aspects, it will be over."

The phone rang. Rainey answered it. "Hello. Yes, she is right here." He passed the receiver to Vienna, whispering, "I think it's your daughter."

"Good morning, Ava. Did you have a good night's sleep?"

"You have another daughter, Mama, or have you forgotten about me?"

Vienna bolted up in bed. "Rosy, darling, how wonderful to hear your voice. I was going to call you later today. How are you, dear? Rainey, it's Rosy."

"Were you, Mother? I thought that maybe you were too busy with your new life."

"Rosy, I will never be too busy for you. Are you angry with me?"

"Perhaps I am just feeling left out."

"Please don't think that, as it is certainly not true. Are you back at Avanloch? We will be home very soon. I can hardly wait to see you and have you meet, Rainey." She beckoned for him to come closer to her.

"Well, Mother, don't hurry because I am not there."

"Where are you?"

"I'm here."

"I know, dear, but where is here?"

"I'm at the airport in Vancouver, trying to get a cab. Can I come to you?"

"What a silly question. Of course you can. Rainey, Rosalyn is at the airport."

"Tell her to go inside and wait at the main entrance," Rainey said. "I'm sending a car for her. Find out what she is wearing."

Vienna relayed that Rosy was wearing a green slicker and a white tam.

"Mother, I am quite capable of arranging my own transportation," Rosy argued.

"Rainey insists. Don't forget to tell the driver that she has long, red hair! Sit tight and wait. Can you do that, Rosy? Now, will you please stop calling me mother? You really are annoyed with me for some reason. I was so hoping that you would be happy for me."

"Oh, Mama, I am! Can you blame me for being apprehensive? Do you know how many times I had to calm you down after your nightmares of this mysterious man?"

"Darling, they were never nightmares and there is nothing mysterious about him. Nothing was ever his fault. I thought Ava filled you in."

"I need to hear and see it from you."

"You will soon. The driver should be there soon and then you will be with us. Ava is going to be ecstatic that you are here. Once you meet Rainey, all your doubts will dissipate. I can guarantee that. He is definitely not the ordinary, run-of-the-mill man."

Rainey grabbed a doorman's cap from the valet room and retrieved his car from the underground parking. He couldn't believe what he was doing. He made it to the airport in record time as the rush hour traffic was done. He pulled into the taxi zone and found Rosalyn just inside the doors.

"Ms. McAllister?" he said. There was no mistaking her long mane of red hair.

She nodded yes.

He picked up her luggage and popped it into the trunk after he had opened the car door for her. He got in and adjusted the rearview mirror, keeping the cap low on his brow. "Did you have a pleasant trip, Ma'am?"

"No, I did not. What is it with everyone? Do I look like a ma'am to you?"

Oh yeah, she is Vienna's daughter all right, he thought. Aloud, he replied, "Just a term of respect, Ms. McAllister."

She didn't speak for a while, content on looking out the side window. Finally, she said, "Are you Mr. Quinn's personal driver?"

"Sometimes." He felt that she was about to start quizzing him, and he wasn't wrong.

"What can you tell me about him?"

"What would you like to know?" He was smiling mischievously.

"Do you like working for him? Is he a decent employer? He's married, right?"

"Yes to all. He is in the midst of a divorce."

She definitely had the Scottish brogue. She was still staring out the window. "By any chance, have you met my mother, Vela McAllister, or my sister, Ava?"

"Yes, Ma'am…I mean, yes, Miss." He didn't want to provoke her.

"And?" She was fishing for something.

"And what?"

"Nothing."

"If I may take the liberty, they are, without a doubt, the two loveliest ladies that I have ever had the pleasure of meeting."

Rosalyn thought that it was a strange thing for a chauffeur to say. She asked him what his name was. He evaded the question by pointing out some of the city's skyscrapers. He asked her if it was her first trip to Canada.

"No, I have crossed over the pond many times, but it is my first time in Vancouver. May I ask you another question? You may choose not to answer it, seeing as how Mr. Quinn is your employer."

Rainey smiled as he watched her in the mirror. He tipped his hat to her. "Fire away."

"My mother is a very delicate and trusting person. Do you have any idea what his agenda is for her? Is he a charlatan? I must protect her at all costs."

He was finding it hard to keep from breaking out into laughter and confessing to her who he was, but decided to keep playing along. "You need not worry, Ms. McAllister. Mr. Quinn is an honorable man. I know for a fact that he is head-over-heels in love with your mother, the beautiful Vienna."

"He has discussed his love life with you?" Rosy was astonished; he had called her mother Vienna! Why did this man know so much about his employer's personal life?

"If he hadn't, then I wouldn't be able to answer your questions now, would I? I know all about their long separation and that the reunion has given him a new outlook on life and love. You will soon see for yourself."

Rainey pulled up to the curb and was met by Sandy, one of the valets. He looked at Rainey suspiciously and wondered what was up with the sky cap.

"Just helping out." He winked at Sandy and handed him a twenty-dollar bill and his keys. He retrieved Rosalyn's luggage and ushered her into the hotel and the elevator. He knocked on his apartment door and was let in by Ava.

One look at him and she started laughing at the same time as she was hugging her sister.

Vienna came out from the bedroom to greet her daughter. "Oh, darling, I am so happy to see you. Rainey, where did you disappear to and what's with that silly hat?" She noticed that Rosy was looking at him with darts in her eyes. "Oh, Rainey, you didn't?" And she broke out in laughter, too.

Ava said, "Rosy, I see you have already met my father, Rainey Quinn."

He removed his cap and did a little bow. "Pleased to meet you again, Ms. McAllister."

Rosalyn saw the resemblance to her sister immediately, but was not amused.

"I'm sorry I deceived you, Rosalyn," Rainey said. "There wasn't time to find a suitable driver. Please don't be angry with me. I meant no harm."

Lord, he is handsome! Rosalyn thought. She watched as he embraced her mother. She had never seen her mother in a man's arms before. Their eyes were smiling. She wasn't going to let Mr. Rainey Quinn off the hook, however. "Well, Sir, you have not made a very good first impression on me! What was the reason you didn't identify yourself to me? Your little game has done nothing to assure me that you are the man Ava says you are." They were all watching her and smiling at her as if she were a child.

Ava looped her arm through her sister's. "Loosen up, Rosy. He was just being Rainey. What's the harm in a little intrigue? I have already given him the third degree, and believe me, he has an answer for everything. Come sit down, we have your favorite tea."

Vienna brought a cup of coffee over to Rainey, who was sitting on one of the sofas across from Rosalyn. "Your sister and I are going to go down and reserve your rooms for another two nights. Can I trust that you are going to play nice? I think a few minutes alone will be good for both of you."

Rainey reached into his pocket, took a credit card out, and handed it to Vienna.

"I think that I can pay for my own room," Rosy stated emphatically.

"It's my room, too, but its Rainey's hotel and he gets a special rate, so don't quibble," Ava told her sister.

Vienna kissed Rosy and winked at Rainey as they left. She said to her daughter, "Don't be too hard on him, honey. He's had a hard life."

As soon as the door closed, Rosy asked Rainey what her mother meant.

"I think that it was her way of saying that I have lived in my own personal hell for twenty years. I have been in love with her for a very long time, and no matter how hard she tries to take the blame for us being apart, I am just as much to blame...perhaps even more."

Rosy picked up her cup of tea and sat back on the sofa. Rainey had seated himself in the identical sofa across from her, the coffee table separating them. He hadn't taken his eyes off her, but she wasn't going to be intimidated by the man who had the same hypnotizing, deep baby blues as her sister's.

"You own this hotel?" she asked. "How long have you lived here?"

"No, that isn't what she meant. I have some privileges. I have lived here a long time—almost ten years—ever since your mother came to see me."

Rosy was astonished to learn that her mother had visited him that long ago. "Mama came to see you? When was this?"

"Let me clarify that. She came to my offices and saw me, but she never let me see her. It's best if she relay the story to you herself."

"I don't understand, but I will coax it out of her."

"You don't have to coax, Rosalyn. Your mother is not keeping secrets anymore."

"And what about you, do you have secrets also? Like why didn't you divorce your wife before Mama came back into the picture? Is your wife suing you for infidelity? Does she know about you and Mama?"

"She knows. No, she is not contesting the divorce. She is not suing."

"Does 'she' have a name? And why is she not contesting the divorce? Do you have something on her?"

"Her name is Louise. Our marriage was over almost before it began. I should never have married her when I was still in love with your mother. It wasn't fair to Louise, but she went into the union with her eyes wide open. Vienna had left me and I needed to try and make a life for myself, never knowing if I was ever going to see her again. Luckily, I have the boys and they have been my saving grace, just as you and Ava have been for Vienna."

"What are your intentions towards Mama?"

"We are going to be married just as soon as possible."

"Are you planning on living here? Because I can't see Mama living in the city."

Rainey leaned forward and took one of Rosy's hands. "Rosalyn, I know that you are afraid I am going to run off with your mother, but we are not teenagers. We have children whom we love very much, and we want to incorporate our families together. We are buying Lily and Joe's house in Bridge Falls because we both love it and we have friends and family there. Then we are going to Avanloch. Will I be welcome there, Rosalyn?"

"I'm not there very much anymore and it is not my house. It is Mama's."

"I think that it belongs to all of you. Just so that you know, I will not be separated from your mother again. I have spent half a lifetime without her and nothing can keep us apart. We have already made that vow to each other."

"Not even me?"

"That's right, Rosalyn, not even you. But why would you want to? Your mother is happy and we have both come to terms with the past. Another thing, I do not need your mother's money. I would live with her in an igloo or a grass hut…it wouldn't matter as long as we were together. I would like your blessing, and in time, you will give it."

"How can you be so sure about that?"

"Because you are your mother's daughter and I am irresistible." He winked at her just as Ava and Vienna entered the room.

She found herself already submitting to his charms.

They had brought lunch with them from the delicatessen. Rosy said she had wondered what took them so long. After they had eaten, Rainey walked Vienna to her hair appointment. She asked him how it had gone with the redhead.

He laughed and said, "About what you would expect. She only has your best interests at heart, so I played it straight with her and I am pretty sure she knows that I am serious about my love for you. She was not at all impressed with my chauffeur act."

Vienna laughed.

Rosalyn had more questions for Rainey when he returned. "Who are your family in Bridge Falls?"

"My parents live in Hawthorne, which is a short few miles away, and of course, my cousin Lara is in Bridge."

She was surprised to hear that he and Lara were related. "Lara is your cousin? Why didn't she tell you where Mama was? Obviously, she knew about your affair."

Rainey smiled at the mention of the word affair. "I can assure you that our relationship was much more than a cheap affair."

"I didn't mean to insinuate that it was 'cheap.'"

"I'm sure you didn't. We didn't have an affair; it was a romance that endured a twenty-year separation. It has been heart wrenching for both of us, but we have forgiven each other. The truth of the matter is that my arrogance caused us two decades. I should never have believed your grandparents when they said she had run off with Jack. I guess I didn't have enough gumption to keep looking for her after my disappointment in Wales. Anyhow, I suppose I was still afraid that she had run off with Jack and didn't love me anymore. Perhaps I couldn't face the fact that she chose another man over me."

"Jack? Who is Jack? Surely, you don't mean Mama's friend from Bridge Falls? And what is this about Wales?"

"Yes. Do you know him, Rosy?"

Ava answered for her sister. "Yes, we both do. I'll fill you in about Wales later, Rosy."

"He lives in Bridge?" All of a sudden Rainey felt ill.

"No, but he still has family there. He is usually home when we are there. Papa Joe told you that they had run off together? Why?"

"He didn't want me looking for Vienna and she didn't want me to find her."

Rosy said, "Did they have a relationship? I thought they were just friends? Though at times, I did think his interest in Mama was more than just platonic."

Rainey turned to Ava and asked her how she perceived the relationship.

"There was no relationship," she replied. "They are merely friends. I don't think we should be discussing Mama's affairs."

"So you do know they had an affair?" Rainey got up and was pacing around the small room. "Does she still see him?"

Ava saw that she had upset her father and was quick to reply. "I didn't mean 'affair' as you are insinuating, Rainey. If you have questions, then you should be asking them of Mama. Why would it matter if they were friends? It's no different than her being friends with Jimmy, is it?"

"She never dated Jimmy."

"Rainey, if anything happened, it was years ago. But I would be willing to bet that nothing ever happened between them."

"He was, and maybe still is, in love with her. Did you know that?"

"No, and how do you know that? Surely, you are not resentful of yesterdays?"

"Lara told me. And you bet I am jealous, especially if she has been seeing him for all of these years. And while we are on the subject, do either of you know a Roberge?"

"Roberge Farradan? How could you know him?" Rosy asked.

"He's another friend of your mother's, isn't he?"

Ava was aghast at what Rainey was inferring. "What's got into you, Rainey? You need to get your facts straight! Mr. Farradan was a friend of Jeremy's and Mama only saw him at social functions. She did have a life you know. You're a little off-kilter today. Is it because of the meeting with the lawyers? You're the only man in Mama's life that I am aware of. If other men cared for her, I know nothing about that. Rosy?"

"Nor I. Perhaps you should stop worrying about the past and live for today."

"You are so right," Rainey replied. "Sorry, girls. I am still not very secure where your mother is concerned. I guess it is time I took my leave. Are you going to wait here for, Vienna?"

"No, let's go get you settled across the hall, Rosy," Ava said.

Rainey picked up her luggage and walked them to their room. He kissed Ava on the forehead and said to Rosalyn, "There's a lot more of those where that came from."

"Is he always so affectionate?" Rosy asked her sister after Rainey left. "Why in the world do you have such a big suite? Were you expecting me? Is that why there are two bedrooms?"

"I had a regular hotel room but Morgan and Mason wanted to stay with us on the weekend, so Rainey managed to acquire these rooms. And, yes, he is always that affectionate. What do you think?"

"That is hardly a fair question. I have only known him for half an hour, unless you want to count that drive from the airport."

"I wish I had been a fly on the window…that must have been some ride! Did 'the driver' give you any insight as to what Rainey was like?"

"Very funny. I think he built himself up sufficiently. I had thought that it was very strange that Mr. Quinn would have discussed his love life with his chauffeur. But you have had much more time to observe him and I can see that you are thoroughly hypnotized by his charms. My only concern is for Mama.

What is going to happen after the novelty wears off? I think he is quite the ladies' man and can't help but think that he has a wandering eye."

"You will soon see, my dear sister, that their feelings for each other are real. Once you observe them together, you will know exactly what I am talking about. They have to be touching all the time, and when one leaves the room, the other follows with his/her eyes. Rainey is worse than Mama; he doesn't want her out of his sight. When we went shopping last week, he insisted that she phone him every hour to tell him where she was. He seems to think that she is going to vanish into thin air. In a way, I can't blame him for worrying that she may disappear again like she did twenty years ago. If I had any doubt about his feelings toward Mama, it was all wiped away when his friends came for dinner in Bridge. Jimmy made it perfectly clear that he could not watch his best friend disintegrate again, so they had better damn well be playing for keeps this time. It was a very emotional evening, especially for Rainey. He discovered that the man he had been talking with when he went to Wales to search for Mama was your grandfather."

"What are you saying, Ava? Have you got bats in the belfry?"

"Mama had told him that she was of Gypsy heritage. She got that notion from Maveryn of course. To her, it was romantic, and she also had told them that Aunt Jannie lived in Wales. His search led him to Papa Louis. He hadn't met Mama yet, and when he finally did, he was almost blind and wouldn't have recognized her anyhow, as she looked completely different from the picture Rainey had of her, and her name was Vela."

"Is this what you meant when you said you would explain about Wales?"

"Yes. Anyhow, your grandfather told Rainey all about you and Maveryn, so he has always known about you, just not that you were connected to Mama. When he figured it out at the dinner, he kind of fell to pieces, knowing that he had been that close to Mama."

Rosy sat down. "This is so strange. How did Rainey come to find Papa Louis?"

Ava filled her in as best she could. "And that is not all. There are other incidents that are just as peculiar."

When Ava was done, she summed it all up to providence, just as her mother had.

"Do you think that all of those stories Mama told us were of her and Rainey?" Rosy asked.

"Are you kidding? Who do you think Emerald and Laddy are? Mama used their middle names to portray her characters."

"I thought that Mama's middle name was Lane, just like yours."

"It isn't. It appears that is just one more thing that we didn't know about our mother."

"So Emerald and Laddy is not a fairy tale. This entire time, Mama was telling us the story of her and Rainey…a true-to-life love story."

"Yup."

There was a knock on the door and Ava opened it to find her mother standing there.

"Is Rosy all settled in? Good, let's go and make a pot of tea."

They both commented on how nice she looked as they walked across the hall to Rainey's suite. Vienna asked if everything went well while she was away, and they told her that it had.

"Rosy, I was a little worried leaving you alone with Rainey but was sure that Ava would keep the peace."

"We all came out unscathed, Mama. I can see by the way he talks about you that he loves you very much and has no plans to leave you. That is all that I was worried about."

"Thank you, dear. You will come to love him. You won't be able to help it."

"That's what he said. I'll put the kettle on."

"Good. I want to change before Rainey gets back with the boys."

The girls went into the little kitchenette just as there was a rapping on the door.

"Now, who could that be?" Ava looked through the peephole to see a woman standing there. She looked harmless so Ava opened the door and said. "Hello."

"Well, so you're the bastard child of my husband!" the woman shrieked.

Rosalyn was there immediately. "What did you call my sister, lady?"

Vienna came bounding out of the bedroom, having heard the accusation, to stand between her two girls.

"And you must be the prima donna who has been seducing my husband. You want him? Well, you can have him." She picked up a binder and threw it into the apartment. "And you can have all of his dirty laundry, too. You have no idea what kind of a man you are involved with…secrets, he has enough to write a book!"

Rosalyn had stepped toward her but Vienna gently pulled her back. "Louise, why did you come here? You are only embarrassing yourself. Rainey is no longer your husband and you have nothing to gain by trying to insult us."

The elevator door had opened down the hall and Rainey emerged with Morgan and Mason. He saw Louise at his door, and he ran down and grabbed hold of her. "What the hell are you doing here, Louise?" His anger at her was most frightening.

Vienna tried to pull him aside. "She said what she came to say and she is leaving, Rainey. Let it go."

"She doesn't get off that easy—not until she apologizes to Ava!" Rosalyn avowed.

The boys had joined their father and were quite alarmed to see their mother confronting Vienna and Ava.

"What have you said to Ava, mother?" Morgan demanded.

Rosalyn answered with malice. "She called *our* sister the bastard child of your father!"

Before Rainey could say a word, the boys took hold of their mother and Morgan demanded that she apologize immediately.

Ava was protesting. "It's okay everyone. I've been called worse. I have a thick hide."

"This is unacceptable, Louise," Rainey said. "I've always known you were a poor sport, but accusing a young girl of something that was not of her doing is even beneath you. Just because you lost today doesn't give you the right to come here and attack them with your unladylike insults. Apologize to Ava, *now!*"

"When they raise the *Titanic*!" Louise shouted.

"Mother, I am so ashamed of you right now. Ava, I apologize for her. Obviously, she has no intention of doing so." Morgan started to usher her down the hall, but not before Vienna retrieved the satchel Louise had thrown at her.

"Don't forget *your* dirty laundry," she said. "Rainey and I have no secrets. Don't ever come near my daughters again." She took Rainey's hand and told the boys to see their mother to the elevator. She closed the door before Louise could utter another word.

Even through the closed door, they heard her uttering, "You'll be sorry, Rainey Quinn. Just wait and see!"

"You certainly didn't need me, did you? I see the McAllister women can handle themselves. I'm sorry. I had no idea that she would show up here. I'm completely baffled." Rainey pulled them altogether for a group hug. "What was in that case?"

"We'll never know, will we, darling? I take it things didn't go well for her today?"

"Everything went according to plan, until she tried for full custody of the boys. I protested vehemently and asked her if she had forgotten our deal. Yes, girls, I had an ace up my sleeve and I would have used it if I had to. Fortunately, her lawyer talked some sense into her and we agreed on joint custody. The boys will be with me—with us—six months of the year, however is convenient for them. Is that all right with everyone?"

"I should say it is," said Vienna. "Rainey, you had better check on the boys."

"Right." He met them at the door and they immediately went up to the girls and apologized profusely for their mother's rude behavior.

Ava formally introduced them to Rosalyn, who encouraged them to come and sit down on the sofa next to them. "There is no need for apology. None of us are responsible for another's actions. You must not be too hard on your mother, for she has lost her family as she once knew it."

Morgan said, "Thank you for your understanding, but we haven't been a family for a very long time, and that still doesn't give her an excuse to berate any of you."

Rainey squeezed in between his two sons. "You're right, Morgan, it doesn't. I am mortified to think that I was ever married to such a cruel person."

"Does that mean that you are divorced, Dad?" Mason asked.

"Not quite, Son. There is a short waiting period, but it is all but done."

Morgan spoke for himself and his brother. "We are happy for you, Dad. But what does this mean for us?"

"It means that you can live with me for six months of the year, however it works for you. In a few years, you will both be old enough to do as you please anyhow. You do understand that to be with me is to be with Vienna, Ava, and Rosalyn, don't you?"

"We were hoping you would say that. Do they want us?" Mason asked shyly.

Ava got up and mussed up his hair, laughing, and said, "Are we ever going to have fun with you two! Are you sure you can handle two sisters?" She winked at Rosalyn.

"Oh yes, we have always wanted brothers to boss around. Ava and I are away a lot, so I hope you will be up to the task of keeping the ghosts at bay when we are not there."

"You can't intimidate them, Rosy. They know all about Avanloch and the goings-on there. They are going to help us find the hidden rooms," Ava told her sister.

"What do we call you, Rosy or Rosalyn?" Mason wanted to know.

"Either; doesn't matter." She turned to Rainey and asked if he would tell them a little bit about Vienna when she was young. Vienna had left to make a phone call.

"It would be a pleasure. First, you must remember that I did not meet her until she was sixteen. She and her family had just moved to Bridge Falls the winter before. Your mother enchanted me from the very first minute I met her. Everyone called her V, as you well know, but she allowed me to call her Vienna. Do you know about the Gypsy fortune-teller?" They shook their heads no. "I'll let her tell you about those predictions herself."

"What do you mean that she enchanted you?" Ava asked.

"To this day, I do not know if she put a spell on me or what."

"What?" Rosy exclaimed. "Are you suggesting that she is a witch and can—?"

"Hold on, Rosy," said Rainey. "You asked me and now I am telling you how it was. Of course, I didn't think of her as a witch...more like a mischievous pixie or imp, as I so often refer to her. She would charm me with her knowledge and her wisdom. She was young but oh so wise. I have never been what one would call a romantic, but I even recite poetry when I am with her and am not even aware that I am doing so. Yes, she definitely can hypnotize me. I use to refer to her as my teenage queen of the hop honky tonk angel."

"Did Mama like to dance?" Ava inquired.

"Very much so and I liked to dance with only her."

"She doesn't like to anymore. She says she hates to have men's arms around her."

Rainey smiled. "That is the best thing I have heard. Obviously, she doesn't mind mine. We dance every night and that is one of the first things she asked of me...if I would dance with her."

The girls sat back and made room for Vienna, who had rejoined them.

"Were you talking about me?" she asked.

"Rainey was just telling us about you at sixteen," Ava confessed.

"Ummm. I just talked to Amma. She said that Uncle John has been trying to track me down; she didn't know why but she got the feeling that something had or was about to happen. Everyone is well, though, and there have been no strange goings-on at Avanloch. I am sure it's about the business, but it will have to wait until we get home."

"Odd," Rosalyn said. "All was well when I was home, but speaking of strange...I think that Ash is off her rocker. She and Uncle John's son, Grayson, seem to have something going on."

"What does that mean? Are they feuding?" Ava asked.

"No, just the opposite. Apparently, they were an item when they were young, but they had a horrendous fight and Grayson ended up going to London and marrying someone else. Did you know about that, Mama?"

"No, but of course, he and Chandler were both gone even when I first came to Scotland. Are you insinuating that Ash and Gray are romantically involved? That would be absurd."

"There is nothing to insinuate. It is obvious for everyone to see. They are always sneaking off somewhere together. Do you think we could have been wrong about her? I have seen her and Gray together, and though they don't act quite as lovesick as you and Rainey, they are coming in a close second." Rosy looked at Rainey and smirked, and he acknowledged her observance with a wink. "She blushes when he talks to her, her voice has softened...does that sound like Ash?"

"What happened to Steff?" Ava asked.

"Haven't the foggiest. Perhaps this is what John wants to talk to you about, Mama."

"Possibly. It is an oddity. We will have to wait and see. Maybe I will be able to get a hold of John later this evening."

Rosy apologized to Rainey and the boys, saying that she was sorry to be talking about things that they knew nothing about.

"That is quite all right," Rainey replied. "I want to know everything about your family. Your mother has told me a little about the history, but I am sure it will take quite a while to adjust to the fact that Avanloch is a castle and the many goings-on there. Now, I think I should inform all of you of our plans. The day after tomorrow, we are going to leave for Bridge and do all of the paperwork regarding the purchase of the house, and then we will fly to Arizona to visit with Lily and Joe for a few days. How does that fit into you girls' plans?"

"I want to go to Bridge with you and visit with your parents again, Rainey," Ava said.

"I may as well go, too, then," Rosy agreed.

"Can we come, too, Dad?" Mason pleaded. "It will only mean three days of missed school. We can come back by bus when you go to Arizona."

Rainey asked Morgan if he wanted to come along, and he said yes. "What do you think, Vienna? Should we let them skip school?"

"As my first official act as an 'almost stepmother,' I say definitely."

Ava said, "Mother, please don't use that word 'stepmother,' as that would make Rosy and me the ugly stepsisters!"

Everyone laughed and Vienna, said, "Hardly, my dear. I am overwhelmed at your acceptance of me and the girls, Mason and Morgan, and I will look forward to your visits to Avanloch. I can assure you that you will love it just as much as we do."

Mason spoke to all. "Promise us that you will leave some of the discovering of the secret rooms for Morgan and me. We will be coming over in March, won't we, Dad?"

"Yes, you will be, Son." He put his arm around Vienna. "Thank you, darling, for bringing us all together. I am looking forward to starting a new life with you at Avanloch."

"Our adventures have only begun." The tears flowed shamelessly from Vienna's eyes.

Chapter Twenty-Three

Avanloch

Rainey, Rosalyn, Ava, and I were waiting in the holding area for passengers at the airport in Tucson, Arizona. We would be flying to Halifax, Nova Scotia, and then on to Edinburgh, Scotland, where we would be taking the train to Waverly and, finally, our journey would end at Avanloch. The girls had wandered down to the coffee kiosk and Rainey and I were alone. It had taken us twenty years to arrive at this point in time. I put my head on his shoulder and closed my eyes and sighed.

"What's the matter, sweetheart?" he asked.

"Nothing. I hate waiting and I hate flying."

"Oh really, Vienna? How do you manage to do it so often then?"

"I have the help of a little white pill, which I haven't taken yet. I thought that having you with me would relax me and I wouldn't need to take it."

"I don't seem to be helping, do I? Do you remember the night we were driving home from Hawthorne and there was a full moon rising over Mocking Mountain? You said that maybe you would become a stewardess and be flying close to the moon one day, and I said that if my architect dream didn't pan out, I would like to become a pilot and then someday we could be sailing by the moon together. Do you remember?"

"Yes, I do, and if we ever get on the plane tonight, it could become a reality. I've lived our past over and over a thousand times, Rainey, and it all leads up to that fateful day that I chose to run away to Scotland. It has been my wildest dream that someday, you would be joining me, and now it is happening and all my foolish actions are being laid to rest."

He took my hand and told me that he was pleased to see that I had chosen to wear the Infinity Bracelets, as they were a token of his love. He said, "I am almost convinced that this is a reality, but then I close my eyes and see myself back in my pathetic world without you. I can't seem to shake the feeling off that you are going to leave me again."

"How can you say that after everything we have been through in the past two weeks? Do you doubt my love and commitment to you?"

"No, I know you love me. Perhaps I will be able to vanquish these negative thoughts when we are safe at Avanloch."

"You will, darling. I promise."

He kissed my forehead, as he so often did. The announcement rang out that our flight was now ready for boarding. Finally, we were on our way. Ava and Rosalyn had the seats behind us and kept us amused with their banter until they both drifted off. I pretended to sleep so that Rainey would relax and close his eyes. There was much left to discover and explore at Avanloch. I had not ventured into the labyrinths of the concealed stairways, and the three secret and mysterious rooms had not been found. How could I have lived at the castle for so long and not know any of this? The only answer I had was that I was preoccupied with raising the girls and perhaps I was afraid of the unknown. It would be different now with Rainey. We would investigate together. I wondered if his permanent presence was going to make a difference to the spirits, just as I had surely done. There hadn't been much action from the netherworld until I arrived on the premises. Were there any surprises waiting for us? I hoped they would all be pleasant ones.

We landed in Edinburgh and I exclaimed, "We're here, we're here!" I jumped out of my seat, forgetting that I was still attached to the seat belt. "Drats!" I unhooked and stood up, saying to Rainey, "Let's go, let's go."

He grabbed hold of me and pulled me onto his lap. "Did the captain say you could unfasten?"

"I don't care. Let go of me, Rainey."

"I don't think so. Why are you so damn impatient?"

I heard Rosy chuckling to Ava. "Isn't it about time that there is someone who can control Mama? Lord knows we had no luck."

Rainey was grinning from ear to ear.

I said, "Very funny, girls. Now get up and go hire us a cab to the coach station."

"Yes, Ma'am!" Rosy saluted me and Ava asked Rainey if he would be all right alone with me. He assured her he would be.

"Do you see what I have to put up with, Rainey? They are two cheeky girls."

"Yes, dear, and you wouldn't want them any other way. Now, do you want to get off this plane or what, or would you rather just sit on my lap all day?"

"I think you know the answer to that, Mister, but let's go anyhow."

Twenty minutes later, we were settled on the train. Rosy and Ava had already gone to the dining coach to see if any of their friends were on board. I opened my purse and took out a little tin container that I kept my hair accessories in. I passed it to Rainey and asked him to pass me the bobby pins one by one as I put my hair up.

"Oh, I see," he remarked. "Now that you are back in Scotland, you want to look as prim and proper as an eighteenth-century schoolmarm. You don't want anyone to see you as the wild and wanton woman that I know." He was grinning again. "Putting your hair up isn't going to make you any less sexy you know."

"Stop teasing me, Rainey! You are making me sound immoral!"

Now he was out and outright laughing. "Oh, darling, you are the most moral person I know. Did you not deny yourself my love for a very, very long time because I was married, and in fact, still am?"

"Well then, I guess I will have to put you in separate quarters at Avanloch because we can't have the staff thinking that I have suddenly lost all my principles." I smirked.

"Well, you can certainly try, but I honestly don't think that you'll succeed, my love."

I agreed with a smile and, as I was so accustomed to doing, laid my head on his shoulder. He was reading a Scottish newspaper when the girls returned and sat down opposite to us. They were disappointed that none of their college colleagues were on board. Rainey talked to them about their studies and future plans. He was not at all surprised to learn that they didn't plan on venturing too far from home. Ava was going to keep up with her illustrative designing and Rosy would stay working at McAllister Shipping while she earned her degree in corporate law.

"We never want to be too far from Mama and Avanloch," Ava confessed. "But if this thing with you and her works out, we won't be so worried to leave her, will we, Rosy?"

"Oh, you think your mother and I have a *thing* going on, do you? Do you really think that a twenty-year passion for each other is going to end any time soon?" Rainey asked.

I smiled and said, "Not if I have anything to say about it."

Winston was waiting for us at the depot in Waverly. I introduced him to Rainey as the two of them were loading our bags into the trunk. He protested that Rainey need not help him, but that was not the way Rainey rolled and he might as well discover that now than later. Winston was our new chauffeur, as Henry had retired several weeks earlier but was still going to remain a welcome presence in our lives. He had taught me to drive and jockeyed the girls around to all of their events for many years. I asked Winston how the retirement party went and he said they had postponed it until I and the girls returned. We were delighted to hear that the party was scheduled for tonight. I thought that he was a little overdressed but did not comment on it, as maybe the formal attire had something to do with the evening festivities.

As we entered Domne, I informed Rainey that the locals did not like the name so the little hamlet was always referred to as the Village. I saw his eyes light up as he caught his first glimpse of Avanloch. We had no sooner passed through the open gates when he asked Winston to stop the car. He reached for my hand and said, "Thank you, Winston. We will walk from here."

"Very well, Sir. The girls and I will continue on."

I knew the architect in Rainey was on full alert. He was a little kid again and I knew it was going to be so much fun watching him discover the wonders of the castle. We walked slowly up the drive and I answered all his questions while pointing out Brackenshire Manor, the stables, barns, and kennels. I pointed the way to the gardens and Willowisp Manor, saying that it was unoccupied, as Amma, Johnny, and family had recently moved into Brackenshire. The carriage house above the garages was where our new groom and caretaker made his home. I did not show him the path to the mausoleum, as I didn't want to think about Maveryn, although I did wonder if she had made an appearance in our absence. Rainey marveled at the way the girls and I talked about her presence, as if there was nothing unusual about it at all. But then, he only believed in tangible facts. He had never witnessed an apparition, but his day was coming.

He asked me what was covered in the middle of the roundabout. I told him that it was a fountain with dozens of dancing fairies, all paying homage to their Queen Loralie. I could tell that he wasn't in any hurry to enter the castle. He was quite content to gaze upon the exterior and marvel at the craftsmanship of the masons' works from another century. I coaxed him into ascending the steps and introduced him to Rosalyn's stone lions, Zeus and Zoar. He asked me where she got the name Zoar from, and I told him what I told everybody. "I have no idea and neither does she."

As I reached for the oversized brass knockers, the two huge doors opened before us. There stood Winston, still in his fine attire, and behind him, straddling the great staircase, was my Avanloch family, although they were hardly recognizable as such. I took one look and burst out laughing, finding my way to the nearest chair. I covered my mouth, as I could not control my hilarity. Rainey looked at me as if I had lost my marbles. Finally, I recovered enough to present him to the strangely attired people in front of us.

"Rainey Quinn, please allow me to present my family to you. You have already met Winston and I am sure you wondered why he was dressed so formally. Well, believe me, I wondered the same thing." I walked over to Amma, who was trying not to laugh. She was wearing a stiff brown skirt and blouse, and a dark shawl hung around her shoulders. Her hair was knotted on top of her head and an enormous pair of spectacles sat on her nose. "This is my dear friend and confidant, Amma." We hugged and I whispered to her, "This is all your doing, isn't it?"

She said that she loved me, too.

Rainey reached for her hand but she hugged him instead, and told him how delighted she was to finally meet him. He replied in kind.

Next in line were the French maids, Shalla, Cyn, Emma, and Millie. They looked very sassy in their short, black and white costumes. They had black web stockings on and little white caps donned their heads. They each, in turn, performed a diminutive curtsey for us. I was very amused with their performance. Rainey had caught on to the ruse and winked at each of them, showing that he appreciated the charade.

Duffy's suit was right out of the eighteenth century and I had no idea what it took to get him into it. I introduced him as the overseer, for I knew not what else to call him.

The three cooks, Mrs. D, Reita, and Mrs. Sharpe, were outfitted in white, starched dresses with matching aprons and chef's hats. I wondered if I could get them to wear the same for our wedding reception and giggled at the thought, as I thought they were pretty uncomfortable and couldn't wait for the masquerade to be over with.

Johnny was next and I said to him, "Just what is your title, Sir? For I am a little miffed."

He was wearing tartan pants that flared out from the knees and an argyle vest over a strange blossomy shirt. He took his flannel cap off and bowed. "Do ye not be familiar with a Scottish gentleman off to a foxhunt, Ma'am? I suppose I should have brought me hunting dogs."

I laughed and took his hand. "May I present Johnny O'Shea, husband to the lovely Amma and father to these three beautiful girls." I acknowledged his daughters standing beside him in their bright, yellow dresses and dainty, blue bonnets. "But most of all, he is my trusted right-hand man and dear friend."

"A fellow Irishman," Rainey said. "I am pleased to make your acquaintance and express my gratitude to all you have done for Vienna."

Johnny shook his hand. "The pleasure is all mine, I assure you, Sir."

"There will be none of that 'sir' business. Rainey is all I answer to."

"And that goes double for me. What's the ma'am all about?"

Johnny laughed. "Well, is it Vienna then?"

"Yes, I am finally Vienna."

"Can we still call you Tia?" the youngest O'Shea asked.

"Yes, darling, you may." I hugged them all and noticed someone standing at the back of the hall. Ava and Rosy came out of the shadows, linked their arms through his, and walked toward me. It was Henry, our honoree. He looked dapper in his Scottish kilt. We had a very long embrace and I asked him if the attire meant that we were in for a playing of the bagpipes, and he teased that I would just have to wait and see.

Amma instructed the girls to cut the ribbons, and upon doing so, a multitude of balloons and confetti tumbled down from the banner that read: "Welcome Home, Lady Vela and Mister Rainey!"

"Now, who is going to clean up the mess while we celebrate?" I queried.

"Leave it to the Brownies. Now, I have a dinner to finish," Mrs. D declared.

"Oh right. Thank you everyone." I could say no more as the tears were falling again.

One by one, the cast of the welcoming committee filed out to do their respective duties. There were more hugs and kisses, and declarations that they would see us at the dinner table. Rainey and Johnny were chatting as if they were old friends. Amma linked her arm through mine and said how much she had missed me and was so happy that I had finally brought Rainey to Avanloch.

"I was in the tower courtyard when you arrived. I watched as you and he alighted the sedan and walked hand in hand up the drive. I imagined that he was trying to absorb the enormity and structure of the castle all at once."

"Yes, he was, Amma. I am afraid my description of Avanloch did not do it the justice it deserves. We are so used to living here that we forget what a majestic building it really is and that visitors are often in awe to its grandiose."

"What do you think my Johnny and your Rainey are talking about? Am I out of my ever-lovin' cockney mind or do you not find a resemblance in the two of them?"

"Oh yes, Amma, I have been aware of that fact from the first time I met Johnny. It wouldn't surprise me one single little bit to find out that they are long lost fourth or fifth cousins. Coincidences abound. You won't believe some of the stories I have to tell you about the twists of fate that kept Rainey from finding me."

"I can hardly wait. I am so happy that the two of you are finally together. I can see how much he loves you and cannot imagine how you had the willpower to stay away from him for so long."

"Neither can I, Amma. Neither can I."

Johnny and Rainey joined us each with huge smiles on their faces. Rainey put his arm around me and said, "You won't believe this, sweetie, but it appears as though Johnny's and my ancestors hail from the same part of Ireland."

Amma and I both laughed, and I said, "Oh really, Rain? You don't say?"

"Why do you say it like that, Vienna?" Rainey asked.

"We were just saying to each other that there is a resemblance between the two of you and perhaps you may be distant relatives." I winked at Johnny.

"Poor bloke, if he looks anything like me! Come on, Amma, let's leave these two to unpack and rest up before the festivities tonight. The good Lord willing, we will have eons to dwell into the past." Johnny gave me a quick peck on the cheek and said to Rainey, "V's the sister I never had and I am so glad you are here to keep her out of trouble. It's been a strain trying to keep her on the straight and narrow, but an enormous delight. Amma and I couldn't ask for a better boss."

I smirked and said the feeling was mutual, but that I didn't like being referred to as their boss. Surely there was a better title for me.

"Well, you don't like it when anyone refers to you as Lady McAllister or ma'am, but somebody has to be in charge. You have to understand, Rainey, that Vela—Vienna, does not like to give orders. She much prefers to ask us if we would like to do this or could we do this for her," Johnny said

"Has anyone ever said no to her requests?" Rainey asked.

"Are you kidding? We may suggest another way of doing something, but no, she has this way of making you want to do anything for her, no matter how mundane the task may be. She is very knowledgeable and has taught us all a lot about tact and understanding."

"I know all about that, Johnny. I can refuse this lady nothing, and, yes, she has been my lady since the day I met her. But then, I am a little bit prejudiced wherever she is concerned." He hugged me and kissed my forehead. "Vienna has told me that she confessed her feelings for me to Amma after returning from Vancouver in 1972 and that Amma told you about me only recently. Vienna and I have decided to put our years of separation to rest and live for the future, and only reminisce about the good times we shared. I want to make something perfectly clear to you, her treasured friends, and that is you can trust me to always keep her safe and happy, for *she is* my happiness and I shall never leave her. I had given up on ever finding love because I had let it slip through my fingers the first time, and now, through some miracle, my beloved has returned and rescued me from the depths of despair. When Vienna chose to disappear, I am so glad she came here to all of you, for I don't believe there is a better place on Earth she could have chosen to make her home and raise our daughter. Avanloch is her home and everyone here is her family, and I can only hope that I will be welcomed as her husband-to-be, for she is my heart and soul, and I am nothing without her. Sorry, I didn't mean to make you girls teary eyed. I just wanted her best friends to know that my intentions are honorable."

"We never thought anything else, Rainey." Johnny reached out and he and Rainey shook hands again.

"Okay then, that is out of the way. Now, when are the Browns coming to clean up?"

"Browns? What do you mean, Rain?" I asked.

"Didn't one of the cooks say that the Browns would be in to clear all this ticker tape and balloons away?"

We tried not to laugh but didn't succeed.

Amma ushered Johnny down the hallway and called back to me over her shoulder. "Have fun explaining that one, Vienna!"

"Okay, what's so funny?" Rainey demanded.

"Do you want to go up the stairs or take the elevator?"

"The stairs, of course."

I walked ahead of him, holding his hand and pulling him along, kicking the debris out of our way. At the first landing, I sat down on the little settee as he inspected the scrollwork.

"Go ahead," he said. "I can listen and examine at the same time."

"Well," I explained, "they are not the Browns but the Scottish Brownies, and according to Scottish folklore, they come to your house after you have gone to bed and finish up the housework."

Rainey turned and looked at me. "Are you pulling my leg?"

"Of course not, darling. This is just one of the many fables you will come across. Now, I am going to go ahead and start unpacking."

"No, wait for me. I will have plenty of time to dwell into this magnificent scrollwork. It seems to be in hieroglyphics."

"Yes, I thought so, too Hopefully, we will discover the origin together."

"Where do you think the girls are?"

"I imagine they are in the kitchen with Mrs. D or setting the dinner table with Shalla and Cyn, or even off visiting Amma's mum, Granny Kay. She is the girls' Scottish grandmother. Anyhow, they will be around soon I am sure."

We had reached the top of the stairs and Rainey stood looking down upon the grand hall.

I pointed out to him the north wing quarters, which had been Jeremy's, and told him that they could be his if he would like.

"Where are your rooms?" he asked.

"In the south wing, at the end of this corridor." I directed him toward my rooms.

"And you expect me to be *down* there? Not bloody likely!"

"I was hoping you would say that."

"Are you worried about us being together here? It won't be the same as if we were alone at the Palace or at my apartment you know." Rainey was scowling.

"Don't be silly! This is my house and my rooms are soundproof, if that is what you think I am worried about. I also have locks on my doors. In three short months, we will be married and what I have will be yours."

He laughed. "I am not worried, darling. And I already have everything I want of yours. I think perhaps you should consider a prenuptial."

"What did you just say, Rainey Quinn? A prenup...? You have to be crazy! That would imply that I didn't trust you and that is certainly not the case. You are Ava's father and I hope that Rosy will someday come to think of you that way, too. If something unforeseen should happen to me, there is no one else I would want to oversee the welfare of Avanloch than you, so if you are up to the task, you are nominated."

"One thing at a time, Vienna. We will discuss this at a further date, and don't ever speak again of something dire happening to you! Now take me to your room, I haven't been alone with you for almost two days. I want to kiss you so badly and my arms are aching from not holding you."

I opened the door and pulled him into my lair. "See that monstrous bed over there? Well, I have slept in it alone for almost twenty years, and I will never sleep in it alone again as long as you are here."

"My lady, I look forward to being your humble lord tonight."

We fell into each other's arms just as we heard giggling and footsteps in the hall outside the door. There was a quiet knock, almost stifled by the chuckles.

"Are you two decent?" It was Rosy.

Rainey opened the door. "Yes, my dear, we are fully clothed. Though how decent, I do not know. What are you *two* up to yourselves?"

Ava barged by her sister. "Don't mind her, Rainey. She is just being Rosy. Dinner will be in an hour, as everything will be ready earlier than planned. Are you all right with that, mama? Uncle John telephoned and asked if you can call him at your earliest convenience. Shall I hook your phone up for you?"

"Yes, thank you, dear. I will call him right away. Did he give you any clue as to what is on his mind?"

"Nope," Ava said. "We'll go and give you some privacy."

"No, please stay. Rainey is going in the shower anyway."

"I am? Yup, I guess I am. Keep your mom company, girls."

"Dial the number for me please, Ava, while I see if Rainey's clothes need pressing. And, Rosy, will you please pick me out a dress to wear? Anyone you like will do. Here, put these on the dressing table for Rainey, will you, honey?"

Ava passed me the phone and I let out a deep breath, as I was expecting ominous news.

"Hello, Uncle John," I said. "I have been trying to reach you for days. Please tell me I have been worried for nothing."

"I am sorry if I have frightened you into thinking that anything was wrong," he replied. "Actually, it is quite the contrary. I have uncovered something that has been a curiosity to me for a great many years and I want the family all together when I reveal what I have discovered."

"You are intriguing me. May I have a little hint?"

"You will just have to wait until tomorrow. Ash and Grayson will be accompanying us. Will you be prepared to overnight us all? I know that you have only arrived today with your young man and we do not want to impose."

"This is the best news, that you will all be here, because I so want you to meet Rainey. He is looking forward to getting to know everyone, too. Don't worry. He is not the type to be overwhelmed."

"Jannie wants to say hello. You will make sure the girls are home tomorrow?"

"Yes, they will be here. Safe drive. Hello, Jannie. I am so happy to hear that all is well, although I cannot imagine what John has to tell us. I probably won't sleep all night."

"Yes, darling, knowing you, you probably won't, but at least you have the love of your life with you. I am so happy for you that I find myself weeping for your happiness."

"Aunt Jannie, you are a love," I said in my best Scottish tongue. "Guid night an sweit dreams."

And she said to me in her favorite good-bye, "*Vaya con dios.*"

Rainey emerged from the dressing room and Rosy let out a low whistle. Ava said, "You look nice, Rainey."

"You do know that I always wear the same clothes, don't you, girls?" Rainey said.

"Not exactly. You have many shades of whites and tans, khakis and browns. You just never choose to wear bright colors. Why is that?" Ava asked.

"Never even think about it. I like what I like and that is that. What in the name of God is that?" A shrill bell had sounded.

"It's just the call bell, dear." I walked over to the small box on the inside of the closet and lifted the mouthpiece. "Hi, you've reached Vienna."

"Johnny here, V. Just calling to see if Rainey would like to join me for a pre-dinner drink in the den."

"Thank him, Vienna, but I will wait for you," Rainey declined.

"He'll be right there, Johnny." I smiled and helped Rainey on with his suede jacket.

"Ava had it pressed for you while you were in the shower." I kissed his objecting mouth. "Will you girls show my fiancée to the den? See you in twenty minutes."

"Bossy, isn't she, Rainey?" I heard Rosy say as I closed the door, and he answered her with a laugh and said he hadn't noticed.

I showered and dried my hair. I didn't have time for a fancy up do, so I pinned it up loosely with curly tendrils encircling my face. I donned a lace petticoat and the long, copper, canvas skirt and yellow silk blouse that Rosy had set out for me. I did the clasp up on the blue teardrop and admired how it still danced in the light. I chose a ring pair of aquamarine earrings and the Infinity Bracelets adorned my wrist. I decided on a pale blush and apricot lipstick. I grabbed a colorful shawl from the closet and slipped into a pair of yellow flats. I ran down the hall and called up the lift. I didn't want to make Rainey anxious, but I first needed to stop by the kitchen and talk to Mrs. D.

I informed Mrs. D that Jannie, John, Ash, and Grayson would be spending a night or two with us and asked if that was all right with her, and maybe Reita could help her again.

"You let me do the worryin' 'bout that, darlin'. Mr. Grayson, eh? The rumors they be true then? Stranger things have been to happen I guess. Now get ye into the dining room as we are a comin' with the vittles!"

I scurried into the corridor and found Rainey and Johnny about to enter the dining room. They each took an arm and escorted me to my chair. Rainey and I were seated together at one head of the table. Rosy was to my left and Ava sat on the right side of her father. Johnny and Amma were next to her and their three girls. Henry and Mrs. Sharpe were seated at the opposite end. All in all, there were twenty friends and family. The supper was superb as usual. There was roast turkey and dressing, and a succulent rack of lamb with a delicate mint sauce. I was sure that every vegetable known to man was on the table. Winter salads and fresh breads rounded out the fare. Glasses were constantly being refilled with wine. I drank my usual sparkling water, as did Rainey, which surprised me, but he said that he didn't need any false stimulation as he had the real thing sitting right next to him. After an hour or so, as if on cue, eight young ladies rushed in to clear the tables and bring in the desserts, which consisted of fruit pies, sweet plum duff, and rich coffees.

"Ah, the Brownies," Rainey surmised.

"Sorry to disappoint you, love, but they be maidens from the village," I confessed.

One young lass I recognized as Kelly, one of my swimming students from years ago, presented me with my own pot of steaming coffee. "Your decaf, Lady McAllister."

I thanked her. Rainey said that he was impressed with the respect of the young people.

Johnny had excused himself, and when he returned, he had Henry's bagpipes with him. Room was made for Henry. He stood up and said, "I wanted to do something special for the Lady of Avanloch, who has been like a daughter to me, but I knew not what. Miss Amma came to my rescue and I have taken the liberty to put your poem, Mollie Magan, to music. With your permission…" He smiled at me and I nodded.

My eyes were already moist. I put my fidgety hands on my lap and Rainey, sensing that this rendering might sadden me, placed his hands over mine. I clasped his tightly. Henry played and Amma recited the words.

"They brought me down to Cardiff Bay
For it was my wish for my last day
I watched the gulls land and fly away
I dipped my feet in the cruel cold sea
The very one that took me Paddy in '33
There be naught for me here then
And I came with little Meg to Gypsy Glen
Now take me back to the land of Avanloch
Where the sprites dance and the fairies frolic
Lay me down in the lavender heather fields
Where the sun reigns down from God's great shield
Let me hear the babbling stream call out my name
As the fireflies light the way from whence I came
My Meg has gone and only I remain alone
If not for you who have welcomed me home
Remember ole Mary as she remembers you
I shall be with you dear friends someday again
Trust in the Lord; this be not the end."

I didn't think there was a dry eye in the house. I stood up and bowed to Henry. Then we serenaded him with a round of applause. He saluted us all. Ava and Rosy collected Amma's girls and they presented Henry with an array of personal gifts. The last one he opened was from us all at Avanloch. It was a huge plaque that displayed his family's coat of arms. He was delighted. It also contained a voucher for a two-week stay anywhere in the world he chose to go. It was for two people, and he looked shyly at Mrs. Sharpe and asked her if she would do him the honor of being his traveling companion.

"What?" she wailed. "No, you dunno have to ask me twice. Mary Queen of Scots, I say, let's get goin' tomoreee before we find ourselves layin' in the glen with Mollie Magan!" She got up and planted a big kiss on Henry's lips.

He said, "Why, Anna Sharpe, I never !"

The room howled with laughter and Amma made an announcement. "I believe that it is time to vacate these premises so the young lassies can do their job. Sorry, Vienna, but that means retreating to the large parlor. Is that all right with you? The boys have a little treat set up for us. Come on everybody. Follow me."

Rainey and I were the last ones out. He asked, "Where are we going and why did Amma apologize to you? I seem to recall you not wanting to talk about one room in the castle. Is this it?"

"You will see." I chose to take him out down the hall and through the main entrance, as I wanted him to see the Harem Room from the front. He looked confused as he followed after me, wondering why we hadn't tagged along behind the rest. I opened the colossal doors and he was met with the full force of the unorthodox room.

He smiled at me in his little boy grin. "So this is what all the fuss is about? Vienna LaFontaine, I never took you to be a prude. I find it all rather amusing." He kept commenting on the décor as he led me to the balcony, where the rest of the troupe had gathered. They had left the front room seats open for us.

"Goody," I said.

"Mother," Ava whispered to me, "there will be no slaughtering of the bulls."

Rainey laughed. "I don't think that is what she is worried about, honey."

One by one, the boys marched in. Johnny led the procession, carrying his fiddle, followed by Millie's and Emma's husbands with their accordions, and Duffy with his tin whistle and harmonica. Winston had a Scottish small pipe and Henry rounded out the procession with his Highland Bagpipe. They took their places on the stage and entertained us for an hour with their renditions of Celtic music. No one had attempted to play the harp or the piano, and at the end, I found out why. The gentlemen all put their instruments down and Johnny motioned for Ava and Rosalyn to join them on stage.

The girls did themselves proud as they performed some of the classic works, which they finessed as both tender and passionate. They finished the evening with their interpretation of "Mademoiselle." Of course, I cried and Rainey wasn't very far from tears himself.

After a robust round of applause for the musicians, Mrs. D announced that there was fresh coffee and pie in the kitchen. Everyone moaned but stopped by the kitchen anyhow. Rainey and I declined, said our good nights, and took the lift to the second floor. As we climbed out, I swooned a little and Rainey caught me.

"What is it, love? Do you feel faint?"

"No, I am just tired. I guess the past weeks have taken their toll on me, then the long trip here, and now all of these celebrations…" I looked into his eyes and silently slipped through his arms to the floor.

The next thing I remember was lying in my bed and everyone hovering around me. I tried to sit up but the room was spinning. Rainey lowered me back onto the pillow and told me to close my eyes. I lay perfectly still for a few minutes until the world quit turning in my head. "What happened?" I asked.

"You fainted, Mama. Rainey caught you and yelled down for us. He already had you in your bed by the time we got here. Are you all right now? You gave us all a scare."

"I think I am all right, Ava. This is not like me at all."

Rosy passed me a glass of water. "Too much excitement, Mama. You need to rest."

Amma agreed and suggested they all clear out. Ava asked if she could stay and help undress me, but Rainey said he could manage. She showed him how to use the call box to summon help if he should need to.

Rainey rolled me over gently, unzipped my skirt, and pulled it and my stockings off. He hung them neatly on the back of a chair. I told him that I would have just thrown them on the floor. He looked at me with his usual amused smile.

"Yes, I know you would have." He unbuttoned my blouse and bra and told me I could sleep in my slip. "This is the first time I have ever undressed a comatose woman. I usually have a little help. Are you through feeling dizzy yet?"

I turned over and whispered, "I was so hoping that we would be married before I became pregnant."

"Vienna, tell me you are kidding." He gently rolled me back over to face him.

I stroked his face. "Yes, I am not pregnant, at least not as far as I know. Just wanted to see your reaction."

"After your black out, I don't think my heart could stand another shock. I am going to hold you until you fall asleep. I love you, Vienna."

"I love you, Rainey."

When I awoke the next morning, Rainey was not in bed beside me. I took my time in standing upright but found I was perfectly fine. The door to my drawing room was open and I ventured in to find Rainey sitting at the desk, musing over some papers, coffee cup in hand. He heard me and glanced up.

"Good morning, darling," he greeted. "You were sleeping so peacefully I didn't have the heart to disturb you. Here, let me help with you with your housecoat." He rose and slipped my arms through the sleeves.

"You are up and already dressed, and have been to the kitchen I see." I beckoned to the steam still protruding from the silver coffee pot.

He poured me a cup and led me to the settee, which he had turned to face the rising sun. "It's going to be a beautiful day, Vienna, and I hope you are up to all it has to offer."

"I am, thanks to you. Please forgive me for my antics last night. I am quite fine now."

"Thank goodness. I hope you don't mind, but I have started to read the letters that you wrote to me."

"How many have you read?"

"I was about to start the third. Your despondency is very evident in the first two and I felt a renewed sadness, for that is just how I felt when I came home to find you gone."

I folded the notes up and returned them to the drawer. "Today is not the time to be dwelling on the sorrows of yesterday. Can we focus on the here and now, the wonders of our love, and the adventures that we are going to share?"

"My sentiments exactly." He squeezed my hand and smiled into my eyes.

We heard knocking on the bedroom door. Rainey opened the door to the vestibule and found Ava and Rosy waiting. They made a big fuss over me and were still not assured that last night was a one-time thing. I sent them on their way to get breakfast started while I got dressed. I had hoped that I would have some time to show Rainey around the castle before Jannie and John arrived.

As we were walking down the hall to the kitchen stairs, Rainey stopped me at the elevator and said that the rooms were not in proportion. He asked me why there were eight rooms on the west side and only four on the east. I told him that I had no explanation, as both sides took up the same amount of space. But the silly little foyer on the east certainly accounted for one room and Ash had two rooms, so that brought the count up to six. I could not explain the far wall beside Ash's suite, as that was all it appeared to be was, a long wall, and no one had ever told me anything different. Yes, of course, we had wondered if one of the hidden rooms was behind it, but we could find no entrance in; not through Ash's or Jeremy's rooms. Ash had told us that nothing was behind it. Rainey said that he was going to take a look from the outside to see how things measured up.

After a modest breakfast, the girls and I took Rainey on the tour. We only had a few hours before company would be arriving. He had already seen the kitchen and the family dining room, so we carried on with the right wing, introducing him to the small and cozy tea room, and then the library and the informal reception room. Outside of it was a large cloak room, next to the outside doors. Now we were back in the grand entrance hall. The girls answered all of Rainey's questions as to who was who in the portraits. He asked where ours were, and we snickered and said in a closet somewhere. We took him back down the great hallway to the McDuffs' suites, the pantries, the closets, and the small maid's room. We were on the left side of the castle now, which was twice as wide as the right and some of the rooms jutted out disproportionally. I was sure the lack of symmetry was not lost on Rainey's architectural mind, but he only would say, "How interesting." The dining room was just such a room, extending some 15 feet out from the main wall, but then it led into a portico and to the main courtyard and pavilion. He admired the short halls between the rooms. He asked what was down the way from the children's playroom, and I told him I was saving that for last. The games room was in the back of the music room, which was of particular interest to Rainey. He remarked on the pattern on the floor, which Ava told him that she, Rosy, and I had just completed last year. We had decorated a circle to resemble a carpet with playing cards. We had chosen the Jack of diamonds, the Queen of hearts, the King of clubs, and the Ace of spades as the large entities, and lesser cards from the different suits surrounded them, appearing as if a card game was in session.

Rosy opened the sliding wooden doors that had been installed to conceal the media room. "This is the only television that you will find at Avanloch, except for the Duffys and the wee one Mrs. D keeps in the kitchen so that she can keep up with her stories."

We crossed the hall into our offices, which were behind the den. It housed two desks and all the organizational files that were pertinent to running the estate. It was basically Rosy's domain, as I had no desire to be involved with the financial aspects anymore than I had to be. I told Rainey that we could make an area available to him for his use. He said that wouldn't be necessary right away, as any dealings he had with his business could be handled by phone for the time being and he didn't want to do any paperwork.

We skipped the Harem Room and started back, as time was dwindling down and I still hadn't shown Rainey the conservatory. The girls left us at the door to check on the luncheon. I asked Ava if she would mind bringing my teardrop down for me, as I had meant to put it on but had forgotten. "Oh, and the bracelets; I don't like leaving them."

"I am sure they are perfectly safe, honey," Rainey said.

"Yes, I know, but they have been alone too long and I miss them when I am not wearing them. I feel naked without them."

"You're right, they have been alone too long…just as you and I were." He opened the doors and said, "So this is your Eden. I can certainly see why you chose to name it that. This really is something! It puts some of the commercial conservatories to shame. You put a lot of love and time into this, didn't you?"

"I only did the ornamental. Johnny is the one who truly brought the place back to life. It had to be rebuilt from the bottom up. First, everything in it had to be scraped—windows, flooring, columns, and most of the ceiling. The only thing that was reparable was the fireplace. Come around the corner and see the swimming pool. We brought a company in from London to construct it. I was very specific on how I wanted it installed and what materials were to be used. The contractor and I did not always see eye to eye. However, he was handsomely rewarded and went away happy. I have to admit this extravaganza of mine cost a pretty penny, but I have no regrets. I could do without the aviary, though. Jeremy kept bringing new species home from his travels abroad and I never had the heart to tell him that I didn't want them. Sometimes, their incessant singing and tweeting drives me crazy. I started leaving their cage doors open so that they can fly about and we are all a lot happier. I never give up the chance to give some of them away, though. For some reason, they keep having babies."

Rainey laughed. "No kidding. Please tell me that you don't keep reptiles."

"Not I, but the girls have snuck a few lizards in. They live over in the sand, among the cactus. This is where I come on my sleepless nights and putter around."

"And I thought you only consorted with the nocturnal ghosts. I suppose they don't like the rainforest. Whose brainstorm was it to install the ceiling water sprays?"

"Johnny's."

"He's quite the all-round assistant, isn't he? Is there anything he can't do?"

Ava interrupted as I was about to answer. "They're here, Mama." She passed me my teardrop and bracelets, and we left to welcome our-much awaited guests.

Somehow, the introductions were made while Jannie and I were fussing over each other. Ash greeted me with a hug, and I kissed her cheek and hugged her right back.

She whispered in my ear, "I see you finally have someone to keep your feet warm on a cold winter's night."

"The same goes for you," I said, smiling. She threw her head back and laughed. I had not seen Grayson for several years and thought he looked remarkably fit and youthful. I imagined that he and Ash were both in their early fifties.

A fire had been laid in the "tea room" and hot beverages and cakes were awaiting us. After a few minutes of polite conversation, I urged Uncle John to tell us his news.

"What I am going to say will come as an enormous shock to some of you, particularly you, Ash."

Ash was fidgeting. "Why me?"

Grayson took her hands in his and said, "Why don't we hear what Dad has to say?"

Uncle John stood up, walked over to the hearth, and pushed a few logs around. He straightened up and continued. "As everyone knows, I have been Jeremy's financial advisor for many years, and his confidant. However, there was one thing which he kept from me. I first became aware of an unaccountable expenditure from his personal finances some time after the passing of his father. I questioned him about it, as I needed the details for tax purposes. The amount was inconsequential. It appeared every month in his ledger as 200 - LB. I took it to mean 200 pounds. His explanation for the expenditure was that it was a charitable contribution to a hospital in Gloucester. He even had receipts. Every few years, the donations increased, until they reached 600 pounds. As you all know, I am retiring this year and want everything in harmony for Grayson and Chandler. Since Jeremy's passing, his personal finances have all been incorporated into the family's coffers and I never thought about the hospital donations. However, I discovered that an amount of 1,000 pounds is being withdrawn monthly from McAllister Holdings and is now making its way to a clinic in Amsterdam in the Netherlands. Needless to say, I was more than a little curious and set out to discover why the amount had increased so much and why it was now being sent somewhere else. I dare say I was not prepared for what I was to uncover. First of all, I ran into a few stumbling blocks, as I was found to be infringing on matters that had been meant to remain private. I am afraid I had to resort to a little chicanery, but I was determined to find out if these monies were of a legitimate matter. The quest has taken up a few months of my time, but I finally have the answer I have been seeking. I have journeyed to Amsterdam with Jannie as my accomplice. Thank heavens she was with me, as what we discovered was quite a shock." He stopped talking, walked over to Jannie, and put his hands on the back of her chair.

We were all sitting on eggshells as to what his revelation was going to be, and I was sure that not one of us could ever have imagined in our wildest dreams the next words that were going to come from his lips.

He looked directly at Ash and then at Rosalyn, and lastly, me. "There is no other way to say this…LizBeth is still alive and living in a specialized clinic in the Netherlands." His words seemed to hang in the air, with no one saying a thing.

Rainey had reached for my hand and was looking at me for some kind of a reaction. I had none, but Ash did.

She stood up, and Gray was right beside her and took her arm to steady her. "How could you say such a cruel thing, John? Liz Beth is dead! She died right in front of me!" She was yelling, and I thought that she might collapse if Gray hadn't been there to hold her.

Jannie went to comfort Ash. "It's true, dear. We have seen her. Although she is still a child in her mind, she is all grown up and the spitting image of your mother. I know it is a lot to absorb, but you have to know that she is being taken care of in a loving and caring facility. The hospital's credentials are impeccable. They are only one of a few in the world that caters to victims of horrible accidents such as near drownings. She can walk, talk, and feed herself, but, unfortunately, only has the capabilities of a three-year-old child. Her brain was deprived of oxygen for far too long."

"How can this be, Jannie? I saw her die. They took her away in the hearse." Ash was sobbing and her body was heaving.

Jannie helped Gray to seat her but continued to rub her shoulders and speak softly to her. "I'm sorry, Ash. Perhaps we should have broken the news to you in private," John apologized. "Do you think you can answer a few questions for us? Take your time; there is no hurry."

Ash smoothed out her clothes and said she was sorry for yelling at him.

John said he fully understood and would have reacted the same way. "I know you were only a young girl yourself when the tragedy happened, but are you up to replaying the incident over again? You said that you saw her die."

"Yes. She was lying on the kitchen floor and Jeremy was bending over her. He was trying to revive her. Mother was screaming. Father came from somewhere and told Mrs. D to get us out of the room. Mother refused and fought with her, saying she wasn't going. I thought at one point Father was going to slap her, as she was so hysterical, but miraculously, Dr. Sheffield…I think that was his name, arrived out of nowhere and he gave Mother a shot to calm her down. Duffy had arrived, and he and Mrs. D ushered us out. I looked back and I swear I saw Liz Beth open her eyes, but I was told it did not happen. I watched from the upstairs window as they carried her out and put her in the doctor's car. We never saw her body again. She was cremated…wasn't she?"

"So the story goes. This is what I have been able to piece together with what little records I was able to access from the clinic. Liz Beth did not die and the doctor thought that she may recover, but he didn't know how much of her faculties she would be left with, so he and your father corroborated the travesty that she had indeed passed away. I am sure, in his defense, he didn't wish to give your mother false hope."

"He always was a heartless bastard!" Ash retorted.

We were all glad to see some of the color returning to Ash.

John continued on with his summary. "Liz Beth's life hung precariously for months and she was eventually moved to the hospital in Gloucester when it appeared that she was not going to make a full recovery. It was 'an end of life' facility. There she stayed and no one knew except your father. When he became ill, he passed the burden of her care on to Jeremy, who, along with everyone else, believed that his sister had died. Your mother had passed away by now so I am in complete ignorance as to why Jeremy chose to go along with the pretense. He certainly never confided in me. As time went on, Liz Beth began to make a little headway and the clinic in Amsterdam was making leaps and bounds with patients who had otherwise been deemed hopeless. Jeremy had her transferred there and he continued to visit her regularly. The staff there told us that she recognized him and was always happy when he would visit her and bring her presents. She called him father.

Ash gasped. "My own brother…how could he have kept it from me? I had a right to know. All these years…she has been alive and alone!" She started to weep.

I finally made my way over to her and knelt down at her feet. "Well, we know now and we shall visit her, and she will never be alone again. Perhaps we can have her moved closer to us. There is a lovely facility in Edinburgh that I think will suit her needs. After forty years, I don't think any clinic is going to be able to alter her situation, and it will be best for all of us if we can have her near."

Rosy and Ava joined me; we all held hands with Ash and she clung to us.

"Do you really mean it, Vela?" Ash asked. "Can we bring her back close to Avanloch?"

"Of course we can! We are the McAllister women and we can do anything!"

"Oh, Vela, thank you. Please forgive me everyone."

"For what, being human?" Jannie asked of her.

Mrs. D had appeared in the doorway. "I don't mean to interrupt...what is going on here? Ash, Vela, what has happened? Miss Jannie?"

"We must tell her," Ash said and, through tears, related the amazing story to Mrs. D.

"Oh my, my, my, is this so?" Mrs. D crossed herself as she so often did when hearing of miracles even though she wasn't Catholic. "One thing be sure then. 'Tis not Liz Beth who tumbled Taty to her death then!"

"Why do you say that, Mrs. D?" Ava asked.

"Well, deary, the living cannot manifest themselves as the departed, can they? Like I said before, if it not be Miss Lizzy, then it be Miss Mary. Come on down to lunch now."

I felt Rainey's arms around me and was thankful that he was here. "You have no idea of what you have stepped into, have you?" I said.

"Life around here gets more interesting day by day. I will do anything I can to help with uniting the family."

"Thank you, darling. I just might take you up on that offer."

The foursome stayed over for two nights. John said that he would look into bringing Liz Beth to Edinburgh and was available anytime any of us wanted to make the trip to the Netherlands. Rosy made plans with Ash and Gray to visit her in the next week.

We resumed with our everyday life. The rains and winds had arrived, so we were forced to be indoors most of the dreary February days. Rainey and I tried to get out even if just for half an hour every day. He had met the magnificent steed that I had bought for him and was anxious to take him over the hills and dales. We had short strolls through the wintry gardens and I had taken him to the mausoleum where Maveryn and Jeremy rested. When the weather wasn't too inclement, we would stroll into the Village and visit with the locals. Much to his chagrin, he had agreed to attend church services with me on Sundays, and just as I had hoped, he and Reverend Peters became fast friends. We spent the evenings with the girls when they were home, playing board games and looking for the hidden rooms. Amma and Johnny were our constant companions. There had been no sightings from the spirit world. Every time we passed room six, though, Rainey would say, "We really must do something about that menace." I would only nod and smile.

I had tried unsuccessfully to contact Roberge Farradan regarding the Infinity legend, but it appeared that he was off on a two-month cruise with his wife and was unavailable.

After the revelation regarding Liz Beth's existence, Ash admitted to us that the fake wall between hers and Jeremy's suites was once her sister's bedroom. Her father had the room sealed, as her mother could be found in it, constantly bemoaning her daughter's demise. He was afraid for her sanity and decided that it must be boarded up. Many people knew of his decision but did not question it, and it was like the room never existed. It was of no deterrence to Lady Audrey Ash, however, as she spent countless hours trying to tear the walls down. Eventually, her heart could not take the abuse and she succumbed to an early death, never recovering from her little girl's accident of which she blamed herself for.

Ash could not remember how to find the entrance, but Rainey assured her that he could find it, and that next time she visited, she could decide what she wanted to do with the room. She thanked him and said that perhaps seeing it would erase some of the repressed guilt that she still harbored. We told her that she had nothing to feel guilty about, and she responded with that maybe she hadn't been a very nice sister. She did not elaborate. And so, another mystery had been solved, but still I wondered why Liz Beth had called out for help when we had played the Ouija. Was it possible that inside that child's mind was an intelligent entity trying to escape? I shook my head. Now who was the fanatic?

We had been at Avanloch for almost a month and I thought that everything was going swimmingly. We were preparing for Morgan's and Mason's visit in a few weeks but still hadn't decided where we wanted them to sleep. Perhaps we would let them have rooms one and two, as they were close to us. Perhaps they would want to share a room, being a big, old, scary castle and all. Rainey doubted it.

We were making the bed. It was ten in the morning. Rainey came around to my side and said, "Sit down, Vienna. I have something I want to tell you."

He was very serious and I did not like the sound of his voice.

"I promised myself that I would never tell you what I am going to," he continued. "But I can't live in this house of love, happiness, and trust any longer without coming clean."

"I don't think I like the sound of this, Rainey. Are you going to leave me?"

"That's funny. Me, leave you? No, but you may want to leave me."

"Never in a million years!"

"Don't be so sure. Will you let me talk? As I said, I never intended to tell you, but if I have learned anything, it's that secrets come back to bite you in the ass. I'm afraid not to tell you. I think I might know what was in the valise that Louise gave to you."

I interrupted him. "I told you, it doesn't matter. I don't need to know."

"Vienna, please…this is hard enough. Will you hear me out?"

I nodded.

"I didn't tell you about my tenure in Italy and I didn't tell you about Priscilla, and the worst mistake I ever made in my life was not telling you that I loved you. I can't keep anything from you that may jeopardize our relationship. I was very good at provoking Louise and I really got her dander up one day when I told her that she was a piss-poor substitute for a mother. She came back at me with, 'Look who's talking? You can't be bothered to see them on Fridays anymore because, apparently, it cuts into your social life!' I told her that I didn't have a social life, and she laughed. I told her that I wanted them to spend more time with me at my apartment and I wanted them on holidays also.

"She replied, 'If you think for one minute that I am going to let you take them to your floosy- infested apartment, you have another thing coming, Mister!' The veins were popping on her forehead; that is how angry she was. I told her that there were no girls in my apartment; not now or ever, and there never would be.

"And she said, 'Ha! You expect me to believe that, you silly boy? Do you think I don't know about your foolish dalliances? Mark my words, Rainey Quinn, there will come a time when you will rue the day that you're sordid sex life comes back to haunt you!'

"It was only Louise sounding off, and as usual, I didn't give her threats much thought. But being here with you, I guess I have finally developed a conscience. I need to get this off my chest and suffer the consequences, as there can be no tomorrow if the past is still weighing heavily on my mind."

Rainey had been pacing the floor and he went over to my dresser and picked up my teardrop.

"You're not wearing this today?" he asked.

I held out my hand and he came over, putting it around my neck, lifting my hair as he did so. I leaned my head against his body but he did not respond to my touch. He tried to smile, but it was a poor attempt. He went over to the window and peered out. He glanced my way briefly and started to talk.

"It was 1977, Labor Day weekend, and we all know how I hate that holiday."

I shook my head, as I did not know that he did.

"Was it not the Labor Day weekend that you first told me that you loved me and I told you to forget me? Did I not put you on the bus the very same weekend the next year, never to see you again? It was also the weekend I married Louise. So you see, nothing good ever happens then. Anyhow, Jimmy and Yates had come down for the Pacific National Exhibition. After a day at the fair, we went out on the town, and I do mean exactly that. I can't tell you how many bars we patronized…a dozen maybe. We ended up in The Yard, an area downtown that caters to exotic dancing and strip clubs. We staggered into the Prohibition Club and partook of even more drink. The boys seemed to enjoy the show. I was numb. The last girl to take the stage was a girl known as Tequila. After her act, she chose to take a seat with us. For some God-forsaken reason, she took a liking to me. Jimmy and Yates, of course, egged her on."

Rainey had now sat down on the window seat. His legs were spread and he leaned forward, head down, and clasped his hands on his knees. He did not look at me.

"Anyhow, after we bought her a drink, she asked me if I would come back and see her next Friday, as that was the only night she worked," he continued. "This Saturday was an exception, being as it was the long weekend. I told her, 'Probably not.' She pouted and pretended that she was wounded. The boys promised that they would return, though that was a lie, as they were going home the next day. I had no intention of ever stepping foot in that place again, but unfortunately, I did. It was the second-biggest mistake of my life…you know what the first one is?" He hesitated and then went on.

I did not know what was coming next and really did not want to know, but I let him continue without saying a word.

"I got into a routine. Every Friday night, I would go to the club, sit at the bar, and wait for her to finish her act. I wasn't interested in watching the escapades of the other girls. Her name was Jorja. For almost three months, I had a relationship with her. Yes, I had given up my Friday nights with Morgan and Mason for her. Very seldom did I ever see her on any other nights, as she was either studying or going to night school. Ha!

"Well, she was busy all right, and one night, I found out just how much. I had phoned her to say that I would not be seeing her that Friday, as the boys had a hockey tournament. As it turned out, the games were cancelled, as half the players came down with a nasty virus, Morgan and Mason included. I thought I would surprise her. As it turns out, I was the one who was in for the surprise. She came to the door, tying up her negligee, and a twenty-dollar bill in her hand. When she saw me, she gasped. A man's voice rang out from the bedroom. 'For God's sake, Jorja, pay the boy and get back here!'

"I barged past her and burst into her bedroom, where I found a fifty-year-old naked man in her bed. The look on his face was one of confusion. I asked him who the hell he was and he asked me the same question. Jorja was sobbing. Anyhow, he jumped out of bed, grabbed his clothes, and retrieved a hundred-dollar bill from her dresser. He said on his way out that he hadn't paid for a threesome. The little tramp was standing there in her flimsy nightie, begging me to listen to her explanation. I felt sick to my stomach as I realized what she was. I asked her when she had time for school and studying, in between Johns? I asked her why she never charged me, and she said it was because she loved me. I asked her if I was her patsy, her way out of her sordid life. I told her that if I had wanted casual sex, I would have gone to a prostitute, someone who made an honest life out of her profession. I told her that she gave a whole new meaning to the word, as she was just a cheap whore. I asked her how much I owed her and emptied my pockets and wallet at her feet. As I was leaving, the pizza boy arrived. I smiled at him and never looked back. I went back to my apartment and was so thankful that I had never brought that filthy bitch to my rooms. I underwent months of hell being tested for every STD. known to man. The fates were on my side, as I came out clean. I would never have been with you, Vienna, if I hadn't. I am not that callous. Are you done with me, Vienna? Have I finally dug my own grave? Do you want me to leave? Do you want me out of your castle and your life?"

I walked across the floor to him and knelt at his feet. "Look at me, Rainey. Do you want to go? Is this place too much for you? Have you had enough of me? Are you hoping that by revealing this unfortunate affair, you have so repulsed me that I would throw you out?"

"My God, no! You are my very being. But you must be disgusted with me."

"I could have lived the rest of my life with never hearing what you just told me, but I realize that you needed to tell it. Now, we shall never speak of this again." I took my engagement ring off my finger and took his hand in mine. His eyes were very moist and the look in them was breaking my heart. I placed my ring as far as it would go on his little finger and said, "Rainey Quinn, will you marry me?"

He collapsed on the floor beside me and took me in his arms. I knew he was trying very hard not to cry. He replaced the ring on my finger and said that he would marry me in a heartbeat, as he was already married to me in his mind. I told him that I wanted to be married in Bridge Falls, with all our friends and family present, on June 11 at 1 P.M., as that would be twenty-one years from the day and time that we had first met. He was amazed that I knew the exact day and time but thought it was a fabulous idea. I told him not to agree too readily, because I then wanted to come back here and be married at Avanloch with our family here. He laughed and said that he would marry me a hundred times over. He said that he loved me more right this very minute than he had the minute before, if that was at all possible. Was there ever a more forgiving person on Earth than me?

I told him once more that there was nothing to forgive. His life before I came back into it had nothing to do with me, and that perhaps, I was the reason that he had done some of the things he had. He made me promise that I would never think that way ever again.

We sat holding on to each other for a very long time, until we heard a knocking on the door. It was Rosy. "Are you two decent?"

"Come in, girls. We are dressed, if that is what you are asking. But just how decent we are, it is anybody's guess," Rainey answered.

"What are you doing on the floor?" Ava asked.

"Planning our weddings," Rainey said matter-of-factly.

"Weddings?" they asked in unison.

"Yes, weddings, with an 's.' Do you want to come?"